The plan was perfect. The plan was in motion. And besides, now it was too late to turn back...

Gravity, Maine, is a small, sleepy town. But there are people with plans. Plans that could change things in Gravity forever.

Bobby Swift and his achingly beautiful wife Noel have been working on their scam for five long years – ever since they stashed two million dollars in a bank in the Caymans. The problem is, the money's dirty, and as soon as they touch it they'll go to jail – or worse.

Which is why Bobby is going to fake his own death with the help of a gullible doctor and a corruptible funeral director, then sit tight in his coffin and wait for Noel to come and dig him up. After that, it's a new life in the Caribbean sun, with all the old heartache left behind.

But even in Gravity, Maine, nothing is ever quite that simple. Not when the human heart hides such depths of passion, depravity and deceit. And not when Gravity's darkest secrets are about to be unearthed.

Haunting, moving and heartstoppingly suspenseful, UNDONE is a novel of unsurpassed power.

Michael Kimball is the author of the critically acclaimed *Firewater Pond*. He lives in Maine, where he is currently at work on a new novel.

Undone

Michael Kimball

First published in Great Britain in 1996
by HEADLINE BOOK PUBLISHING

First published in paperback in 1997
by HEADLINE BOOK PUBLISHING

A HEADLINE FEATURE paperback

16 18 20 19 17

ISBN 0 7472 5535 0

Typeset by Keyboard Services, Luton, Beds

Printed and bound in Great Britain by
Mackays of Chatham PLC, Chatham, Kent

HEADLINE BOOK PUBLISHING
A division of Hodder Headline PLC
338 Euston Road
London NW1 3BH

For Glenna

PROLOGUE

H e was aware of nothing at first. Then eight tiny beeps sounded from his wristwatch, and his heart started, a faint beating. He heard the swish of blood in his ears. He became aware of light on his eyelids. He heard Noel speak his name, like a sweet, faraway song.

'*Bobby?*'

Bobby Swift lay, surrounded by velvet crepe, inside the finest mahogany casket at Wicker's Funeral Home. He took a breath that was nearly imperceptible. He knew that Eliot Wicker was standing there too. He heard the lanky funeral director say, with no emotion, 'Here he comes.'

He felt the cold inside him like the frost in a hard winter ground. He wanted to tell them he was freezing, but his jaw wouldn't work, nor were his lungs able to push a single sound through his vocal cords.

'Temperature's down,' Wicker said, bending so close that his breath felt hot on Bobby's neck.

A second shadow moved in from the left: Noel. 'Should I get a blanket?'

'Here he comes,' Wicker said again.

Cold! Bobby tried to say the word.

'Bobby?' Noel's voice sounded near, and now her hands were under his neck, hot. His heart thumped, and a fierce chill jolted him.

1

'He's having convulsions!'

'He's shivering,' Wicker replied. 'Go up and run a bath, lukewarm.'

Bobby watched as Noel's shadow pulled away, and then Wicker moved in, hot hands on Bobby's ears. 'You're too cold, Bob!' he said in a loud voice. 'I'm going to carry you upstairs.'

Bobby tried to make himself heavy. The thought of Eliot Wicker carrying him anywhere was a sour one, but he could do little to prevent it. He could not even stop his own shaking. The undertaker's hands went underneath him inside the casket. He heard Wicker grunt, repositioning himself, and suddenly Bobby was lifted in the air, slung over Wicker's bony shoulder. He watched the backs of Wicker's boot heels take the stairs. He muttered an objection.

'Hold on,' Wicker said, straining. When they reached a landing and went around a corner, Bobby heard Noel call from upstairs. Wicker's reedy response carried through Bobby's chest: 'I got him.' Bobby reached for the wall, not wanting Noel to see him helpless like this.

'Put me down,' he slurred.

'Be another second, Bob.'

'Now,' Bobby told him, and then there was brightness, gleaming white floor tiles. He heard the rushing of water, and suddenly he plunged into a great aching steam, a crushing pain. He let out a cry and exploded out of the water, clutching the towel rack. 'You're gonna kill me for real!' he cried, fighting to stand, pulling himself up to the showerhead. The water thundered out of the faucet, splashing off his shirt. His entire body shivered. His heart pounded. Humiliations compounding, here he was urinating into his waterlogged pants.

All at once he surrendered, his convulsions peaking in a single violent shudder, a loud, quavering moan. He laid his face against the shower tiles. Another tremor followed like an aftershock, another moan.

'It might be hypothermia,' Noel said.

Bobby hit the drain release with his foot, watched the vortex start between his legs. He heard Wicker croak, 'He's okay, get him a towel.'

Pain subsiding, Bobby reached down and made the water warmer, lifted his face against it. Standing in the cascade, he opened his eyes, turned to Noel and grinned. 'How'd I do?'

She turned away from him and opened the third of a bank of drawers built into Wicker's beige bathroom wall, retrieving a thick brown towel. Bobby watched the backs of her long legs through the shower, the muscles of her thighs. She was barefoot. As she turned back to him, she used a corner of the towel to wipe the water that dripped down her own neck.

'You were dead,' she replied.

Noel Swift was the most beautiful woman, without a doubt, that Gravity or any other Maine town had ever seen, a rare cosmopolitan out here in the sticks. Her eyes, which were the startling green of emeralds, seemed to shine when she was aroused, and they were shining now. Her lower lip was heavy, dark with lipstick; her orange hair lay in a sheet beside her right eye, a wet strand tangled on her cheek. Today, on what was otherwise a typical Wednesday in May, she was wearing a cream-colored muslin dress that ended near the tops of her thighs. Bobby loved her wholly, longed for her constantly, even though she was already his. He wanted to pull her into the shower with him – and would have if Eliot Wicker weren't standing there. He had an urge to, anyway, just to spite the undertaker.

Then Wicker reached in and turned off the shower. 'Not clinically dead,' he said. 'But passable to the naked eye.'

Bobby peeled his shirt off his back, balled it up and tossed it in the sink. 'Be the richest dead man alive,' he said, giving Noel a look as he unbuckled his belt – 'clinical or not.' At thirty-three, he had the physique of a swimmer and the dark good looks of a movie star, topped off by a disarming laugh that came so easily and so often that laughing seemed a part of his normal speech. For an edge, he'd had a red rose tattooed on the back of his right hand. 'You got something dry?' he said to the undertaker. 'I don't want to catch a cold for my funeral.' He stared at Wicker and laughed, then turned to Noel, grinning. She returned a look of her own: shining. He dropped his pants.

Downstairs in the casket selection room, Bobby knelt beside his casket, dressed in Wicker's bathrobe. He worked his hands under the velvet and snugged the Velcro strap around one of the oxygen tanks. There were two – slender green tanks lashed to either side at the head of the casket – and, concealed by the closed lower lid, a pair of eighty-pound scuba tanks fitted with a T-bar connector. Bobby's legs would rest on top of the scuba tanks.

'If I gotta be tilted for the show,' he said, adjusting an oxygen tank, 'this one digs into my side, makes it harder to concentrate.' He added, 'At least I won't have to worry about falling asleep. Could you see that, I start to snore?' He looked at Wicker and laughed hard. In another basement room, the undertaker's clothes dryer hummed.

'Do you really have to bury him?' Noel asked, strolling an adjacent aisle of showcase caskets. Her concern warmed Bobby, even though he knew what Wicker's response would be.

'Oh yeah, like the pallbearers aren't going to know the casket's empty.'

'You could bury bricks. Or rice.'

Wicker shook his head. 'Not a possibility. Once the organ

4

music starts, this box won't be alone till it's underground.' He knocked on the mahogany with one knuckle. It made a solid sound. 'Call it off now,' he said. It was a clear threat, not without mocking.

Bobby stood, put his arm around Noel, his hand on her warm hip. 'I did forty-five minutes today—'

'Forty-three,' said Wicker.

'Tomorrow I'll do an hour for the doc, no sweat. Fire up that heating pad and I bet I go two by showtime.'

'You're gonna be underground five.' Wicker again.

'And we got three hours of air in the tanks, normal breathing. Tranced out, I can stretch it to six, eight hours, no sweat.' Bobby turned again to Noel, spoke reassuringly. 'You got plenty of time to dig me up, Babe. But then you're going to have to do something to get me warm.' He looked at Wicker and laughed as he ran his hand up her side. Wicker averted his eyes. 'Seriously, though' – Bobby was still talking to Noel but now he was watching Wicker – 'you'll have a couple of hours to dig me out.'

Wicker said: 'You're up on the west end of the cemetery – all gravel. She could dig it with a spoon.'

Bobby nodded, giving Noel's side another squeeze, reassuring her. But at the edge of his mind, something was agitating him. 'Come on,' he said. 'Let's give the man his down payment and hit the road.'

They went through a door into the burgundy-carpeted office, where Noel's green silk purse was slung over the arm of a velvet couch. It was a comfortable room, softly lit and noticeably, forcefully, quiet. Framed prints of snow-covered city streets hung on the walls, intermingled with Wicker's funereal certificates. Noel opened her purse and withdrew a bulging white envelope, lifted the flap and slid a stack of twenties and fifties onto the desk. Wicker checked the window behind him.

'Make me look good,' Bobby said, 'and there'll be a bonus for you.' He grinned at Wicker.

The undertaker's gray eyes, half-closed, met Bobby's with a measure of acrimony. Eliot Wicker was an efficient funeral director. His chapel was sweet smelling, and his recorded organ music always understated. But the man was no artist, and on the rare occasion that a mourner remarked how good a client looked, anyone in town would know it was a conspicuous lie. Of course Bobby could have gone closed casket all the way, except it wouldn't have been Bobby. He wanted to know, in his next life, just what he had pulled off.

But tonight, as Noel drove home through the quiet town, something was bothering Bobby, something more than the risk. He couldn't put his finger on it. After they had driven a mile, he said to Noel, 'Call Sal. I mean, if anything gets screwed up.'

Noel drove silently for a few seconds. 'Did you tell him?'

'No. I'm just saying, if something goes wrong, call Sal.'

'Nothing's going to go wrong.'

'I'm just thinking here – you get a flat tire on the way to the cemetery, you throw out your back digging me up, somebody finds the shovel in the woods. Anything happens, you can call Sal. He's the reason we came here in the first place.'

'We came here because the locals still don't seal up their dead in concrete vaults. Nothing's going to go wrong.'

Bobby let a few moments pass.

'I don't see any other way to get at the money. The IRS is watching me, the Treasury Department is watching me, the people from the Resolution Trust. The bank wants their money back, they got their loan officer in prison. He gets out, he's gonna come looking for his share ... or he's gonna send someone. So they hear I'm dead, they'll all have a drink and a lousy night, and then get on with their lives, right?' Bobby laughed. Noel didn't.

He opened the window, let the chill night air swirl through the car. The peeping of tree frogs came and went as they passed a bog.

'I feel important,' he said. He put his hand on her inner thigh. Her legs closed. Houses they passed were dark. He took his hand off her leg, turned in his seat and faced her. He said with a grin, 'You're nervous.'

Seconds passed. Then her legs opened again and she said to him, 'Bobby, I'd rather be stuck in this horrible little town for the rest of my life than have anything happen to you.' She returned the accusation: 'You're nervous.'

He gave a shrug. 'This isn't like jumping from a plane. Up there it's wide open, you're in control.' He paused and let the vision grow. 'But this . . . you do get edgy when that lid comes down.' He laughed a little, nervously.

'Call it off,' she told him. 'We're paying the bills with what we earn from the store.'

'I *will* miss Blueberry Blossom Day,' he said, giving her a grin.

'You'll miss Sal Erickson.' She continued watching the road, her back rigid.

'Babe, I didn't say anything to him. My point is, if anything comes up, we can trust Sal Erickson—'

'We trust *no one*.' She responded so fast that her words overlapped his. And the silence that followed set those words in the air between them as if they'd been solid.

No one.

And she was right. Who in the world could keep a two-million-dollar secret?

1

'No one can forgive me but my baby.'

—Tom Waits

'*Sal?*'

    Salvatore Erickson was awakened by the harsh whisper, the beam of light brushing his face.

'*Sally—*'

Someone at the window with a flashlight. Sal sat up fast, heart thumping.

'*Come on down.*'

Sal caught his breath. 'Bobby – Jesus—'

Beside Sal, Iris stirred.

'It's Bobby,' Sal said to her. He tucked the sheet under her chin.

'Bobby?'

She groped the nightstand for her glasses.

'I'm on the ladder,' Bobby explained.

Sal kissed Iris's thumb. 'He's on the ladder. Go back to sleep.'

'Come on down for a minute,' Bobby said.

'It's one-thirty, Ace. We gotta work tomorrow.'

'That's okay, come on down.' Bobby was gone from the window before Sal could object again.

9

Michael Kimball

With a labored sigh, Sal folded the covers back and set his feet on the carpet, grabbed his underpants and corduroy trousers off the bedpost.

'Sal?' said Iris.

'It's okay, I'll only be a second.'

Stepping onto the floor and into his pants, Sal heard the sleepy plod of Davey's feet outside his room. The landing light came on, and then his fair beanpole of a girl was standing in the doorway. 'I heard talking,' she said in a breath, squinting against the light.

Iris smiled. 'Oh, love.'

'How come Daddy's getting dressed?'

'Hurry back to bed, hon,' Sal told her. 'Mommy has to get a good night's sleep. She's got a final exam tomorrow night after work.'

'Tonight,' Iris corrected. 'It's already today. And I'll be delivering a baby, too, when Trudy decides she's ready.'

Dazed, Davey looked in at her mother. 'I'll go back to bed so you can study.' Joking.

'How about a hug first?' Sal said, pulling a sweatshirt over his head.

In a single motion Davey swept across the bedroom floor and wrapped her arms around him, delicate limbs that seemed to grow longer every week. Sal moaned sleepily, lifting Davey to give her a kiss. 'You're getting so big,' he said, as he set her on the bed beside Iris. 'Give Mommy a kiss now and then hurry back to bed.' He touched Davey's hair.

'See you in the morning,' she told him, extending a lazy arm.

'See you in the morning,' he returned. Then to Iris he said, 'I'll be right back.' As he turned to leave, his sweatshirt snagged. He reached back, found Iris's hand there. He removed her fingers gently, lifted her hand to his mouth and

10

gave it a kiss. 'Don't worry, okay?' he said, then leaned over to kiss her mouth before he left the room.

Holding her daughter in bed, Iris listened to her husband go down the same worn stairs she had climbed for the first eighteen years of her own life. After a few seconds she heard the kitchen light click on. Then the familiar squeal of the kitchen door.

'Hey,' Davey whispered. 'You gonna let me go so I can get back to bed?'

Iris smiled, unclasped her hands from around Davey and kissed her cheek. Davey rolled off the bed and glided silently from the room.

Another summer coming, Iris thought, steeling herself.

Outside, the night bristled with spring – the clean chill of the air, peepers chirring off in the distance, the smell of worm-perforated soil. Sal came out quietly, pulling his corduroy sportcoat over his sweatshirt. 'Kinda late, ain't it, Ace?' he whispered to Bobby.

Sal was thirty-four, a year older than Bobby. They had grown up together outside of Providence. Like Bobby (whose maternal grandfather, Sordillo, had come from Italy), Sal was dark-eyed and dark-haired, his mother's Italian blood easily overpowering his father's Scandinavian. In fact, the only legacy Sal carried of his Swedish father (besides the surname) was his strong Nordic jaw.

'Come on,' Bobby said. Dressed in his leather jacket and black jeans, he started across the road.

Sal held back. 'What's up?' he whispered.

'Nothing, I gotta talk to you.'

'Yeah, don't wake up One-Eye,' Sal whispered. The mongrel belonged to Iris's father and brother, Otis and Jerry Royal, who lived in the small blue house across the road. The old dog had spent his life chained to the ramshackle garage that was attached to the house, presumably to keep thieves away from Jerry's collection of car parts and appliances that littered the property, or the blue gospel bus parked on the knoll, or the chickens that roamed free (one of whom, long since deceased, had given the dog its name). Roused, old One-Eye could bark for hours.

'Come on, let's go down to the falls,' Bobby said.

'Talk here,' Sal answered, but Bobby was already crossing the road, leaving Sal little choice but to follow. They joined the worn path at the left corner of the Royals' lot and started following it through the scrub field, when they heard the sudden snap of One-Eye's chain. Sal caught Bobby's arm.

'Stay still,' he whispered.

The dog, blinded by the 200-watt floodlight over his head, stretched his short chain, sniffing the air.

Bobby reached down with his hand, felt around in the grass and came up with a rock in his hand. 'Don't screw around,' Sal told him. 'They're crazy in there. They've got guns.'

Bobby laughed softly, drew his fist behind his ear.

'No,' Sal whispered, too late.

The rock arced into the night, shot like a meteor through the zone of floodlight before rejoining the darkness again, and then in the gospel bus, window glass jangled.

The dog spun, sprang at his chain, barking.

'Come on,' Bobby said, and the two men hurried along the path, their footsteps covered not only by the barking and chain-snapping but by the sudden, gravel-throated shouts from inside the house.

'SHUT UP! YOU SHUT UP, GODDAMMIT!' A light came on in the back of the house. Bobby laughed as he ran. One-Eye's barking grew more frantic. A door slammed. 'SHUT UP! HEY! HEY! *HEY!*'

As Bobby and Sal reached the river, a gunshot sounded.

The barking ceased abruptly even as the gunshot echoed off the trees, leaving the night air suddenly full of other dogs barking in the village, while Otis and Jerry Royal howled at one another inside the house. Amidst all the noise, Sal and Bobby veered away from the open river and headed right, into the woods toward the fishing pool.

They made their way through fifty feet of sparse, second-growth pine, where two of Jerry's old station wagons lay, not yet overgrown, Bobby aiming his tiny penlight beam in front of him, breaking through low, dead branches to what promised to be a moonlit riverbank.

However, the nearer they got to the river, the heavier the mist grew. By the time they reached the bank, it was like walking into a heavy cloud. The moon was a mere smudge above them, while all around sang the full, keening chorus of peeping frogs, the river whispering off to their left. Bobby slowed up, handed the penlight to Sal and said, 'Here, you know the way.'

Sal shone the penlight into the fog (for what little good it did) and led the way down to the bank.

'I think he shot his dog,' Bobby said aloud, and he laughed.

'Shh.'

Sal stopped at his fishing rock, a flat granite slab overlooking a shallow bog. Bobby put a hand on his back. 'Low tide,' Sal whispered, 'watch your step. It's not deep, but the bottom's like quicksand.'

They were at the head of the reversing falls, the phenomenon for which the town of Gravity was named. Every high tide, the river gradually slowed and deepened and then turned back on itself, the estuary waters washing inland, creating small, noisy rapids over the rocky incline just below them. When that happened, the reversing river overflowed its banks and transformed the bog they were standing on into a wide, waist-deep fishing pool.

13

Now the tide was low, and that was fortunate. Because at low tide rocks and tussocks rose out of the water, making the bog traversable.

Sal shone the penlight against the mist, looking for his first step. 'Ready?' he said, and he left his fishing rock, landing on a wide, firm tussock. He got his balance, made room for Bobby and shone the light down at his foot. Bobby stepped, landing right behind him. He took hold of Sal's arm to keep from falling.

Off to their right they heard a car pass on the road, obviously in response to the gunshot and the shouting. They could hear traces of men's voices.

'Nice of us to give the locals something to do,' Bobby croaked, chuckling. 'Fuckin crazy Jerry, I think he shot his dog.'

'Shh.'

Sal looked for the next step, a high flat rock. He saw it, barely, and was about to step off when Bobby grabbed him. '*Jesus!*'

Sal reeled with his free arm to keep from falling.

'*Jesus Christ!*' Bobby said again. In response, the peepers stopped trilling.

'Shh! What're you doing?'

Bobby snatched the penlight from Sal and shone it behind them. The beam was barely two feet long. Up in the village, dogs continued barking.

'*There's a body.*'

'What body?'

Bobby moved the penlight through the fog, illuminating a couple of plastic bottles floating under the bank. 'I'm not shittin you, Sally.' His voice was a whisper. 'I saw the ass cheek in the moonlight. Over there.'

'Ass cheek in the moonlight—?'

'Stickin out of the water. Ass and thigh.' Bobby leaned over the tussock and followed his shivering penlight beam until the light stopped on something. Sal held Bobby's leather jacket to keep him from falling.

'That?' Sal said. 'That's a milk jug. A plastic milk jug.'

'That wasn't it, Sally.' Bobby moved the light back, over a plastic bag, a slab of light blue Styrofoam, a plastic soda bottle. The pool had a habit of collecting whatever litter hadn't been carried to the ocean when the river reversed. The stuff backed up and then settled in the cove after the pool retreated with the next tide.

'That?' Sal took Bobby's hand, guided the beam to their right. 'That's a kickball, a kid's broken kickball.'

Unconvinced, Bobby pulled back to the left, moving the light through the fog. 'You know what they say about this place, Sally, how the Indians used to see things all the time. Spirits down here.'

Sal snickered. He'd never seen Bobby this shaken over anything. Bobby Swift, who'd raced motorcycles in high school, test-piloted F18s in the navy and then opened a sky-diving school when he got out – Bobby Swift afraid of ghosts?

'Right out there,' Bobby whispered. 'It's gone now.'

'The ass cheek of a ghost—?'

'Buttock and thigh. Fuck you, I know what I saw.'

Abruptly leaving the tussock, Bobby stepped down into the water and went slogging noisily for the bank.

'Hold up, I can't see,' Sal called in a whisper, but it was clear that Bobby wasn't stopping. Without the aid of the light, Sal had little choice but to step off the rock and follow, a dozen ankle-deep, foot-sucking, methane-releasing steps, until the bank rose firm and dry, and the river narrowed to their left and was loud again. Bobby waited on the path, his penlight a faint yellow dot in the mist.

When Sal climbed up alongside, his sneakers sloshed like sponges and smelled like raw sewage. 'Make sure you come get me next time you feel like talking to someone,' he said, taking the penlight from Bobby and following the path upstream. Bobby stayed two paces behind, the noise of the river easily outdoing their footsteps. Momentarily the peepers resumed behind them, and the two men were swallowed by their song, by the river sounds, the night and the mist. As the bridge began to emerge ahead, vaguely silhouetted by the lone streetlight in the village, the trees on the bank receded, giving way to piles of disused concrete supports, rusted tentacles of rebar twisting out of their sides. Beside the bridge a worn path led up to the road just below Bobby's store. Sal headed for the path. On the bridge above, a car rumbled past.

'Hold up,' Bobby told him, 'let's catch our breath, wait'll things settle down.' He sat down on a block of concrete.

Sal came back a few steps, crouched on the ground beside the concrete. He could smell Bobby's boots.

Bobby lowered his head and laughed softly. 'You hear 'em back there?' he said. 'Fuckin Jerry, man, you got some dangerous relatives.' He looked at Sal through the darkness and gave another laugh, high-pitched, nervous.

'What's up, Ace?' Sal said. It was what they used to say to each other when they were both drinking. He pushed to his feet and took a seat beside Bobby.

'I don't know. It's good to have somebody you can do this shit with. It's important.'

Sal couldn't remember a time when he had seen Bobby so serious.

'Everybody needs one person they can trust completely,' Bobby told him. 'You know what I'm saying? I mean trust with your life. Your wife, friend, I don't care. One person.'

Since Sal had quit drinking, he'd found such alcohol-fueled conversations exasperating. 'You've gotta trust yourself,' he replied, even though he knew it wasn't what Bobby wanted to hear.

'Come on, Sally, who do you trust?' Bobby stared at Sal through the darkness. 'I mean, completely. Implicitly.'

'Completely? Myself.' Sal knew by Bobby's persistent stare that he wouldn't settle for that answer. So he said, 'My wife, alright? I trust Iris.'

'Trust her with your life,' Bobby said, staring.

'Yeah.'

'With your life.'

'Yeah, why not?'

'Well.' Bobby, head lowered, nodding, resigned. 'I guess that's the way it's supposed to be.' He rubbed his palms on his pants, which meant the conversation was over, then he slid off the concrete onto his feet. 'Whaddya say, Ace? Let's go join the search party.'

When they emerged at the foot of the bridge, they walked a few feet down to the stop sign. On the road to their right, Sal's road, three men were walking toward them with a flashlight. A ways beyond the men, the blue light from the constable's car was flashing in front of the Royals' house, and silhouettes of more men crossed back and forth in front of the car's headlights. Bobby pinched a Camel from his shirt pocket and lit it with a lighter, then called to the men as they approached, 'See anything down your end?'

'Hey, Bobby!' one of them answered. It was Jerry Royal, carrying a flashlight in one hand and a 16-ounce Pabst in the other. His flashlight beam found Sal's eyes, remained there longer than necessary. Although the two men were brothers-in-law, Sal and Jerry hadn't spoken since Sal and Iris had moved from Providence eight years earlier and taken over the family house, which the town was about to confiscate for back taxes.

Jerry said to Bobby, 'We ain't seen a thing on our end. How 'bout you, down here?' (With Jerry, the word *here* had two syllables: *hee-ah*.) 'Anyways, whoever it was cost me a dog.'

'He shoots his own dog,' one of Jerry's companions said. 'I still can't believe that.'

'So?' Jerry replied lightly. 'Weren't my fault.'

His flashlight beam returned to Sal, moved down his corduroy trousers to his muddy sneakers. Then, with his other hand, Jerry dropped his empty beer can into the grass behind him. When his hand returned to his front, he was brandishing a small snub-nosed revolver. Sal felt a rushing through his chest, a tensing of muscles. He tried not to show it.

'Got my shotgun confiscated,' Jerry said. 'Imagine the town constable scared of a little honest justice?' His flashlight beam moved over the asphalt to Bobby's black boots, which were also mud-caked.

Bobby covered smoothly. 'We checked down the river, Jerry. No sign of 'em there.' He dropped his cigarette on the road, scuffed it out, then said to Sal, 'Well, Ace, we did our part. Guess I'll go in and get some sleep.' He turned his eyes up the hill to his store, where a light was on upstairs. 'Then again, it looks like Noel's awake. Maybe I won't be sleepin after all.' He looked straight at Sal and gave a laugh.

'I like the sounda that,' Jerry said, sticking the pistol back in the waistband of his jeans.

Bobby took Sal by the arm, led him aside. 'You be good,' he said. He gave a squeeze and then started for home.

Bemused by Bobby's good-bye, by the entire episode, Sal stood for a minute with the other men and watched Bobby walk over the bridge. Then Sal turned and started walking down his own road.

'Take 'er easy, Bobby,' Jerry called. The other men bade similar good-byes – to Bobby. It was a fact of Sal's life with Bobby, from childhood on: Bobby fit, Sal didn't. Heading toward the car lights and commotion in front of his house, Sal put his hands in his jacket pockets, felt a chill on his neck and thought of his hat, the old tweed touring cap that he'd lost the summer before. When he reached his house, Otis Royal was still in the road raising a ruckus with the constable while a rough semicircle of men looked on.

Sal stayed to the left, out of the light, and cut quietly across his front lawn to his back door. In the kitchen, in the dark, he took off his sneakers and socks, took off his sportcoat and laid it over a wooden chair, then made his way up the stairs. In his bedroom, he pulled his sweatshirt over his head and draped it over the bedpost. He undid his belt and stepped out of his trousers and underpants, hung the trousers over his sweat-shirt. He could hear by Iris's breathing that she was awake, waiting for him. He nestled beside her under the covers, found her face with his hands and kissed her on the mouth.

'We should really start spending more time with your family,' he said.

She made a sound in her throat. 'Did they shoot at you?'

'I wasn't the one barking.'

She sighed.

'Don't worry, okay?' He kissed her again.

The seconds passed silently, until she said: 'Bobby's going to get you killed someday.'

His hand, chilled from the outdoors, went underneath her T-shirt and found her warm breast. She curled away from him. He pursued her.

'Sal, we have to get up in three hours.'

He pulled the blankets over her shoulder, then massaged the back of her neck with his thumbs until he could feel her muscles relaxing and hear by her breathing that she was starting to fall asleep.

Outside the house, the episode ended in stages. Car doors opened and closed, car engines started, revved, then died away. Up and down the road, house lights blinked off one by one until once again the singing of peepers and the whisper of the river were the only sounds in the long bright night.

Sal lay there, his fingers tenderly working Iris's muscles, hearing all of it, hearing none of it. He was thinking about Bobby and the way he had said good-bye. Most of all he was thinking about their conversation under the bridge.

'Who do you trust?' Bobby had asked him. Sal knew the answer Bobby was looking for – he'd known it at the time too. There was something Bobby had come to tell him, some reason Bobby was asking for his confidence, and Sal had withheld it.

Silently, he lifted the covers and slipped out of bed, took his bathrobe from the bedpost and padded out of the room, putting it on. Feeling his way down the dark stairs and around the corner of the living room, he turned on the light over the kitchen table and picked up the telephone.

It was only after he began dialing Bobby's number that he thought of the hour and hung up again, telling himself that he'd go see Bobby after work. In days to come, when he thought of Bobby Swift, he'd remember this night. He'd remember the conversation under the bridge, the phone call he'd almost made, and how he had let Bobby down.

2

Gravity, Maine, boasted a population of one thousand people, give or take – more in the summer, fewer in the winter. The town supported an elementary school, a health clinic, a volunteer fire department and a grange. Roads were narrow in winter and buckled with frost heaves in spring. Blueberry fields comprised a good deal of the land in town, certainly most of the farmland, but blueberries didn't make money anymore, not for the family growers. Gravity was a poor town, by national standards, as it always had been. Houses were old, barns patiently caving in, boats in need of painting. But by Maine standards, people were not wanting. Nearly half the adults in town had jobs; the other half were unemployed or self-employed (mostly as fishermen, lobster-men, clammers) and did enough business to get by, same as townsfolk had done for decades.

The Gravity Superette was a two-and-a-half-story, white-shingled building built across from the firehouse in the village, just above the river. Bobby and Noel Swift had bought the old store with the profits from the sale of their Boston condo, and in three years (which was two years longer than Noel had planned to stay) Bobby had turned the mom-and-pop into an enviable business, all the while biding his time. Nurturing the Plan.

The Superette was the center of town life. If you needed

gasoline, kerosene, groceries, beer, wine or liquor, fishing or
hunting gear, work clothes, plumbing or electrical supplies,
hardware or rental videotapes – you could find it at the
Superette. The town's fire phone was located there. A lunch
counter and six fountain stools ensured that mealtimes were
lively with men's gossip and local politics. Although Bobby's
fish chowder was the biggest seller, according to Herb True
(whose wife Bonnie worked at the store) it wasn't the chowder
that kept the fountain stools occupied but the fact that Noel
Swift served it. Herb liked to say that Noel probably caused
more unplanned births in town than the pope.

Bobby and Noel lived upstairs from the store, in a spacious
apartment that Noel had decorated entirely in African. Tribal
ritual masks hung on the walls, animal icons peered down from
shelves and corners, and every window was surrounded by
lush green jungly plants – an oasis of high life in this poor
fishing town. Down behind the building, facing the garage
(and surrounded by woods on the other three sides), was
Noel's in-ground swimming pool; word was that in the
summertime she swam naked every night after the store
closed, although no one actually claimed to have seen her – no
one whose word was good, anyway. The basement was
Bobby's – the garage where he kept his Corvette and his
Harley, the workshop where he kept his tools, and the small
gym where he died.

At noon on Friday, after lunch, Noel drove to Bangor to buy
paint for the bathroom. She didn't kiss Bobby when she left
because she never did; although today Bobby would have liked
that. At 3:30, after high school let out, Erica and Chad came to
work as they always did, and Bobby went downstairs and
changed into his gym clothes. He usually kept the thermostat
off, but today he needed a cold sweat, so he turned it up to
eighty.

At 4:00 Eliot Wicker came in for his afternoon coffee. At

4:30 Noel called from a Bangor hardware store and asked for Bobby. He's not answering the phone in the apartment, she told Chad, maybe he's down in the gym.

The baby-faced, broad-shouldered boy – Chad was captain of the school football team and a churchgoing Baptist – hurried downstairs and knocked on the gym door. He called Bobby's name. When he got no answer, he pushed the door open and saw his boss on the carpet beside his exercise bike, one foot stuck in the stirrup, his face contorted in pain. In the first instant, Chad was dumbstruck. Then he ran to the bike and dropped to his knees, knocking into Bobby's arm, and struggled to pull Bobby's foot out of the stirrup, hoping the stuck foot was the extent of his problem. 'Bobby, you okay?' he said.

But Bobby's arm was clammy to the touch, his eyes slack and unfocused.

'*Bobby?*'

Chad took Bobby by the shoulders and shook him. Bobby's head flopped lifelessly.

'Wait a minute!' Chad blurted, and he looked wildly around the room. 'Wait a minute!' he said again, then ran out the door, glancing hard off the frame.

Now Bobby relaxed, let every molecule of his body fall into a calm of keen concentration. Chad was a smart boy. He'd call the emergency number posted on the store phone. After 4:30 on Fridays, Walt Moody was the only doctor at the clinic. The young man had twice in the past half-year listened through a stethoscope while Bobby made his heart turn somersaults. Both times he had rushed Bobby to Downeast Memorial, where the disorder was diagnosed as cardiac arrhythmia; and so it was charted at the Gravity clinic. Bobby's history listed a grandfather who had died of heart failure before his fortieth birthday – a fiction, but part of the official record, nonetheless. With such a background, and a God-fearing football captain as a witness, there'd be no cause for suspicion, no reason for the insurance companies to request an autopsy. Doc Moody, who was known to tremble in the presence of death, would gladly stand aside for Eliot Wicker, who was already on his way downstairs. Without complications, Bobby knew that he'd be on his way to the funeral home in a half hour.

Bobby let go of his body, let go of his mind and went deep into himself. This was not sleep, but *focus*, pure and total, the way he had been taught by the Brahman, the way he had trained for the past four years. He let his bladder empty into his sweatpants. He *became* his heart, *became* his lungs, and he brought himself to rest, quelling his body's panic with masterful control, so that even when his heart began slowing and his lungs shutting down, he could hear the undertaker's throaty voice rising above the rumble of footsteps coming down the stairs. 'No one allowed,' Wicker was saying. 'No one allowed.' Bobby was at once totally aware and totally unaware of it all.

Sal Erickson's headaches were nothing new, but today he had a beauty. The annual Blueberry Blossom Pageant was Sunday night, and his only schoolwide rehearsal had been a disaster. Children didn't know how to line up on the stage, they didn't know words to the songs, and their singing was brutal. It was the same every year with these shows: kids acting up, stressed-out teachers buzzing around him, *Mrs Bonnevill's class has the best songs again this year*, *Mrs Perkins never did it this way*, day after day, week after week, a thirty-four-year-old man spending the best years of his life corralling little kids onto a rickety gym stage, the same man who, ten years earlier, had toured Europe as a featured soloist in Woody Herman's Thundering Herd, whom *Downbeat* had called 'one of the brightest young trombone players in the east,' Mr Sal Erickson, ladies and gentlemen, now performing a little number about pussy willows, pufferbellies and flying fucking unicorns.

When Sal got home after school, the cat was on the counter drinking milk that Davey had spilled, and Davey was sprawled on the living room floor watching cartoons. Sal took off his corduroy jacket and tossed it on the couch.

'Tough day?' he said.

She took her hand out from under her chin and rocked it a little, never taking her eyes off the television.

'Take me fishing?' she said.

'You talking to Bugs Bunny or me?'

She wiggled her skinny butt at him.

'I gotta make supper, hon. Mom's got her big test tonight. Besides, I bet you didn't weed the peas like I asked you.' Davey wiggled her butt again. 'Or practice your piano.'

He went into the bathroom and stepped out of his trousers, hung them on the towel rack, then took his black sweatpants out of the hamper and put them on. Sal had been a good athlete in school. He still had an athletic body, able and well-proportioned. In fact, with his thick neck and coarse, cropped black hair, he looked more like a football player than he had a musician – or a music teacher, as he had come to acknowledge himself. He unbuttoned his shirt, pulled it over his T-shirt and pitched it in the hamper, then went into the kitchen to find his sneakers.

'I'll take you fishing tomorrow morning,' he called to Davey as he laced up, 'but you gotta do your piano and peas.' He stepped out the back door, where he saw Jerry Royal across the road, working over a smoking trash barrel. It was where Jerry incinerated his oily rags and trash and the occasional chicken that got flattened in the road. Jerry was stirring the fire with a charred piece of two-by-four that was also on fire, by the looks of it. By the stench, Sal guessed that Jerry was burning the dog he had shot the night before.

Aware that his brother-in-law was staring at him through the smoke, Sal turned right, toward the village, checked his watch and started jogging. Actually, what Sal did couldn't be called jogging. From the start it was a flat-out, lung-singing sprint. A straight half mile in 2:10. 'Like someone was after him,' their neighbor Martha Abraham would tell people at the post office.

Sal's lungs were already burning as he blew past Mrs Abraham's house, past the lone apple tree in her field. He pumped hard, his lungs stretching beyond their limit, his heart pounding in his chest. Then he pushed even harder, certain that he had never run as fast, chasing his own elongated shadow up the frost-heaved asphalt. He could hear Thelonius Monk in the whistling through his teeth. *Little Rootie Tootie*. Yeah, they're chasing me now, Mrs Abraham.

Behind him he heard a car coming fast. He thought wildly that he could keep pace with it, and he opened up even more, incredibly, until he felt as if his heart might explode – and then the vehicle passed him. It was the undertaker's black Suburban, Eliot Wicker heading to the Superette for his afternoon coffee.

At the junction of the Village Road Sal slowed to a jog, to a walk, then bent at the waist, panting. He checked his watch. Two-ten, a new record. He walked a wide arc in the road, hands on his hips. His face burned, and his lungs replaced air like a two-stroke engine. Off ahead of him, the sun sat low above the trees, a warm, smiling peach, while the surrounding sky had become the kind of promising blue that only happens in spring. Sal felt good about that, felt good about noticing it. A lone peeper began chirping down at the river, getting a start on the evening. Sal felt good about that too. Six months since he'd quit drinking, to the day. He felt strong, every day stronger.

He and Iris were getting along better than ever. Davey was happy and healthy and doing aces at school. His Sunday concert, he knew, would go fine. In fact, the only unsettledness in his life, as he saw it, was whatever he had left hanging with

Bobby the night before – and now, while he had a few minutes, he was going to take care of that. Heading up the hill to Bobby's store, he sprang into a run, bolting straight up the middle of the grated bridge, pushing with everything he had left.

'No one allowed,' Wicker sang, his spindly arms outstretched to the stairway walls. Sal pulled on the undertaker's shoulder, trying to push past. 'No one allowed!' Wicker said again, shaking him off. But on the landing Sal shoved past Wicker as if the man were a turnstile.

'You can't go down there!' Wicker told him, as Sal took the remaining stairs two at a time, then swung around the half partition and charged through the door that led into Bobby's gym.

'It's his heart!' Chad called from behind Wicker.

Sal flew into the room, crouched over Bobby. 'Call a doctor! Did somebody call a doctor?' he shouted.

'You either!' Wicker said, banging into the small room, attempting to close the door on Chad.

Sal lifted Bobby's head into his hands and spoke into his face, as if he were waking his friend from a nap. '*Bobby?*' The hair that hung over Bobby's neck was wet. His skin was chilled. '*Come on, Bobby!*'

'Let me in there, leave him alone!' Wicker snapped, slapping his hand down on Sal's shoulder, his fingernails digging into Sal's skin.

Sal disregarded him. He slid his leg under Bobby's neck to keep his head from falling. With his left hand he raised Bobby's shoulder, cradling him. 'Bobby, you come on now!' he cried. With his right fist, he thumped Bobby's chest.

Bobby gasped. His eyes gaped. His body stiffened, trembled for a second and then fell limp, even though his eyes held their same stark surprise.

'Get him off!' Wicker yelled, wrapping his arm around Sal's neck and pulling back.

Now another pair of arms grabbed Sal from behind. 'Mr Erickson!' It was Chad, much stronger than Eliot Wicker. Together they hauled Sal back across the carpet, Bobby sliding with him.

'Let him go!' Wicker strained, locking his arm around Sal's arm and pulling back. 'You probably killed him yourself!'

'No, he's coming out of it!' Sal shouted, not relenting. He reached to pound Bobby's chest again, but with Chad wresting his arm back, he managed only a glancing blow. And then he lost Bobby, as Chad drove him back against the door. 'Mr Erickson, you gotta stop!' he said.

'*Somebody call a doctor!*'

'I called the ambulance!' Chad said.

'It doesn't matter!' Wicker shouted. '*He's dead!*'

The words stunned Sal. For the moment he lay against the door, motionless, looking over Chad's shoulder, while Wicker knelt beside the sprawled body, holding Bobby's wrist between his thumb and first two fingers, his other hand on Bobby's heart, his ear pressed to Bobby's open mouth. The picture of concentration. After a few seconds, the undertaker raised his head and took a deep breath. He looked over at Sal and gave a shrug, his teeth clenched hopelessly.

'I'm sorry,' he said, bringing all his funereal compassion to bear. 'He's gone.'

'No, he breathed,' Sal asserted, Chad still pinning him against the door, digging the sides of his sneakers into the carpet.

Wicker shook his head with a patronizing smile. 'Reflexes,' he explained. 'You knocked the wind out of a dead man.'

Sal didn't get home until ten that night. When he walked in the living room, Davey was sitting in the rocking chair, wrapped in a quilt and watching TV. Iris, already back from school, was asleep on the couch, her notebooks and textbooks and pager spread on the coffee table and floor. Sal lifted Davey off the chair. As he carried her up the stairs, she said sleepily, 'Where were you?'

'Something came up,' Sal told her. He carried her into her bedroom and put her in bed, tucked her in.

'Mommy had to get Melissa to stay with me while she went to take her test,' Davey said to him, giving him a worried look.

'I know,' he said. They kissed lightly on the lips, then Sal shut off her raccoon lamp and started downstairs.

'See you in the morning,' she sighed.

'See you in the morning.'

Downstairs he kissed Iris awake. She opened her eyes placidly, then adjusted her specs and held up her middle finger for him. He kissed the finger. 'How was your test?'

She held the finger in place.

'I get the message.'

'Just making sure,' she said.

She looked at him curiously. Her soft eyes sharpened and her finger went slack.

His words fell like wood. 'Bobby died.'

She drew a quick breath. 'Bobby Swift?'

'He had a heart attack, working out.'

Iris raised herself on her elbow, eyes glistening. She took another breath, let it out. She reached for Sal's arm, took a fistful of his shirt and pulled him down on top of her. He kept a knee on the floor.

'Are you okay?' she asked him.

'Yeah,' he answered, with some surprise. Actually he *was* okay; stunned, maybe, but not distraught, as he thought he'd be. (As he thought he *should* be.) He had already stopped wondering if there was any psychic significance to Bobby's late-night visit the night before, or to the way Bobby had said good-bye. He started to kiss Iris again and, without planning to, opened his mouth and found her tongue with his own. He took hold of her small breast, took her nipple between his thumb and finger. Her body rose into his. She took his hand and broke the kiss.

'We don't want to do this now.'

Involuntarily, he drew a long breath, thinking he might finally cry. But he didn't. He ran his hand up under her cotton jersey, found her nipple hardened, and he manipulated it again.

She took his hand. 'Sal, we wouldn't be any good.'

'I don't know about that,' he answered.

He thought he should feel some shame for the way he wanted her now, but now he felt so grateful to have her. They went into the bathroom and brushed their teeth together, then climbed the stairs with only the moon through the window below lighting their way. Once in bed, they had tumultuous sex for an hour, their first in weeks.

3

Bobby came to in Wicker's black Suburban, zippered in a white body bag. As he had done the night before, he once again broke into uncontrollable shivering. His wet sweatpants didn't help. He rattled the plastic bag, clattered the collapsible stretcher and then heard Wicker shout at him to keep still. When they got to the funeral home, Wicker wheeled him on the stretcher into the laundry room, where he unbagged Bobby and wrapped him in an electric blanket. Despite its low heat, the acclimation was just as painful as when he'd been dropped into the bathtub.

But it was nothing compared to the boredom that followed – the seemingly endless thirty-six hours closed in that laundry room, lying on a pile of wool blankets reading *Money* magazines and ten years' worth of *American Funeral Director*, or periodically going into the toilet enclave and masturbating, imagining Noel.

The confinement was brutal. But Wicker had threatened to expose the whole scam if Bobby so much as opened the laundry door, and Wicker was nervous enough to do it. He had kept Bobby awake for most of the first night, clearing his throat upstairs, a meticulous, continuous dislodging of phlegm. The more Bobby tried to ignore it, the more aware of it he became, so that his own sleep was fitful at best – and he needed to be rested.

The only respite from the boredom was an hour on Saturday morning, when Sal came with Noel to choose the casket. Hearing Sal's voice through the wall, Bobby was saddened to think that he was losing his best friend. At the same time, he was revisited by the unsettling suspicion that something was slipping his mind, and he wished more than ever that he had included Sal in the Plan.

When the voices came closer, Bobby cupped his ear to the wall and heard Sal say something about the teachers' retirement fund – offering to help pay for the funeral. And Noel refusing.

'Just send me the bill,' Sal said to Wicker.

'If Mrs Swift is comfortable with that,' Wicker replied.

'Send me the bill,' Sal said again.

Noel was wrong. Sal they could trust. And, after all, things *could* get screwed up. Noel could get in an accident driving to the cemetery. Kids could be up at the cemetery raising hell. With Sal as backup, they'd be able to handle it.

'If there's anything else I can help you with,' Bobby heard Wicker say, getting rid of them. Bobby slid to the door. He could do it now. He could open the door and—

'We make this as easy as we possibly can for the bereaved,' Wicker continued. Bobby could hear their footsteps moving past. The thought of telling Sal what he was pulling—

He took hold of the doorknob.

Now or never. Include Sal. Sneak up behind him, scare the shit out of him, take a picture of the look on his face and laugh like hell.

A door closed, and Wicker's voice went away. 'Times like these . . .'

Yeah, tell Sal. And then leave him here.

Another door closed, the voices becoming thin tones through the wood paneling.

Because if Sal knew that Bobby was alive, he wouldn't be

able to leave it like that. Not for the rest of his life. Someday, maybe ten or twenty years from now, when he thought it was safe, Sal was bound to find a pay phone somewhere. Or take an innocent Cayman vacation. If suspicion ever arose, if the government got more proficient at tracking down every missing pebble in their mountain range of defaulted savings and loans, all they'd have to do is take a look at Sal. Question him on the wrong day, threaten to separate him from his family.

Noel was right. The Plan was perfect. He winced to think how close he had come to blowing it. All his life Bobby had thrived on risk and fear, had burned it like fuel. But it had never worried him like this.

Maybe it was because he had never had to rely on anyone else. And now his life depended on Noel. So ... The Plan was perfect. The Plan was in motion, and, besides, it was too late to turn back.

For the rest of the day – and all through that long second night – Bobby lay sprawled on the heap of blankets, with-standing the odor of detergent, listening to the footsteps pacing above him (and the incessant throat-clearing), going over it again and again.

The shovel and pitchfork were waiting in the woods near his plot. The rental car was reserved at Bangor International Airport (in the name of Dale Newman, who had also reserved a hotel room at the Logan Airport Hilton in Boston). Once closed inside the casket, Bobby would open the tanks in succession: the scuba tanks first, then the oxygen tanks. He would set his watch alarm each time he opened a valve in order to rouse himself when it was time to start a new tank. Sometime before the third alarm sounded, Noel would be there digging him out. She'd awaken him with a whisper. She'd have a suitcase of new clothes (they'd leave his burial outfit in the grave). In the suitcase would also be scissors, hair dye, tortoiseshell glasses and his new wallet, along with Dale Newman's plane ticket, passport and birth certificate – courtesy of a Brookline counterfeiter Noel had met in her modelling days. In the new wallet was Dale Newman's driver's license and an identification card issued by the Atlantic National Bank and Trust, where two million dollars waited in an offshore Cayman account shared by Bobby Swift and Dale Newman. Now that Bobby Swift had passed on, the account belonged solely to Mr Newman. New man indeed. He'd make his first withdrawal Monday morning. Buy a bicycle and some diving gear and start his new life.

When the life insurance settlement came in – twenty-five thousand, not enough to cause suspicion – Noel would take a vacation, leave the store in Herb and Bonnie's hands and go on a cruise out of Tampa. She would write back that she'd met a wealthy man on the boat and fallen in love. She'd hand over the store to Bonnie True, lock, stock and videotape, and then disappear.

From then on, the Newmans would be islanders. Their leased condo stood two doors from the water. Once they won approval as Cayman residents, they'd buy beachfront, invest the rest in conservative mutual funds and live fat and free for the rest of their lives. They'd ride bicycles with straw baskets on the handlebars, they'd dive every day down the bottomless reefs. What else was there to do on Grand Cayman but scuba dive, bask, feast and hide your money? They'd eat fresh fruits and fishes, drink rum punch and fall asleep every night in each other's arms, listening to the hush of the surf, knowing they were safe in the vast, warm hold of the Atlantic. Except

the coughing—

Except for Eliot Wicker.

That was it.

Noel's words came to Bobby with a cold slap: *We trust no*

one. A single vision chilled him: shiny black wingtips scuffing through beach sand.

At five o'clock on the morning he was to be buried, Bobby Swift opened the laundry door and came into Wicker's office with his penlight. He stole through the embalming room, through the casket selection room and into the chapel, where his own mahogany casket sat up in front of fifteen rows of chairs. Only the viewing lid was open, as it would remain during the funeral. The room was windowless, airless.

He opened another door and crept into the arrangements office, where ivory dawn light lined the venetian blinds. He moved to the window and quietly parted two slats. The sky was softly lit. Brighter was the white sign on the front lawn – WICKER'S FUNERAL HOME – as was the parking lot; the double lights on the single pole swarmed with insects. Why any funeral director needed to advertise, why he needed to light an empty parking lot—

But of course Eliot Wicker wasn't advertising – or helping customers park their cars. He was afraid of the dark, plain and simple. He was afraid, and he would break, Bobby was sure of it now. Once Wicker's share of the money was spent and all he had left was his gnawing envy and that throat-clearing fear – he'd spill it all. Maybe to some out-of-town therapist, maybe to his mother, maybe he'd go straight to the police, or he'd gas himself in his spotless Suburban and leave a note. Whichever way Wicker wanted it, there'd come the day when the black shoes would appear at Bobby's beach blanket, double-knit cuffs fat with sand. He pictured Noel being led off the beach in handcuffs. He pictured himself killing Eliot Wicker.

Pistol shot to the head, knife through the heart – he allowed the notion to grow. He even caught himself trying to justify it: Wicker was greedy and heartless, and the world would be a better place without him. But that wasn't the point, and Bobby knew it. Murder was murder, and Eliot Wicker was standing between this dead man and a lifetime of bliss. It could be quick, it could be done tonight, after the resurrection, before Bobby left for Boston. Noel would never need to know.

Murder.

And who better to commit the crime than a dead man? Bobby waited for some pang of remorse, but none came, even as he turned back into the building (wiping doorknobs with his shirtsleeve) and slipped into the embalming room, where he pulled on a pair of latex gloves and went quietly opening drawers until he found the two things he was looking for: a tiny screwdriver and the weapon. He didn't know the object's real purpose, but it was assuredly built to do the deed – a hollow steel shaft, sixteen inches long and pointed at the tip. A touch of irony – the word SLAUGHTER was engraved on its side.

Murder.

He crept back to the chapel and hid the thing in his casket, under the velvet, under the scuba tanks, beside the six-volt lantern battery that would power his heating pad.

Then he went back to the arrangements office, lit brighter with the dawn. There was a black plastic panel of four switches on the wall. They were labeled MUSIC, SIGN, PARKING, CHAPEL. Penlight in his mouth, Bobby unscrewed the panel cover, saw the red wire he wanted and leveraged it off the terminal with a spark. He looked out the blinds and saw the parking lot lights extinguished, then tucked the wire back in the box and replaced the panel. He returned the little screwdriver to its place in the embalming room and headed back to the laundry room, where he continued his preparations. In the enclave, up by the ceiling, there was a small casement window. Bobby stood on the toilet seat, reached up behind the venetian blinds and unlocked it, then he settled back on his bed of blankets to sleep. Murder, indeed. The notion made him slightly more nervous than his burial, and now he found himself clearing his own throat. He heard Wicker's cough like an answering call, and he answered back noisily, wondering with a quiet yet persistent laugh if the undertaker was stretched out on his bed, staring at the ceiling, thinking the very same thing: that there was almost nothing a dead man couldn't do.

Rest Awhile, the hillside cemetery was named. Grass was thick here, and trees crowned with a lofty iridescence. Sunday morning, Blueberry Blossom Day, the day of Bobby Swift's funeral, Sal's school concert. The walking calmed Sal.

Watching Iris and Davey stroll ahead, Davey touching each windsmoothed tablet as they walked, Sal was touched by the similarities of mother and daughter: the shiny, oaken, pageboy hair; the slight, agile bodies. They even walked the same, upright, with short tentative steps, like sprinters saving something. It was here that Sal and Iris sought to smooth over whatever crags Bobby's death had cut in Davey's young philosophy.

For his part, Sal was handling it judiciously – although he remained unable to thoroughly absorb the simple fact: Bobby was dead. Over the two days, he'd found himself repeating it – Bobby is dead. Bobby is dead. But it wasn't sinking in, even when he'd revisit the experience: Bonnie True's watery eyes when Wicker wheeled the body out the garage door; the way the regulars sat at the counter, back-to, bitterly reviewing the warning signs they had missed; or the smart, fatalistic look Noel had given him when she had arrived, and the way she'd hugged him, seeming to be offering comfort rather than accepting it.

'Remember when Thelonius died?' Iris's voice broke the silence. 'And we buried him out back, with his little gravestone?' With the black clip of a pager stuck to her pocket (one of her midwifery mothers from Oyster Cove was due today), she reminded Sal of a tour group leader, the way she seemed to glide over the lawn, conducting this family lesson in mortality.

'Is Thelonius in heaven?' Davey asked.

'Imagine,' Sal said, 'a heaven full of cats.'

With a backward glance at him, Iris answered Davey: 'If you think about it, cemeteries are really for those of us who are alive, so we can remember the people and pets we loved.' Iris seemed unmindful that the other members of her family, Otis and Jerry Royal, were at the top of the hill, digging Bobby's grave. Sounds of their arguing wafted down the hill.

'Is that where they're burying Bobby?' Davey asked, looking up. 'Way up there by himself?'

'Mm-hmm.'

Sal wondered, as he often had (as many townspeople had), how Iris and Davey could have come from the same gene matter that invested Iris's father and brother.

'I know where my grandmother is,' Davey said abruptly, breaking away from Iris.

'We really don't have time, love.'

'Daddy showed me once,' she said, venturing deeper into the cemetery.

Iris looked back at Sal, who called to Davey, 'Come on, hon, we've got to get you to Kristin's.' But Davey had already found the marker in the ground.

'I found her, Mommy. Leonna Royal.'

Sal climbed the terrace, walked to Davey's side and rested his hand on her head.

'She's got killed in the bus crash, right?'

'Yup.'

'But how come there are no flowers?' Davey looked back at Iris. 'You said cemeteries were to remember the people we love.'

Iris joined them, her arms folded. She glanced back to see her father at the top of the hill, leaning on his shovel, looking down at her. 'Sometimes people don't have good memories,' she said.

Davey scowled. 'Was she mean?'

'Not mean, just sort of – hollow.'

'*Hollow—?*'

'Empty,' Iris attempted, 'unforgiving . . . love, I really don't remember.' She turned toward the road, caught a breeze in her face. She held her hand out. 'Time to go,' she said. Davey took hold and they started back toward the gate. Sal hung back to give them time.

It was the blue gospel bus, the dented shrine that sat on the knoll beside her father's house. Sal had learned some of the story from Iris, more from Bobby. The Royals had been returning from a gospel jubilee in New Brunswick. There was a photo in a scrapbook at the town house, autographed. Iris, who was eight, played mandolin. Her father played fiddle, her mother played guitar. Jerry, at fifteen, was the grinning star of the band, slapping a big upright bass, THE ROYAL FAMILY decaled in white letters on its face. GOSPEL TROUBADOURS.

The kids were asleep when the bus left the road, Otis too drunk to manage a curve. The bus rolled only once; in fact, the vehicle escaped with minimal damage. But inside, the Royals and their equipment were tossed about like bingo pills. Only Iris, tucked into bed, was not seriously hurt. Jerry broke his leg; Otis fractured his skull, broke both wrists and several ribs, and was unconscious for two days; Leonna, who had just put Iris to bed, broke her neck and died instantly.

'I'd be sad if you were killed in the accident,' Davey said to her mother, then deadpanned with a backward look at Sal. 'Then again, I guess I wouldn't be here to be sad.'

'Clown,' he said, catching up to her and wrapping an arm around her neck. She grabbed his hand and pulled it around her shoulder.

Michael Kimball

'Anyway,' she said to him, 'I still don't see why I can't go to Bobby's funeral. How old were you when you went to your brother's funeral?'

'Are you still playin that old song?'

'Mm-hmm.'

'I didn't go to my brother's funeral,' he told her.

'How come?'

Sal shrugged his shoulders. 'I wasn't invited.'

Davey looked up at him. He shrugged again. She sighed, her eyes wandering over the ground.

'What's up, hon?' he said, pulling her against him.

Davey shook her head, scowling. 'I really miss Bobby,' she said in a small voice, no longer clowning. Sal lifted her off the ground, put his cheek against hers and resumed walking. She wrapped her arms around his neck, her legs around his waist. He heard her sniff. Bobby is dead, he said to himself. *Bobby is dead.* But all he could feel was the warmth of Davey's face on his, the warmth of the sun on his back and the wonderful quiet of the morning.

'What the hell did she send this monkey suit for?' Bobby complained. He and Noel had argued about the tweed suit ever since she'd brought it home for him a year ago, in preparation for the funeral.

'Close your eyes,' Wicker told him.

Bobby lay on the embalming table, dressed in tweed slacks and a sleeveless T-shirt, his face stiff with foundation. Wicker had spent almost ten minutes working on his hair, bent over him, sighing, grunting, holding his breath. The service was two hours away.

'Close,' Wicker said again. Bobby did, and the undertaker rubbed his thumbs on Bobby's eyelids. When he finished, Bobby opened his eyes and saw him screwing the cover on a large white jar. EYE SHADOW, the label said.

40

'Wait a minute,' Bobby told him. 'Gimme a mirror.'

'Be quiet. You've got to have color.'

'I've got color, I'm alive. Just give me a fucking mirror.'

'I don't have a fucking mirror.' Wicker turned and picked up a small bottle from his tray. 'This is for your lips,' he said.

'No way, no lipstick,' Bobby told him.

But as Wicker unscrewed the brush applicator, it was clear that he wouldn't be swayed. 'It's not lipstick anyway, keep quiet.'

Bobby grabbed his hand. ZIPLIP, the label said.

'It's to keep your mouth shut,' Wicker told him. There was some satisfaction in his voice as he brushed the vaporous liquid on Bobby's lips. 'Close,' he said. 'Breathe through your nose.'

Fortunately, Bobby's nostrils were clear, and the fumes from the glue cleared them more, but that still didn't quell the slight panic he felt. He snapped his lips apart. 'Am I gonna be able to get this stuff off?'

A door closed in the next room. Wicker's hand shot out, clenched Bobby's jaw. The grip was firm; the hand trembled. Footsteps approached loudly. Bobby closed his eyes. The door opened. A voice said, 'I come over early, Eliot. Think we might need more chairs.' *Chayuhs*. It was Jerry Royal, the odd job man.

Bobby heard satisfaction in Wicker's response: 'I don't think we'll get that many today.'

There was a protracted silence then, and Bobby knew that Jerry's eyes were on him. Under Wicker's perfumed hand, Bobby's teeth dug into his lip. 'Awful young,' the voice said.

'Jerry,' Wicker replied, 'knock, okay?'

'No problem.'

The door closed. Wicker's hand left Bobby's mouth, and Bobby tried his lips. The cement had set. Wicker began to hum as he unscrewed another jar. When Bobby opened his eyes, he saw Wicker's two fingertips, smeared with red, coming down to his face.

'Oops,' the undertaker said happily, as he began making small circles on Bobby's cheeks. ROUGE, the jar said.

Bobby grabbed his hand. It wasn't to stop him, as Wicker thought when he first tried to pull away. It was a handshake, a pact. A grip of faith in another human being. Bobby's eyes, burning from glue fumes, locked onto Wicker's. His fingers locked around Wicker's hand, held it strong.

The undertaker twisted out of Bobby's grasp. '*Okay,*' he whispered.

It was at this moment that Bobby knew for sure that he would return tonight to kill this man. He hoped he wouldn't enjoy it.

Sal avoided looking at Bobby's casket as they made their way into the cool chapel. Likewise, he avoided Noel, who stood surrounded by flowers and mourners in the front corner of the room.

There was no question that she was as striking a widow as Gravity had ever seen. Her dress was camp, a black lacy tribute to the '40s, the sleeves a membranous skin that hugged her wrists to the heels of her black lace gloves. She accepted sympathy straight-backed, almost defiantly, presenting the rich façade that no townsperson had ever come close to penetrating.

Taking a seat at the end of a row of folding chairs, Sal kept his eyes on his own fingers in his lap. Sitting this quietly, he felt the tremor playing deep inside him, as he knew it would. He tried to ignore it by concentrating on the recorded organ music, the soft talking.

He had been to only one funeral in his life, his grandmother's, when he was too young to be impressed. Although he was ten when his younger brother Anthony drowned, his parents went to the service without him. And then neither of them ever again mentioned Anthony's name in his presence.

The boys had been walking through the woods near their house when Anthony walked out on a section of frozen river. Sal had told him not to, but Anthony laughed at him and went out further. That's the way Sal remembered it, anyway. When Anthony broke through, it was only up to his waist, and Sal laughed right back at him – at the way Anthony's mouth and eyes flared from the cold – but then Anthony slid under. He was wearing a red hooded sweatshirt, and Sal watched the color travel beneath the ice, limp as a flag. Sal screamed Anthony's name, he stood helpless for a second or more. Then he ran down through the trees thirty feet or so to a spot downriver where the banks widened and the ice opened up in the middle. He got there before Anthony did. The ice, which grew in around the rocks along the bank, was maybe a half-inch thick. But where the river deepened and the channel got stronger, the ice thinned to a film and then gave way to moving black water. Sal made his way out to the furthest rock and, as he did, Anthony emerged in the open – facedown, hands dragging the bottom. Sal stretched his arm as far as he could. He leaned his hand on the film of ice until it broke through. But his little brother floated past, out of reach, and once again started to slide under the ice. Sal screamed at him to stop. He shifted his body on the rock and kicked his heels through the ice, intending to go in after Anthony.

But the river was dark and frigid, and it poured into Sal's boots like fire, trying to pull him under too. So he sat there with his legs in the water, clutching the rock while he watched his brother disappear for good.

For a number of seconds, or a number of minutes, he sat motionless, letting the icy river tug at his feet. He was stunned by the cold, by the clean, bright silence of winter. In fact, it amazed him how peaceful the woods and river seemed, with

Anthony tumbling away under the ice and his own senseless legs dangling in the river. Finally he lowered himself off the rock until his feet hit the bottom and the water reached his waist. Holding the rock dearly, he lowered the rest of his body in, dropping to his knees and letting the icy river pour over his neck and head. He came up screaming again because it hurt so much, and because that's all he could do. Scream and run for home, the frozen survivor.

It was a mile downriver that Anthony finally stopped, snagged by a half-submerged shopping cart behind the town pizza place. The boys' Italian mother didn't speak a word for almost a year but sat in her living room and watched television hour after hour. Sal's father, a Swedish stonemason who had never talked much anyway, began spending his evenings in the cellar, where he carved duck decoys and listened to Lutheran radio broadcasts from Chicago. Sal – ten years old, eleven years old – stayed outdoors as long it was light, playing pickup sports in the neighborhood. At night, when he came inside, he would shut himself in his room and practice his trombone. When the family ate together, it was in silence. The morning his mother finally spoke, it was to a glass of orange juice that Sal had knocked off the table. 'Sock it to me,' she said.

Sal felt inside his sportcoat pocket for the pills. The Librium had been part of his detox therapy the previous winter. Before leaving the house for the cemetery, he had stashed three or four in his pocket. Not that he was craving a drink, but a raw unsettledness had been growing in him since Bobby's death, like a caffeine overload. He reasoned that it was stress. First Bobby's death and now the funeral, not to mention his school show later in the evening. No reasoning about it – an icy vodka martini danced on the fringes of every thought. He let the pills slide through his fingers and removed his hand from his pocket. He'd gone six months without needing one; he didn't want to start now.

Without meaning to, he looked up and saw Bobby. The pink, mannequin face. Lying there in a coat and tie. Christ, Bobby hated neckties. Leashes, he'd called them.

When I die, Bobby had said once, *I want my body to be dropped on the White House lawn from twenty thousand feet. No chute. Bam! During a press conference, the president up there, a note around my neck saying, 'Bullshit.'*

Sal's chest jumped with a laugh, thinking of the way Bobby had laughed when he'd said that. He shifted in his chair, noticed Eliot Wicker in the corner of the room, standing stiffly beside the minister, his hands folded solemnly in front of him while his eyes darted around the room, eliciting nothing but a cold, indifferent greed, just the kind of man to escort you from the world.

By now the mourners were crowding in both doors, while Jerry Royal, stuffed into a light blue leisure suit, pushed up the aisles carrying more chairs.

Now Sal could hear weeping, and he looked to his right, where a broad-backed teenage boy was hugging a sobbing girl with a blotchy face. It was Chad and Erica, from the Superette. Chad seemed to be holding the girl up. That touched Sal.

Still, he wasn't close to tears himself. He figured – not for the first time – that this too was due to his alcoholism. Here he had just lost his best friend – his only friend – and he felt nothing so much as the low, steady drumming of his vodka god.

As the minister asked everyone to stand for a prayer, Sal slipped his hand in his pocket, pulled out a Librium and stuck it in his dry mouth, forced it down.

It was late afternoon when they buried Bobby. Sal and Iris stood together in front of the casket. Noel and the minister stood beside them, casting long shadows. The sound of an occasional car passing on the road below was audible only during the silent meditation, and then only when the wind stopped.

Sal spotted Iris's father waiting under an oak tree with a shovel and pitchfork in a wheelbarrow. Otis was a fat man, white-haired and pink-faced, wearing a white T-shirt that showed his pinkish gut. He was making noise with his tools, probably because Iris was there.

It was over quickly. The minister blessed Bobby and blessed the mourners, and the townspeople filed past, some stopping to lay a flower on the casket. Sal, subdued by the Librium, stood at the grave until the last person left.

Noel came up behind him and took his arm, and then she took Iris's arm and worked her way between them both. 'You guys are coming over, aren't you? Help me get through this?' Iris started to say that, no, she had a baby to deliver in Oyster Cove, when Noel abruptly let go of Sal's arm and turned Iris toward the cars. 'Keep walking,' she said.

Sal saw the reason. Otis was coming toward them, his tools clattering in the wheelbarrow, his round gut bouncing like a sack of feed. Sal was impressed, but not altogether surprised, by how deftly Noel had read the situation. He noticed Eliot Wicker standing by a black limousine, holding the back door open, watching the women. Wicker cleared his throat pointedly. Noel turned, then gently released Iris and said to Sal, 'I'm supposed to ride in the limo. I'll see you there.'

When his wristwatch started to beep, Bobby started his heart. He drew a shallow breath through his nose as he rose slowly to consciousness. His eyes opened to blackness. Close to his face he could hear the dull, uneven rhythm of gravel piling onto the coffin. Another sound – his scuba tank sputtering – meant he had stretched a half hour of air to an hour and a half, right on schedule. His body began to shake, but not as badly as it had in the past two days. The heating pad helped. In fact, the lower part of his back burned from it. By contrast, the backs of his legs were cold from the scuba tanks. He allowed himself a deeper breath, and that's when he remembered that his lips were sealed. He quelled a slight panic, focused on calming himself and was able to breathe easier.

He wanted to move the heating pad but found his arms pinned against the oxygen tanks; likewise his knees, propped on the scuba tanks, were pressed against the casket lid. Once again he had to calm himself, concentrating deeply, to quiet his heart before it had a chance to beat any faster.

He guessed the dirt on the casket was a few inches deep by the muffled sound of its falling. In this total darkness he could picture the Royals up above in the sunlight, father and son shoveling furiously so they could brag at the store later how they made thirty bucks an hour, cash money, and that's no horseshit.

Bobby shifted his right shoulder a bit, appeased himself with that small movement, and then reached between his legs for the T-bar connector, which linked the diving tanks. He opened the left-hand valve a half turn until he heard hissing, then backed off a bit. He noticed that his shivering had already subsided, and he was glad for that, glad for the heating pad.

He raised his hip an inch and managed to withdraw the penlight from his pants pocket. Flicked it on, and his heart took a thump. The velvet was inches from his face. He felt terribly closed in, felt his nostrils constrict. He tried to separate his lips with his fingers, but they were sealed tight. He wanted to wet them with his tongue, but his mouth was dry. He reached down and opened the valve a little more, then lay back to calm himself with logic. Yes, he was underground, but less deep, actually, than most people's basements. He was comfortable, relatively so. In four hours Noel would be there, opening the lid. And they would be wealthy and free.

When he felt calm again and able to breathe easily, he checked his watch to make sure the alarm was set for another two hours. He calculated his pulse. Then he reached down and turned the air to a bare whisper. He flicked off the penlight, tucked it into his shirt pocket and set his mind to relaxing every muscle. Simultaneously, he focused on his heart. The sound of dirt hitting the casket was dying now, replaced by his own blood slowing, like a wind dying, like a gentle surf sizzling off island sand. He was lying under a dome of blue sky, the burning on his back was sunshine, and the waves grew so quiet that he finally strained to hear anything at all, until what he heard was—

a snore.

He snapped awake, heart pounding. He had nearly fallen asleep. He pinched his stomach. Hard. *The one thing he could not do was fall asleep.* Sleeping, he'd miss his alarm. Sleeping, he'd suck his oxygen dry. Sleeping, he might never wake up. He thought of how Eliot Wicker's coughing had kept him up for two nights, and his hands tingled. He reached down and opened the valve again, let the compressed air breathe freely into the casket. Taking in two big lungfuls to clear his head, he replayed the murder once more, to heighten his senses. He sinks his thumb into Wicker's throat, he sees those expressionless eyes flare, hears the startled, strangled gulp as he thrusts the weapon straight into Wicker's heart. *An embalming tool.* That's what he'd taken from the mortuary, now he could feel its blunt end against his butt. That's why the thing was hollow, for pumping embalming fluid into corpses, or for draining body fluids out. So tonight he would embalm the embalmer.

When his own heart was once again pumping normally and his brain was sharp, Bobby felt for the valve and turned it down. Confidently in control again, he focused on his respiration, his circulation, and he slowed them both, shutting down completely, silencing his mind, becoming keenly aware of nothing.

When the first tray of finger sandwiches was empty, Noel sent Chad down to the walk-in cooler for more. The store had closed at three for the funeral and would remain closed to the public for the next two days. However, beer and wine were available to anyone who showed up for the reception. As it turned out, so many townspeople came to pay their respects that most of the men ended up down in the parking lot, sitting on tailgates, smoking cigarettes and drinking the free beer. Jerry Royal, already back from the cemetery, was busy needling the clam-diggers. 'Forty-five dollars an hour, cash money,' he told them every so often. 'Your plumber don't even make that.'

Upstairs, Noel's kitchen counter was lined with bottles of wine and liquor. To avoid temptation, Sal stayed in the long corridor that connected the kitchen to the living room, drinking seltzer and watching as the number of guests increased, passing from one end of the apartment to the other and eventually overflowing into both ends of the corridor, trapping him in the middle. Had Noel not asked him to stay, he certainly would have gone home. But home alone, he reasoned, he would only be nervously counting the hours until his school concert. Besides, the Librium he had taken at the funeral was making the reception bearable. Mostly he passed the time looking through the long bookcase that stood against the wall, housing Noel's showpiece books that had outlived their time on her coffee table: books about whales and witches, erotic massage, Zen Buddhism, rain forests, American Indians, American women, angels. Beside the bookcase, a short hallway off the left wall led to the bedroom and bathroom, which people began using with more frequency.

At one point, while Sal was thumbing through a book on French impressionism, a couple stopped and the man said he understood that Sal had once played with Woody Herman. Before Sal could respond, the man's wife said, 'McHale's Navy?' to which the man replied, 'No, that's Ernest Borgnine. We're talking music, dear,' to which the woman responded pointedly that she didn't have time for music, and the couple went away in opposite directions.

Sal pulled out a thin paperback, its bright red spine block-lettered SABOTAGE! The cover read, A GUIDE TO RADICAL ENVIRONMENTAL ACTIVISM. Inside were pages crammed with typewriter type and crude drawings of mechanisms for immobilizing logging equipment, or recipes for concocting explosives from fertilizer and sawdust. Sal was reading about brewing a delayed-ignition fire starter using swimming pool cleaner and hair cream when a hand touched his arm, a black glove. 'Thoughtful custom,' Noel said quietly. 'Your husband dies and everybody comes over and drinks all your liquor.' The glove, intricately laced, held a champagne glass by the stem, but it wasn't champagne she was drinking. Sal could smell the vodka martini on her breath.

'That's not Dom Perrignon,' he said to her.

'I needed something stronger today. Does it bother you? I probably shouldn't have brought it over.'

'I'm okay,' he told her, actually impressed at how the Librium seemed to deaden his craving for the drink. 'How're you doing?'

She gave him a dead-on look that said she'd rather be anywhere than here. 'You'll stay to the end, won't you?' she said.

He looked at his watch. 'My show's in two hours,' he answered, and he felt a twinge of anxiety.

'Situational ethics?' a voice interrupted. Eliot Wicker.

Sal didn't know what the mortician was talking about until

Wicker took hold of Sal's book and tilted it up, reading, 'A guide to destroying the destroyers.'

'They're recipes,' Noel explained, 'for fucking up bulldozers and burning down billboards.'

Wicker gave her a patronizing look. Dressed in a white shirt and black bow tie, he sipped champagne from a wide-brimmed, stemmed glass. 'More like recipes for killing off the human race so that genetically inferior species can prolong their imminent extinction,' he said.

Roundly ignoring him, Noel turned and walked down the corridor toward the living room, exiting before Wicker had finished the sentence.

'I love women, don't get me wrong,' Wicker said quietly to Sal, 'but something in the cognitive reasoning department—' He raised his brow in a show of futility, took another drink from his glass, then launched into a racial interpretation of Darwinian theory that would have given Hitler insomnia. It wasn't long before Sal pinched another Librium into his mouth. He considered dropping one in Wicker's champagne, wondering if the undertaker was always this agitated after a burial, or if Wicker considered the confrontation that had occurred between them in Bobby's gym a sort of bonding experience. In Sal's mind the feelings lingered that Wicker could have done more to save Bobby's life. Now the man was recounting some of the more ironic deaths of his other clients – and there were many.

While Wicker talked, Sal lost track of time. When he looked at his watch, it was 6:00 and Wicker was still talking. Thinking that the second Librium wasn't working, Sal dropped another while he pretended to cough.

'... tractor rolled over him three times, veritably pinning him against the very same apple tree that his father had planted for him when he was a baby – exactly sixty-two years to the day, as God is my witness...'

Sal smiled pleasantly, actually felt quite pleasantly numb, drifting in and out of attention while Wicker pontificated about taxes, welfare, crime and capital punishment.

Just before 7:00, Noel appeared, stepped between the men and led Sal aside. Handing him a half-filled vodka martini, she pressed against him so only he could hear and said, 'I've got to get out of here. Can you take away everybody's drinks and tell them to hit the road?'

Sal nodded. Looked at his watch. 'I've gotta go myself,' he said.

She brushed the side of his neck with her lips and whispered, 'Are you having fun talking to the undertaker?'

In response, Sal looked straight at her, brought the martini to his mouth and tossed it down.

Staring at him darkly, Noel gave a hint of a smile.

The heat took his breath away.

4

Once again Blueberry Blossom Night had fallen in Gravity, Maine. The moon shone full and bright in the sky, the night air scented with springtime pollens and grasses. At the school, cars and pickup trucks overflowed the parking lot into the road. In the east, sporadic firecrackers sounded where bingo was getting underway at the Baptist church and a contra dance was about to begin at the Jolly Hollow Grange. There and all over town, young Gravity men were working at prodigious volumes of beer in preparation for the annual outhouse burning. Word was, the fire would be outside the Superette this year, in memory of Bobby Swift.

Alston Bouchard, the town constable, was out cruising the roads in his yellow Subaru wagon, ostensibly to prevent the immolation. But the town's older men (who had long since burned their last outhouse) knew what Bouchard was up to. He'd let the boys outsmart him tonight, same as every year. He'd be a fool not to, and everybody knew – the smarter ones, anyway – that Bouchard was no fool. Laid back, maybe. Lazy, some said. But he had outfoxed enough of them in his twenty years on the job that at least they knew he had a brain.

At just before 8:00, when her apartment was finally empty, Noel walked down her back stairs into the garage. She flipped a switch on the wall, and the garage door opened behind her.

53

She walked quickly to her Volvo and opened the door. As she was about to climb inside, a voice startled her.

'Don't shut me in.'

Jerry Royal, lumbering through the door of Bobby's gym.

'God, Jerry,' Noel said, her hand on her chest. 'I thought everybody had left.'

'Noel, I feel just awful,' Jerry said, approaching her.

She stood behind her car door. 'I'll be okay, Jerry.'

'No, that too, but I mean about using the toilet in there. We were outside yakkin and I had to go, and it wasn't something I could do in the bushes, if you know what I mean, and I knew Bobby had a toilet down here, but then when I'm in there I'm thinkin, where he, you know, and I'm on his toilet, I shoulda found someplace else, whatever—'

'Jerry, it's okay, really.'

'I know. You're being brave. But you oughta know: Bobby was a friend to everybody, rich, poor, whatever. Matter of fact, just tonight we were up there discussin about getting a statue made, settin it up there by the firehouse.'

Noel smiled. 'He'd appreciate that, Jerry.' She lowered herself onto the car seat, waiting for him to leave. He took the door from her, leaned over the top.

'No,' he said, close enough so that she could smell the beer and cigarettes on his breath, 'I just wanna say that, *whatever*, you ever need anything, *ever!* 'Cause I know you're gonna find another man, no problem there . . .'

He moved around to the edge of her door. She took hold of the armrest, to close it, but he wouldn't let go.

'You know what I'm sayin,' he told her. 'So, where you off to?'

'Just – nowhere.' She looked at her watch. 'I need to take a ride, to clear my head.'

'No, but if you need company—'

Noel smiled at him. 'Thanks, Jerry, I'd rather be by myself.'

Without warning, he leaned in and smothered her in a one-armed hug. As big as he was, her face ended up at his armpit. At first it didn't seem like he was going to let go, but she managed to slip his clutch.

'So, okay,' he said as she shut the door. She started the engine and quickly shifted into reverse. While she backed out of the garage, he hurried around behind the car and back-pedaled toward the swimming pool, directing her. 'You got it, you got it, you got it...'

She shifted into first.

'Go for it,' he told her, 'I'll get the door.' But she was already closing it with the remote control attached to her visor. 'Okay, you got that thing,' he said, as she drove up her driveway and headed for the cemetery.

In the school gymnasium, the town's children were herded, one classroom at a time, onto the old stage, while teachers assembled them onto three risers, smiling gamely while cameras flashed over and over, while parents carried on scores of conversations in the audience, sometimes from two and three rows apart. As usual, many of the fathers refused to sit in the seats, preferring to mill around the gym door in T-shirts and caps, discussing work and local politics as their children sang. For Sal, it was bearable tonight. No, tonight it was a genuine kick.

Only Mrs Abraham, the accompanist, seemed distracted, worrying over the talking, the out-of-tune piano, the astounding cacophony of the children's singing. But she was new in town, unaccustomed. During the applause for the second-grade finale, a particularly jarring 'This Land is Your Land,' Sal crouched at the edge of the stage and said to her, 'Don't worry, no one listens anyway.'

Then, rising effortlessly – demonstrating his impeccable balance – he strode across the stage to wait for the next class.

He noticed the school principal, Avery Bingstream, slender and straight-backed in his brown business suit and big square glasses, standing in the side aisle, beaming. Sal considered going to the microphone and asking for a round of applause for the principal but decided against it. He ducked around the curtain, reached behind an empty paint can, found his mug and took a drink. The Russian vodka shone through the Librium like a midnight sun on snow: frigid, bright and blinding.

In darkness and silence that were absolute, Bobby's penlight came on. He shivered from the cold. He saw burgundy velvet. He stared. He was wet with perspiration, panting hard, forcing air in and out of a nose that was badly clogged. With some effort he bent his elbow and looked at his watch. 8:15. His heart surged. His alarm had gone off over an hour ago and he had slept through it. His nose breathing accelerated, but he couldn't catch his breath. There was no oxygen left in the casket, he realized. He opened both valves on the scuba tanks, heard nothing. He wondered how he had awakened at all.

He reached around under his left arm, fit his hand under the velvet to unfasten the Velcro strap, and rolled one of the slender oxygen tanks up onto his chest. He twisted its valve until he heard the faintest hissing. He took a breath through his nose. Another.

Now he concentrated on calming himself. Noel would be opening the lid in an hour and a half. He had the two E-sized tanks left – pure oxygen. Each held about twenty minutes' worth, normal breathing. With slow breathing, he could double that. Tranced out he could make the air last three to four hours – as long as he didn't sleep again.

His toes felt icy, his legs asleep. He wanted to take off a shoe and warm his feet with his hand, but his knees were pressed against the coffin lid by the scuba tanks (which were worthless now – worse than worthless, they took up space). His cold feet might as well have been a mile away.

More distracting, his nostrils were nearly shut. Once again he tried to open his mouth with his fingers, but the cement held fast. With both hands he took hold of his lips and gave a quick pull, ripping some skin. His eyes teared from the sting, but his lips remained welded. He realized he'd have to separate the lips somehow. He thought of the embalming tool he had stashed for Wicker. He lifted his right hip, reached a hand under the velvet and brought the cold instrument up. He laid the penlight on his chest while he directed the point of the thing into the center of his pursed lips. The tip was icy. He opened his teeth inside his mouth so he wouldn't strike them, and then with a painful grunt, he pushed. His eyes stung. He shut them tight. He leaned into the tool until he felt more skin tear, but still he failed to break through. Suddenly, as if to surprise himself, he gave a short, hard thrust. The shout came out his nose, muffled instantly inside the casket. The oxygen tank rolled off his chest. The shaft had seared through his lips, and the tip sliced the underside of his tongue. He withdrew the instrument, tasted blood seeping in his throat. To his relief, he was able to draw a whistle through his mouth. It burned.

He cupped the tank in the crook of his elbow and, under his penlight beam, set his watch alarm for an hour and a half, certain that he wouldn't need it, confident that Noel would be there rousing him from his trance. He pictured the look on her face when he opened his eyes, the feeling of her hands helping to lift him out. In all the world, he thought, no one had ever loved a woman the way he loved Noel.

He brought the oxygen valve close to his face and looked at his reflection in the chrome plating. A twinge of fear gripped him. Wicker had made him a death mask of white, then compensated with a powdery pink. Twin circles of rouge dotted Bobby's cheeks, and his lips were deeper red, darkened with a puddle of blood in his blowhole, which bubbled with each little breath. Worse, his eyebrows were lined, his scowl wrinkles caked, eyelids shaded blue. He thought of Noel seeing him like that, of Sal, and everybody else in town. This is how Bobby Swift would be remembered, like a fucking transvestite—? He felt the bottom of his rib cage with his middle finger, then ran his thumb up his chest until he felt his heartbeat. He gauged the distance between the two and calculated the angle. That's how he'd kill Wicker, under and up.

He should have told Sal, he thought again. He could always count on Sal. They were like brothers, best friends since childhood. Of course he could count on Noel too. After all, he had trusted her with his life. And why not? Encased as he was inside this tight, black tomb, he allowed no thought of mistrusting her.

In his imagination a picture appeared: Noel working above him with her shovel. He wondered if he could really see her, if their minds were that finely attuned. He tried to listen for her but heard only the whisper of oxygen.

He closed the valve down until he could barely hear the air flowing, and then he held the canister in his hand like a baby's bottle, aiming its breath of air at his little mouth. He shut off his penlight and commanded his muscles to relax. He slowed his heart. He cut his breathing in stages...

Noel, he thought ... Noel would take care of him.

She had a way of always getting the best seats at a show, the best table in a restaurant. It was that certain tone she took with maître d's and ushers, something of a promise in the look she gave them, a promise she had no intention of keeping. She did lie, after all, when it suited her. In small ways.

Without intending to, Bobby imagined the sensation of breaking out of the casket into the crushing, suffocating blackness around him, where the weight of the earth on top was equaled by the pressure of gravity below, so that, with only seconds of air in the lungs, completely disoriented, you claw against the blackness and end up burrowing deeper...

Bobby's chest heaved. He cleared his mind. Total silence. Lying in the relative comfort of his casket, he oriented himself: up from down.

A picture of Eliot Wicker intruded on him, tall and toothy, hair perfectly combed and parted, asleep in his bed. The undertaker would awaken with a start when Bobby shined the light in his face; say something like *What the hell are you doing here?* And Bobby in his tortoiseshell glasses and brown hair would reply, 'Saying good-bye,' and then squeeze that scrawny white throat in one hand, and with the other, *PLUNGE* – under and up, under and up—

Bobby caught his heart racing again. He forced Wicker out of his mind completely. He listened for Noel's digging again and actually thought he could hear her now, standing above him. He pictured her face and felt the onset of a beautiful peace. The next time he opened his eyes, he knew she'd be there, the pale moon over her shoulder, her warm hands on his face. Pale moon over her shoulder, warm hands on his face. Warm hands on his face.

Eliot Wicker had just kicked back in his recliner to watch the Red Sox, when a sudden loud knocking threw him to his feet. Pacing through the kitchen, he could only believe that something was wrong. He imagined it was Noel. He eased the door open with a lazy, ominous look. But it was Alston Bouchard standing in the yellow breezeway light.

'Hello, Alston!' he said, acting aboundingly happy to see the constable. He turned and headed back inside. 'Come in, you want coffee?'

'Nope,' answered Bouchard, catching the door.

Leaving him standing in the kitchen, Wicker went into the

living room and turned off the TV, then rejoined Bouchard again in the kitchen. 'I hate the Red Sox,' he said. 'You?'

'Not especially,' answered the constable. Alston Bouchard was a dark, uncomfortable man who seemed to add darkness to himself as a way to hide. A black John Deere cap covered black hair that grew densely behind his ears, and his marbled black beard covered the rest of his face and neck except for his dark, humorless eyes, which were themselves covered by the thick lenses of his black-rimmed glasses. He rarely spoke, rarely smiled; mostly he'd just stand in a room, watching, listening, making people wonder what wrong thing they might have done, though that was never his intention.

'So,' Wicker said, 'busy day.' He did not hide the nervousness well, and he knew it. Looking Bouchard square in the face, he might as well have said, *Look, I'm completely natural.*

Bouchard put his hands in his pockets. 'Too bad about—'

'—Bobby, you know it. Town's gonna miss him.' Wicker swung his long leg over a bar stool and then started to cough. 'Sit down, Alston, you want to sit down?' The constable remained standing. Wicker coughed harder. 'Fuckin postnasal drip.'

Bouchard moved a couple of steps toward Wicker's bulletin board, a patchwork of bills and business cards beside the wall phone. 'Nope,' he said. 'I'll set when I get home.' He had a deep voice, deeper than even his considerable bulk suggested, but he spoke softly, as if he had learned to do so to avoid frightening people.

Wicker wondered if anything incriminating was on his bulletin board. He wondered what Bouchard was doing there. He decided that it was natural to ask. 'So, what, Alston, my landfill permit's expired again?'

'Just' – Bouchard jerked his thumb toward the window – 'you know your lights are out?'

Lights—? Wicker stared at Bouchard while his mind raced,

trying to understand how lights might implicate him. 'What lights?'

'Parking lot,' Bouchard explained. 'Your sign too.'

'Maybe a circuit breaker, I don't know.' Wicker swung off his stool and looked out the window toward the road. Was he acting defensive? By Bouchard's silence, he guessed he was. So what? Defensive, for him, was natural. Besides, any other night of the week he would've wanted the man out of his house. He moved toward the door, meaning for Bouchard to follow. 'I'll look into it, Alston. Was there anything else? I'm kinda watching that game.'

Bouchard shook his head. 'Just thought you might want to know about . . .' The constable had a habit of ending sentences with a gesture rather than words. He aimed a thumb at the door, meaning the lights. 'The boys are gonna be out rammin' tonight. They can be . . .'

'Yeah, they do get wild.' Wicker opened the door and stepped out into his breezeway, holding the door for Bouchard. 'They get their outhouse yet?' he asked, offering the constable a little small talk for the road. He could see that his parking lot was indeed dark.

'Not yet,' Bouchard said, finally joining Wicker in the breezeway.

'Oh, well, harmless enough, I suppose.' It was an exit remark, which Bouchard failed to read.

'I imagine one of these days someone'll miss 'em,' Bouchard said.

'Who? Miss who?'

'The outhouses, I mean. Where so many have indoor plumbing now.' Small talk was awkward for the constable. He hesitated at the breezeway door, took off his cap and combed his fingers carefully through the few long strands of hair that covered his head. He replaced his cap, pulled it down and asked, unexpectedly, 'You planning on staying in tonight?'

'What, I can't stay home?'

'Nope,' Bouchard said, 'you can.' He walked a few steps down the walk and then turned around the corner of the house, heading for the parking lot.

Wicker called after him, 'I mean, Christ, Alston, a man should be able to stay in his house on Blueberry Blossom Night without someone making a federal crime out of it.'

Just as the oxygen began to sputter, Bobby's watch alarm beeped. He came to, found his penlight and switched it on. Looked at the time. 9:30. He listened for Noel digging above him, but all he could hear was the sputtering. He closed the valve to silence the tank, then held his breath to listen. She was there, he knew she was. He turned off the light, thinking the darkness would help him hear. But total silence pressed in around him. He flicked the light on again, looked at his watch. 9:32.

He'd gone an hour and a half on twenty minutes of oxygen, right on schedule. With one more tank, even without trancing, they'd have plenty of leeway in case the digging was a little hard or she'd been delayed. Obviously she'd been delayed. 9:33.

He pushed the spent tank down his chest, beside his leg. It made a bright ring against the empty scuba tank. Pulling the other tank up from beside him, he felt a pleasant relief at the shoulder room he had now. He opened the valve, heard the oxygen hiss out. He backed off again, then pulled a deep, calming breath through the little hole in his lips. Closed his eyes and listened for Noel. Even if she were digging down, he thought, two feet above the lid, he wouldn't necessarily hear, soil being such a good insulator. She could have been six inches away from him. He flicked on his light again and checked his watch. 9:35.

He shut off the penlight, closed his eyes and opened the valve once again, proceeded to slow his heart. He turned his thoughts to the island, the long, wide, sunlit beach. Lying there on a blanket with Noel. She'd raise a finger and the waiter would come down with another margarita.

He thought of the horse in their living room – the bronze-plate sculpture she had bought from the Boston importer. Four hundred dollars, she had told Bobby it cost. They'd lived with the thing for a month before he found out she had actually charged twenty-eight hundred bucks to his Visa account.

So she did actually lie, even to him, on occasion. When it suited her. But he'd never considered that kind of brazenness anything but endearing. He liked street smarts in a woman, especially in a woman like Noel. Even now, as he felt himself drifting off, he snickered a little, the way that bronze horse stood in his living room with that little smile on its face, while he was down here picturing it.

While the audience talked on, the third graders stood on the risers and waited for Sal to return to the microphone. He was in control now, completely and confidently so. Striding out from the curtain, perfectly balanced, he reached for the microphone and his fist struck the stand, making an explosion in the gym. Seeing the mike leap from its holder, he flashed out a hand and snatched the mike from the air, then brought it to his mouth as if the move had been choreographed.

'Ladies and gentlemen,' he began. He heard a little laughter and acknowledged it with a warm Mediterranean smile (Tony Bennett eyes, Iris used to say about his crinkled smile). He glanced back at Davey. She knew. No, she didn't. He gave her a wink. She fidgeted. The audience grew louder.

'Okay, folks,' he said, 'let's quiet down.'

The talking subsided a bit. Microphone in hand, Sal felt like Jerry Lewis – all he needed was the tuxedo and cigarette. He looked around the audience, spotted Iris. Gave her the smile.

Thought of dedicating the show to Bobby, decided against it. Thought about talking to the crowd about the pleasure of actually *listening* to music for a change, but decided against that. 'Erie Canal,' he said finally, 'Erie Canal,' and replaced the mike in its stand.

He looked behind him at the third graders, then turned to Mrs Abraham and counted off the song. She played the intro, and the children began to sing about the mule named Sal, and Sal laughed at that. But by the end of the first verse, their voices were already at war with one another. 'Low bridge' sounded like the mule might have been trying to cough up a slug of barbed wire. Standing in front of them, Sal bent his knees and made a pulling gesture, as if he were helping the animal dislodge the obstruction, but his pantomime was lost on the crowd.

Then, afraid they might think he was making fun of the children, he said into the mike, 'Very nice,' which the audience took as a cue to applaud, which in turn caused the nervous accompanist to think he was abandoning the whole thing and stop playing. 'No, keep – keep—' Sal wheeled his hand and Mrs Abraham resumed dutifully. The problem was, by now the singing had also stopped, and the audience talking started up again. Mrs Abraham's eyes, hard on Sal, gelled with fear.

That's when Sal got the idea that would change his life. He said to her, 'Keep playing,' and then said to the audience, jokingly, 'You quiet down.' They did. All the while, he held out his hand to the children, keeping them from singing. When the last line of the intro came around, he nodded to the singers and said, 'Hum it this time, you know how to hum?' They grinned at him, their lips clamped. He tossed his hand and they began, their voices sailing over the noisy gym like a swarm of happy bees.

'Don't stop,' Sal told them. 'Don't stop,' he said to Mrs Abraham, and then he made for the wings.

Undone

Noel climbed the terraces close to the tree line, shaded from the light of the full moon. She had left her Volvo in the woods just below the cemetery, on a gravel turnoff to the river, where it wouldn't be seen. The contra dance and bingo game were in full swing on the east side of town – she could hear distant sounds of cars and firecrackers. This part of town was quiet, however, with the town's children and their parents all ensconced in the school gym. Not a single car passed.

All along the hillside the polished gravestones reflected the moonlight, winking at Noel as she walked, their shadows sharp on the flat grass. When she left the tree line for Bobby's lone grave, a car did pass below, soundlessly, just a trailing of taillights over her shoulder. She walked around Bobby's plot and headed for the forked limb of a tall maple, then pushed into the woods on its right.

She switched on her flashlight and aimed the beam ahead of her, at three birch trees. Everything else was darkness. She stepped carefully over a small deadfall that Bobby had laid in the way, then deflected some pine branches with her shoulder. In the spot of her light stood a lichen-encrusted wall of rock, too wide to be seen in its entirety. At the near end of the boulder she reached down and pulled aside a couple of pine boughs and then lifted the shovel and pitchfork, their handles aligned, wrapped in a dark wool blanket. Evidence of her crime. Gripping the bundle tightly so it wouldn't make a sound, she turned back and pressed for the moonlight.

In the gym, the audience watched in rapt silence as the third graders finished humming the fifth chorus of 'Erie Canal' and then began an sixth. A couple of fathers paced nervously by the door. Several had already left the building and were smoking cigarettes in the parking lot. Mrs Abraham, still accompanying the song, kept her smile up, but it had hardened considerably.

65

All at once the gymnasium was shattered by the blare of a trombone, a bluesy fanfare, as Sal strode in stage left, doubling the hummers' melody on his instrument. There rose a small outburst of applause and laughter, mixed with a low, indignant cheer. The hummers grew louder. Sal stopped for a moment, looked out in the crowd, then shut his eyes and played a scorching Dixieland counterpoint on his horn, cakewalking around their tune; capsizing it.

'Don't give up,' he told the kids as he approached the microphone, waving the piano on to another chorus. He drew a voluminous breath, tossed his head back and blew a dissonant squall, blew it loud and long until his face grew red and veins bulged at his temples. His heart pounded. It had been so long since he'd played – really played.

'What are you doing?' Mrs Abraham sang at him, still smiling, struggling to keep the song in motion. Sal ignored her. He looked back at the risers and saw Davey stiffen, her eyes glistening. He closed his own eyes again, raised his face and let go with a long, plaintive wail. He was saying to Davey, *These are tears, honey.* He blew another one, let it arc and sail over the room ... for the rest of the town. Hell, everyone knew Bobby. They'd know what Sal was feeling. He almost lost his footing then, staggered back a step – but he did not fall. *Balance*, ladies and gentlemen. Sal Erickson is in complete control. Then another one for Bobby, a long, strident blast to shake him from the clouds. Sal shook it, gritty as you please, then shuffled it into a raunchy, strutting blues. Bobby's Song. He played it loud, played it fat and slow.

He became dimly aware that he was soloing. The piano had stopped at some point, he didn't know when. The children had stopped humming too. He opened his eyes and saw parents and teachers escorting the kids off both sides of the stage. Christ, they were tiptoeing, some of them. Sal wailed on, soaring, gone, pure and total. In a small part of his mind he could see the exit doors bottlenecked with townspeople, Philistines escaping the fire, but all turning back for that one last look. He could see Iris's white uniform for an instant, and the back of Davey. Too late for losers, he was gone. And now some smart-ass pulling the curtain closed in front of him – like that was going to stop him. He glanced into the shadows and saw Charlie Walker at the ropes, the custodian. He made a move toward Walker, and the old man retreated.

Behind the curtain now, Sal continued blowing. Jazz, people! Monk, Diz, Bird, Miles, Satch. *Jazz!* When his slide found the break in the velvet, he followed it through and almost stepped off the stage into the seats. He teetered for a moment, but he didn't fall – not a chance. *Balance, baby.* And suddenly the gym was practically empty, just the fat men in T-shirts milling around the perimeter like dogs, waiting for him to fall. Not a chance. For them he stood on the very edge of the stage and rocked back and forth. For them he reached into his animal brain, gave them something gristled and warlike to chew on.

And, right on cue, here came Avery Bingstream, the principal, striding up the center aisle in his gray suit, watching his shoes. There was a careless bounce in his step, which meant that he hadn't thought this thing through. Sal matched his footsteps with his horn. Then the stage went dark and the houselights started blinking off, a row at a time – that son of a bitch Walker again. Sal started to turn, but then Bingstream was already mounting the stage stairs. The timing was off. The rhythm was building. Sal took it up a key, warned Bingstream back with a growl. The principal kept coming.

Sal stepped back, into the curtain. Spread his legs for balance. His music was industrial now, he wished somebody was recording it. Ornette meets Igor, right? On the top step the principal stopped; straightened his glasses. Picked up the microphone and replaced it in the stand, giving Sal his most placid smile. But Sal could read the flurry of lines behind those big square glasses: uncertainty and fear. He shook a fierce glissando at the man.

'Well,' Bingstream said, working off a shrug, 'I guess it's—' Centurion hoedown, right in his face.

'—time to go home, put the feet up, have a rest.' The principal reached his hand out slowly, as if he were disarming Sal.

Sal warned him back with an eyebrow, pumping the slide back and forth, back and forth, but then Bingstream caught the slide in his hand. The note exploded from the bell as the slide pulled out of the instrument. The surprised, gravity-stricken principal, reeling with his trophy, caught the mike stand with his other hand, hugged it like a crooner as he back-dived off the stage and hit the floor below with an amplified WOOF! A folding chair spun on one leg then crashed. The mike stand rolled away. Bingstream sat up fast, but then just remained there clutching the trombone slide, staring at his shins.

Sal closed his eyes and leaned back against the curtain, which failed to support him – he didn't fall, though. Never fall. He felt the warm velvet sliding up his back, massaging his shoulders. *Balance*, ladies and gents, he had it in spades.

But someone is laughing in the dark – the bronze horse is snickering like crazy. The penlight makes a faint, beige dot. Bobby makes a whistle when he laughs. He's sweating, whistling like a locomotive in a runaway laughing panic, and the horse can't breathe. Bobby can't find his consciousness, that's the trouble, he's stuck in this idiot dream! Or is he even asleep? The velvet crepe is moist, burgundy, a delicate floral pattern in front of his eyes. The whole world is cold, extremely cold, and he's wet with perspiration. His throat is dry. He's whistling, in and out, faster and faster. It's because there's no more air. It's because his nose is clogged and he has only a blowhole for a mouth. It's because he's a fish out of water! He whistles faster when he pictures this. He flips like a fish, *sees* himself as a fish. He laughs at this, whistles like a fish. The oxygen tank is laughing too, sputtering madly. Empty or full, he can't decide.

Or else it's the shower that's hissing. He's standing, fully clothed, in Eliot Wicker's shower, and Noel turns away from him to get him a towel.

Too much oxygen – that's the problem. He shuts down the valve. That's right, save what's left. The tank gets quiet. But he's still whistling up a storm, panting like a horse. Sea horse. Sea horse metabolism – his little lungs are on fire. He puts his knees up to the velvet, and it gives. He thinks he's pushing the casket lid open. He thinks he's up on the hilltop, free. But it's his muscles, not the lid, giving out. Then he hears her digging.
Noel.

He makes a little sea horse squeak in his throat that embarrasses him – and he hopes she hasn't heard. His knees are pumping together furiously, the way a sea horse swims. Or are they? He can't tell. No, he's lying perfectly still, *thinking* about swimming. Don't panic! It's his inner voice. Bobby Swift is telling the sea-horse-man to think. *Think.* He listens to the oxygen tank again but hears only his own rapid back-and-forth whistling, like someone sawing wood, like those little ornamental woodcutters, dutifully driven by the wind; though Bobby's lungs are sawing at nothing. His chest is collapsing. He thinks the tank is dead – can't remember if he closed it down. The penlight flares. He shakes the oxygen tank like a deodorant can, the valve cracks his jaw, his knuckles brush the low ceiling, he listens again, hears his own sputtering whistle, then he remembers—

The other oxygen tank, *the other tank*! It wasn't completely empty when he changed over, still time left, party time, party time. He reaches for it, but it's not there.

'*It might be hypothermia.*'

It's Noel's voice he hears, but then he's not sure. His head is swimming in voices, whispers. 'He's okay,' Wicker says. 'Get him a towel.' Bobby feels for the tank. The penlight rolls off his chest onto the floor, glows brilliantly. The casket is floodlit. He tingles in waves. He snugs his body down, butt against the T-bar, knees against the soft lid, his body is swimming on its own now. He feels for the tank, his body doubled up, his knees jammed against the side of the coffin, and the valve is in his hand suddenly, it's been there all along, he thinks it's a handful of change at first, to put in his pocket, but see he knows he's hallucinating. He's a bronze horse stuck in its shipping crate, he laughs at the thought, snickers through his blowhole, can't whistle any faster, but he does. He's a bird, he's a peeper. He opens the valve, and it whispers:

Noel.

She turns away from him, opens the third drawer and pulls out a thick brown towel. She's barefoot, and when she turns back she's wiping the water off her own neck, her green eyes are shining, shining. 'You were dead,' she tells him.

He kisses at the valve, forces the cold steel against his burning lips and sucks the oxygen deep into his lungs until his head glows inside. *Noel*, he thinks, a prayer. He takes her in, fills his lungs, fills his bloodstream, and then the whisper goes away. He opens the valve until all sound stops, turns it both ways, but there's no whisper left. He sees stars. Stars everywhere. And suddenly he realizes that everything is perfect.

Everything is fine. Because Bobby Swift is master of his heart. And one breath of oxygen is all he needs. He rolls onto his back to relax. Master of his heart. His back is arched, his lungs are filled. No, it's his face – his face is expanding like a balloon. His heart is beating jungle drums in his chest.

And then he feels a kick, a terrible beat – a belch of pure white light. And Bobby Swift's last thought is clear as the full brilliant sun going off in his head.

Noel knew where Eliot Wicker kept his bath towels.

5

'I don't care,' Eliot Wicker said into the phone. 'I've got to see you.'

Pressing the telephone to her ear with her shoulder, she tipped the suitcase upside down, spilling Bobby's summer clothes onto the bed.

'Noel, I'm a nervous wreck over here by myself.'

'Don't be,' she said.

'After what we did?'

Shirts and trousers, she reached into each pocket and ran her fingers along the linings. The plane ticket was gone. So was his wallet.

'Come on,' Wicker said. 'No one'll see me. I'll leave in the morning before it gets light.'

Had Bobby stashed them in the casket and forgotten to tell her? Or made some last-minute arrangements with Wicker? Impossible.

'Okay, you come over here then,' the undertaker said. 'Come in the middle of the night, I don't care. You've got a key. What the hell are you doing, Noel? Say something to me.'

A moment passed, then she said softly, 'Don't call me anymore.' And hung up.

Sal marched past his house a second time. He couldn't go in,

71

not yet anyway, certainly not with the bottle in his hand. Iris had vowed that if he ever drank again, their marriage was through. That was six months ago. The way he felt right now, the night so full of promise, what did another broken marriage matter in the whole magnificent, spiraling cycle? He lifted his face and smelled the river, the red oak, the white pine, the bracket fungi, the whole awakening world. He heard a car horn far in the distance, barking dogs and the paper-thin sounds of music. The night pulsated with rhythms, a thick heartbeat rising up from the earth, a long, seductive breathing above. The spring was fully upon the town, and Sal was certain that in his entire life he had never felt half this good. He unscrewed the cap and finished the vodka, then set the empty bottle gently in the mailbox at the foot of his driveway.

Tires squealed. He looked up. Headlights flashed as a pickup truck bore down on him from the village. He stared into the lights as it came, transfixed, until the truck went fishtailing past him, boys whooping out the windows. Which meant the outhouse raid was about to begin. He waved, shook a confederate fist above his head.

And here came the blue flashing of Alston Bouchard's dashboard light. The truck had been an obvious decoy, meant to lure the constable away. But he came on anyway, the dour Acadian, not quite fast enough in his old Subaru. The annual rebellion. Raise hell one night a year, mind your manners the rest. Yes, Sal thought, it was a wonderful town.

He was tempted to go down to the store and raise a little hell himself. And before he knew it, he was doing just that, springing up the road, his lungs effortlessly exchanging air with the cold, moonlit night, blowing past the sleeping houses like a phantom, and then he was turning up the Village Road, jogging over the iron grate bridge, pumping up the hill until he reached the store, where he circled the parking lot to catch his breath.

'Hey, there!' *They-uh.* It was Jerry Royal, coming up from the right corner of the building, where the driveway went down. 'Hear ol' Mister Music got into the sauce but good tonight.' Jerry laughed – a cartoonish guffaw. He was zipping his fly.

'What the hell, it's Blueberry Blossom Night,' Sal replied. 'How are you doin?'

'Oh, I dunno, 'bout as happy as a bastard on Father's Day, I guess.' In eight years, since Sal and Iris had moved to Maine, it was the most the two men had spoken.

'So, whatchu doin out past your bedtime?' Jerry continued. 'The old lady won't let you back in the house?' At this Jerry belted out another gutful of laughter. 'Join the club. She won't let me in that house, either! Me *or* the old man, and he's been dry ten years.' He chortled again, then drained his beer and crushed the can flat in his fist, tossed it into the road.

A window raised above their heads. 'Come on up,' Noel said through the screen. 'We'll get some coffee into you.' Both men knew that she was addressing Sal, not Jerry.

'That's an invitation I wouldn't deliberate on long,' Jerry remarked quietly, then added, with some remorse, 'I shouldna said that, under the circumstances.'

All at once a truck came squealing up from the River Road, blowing its horn as it crossed the bridge. It slowed, approaching the store, then stopped, revving its engine. 'That's my taxi,' Jerry said, and he skipped onto the running board, slapped the roof and the truck sped away. The night became remarkably quiet then, just the river singing off to the right, the river and the peepers.

'I could use the company,' Noel said. Her silhouette was softened by the screen. 'Go around to the garage. I'll let you in.'

Noel's driveway led down along the right side of the

building, then turned around the back, where there was a set of double garage doors and, to their right, a window-paneled entry door.

When Sal got down there, the garage was dark. The only light came from the stairway, which was concealed behind a partial partition on the right-hand wall. He looked in the door window but saw only his own reflection against the sky. Suddenly the door opened and she was there, barefoot, dressed in red spandex leggings and a plain black T-shirt. She turned without saying anything and made for the stairs. As Sal followed her up, he became fixated on her buttocks. Although he wasn't especially attracted to women's backsides, Noel's was singularly stunning: high, round and compact, cheeks that strutted in front of his face all the way up two flights.

As they reached the top, Noel reached back and patted herself. 'Good for the derrière,' she said.

'I can see,' Sal replied, teasing. She waved her hand, a playful slap meant to miss him. It was their customary, innocent flirting and nothing more. Of course, Sal was completely faithful to Iris; and he would never have touched Bobby's wife. But he had occasionally fantasized about Noel, wondering how far she'd take it. He'd always been the one to back off.

The kitchen already looked like a single woman's kitchen – no tools on the counter, no boots by the door. The bottles and trays of food from the reception were gone. Except for the flowers, there was no evidence that Bobby had ever lived – or died – here. But then Sal couldn't have expected differently; Noel was not a sentimental person. He liked that about her, certain that most women in her spot would have felt obliged to wear their sadness like an overcoat so people wouldn't think them heartless.

74

She opened a cupboard and stretched high to reach something, her bright red legs lithe and long. He remembered her saying once that when she was a girl she liked to wrestle with boys. He bet she didn't often lose.

She took down a canister and measured fresh coffee beans into a small electric grinder, then sank the plug into the outlet, all the while giving Sal an icy stare. The grinder screamed as she pressed its top. Still she never took her eyes off him, and it became an effort of growing pleasure to hold her gaze with his own. Was she teasing him? Testing him? Suddenly the screaming stopped.

'What's that look?' she asked.

'What look?' he replied.

Noel turned to the door. Footsteps came out of nowhere, and before either could react, the door flew open and Eliot Wicker stepped in. Sal looked at Noel, her face a sheet of neutrality. Wicker, in turn, looked at Sal, fairly dumbstruck. Then he turned back to Noel and said, 'I thought I'd look in on you, make sure you're okay. It's part of my job.' His eyes fell to her legs.

'I'm fine,' she said impassively. Her lipstick, Sal noticed, was not the bright red he thought she usually wore, but a browner tone, more like the red of a medium roast.

Wicker appeared short of breath, and his face glistened with perspiration. 'I heard they were on their way over here tonight, with this outhouse business. I wanted to make sure it didn't get out of hand.'

Sal saw that Noel's blank expression hadn't changed. Then he realized why she was silent – and he felt embarrassed at being found there, as if he were making a play for his best friend's widow. He moved toward the door and said, covering, 'Noel, anytime you feel like talking, Iris and I are always there, you know that.'

She gave him an odd, bemused smile, while Wicker opened

the door for him, looked him over in a way that made Sal stop on the threshold.

'You got a problem?' Sal said.

The undertaker folded his arms and replied, with utter disregard, 'No problem in particular.'

Sal nodded. He could see the man wasn't too bright, the type that got shafted as a boy because of his deficiencies and now spent his life getting even with the world. He held Wicker's listless stare for another second or two, then said, 'My mistake.'

'Hey,' Wicker answered. He pointed a finger at Sal, a sporting gesture, then shut the door behind him.

Wicker stared at the door. He listened to the footsteps as Sal walked down the stairs. When he heard the basement door close far below, he pushed the lock on the apartment door, then turned and brushed past Noel, walked down the hall to the living room and looked out. In a moment he saw Sal, under the streetlight, walking down the road toward the bridge.

'What's he, got another woman waiting for him down there?' Wicker asked, hearing Noel enter the room behind him. 'Move away from the window,' she said.

Wicker stepped aside and lowered the venetian blinds, taking his time doing it.

'Do you know anything about Bobby's wallet?' she said. 'Or his plane ticket?'

'What exactly am I supposed to know?' he answered.

'Do you?' she shot at him.

He turned around and stared at her, eyes half-open, appearing disinterested, as he always did. 'No, I don't,' he said. 'Do you know I almost killed myself coming over here?'

'And?'

He held up his right hand, scraped raw. 'I almost fell down the bridge embankment. Goddamn Grand Central Station out there.'

Noel looked at him with disbelief. 'Jesus, don't you understand?' She stopped, turned up her palms and said, '*Murder*.'

'Don't worry, Noel, nobody saw me. But I do think I deserve to know what that guy was doing here.'

She threw a finger toward the window. 'That guy saw you here.'

'So what was he doing?' Wicker stared at her, thinking his persistence seductive.

She shut her eyes.

'Alright, maybe I'm overreacting. I *am* overreacting, okay? But I think it's best to straighten these things out at the outset of a relationship. Do we want to see other people or not? My vote is no.'

She crossed to the floor lamp and turned it off, so that only yellow light from the hallway entered the room. 'I'm leaving,' she told him.

'Come on. Where are you going this time of night?'

'Leaving. Going away.'

He paused to take this in and determined quickly that it was part of their argument.

'I guess I've just got to get used to it,' he said. 'God knows how many guys are going to be coming onto you now that they think you're alone.'

Noel turned and walked around him, stopped beside the bronze horse. She took a breath, then turned to face him, fingers folded in front of her, businesslike. 'Eliot, your money is at the Prince First Federal in Nassau. On the first of October I'll give you the account number, just as we planned.'

He took another moment to respond. 'I said I was sorry, okay? I was out of line. I know you weren't up to any hanky-panky, come on.'

She narrowed her eyes. 'I was going to fuck him,' she said, 'until you came.'

His breath left him in a sort of laugh. But he wasn't smiling, just staring at her with those sleepy eyes.

'Eliot, go.'

With his long fingers he scratched his long stomach. 'Okay, you want to move, we'll move. Anywhere. That's the beauty of my business.'

She stood rigidly. 'Listen to me,' she said. 'All we are, all we've ever been, is business partners. Now go.'

He laughed, a self-assured snicker. 'Sorry, not after the other night ... you can't tell me that.'

'The other night,' she said, 'was business.'

'Some business.' He attempted a smile, reached out and took hold of her arms.

A car pulled into the lot below; they heard a country song, a burst of laughter. She twisted out of his grasp. 'Listen,' she said, 'you repulse me, do you understand? You're shallow and bitter, you speak like bad television. And you're going to get us caught.'

Stunned, he continued staring at her. The smile died on his lips. Now it looked like he was about to cry.

'Give me your hand,' he said, his voice shaking. She began to object but he grabbed it, pressed her palm to his chest. 'Can you feel that?'

She could. His heart was beating.

He glared at her, his translucent eyes for once fully exposed, and she thought for a moment that he was going to hit her. He whispered, 'I *killed* for you, goddammit, and I would die for you. But there's one thing I will not do!' His voice was rising again.

'Shhh,' she said, her own voice starting to shake.

'*I will not let you go!*'

Undone

He could see that he was beginning to scare her, and it boosted his confidence.

'Noel, I'll say it simply. Life without you would not be worth living – and secrets would not be worth keeping.'

A silence fell over the room. Noel, looking down, gently wrested her hand from his heart. She spoke quietly. 'You're not being clear, Eliot. What is it you're trying to say?' Another truck pulled into the lot down below, male voices laughing and loud.

'I'm saying that if you leave me, I don't care anymore. I'll expose us, I don't care. Noel, you've got to give me a chance.'

She took a quick breath, but spoke deliberately, almost lightly. 'Eliot, when you say "expose," what exactly do you mean?'

'Expose,' he said, and a volley of firecrackers rang out. 'Tell.'

'So you'll tell.'

He leered at her, giving her a taste of his newfound power.

She backed up a step. 'And they'll dig up Bobby's grave,' she said. 'They'll find his body, they'll find oxygen tanks, scuba tanks, a heating pad and flashlight. And it will become abundantly clear that Eliot Wicker knew he was burying a living man.'

Wicker nodded confidently. 'You got it.'

She closed her eyes slowly, and when they opened again they were cold and steady. Wicker was still nodding, but now he was beginning to pay attention too.

'Think,' she said. 'Was I there when Bobby died? Did I bury him? Can you think of a single shred of evidence in that casket, or anywhere, that could implicate me?' Her face became a mask of innocence.

Wicker stared.

She said, 'Bobby planned this whole thing with you so he could get away from me.'

'Alright, why did I double-cross him, then? What was in it for me?'

'Me.'

He attempted a laugh, but his eyes betrayed him.

'You had a thing for me. Isn't it obvious? Running up at midnight. And now we have a witness. You just won't leave me alone.'

He gave a small laugh that was meant to ridicule her, but it was a pitiful sound.

'Do you actually think a jury could believe that any woman would leave Bobby Swift for you?'

Wicker remained stationary, even as his insides collapsed. He felt himself swaying.

'For me,' she continued, 'life with you would not be worth living. So go right ahead, Eliot. *Expose.*'

She held him in her triumphant gaze and he stared back at her, numbed. More voices sounded below them. The undertaker turned mechanically and took hold of the doorknob.

'I don't think you want to go out the front,' she said.

A volley of firecrackers rang out, followed by a chorus of whooping. Wicker paused, then swept dizzily past her and marched down the hall toward the kitchen. She heard the back door open and close again, quietly. Now a glow appeared on the front blinds, a soft, flickering orange. Outside, horns started blowing and boys started whooping. Flames crackled. Noel opened the slats and looked down. In the middle of the intersection, the outhouse shot flames into the sky like a giant candle, belching thick, asphalt smoke off its slanted roof. Suddenly the country boys scattered to their pickup trucks, and in seconds they were gone, escaping in two directions. From the left, Alston Bouchard pulled up in his Subaru wagon, blue dash-light flashing. He circled around in the parking lot and then parked across from the store, on the other side of the flaming outhouse. He turned off his lights and his engine and then just sat there, to wait out the fire, while horns sounded gleefully in the distance.

Noel stepped away from the window. Another Blueberry Blossom Night had ended in Gravity. For Noel Swift, she thought with great relief, it would be the last.

Eliot Wicker's shoulders ached before he was two feet deep. But he was driven – worlds beyond heartsick – fueled by a white-hot rage. He didn't know exactly what he'd do about Noel Swift, but he sure as hell wasn't going to let her dump him. Not without the fight of her life. So he stood in the moonlight and stabbed the earth with his spade, again and again, piling dirt on the tarp he had dragged up from the toolshed.

He had been bluffing, of course, when he'd threatened to expose their crimes. But he feared she wasn't bluffing at all. For down in that casket there was more than enough evidence to screw him up, but good: oxygen tanks, flashlight, heating pad. It would be obvious that he had cooked something up with Bobby Swift. So, after tonight, let her talk. See where it would get her. They'd open the casket and find – *voilà* – Bobby's Swift's corpse and nothing else. So let her talk.

Wearing his navy blue windbreaker and brand-new jeans – *which he'd bought just for her!* – he had marched two miles from his home to the cemetery, actually running half that distance by necessity, darting from cover to cover so he wouldn't be caught in a clearing, should a car pass: But now it was well after one and the town was fast asleep. The entire way over here, he'd seen only two cars, a couple of diehards going home.

Originally he had considered sneaking the body back to his morgue for a proper embalming, but he decided it was too chancy. Anyway, there was no need. If they ever did exhume the body, Noel's story would be blown at first sight. *Where's the oxygen tanks, lady? Where's the scuba tanks?* She'd be instantly discredited, and they'd close the casket and be done with it. Granted, the corpse would be profoundly decayed, but no one expected Wicker's work to be perfect.

By the time he had dug little more than three feet down, he was shoveling with one knee on the ground, barely able to fill the spade. Distasteful as it seemed, he was forced to step down into the grave, where he kept digging until finally he stabbed the casket lid with the toe of his shovel, eight or ten inches down. 'Fuck you,' he grumbled to himself as he scraped the dirt off the polished, arched wood. 'Fuck the both of you.' His hasty plan was to free the viewing lid only, hoping to accomplish his mission without having to open the whole thing. So he stood in the lower half of the grave and pulled the dirt toward him, mounding it under his feet, each shovel clearing more of the upper lid. When enough wood was exposed, he knelt in the dirt and reached down for the latches. Strangely, he found them already turned.

A rotten suspicion weltered up inside him. He straightened his back, got his fingers around the edge of the lid and pulled with every molecule of strength he could muster, straining until the lid turned up in his hands. He swung it open, spilling dirt down his sleeves. When he looked down, his heart walloped inside his chest. The body!

Bobby Swift was gone—

'SHIT!' Wicker cried, even before be began to understand the implications. He ducked down in the grave, hoping no one had heard his shout.

Gone—

The thought sent a hard chill through him. Gone where?

No man could burrow his way out of a closed casket six feet underground. Not even Bobby Swift. Then what if – Wicker visualized this with a shudder – what if Bobby had broken his way out, started crawling into the earth and died there? It was a horrible thought, but one that had to be true. Wicker felt along the dirt wall, looking for a hole, expecting to find – what, Bobby's foot? – when he heard a sound.

He fell back and whipped his gun out of his windbreaker pocket, a Colt .38 semiautomatic. He quietly pulled back the slide, chambering a round, then he rose to the surface, moving his aim in a slow circle. Out in the night, everything lay still. The moon poured a wide, stark light over the cemetery below. The woods that wrapped around behind him remained perfectly quiet. He could even hear the river, nearly a mile away.

Pocketing the Colt, he turned his flashlight back on, then stepped down inside the casket, reaching his toe beneath the lower lid. He could feel the scuba tanks and both oxygen tanks, all covered with a dusting of dirt. Everything in place except the corpse—

That's when it hit him:

She had dug him up after all! Or else she had hired someone to. Wicker's breathing intensified. His face filled with pressure. Bobby Swift, alive! Probably far away by now – Cancun, Belize – Wicker was sure it wasn't Grand Cayman. No, they were too smart for that. Wherever Bobby was, Wicker knew damn sure that Noel was getting ready to join him.

And Eliot Wicker – once again, folks – Eliot Wicker gets screwed.

Oh, he wanted her now. Those icy green eyes, that crooked, haughty mouth, he wanted her worse than ever. And what could he do about it? He squeezed a handful of dirt so hard that his arm trembled. Here she had him sitting asshole-deep in an empty grave, surrounded by the evidence that could put him away for life. And for what? The crime of stupidity, of desperate, stupid love.

But she wouldn't get away with it, no way. He didn't know exactly what he would do, but he did know this: he would get her somehow, no matter what the cost to himself. He lifted one of the oxygen tanks out of the casket, flung it onto the turf above with a hollow ting. The other tank he hurled over his shoulder into the sky so high he could feel the impact through the earth when it came down.

Even if it meant he'd lose his license, he didn't care. If he had to do years of hard time, she'd pay. Oh, how he wanted the day to come when he'd be standing on the free side of a bulletproof pane, telephone in hand. What would he say? Something simple. Fuck you. Yeah, the big fuck you. Twenty-five rotting years in some hellish asylum, and he'd visit her every day just to say it. Fuck you, baby.

He struggled with the twin scuba tanks, got them up over his head and heaved with all his might. They made a ring when they hit the ground, which was a remotely satisfying sound. He bent down, felt under the closed lid for anything else, and found – luckily – the dead penlight. He threw that into the sky as far as he could, heard it snicker through the trees. Lying bitch. Next he snagged the heating pad, followed its double wires to the battery, bundled the whole thing and threw it so far into the sky he never even heard it land. He imagined it coming down over the cemetery like a parachute. He imagined Bobby Swift, prison pants down by his ankles, being buggered up the ass by some grizzly 300-pound Colombian drug lord. You too, Bobby. The casket would be clean.

Clean as his own alibi: The man was never buried, he'd say – if it came to that. Simple. Bobby Swift had tricked every-body. Otis and Jerry Royal had lowered an empty coffin into the ground; they were too drunk to notice, that's what he'd say. As for his failure to embalm Bobby—

He'd have to think about that one.

He got down on his knees with his flashlight and swept his hand around in the loose dirt, feeling for anything else, when something pierced the palm of his hand.

'*Bitch!*' he spat, blaming Noel for this, too, and then pulled the thing out of the dirt. A trocar – his embalming tool.

He shone the light on its dirt-encrusted tip, trying to make sense of the thing, when one of the oxygen tanks rolled back into the grave and glanced sharply off his head, knocking him onto his hands. He pressed his forearm to his head, the pain throbbing over his entire skull. And this, finally, was more than Eliot Wicker could stand. He threw his face into the air and—

Somebody was standing over him, at the edge of the grave, holding the other oxygen tank.

Wicker's first thought was to explain himself. 'I'm just reconfirming,' he said.

His second thought was to get at his Colt. In a flash he went for his pocket and brought out the gun, but then the oxygen tank came whistling down. There wasn't time to duck. Its impact on Wicker's head made a vicious PING. It was the last sound the undertaker would ever hear, if he ever heard it at all.

6

Sal opened his eyes when he heard the door close. A heaviness rolled over him like faraway thunder, the drone of an engine: the school bus driving away. He realized he was lying in front of the living room couch. A cushion lay on his side...

'Iris?'

He heard the refrigerator close. He sat up, and the heaviness in his head thickened. Then the back door closed. Dizzily, still dressed, he tossed the cushion off him, got to his feet and went into the kitchen, opened the door. She was getting in her car.

'Why didn't you wake me up?' he said. 'I'm late.'

The look she gave him was short, but long with sober resolution. She started the engine and backed out of the driveway. A sickening fear shot through him as he watched her drive away.

Numbed, Sal tried to remember the previous night; failing that, the previous day: Bobby's funeral, Noel's reception ... His conversation with Eliot Wicker faded in a Librium haze. His show? He knew it was useless to try.

'Just like this when we found it,' Jerry Royal said.

Alston Bouchard stood beside him, looking down at the cemetery plot. Otis, Jerry's father, sat sidesaddle on the riding lawn mower beside them both, his stomach sagging over his lap. A swath of mown grass stopped abruptly beside Bobby Swift's grave site, where squares of sod fit neatly together – except for one square, pushed up at its corner. But that wasn't what bothered the men. It was the blue-black barrel of a pistol that poked up, aimed at the sky. Otis leaned forward and pulled the sod back, and they could see that the pistol protruded from the earth to the trigger, which was squeezed in the firing position by a dark, greenish-red index finger with a manicured nail.

'Prob'ly rubber,' Jerry said, picking at the finger.

'Jerry,' Bouchard told him, 'maybe you best not...'

'Jumped the bejesus outta me, that thing,' Otis declared. Dressed in a sleeveless T-shirt that was stained with his sweat, Otis was testimony to the overwarm day.

'Somebody's idea of a practical joke,' Jerry said. 'No doubt.' Bigger than his father but not yet as heavy, Jerry was nonetheless obvious progeny. 'Like I said, tamp it down, let the sleepin dog lay.' He set the heel of his shoe on the pistol, attempting to push it down.

'I don't think you ought to do that,' Bouchard told him. He crouched down to get a closer look, picked a bullet casing out of the dirt, then peeled the sod back and found five more in a cluster.

'Thirty-eight,' Jerry said. 'I already checked.'

'Looks like he was trying to get somebody's attention,' Otis said.

'Either that or duck-huntin,' Jerry added, looking for a laugh.

'You boys move anything?' the constable asked.

'Just like this when he found it,' Jerry said again.

Bouchard sniffed the casing. It was around 6:30 in the early evening, a hazy, oversized sun melting over the western hills. The Royals had waited until late afternoon before mowing, hoping for a cooling breeze, but it never happened. The air sat over the town, dead heavy.

'Want us to dig it up, Alston?' Otis asked. 'While we're on the clock.'

'Too hot for that shit,' Jerry answered.

'I don't think yet,' Bouchard said. 'Either you boys talk to Eliot Wicker today?'

'Not me,' Jerry replied, and Otis grunted the same, as he scratched under his arm, then wiped his hand on his belly. 'Awful warm, Alston, you don't need us anymore.'

'I don't.'

'Want to leave the lawn mower, for evidence?'

'Leave it.'

'Okay then.'

As father and son lumbered from the grave to their new Chevy pickup, Jerry's black shotgun hanging in the rear window, Bouchard called out to them, 'You got a shovel here—?'

'Down the shed,' Jerry told him.

Bouchard rose to his feet, said, 'I'd appreciate it if you boys would keep this to yourselves. It'd likely upset her.'

'No doubt,' Jerry said, sliding into the truck. As they drove down the hill and turned out of the cemetery, the man who had arrested both of them countless times over the years stepped away from Bobby Swift's grave and looked up at a branch of an old maple tree, where something peculiar was hanging.

'They'll believe you,' Sal said again, but he was getting nowhere.

Iris, her back to him, poured a glass of water from the kitchen tap and drank it, fortifying her resignation. It was almost seven and still ninety degrees outside; even hotter inside. Still in uniform, Iris was just back from work.

'I need to take care of Davey,' she said, 'and I need to take care of myself. You need to take care of yourself.' Her words were laced with a maddening indifference, as if she were talking to a stranger – or firing an employee. She stuck her glass under the tap for more water.

He started to respond, but then he stopped. He wanted to tell her that he didn't know how it had happened, but he knew that anything he could think to say would be futile. More maddening, he actually didn't know what he had done. That he had gotten drunk was obvious – he remembered the first sip at Noel's reception. He remembered making another drink in her kitchen once everyone had left. After that, between the Librium and the vodka, the wall was up and there was no penetrating it.

'Iris, are you sure about this?'

He was speaking matter-of-factly, showing that he could be resigned too, hoping that she would rescind. But she stood with her back to him, unyielding.

'It was a bad night,' he said. 'It was the Librium, it was Bobby's funeral, it was a mistake.'

She sighed. 'It was no mistake, Sal. You knew what you were doing before you took the first drink. You knew what the outcome would be.' She turned and looked directly at him, her sea-gray eyes steady behind her lenses. 'I want you to leave,' she said.

He took a deep breath of the stilted air, feeling like the oxygen had been sucked from the house.

'That's it, then,' he said.

Her expression didn't change.

'What are we going to tell Davey?'

'I don't know yet.'

He went to the counter, picked up his car keys.

Iris didn't budge.

'I know that was the deal – I agreed to it,' he said. 'But we need to be realistic for a minute. If you don't go to that school board meeting with me, I'll lose my job, and then you and Davey end up passing out food stamps at the store like the rest of your family.'

She turned away from him again, stared out the window – a reaction at least, but he cursed himself for saying it. He went to touch her, to put his hand on her shoulder, and then he saw what she was looking at: Davey, in the garden, weeding peas.

By the time Sal and Iris reached the school, word of the green hand and the pistol had spread around town. The story was, teenagers had stolen a mannequin's arm from the Bangor Mall and buried it in Bobby Swift's grave, along with a stolen .38. In the school library, George Web was relating the tale to the other board members, but he stopped when Sal and Iris entered the room.

The couple was asked to sit in small wooden chairs on one side of a long library table. Despite the heat, Sal wore his usual corduroy jacket over a gray jersey. Iris wore her uniform. The five school board members sat behind the table along with the principal, Avery Bingstream, whose left arm was set in a white plaster cast and sling. Sal guessed that he was the cause. A mediator from the Maine Teachers' Association, a young man sweating liberally in a three-piece suit, sat at the head of the table, symbolically between the two factions. As the meeting went on, he removed the coat, then the vest, and then his tie, apologizing each time.

'What you are telling us, then, Mrs Erickson, is that Salvatore was, in fact, under the effects of antianxiety medication—?' This was Helen Swan, a retired psychiatrist from New Haven and head of Gravity's school board. White-haired and unadorned in a meticulous way, Helen was a former summer resident who had settled in town permanently four years ago to be near her son and granddaughter.

'Librium,' Iris confirmed, her hands in her lap. 'Sal was

under a lot of stress with Bobby's death. We had the bottle in our medicine cabinet – sometimes I need help sleeping.' With the proper self-effacement, Iris covered her lie with a smile for the woman.

'I see,' Helen Swan replied tentatively.

'That's understandable, with stress,' George Web piped in. 'Tough thing when you lose a friend.' George was the only man on the board, a subsistence-level carpenter and blueberry farmer and the member with the most seniority. Sal knew he could count on George's opposing Helen Swan on any matter.

'I told him to take two or three,' Iris added, embellishing her story. 'I didn't know he'd have such a reaction.'

Sal looked down at her clenched fingers, and he felt a sudden longing, like it was years ago and they were united against the world. He did not want to believe he could lose her. He took hold of her hand, which became lifeless in his.

'The truth is,' he said, 'Iris warned me not to take them before the concert. I didn't think it would be a problem.'

He looked up to see Helen Swan holding a coffee mug. 'MY FAVORITE TEACHER' was printed on it, a Father's Day gift to him from Davey. The woman peeled cellophane off its top. Neither Avery Bingstream nor any of the board members needed to see what was inside. Neither did they watch Sal. They kept their eyes on Iris, who twisted her hand out of Sal's. The mediator shifted in his chair.

'It was backstage,' Helen said.

Sal's stomach clenched. He knew what the mug meant. Helen tipped it forward, offered it to him. He did nothing. She slid the mug to the mediator. 'People in the audience saw him drinking from it.'

The young man dipped his finger into the liquid and touched it to his tongue. He sniffed at it and then cleared his throat. 'Vodka?' he asked. No one responded. 'Mr Erickson, would you care to say something on your behalf?'

Sal shook his head no.

'Mrs Erickson, is there anything you'd like to add, or change, regarding your testimony?'

The panelists waited quietly. Avery Bingstream ran his plaster cast across five or six inches of the wooden table, making a dry, scraping sound. The fan in the doorway grew louder. Sal felt the heat surge over him. Beside him, Iris stared straight ahead, almost entranced, humiliated beyond words.

'Please, let's not prolong this,' Mrs Swan said. 'Unless anyone has anything to add, I believe the board is prepared to vote on dismissal.' The other members nodded uncomfortably.

Sal stood up. 'I'll save you the trouble,' he said, pushing his chair neatly under the desk. 'I'll hand in my resignation in the morning.'

Helen Swan looked briefly at the other members, then replied, 'I'm afraid you don't have that option, Mr Erickson.'

Alston Bouchard worked alone. Protocol dictated that he call the state police, but he wanted to know what he was reporting before making the call – he didn't want to be the brunt of a Blueberry Blossom Night prank. By the time he discovered that the hand was indeed attached to an arm, he had also uncovered the head, the hair, and then the face, of Eliot Wicker – but then he noticed a leather belt wrapped around the dead man's neck and the tops of two shiny tanks behind his shoulders . . . so he continued digging.

It was dogged, drenching work. He kept a gallon of water on the ground beside him and assuaged his thirst every few minutes. With each shovel of dirt, perspiration poured off his nose and streamed down his glasses, rippling his vision. Now it was almost eight and darkening, and he was down to Wicker's jeans, far enough to see that it was Wicker's own belt that held the scuba tanks to his back – and that whoever had buried him had also taken the time to poke a flashlight out of his fly.

The local undertaker dead and buried with scuba tanks, a shining erection and a gun. And a missing corpse. Some prank.

The constable stopped digging. He took off his glasses and splashed water on his face, and then he looked out over the horizon. An hour earlier, orange-tinged cumulus clouds had begun billowing straight up in the western sky. As the sun had disappeared, the air had settled to a standstill, birds had stopped singing, and now an ominous quiet hovered over the hill. Thunderstorms had been predicted, but Alston Bouchard didn't need a weatherman to tell him that. Heat like this – in May? – could only mean one thing. When the first rumble crawled across the western sky, he decided to make the call.

Sal drove past their house, past the village, and then turned onto the Townhouse Road. He drove down along the blueberry barrens until they were within sight of the cemetery, and there he pulled over and shut off the engine. The sky, darkening in the west, fluttered with lightning. He waited for Iris to begin, knowing it was useless to apologize.

She didn't speak right away but waited while thunder grumbled across the horizon. Then she sat longer.

Looking absently at the lone man working up at the top of the cemetery, Sal gave no thought to the fact that the man seemed to be digging at Bobby's grave. Rather, he was beginning to finally understand that his life was over, difficult as it was to fathom how it had ended so fast: his marriage, his family, his career.

He had met Iris in the spring ten years earlier, the night the Thundering Herd played the Ellsworth Auditorium. After the concert Sal and the drummer went to a Bar Harbor pub, where a hot local dance band was playing. Iris, two years into nursing school, was there with two friends and phony IDs. She told Sal later that she was attracted to him not because he walked up to the stage with his trombone and roared through an incredible five-chorus solo that brought the crowd – and the band – to a frenzy, but because of the way he slunk back to his seat when it was over; because of his darkness; because of the way he seemed to be hiding inside his tweed cap and overlarge corduroy jacket. His manner didn't fit the ferocity of his music, and she'd told him that she wanted some time to figure him out.

After they had learned more about each other, Iris would say they were attracted to one another by a bond of childhood tragedies. But the real reason she was attracted to him – and they had each grown to see this independently – was because of the drink. Back at his table, two vodka martinis were sent to him, and he'd downed each with a tip of the glass to his benefactors. The second was from Iris, and he'd looked twice.

Now, as they sat listening to the thunder, her indifference was astonishing. He had, with a single act, become just like the other men in her life, her father and her brother: Gone.

'When we get home,' she told him, 'you'll need to pack some things. I don't know where you're going to stay—'

'I'll find a room in town,' he said.

'On the weekend you can come back for whatever else you need, and we'll work out the arrangements. If we can't agree, we'll have to get lawyers.'

She looked out the windshield, finished. Just like that. Like they were scheduling a brake job for one of their cars. A flurry of lightning lit her face, and the night seemed to grow instantly darker. Five or six thick raindrops splattered against the windshield, while a distant roll of thunder went on and on. She refused to even look at him.

He had managed to stay dry for five years after coming to

Maine – until Bobby and Noel came to town. It was that first summer, three years ago, when he took a part-time job at the store during his school vacation. That's when he started again. Closing time, they'd have a drink or two, he and Bobby and Noel, and as the summer wore on, he began staying later and later. In July he found himself in the county jail one morning after he and Bobby had torn up an Ellsworth tavern (that's what they'd told him, anyway). Somehow Bobby – who had instigated the brawl – managed to keep it out of the papers, but that didn't smooth things between Sal and Iris. In August, to help Sal sober up, the two men canoed up the 100-mile Allagash waterway in northern Maine, dry. It was an eight-day trip, during which Sal was constantly haunted with vodka cravings – and Bobby, who didn't have the addiction, stayed awake with him every night, talking and tending the campfire. When Sal returned home, he promised Iris that he'd never drink again, and he kept his promise – until the next summer, when he went to work at the store again (over Iris's objections) and fell quickly into another ten-week binge. Some nights he didn't come home at all, nor would he remember where he had been or what he had done. Iris, depressed and angry, told him she had had enough. So he and Bobby canoed the Allagash again at the end of August – but this time Sal wasn't able to kick, and his drinking continued into the school year. In November he checked into a Bangor detox ward for six weeks. Upon his return, she promised him that if he ever drank again, she would divorce him. He agreed to the terms. Now she was keeping her promise.

He started the car, punched the shift into first and started to pull onto the road, when headlights flashed in his rearview mirror. He kicked the brakes as a police car swerved around him, red brake lights glaring through the rain-spattered windshield. The cruiser turned into the cemetery, taillights making their way up the terraces.

Impassively, Iris reached over and flipped on the wipers. 'Davey's home alone,' she said. 'She doesn't like the thunder.'

Back home, Sal sat at the kitchen table while Iris put Davey to bed. When he heard Iris's footsteps cross the landing, he went up. He wanted to pretend nothing was wrong, but Davey was on to him. As they kissed goodnight, she clasped her fingers around the back of his neck and wouldn't let go. 'Come on, hon,' he told her, separating her fingers, 'get to sleep now.' He shut off her raccoon lamp and started to close her door.

'Love you,' she told him.

'Love you too.'

He crossed the landing and went into his bedroom, closed the door behind him. His suitcase lay opened on the bed beside a neat stack of his clothes. Iris was folding his handkerchiefs and laying them in.

'I'll do that,' he said to her. Then the door opened behind him.

'Daddy, I almost forgot,' Davey said, looking in. Seeing the suitcase, she sang, 'Are we going on vacation?'

'Honey, what is it?' Sal said.

'Just – Noel Swift called when you guys were out. I didn't write it down because there was too much, but she said to tell you to come over because she's got something for you, and this time you won't get interrupted.'

A stillness overtook the room.

'Honey, go back to bed now,' Sal told her, then added the lie: 'See you in the morning.'

She pouted.

'Go ahead.'

'See you in the morning,' she muttered, and left the room.

Sal picked up a couple of shirts, folded them and stuffed them in the suitcase. Iris busied herself in the closet, rattling hangers. Outside the walls, thunder murmured. Inside, the silence escalated. Sal picked up a pair of corduroys, folded them and set them in beside the shirts, then grabbed a handful of jockey shorts from his bureau drawer and bunched them on top.

'Did you even wait for the funeral?' Iris said finally.

'Don't start that,' Sal shot back, 'you know there's nothing going on between Noel and me, you resent her because she's an *out-a-statuh*'—

—'obviously enjoy her flirting'—

—'like maybe I resent having to live in your stupid hick town!'

—'Your choice, Sal, your decision'—

—'No, your choice. Your ultimatum! I gave up a career for you'—

—'You got fired from every band'—

—'*Downbeat* called me the best'—

—'*Downbeat* didn't have to put up with your drinking'—

—'Yeah, well I wasn't a drunk till I married you.'

Slamming the suitcase shut and latching it, pulling the suitcase off the bed, he sought to leave her with that. But she followed him out the room to the top of the stairs as he went down.

'My whole life I've put up with drunks,' she told him.

'That's right,' he replied, and he stopped at the bottom to give her a last look. '*You came looking for me!*'

The Superette was closed when Sal drove by, and Noel's apartment was dark. He hadn't intended to stop, but he could see by the faint glow in the storefront window that a light was on in the stockroom, which meant that Noel was back there working. And since she, after all, had just lost her husband – and now that he was in need of a sympathetic ear himself – he pulled down her driveway.

Fully dark now as he stepped out of his car, the night

weighed down heavily, while miles above, monstrous clouds tossed electric bolts back and forth, toying. Although the brief rain had stopped for the moment, the water in Noel's swimming pool swayed plaintively, as if sharing some secret relationship with the storm.

Thinking the door would be locked, Sal tried it anyway and it opened. The garage was blessedly cool, and pitch-black. He closed the door, reached out his hands and felt his way around Noel's Volvo. He could hear soft music upstairs, a saxophone and trumpet. Coltrane and Miles, from *Kind of Blue*, Bobby's favorite. Sal had never heard Noel play it before. She prefered world music, pan-global, whatever she called it. Drumming on goatskin, tribal chanting, stomping in the dust.

From the darkness he called hello, but only the saxophone responded. He made his way around the half partition and started up the stairs, climbing noisily, not wanting to startle her with his sudden appearance. After a few steps he arrived at a landing and had to turn right, feeling his way up the stairs with the toes of his sneakers and the handrail. With every step the air grew warmer, and then he emerged on the second floor, where the music was louder and a line of dim light leaked under the stockroom door. Sal took hold of the knob and pushed the door open, and he felt a rush of stifling heat.

He was in the stockroom, a wide-open, dusky, cardboard-smelling, windowless area filled with unshelved merchandise. He looked down a straight avenue created by two rows of cardboard boxes on wooden pallets. Similar aisles stretched toward the store on his left and right. Somewhere to the right of the center of the room, a soft spot of light shone on the wood ceiling. The saxophone sounded from that direction too, sailing over the low, arduous hum of the industrial-sized floor fan that Bobby had kept back there.

'Hello,' he called. The music quieted suddenly, and then he heard her voice.

'How did you get in?' she said.

'Through the garage. The door was unlocked.'

He entered the wide main aisle just as she stepped into the light about halfway down, between two pallets of boxes. She seemed to study him as he approached her, almost as if she didn't believe him. She was barefoot and barelegged under a short denim skirt and lazy beige tank top. Her tangle of orange hair, lit from the right, shone like fire. She held a tumbler in her hand, full of ice.

When he had almost reached her, she looked down at her drink self-consciously and gave an apologetic shrug. 'It's murder up here,' she said. 'There's no air.' Her arms were shiny with perspiration.

'It is hot,' he agreed. As they came together he stopped short of giving her a hug, feeling uncomfortable about touching her, the way she was dressed, the fact that they were up here alone. Seeming to sense his discomfort, she turned away from him and walked around a tall stack of cardboard cartons to her desk, a wide cherry affair covered with invoices, receipts and an accounting book. On the corner of the desk stood a pewter ice bucket; floating in the ice, a pint bottle of Stoli.

'I hope you don't mind,' she said. 'Should I hide it from you?'

Sal shook his head, and a drop of perspiration ran down his cheek. He wiped it with the back of his hand. 'I'm okay,' he said.

She gave him a sort of smile. 'You look great,' she replied. If sarcasm could be seductive, she had it down.

'It's the heat,' he replied. 'Or I'm in shock – I don't know – everything's out of whack.'

She swung the desk chair around for him, then slid herself back on a carton of vegetable oil. In the same motion she reached back to turn off the floor fan, briefly exposing a side of her breast, a smooth, white softness. 'I'd rather have the heat than the noise,' she told him.

He sat facing her with his back to the desk. 'Iris and I—' he began, but then he felt like he was blurting.

Her green eyes sharpened on him.

'We had an agreement...' He raised his fingers off his thighs, helplessly. 'And I blew it. So I'm gone.'

She gave him an odd look: even though her eyes narrowed with concern, her burnished lips turned into a slight smile. It was a feature of knowing Noel, that her mouth was often at cross-purposes with her eyes. She took another sip of her drink, ice cubes chiming against the crystal. A bright green circle graced the front of her tank top, the orange word BOTSWANA scrawled across it. 'Give her time,' she suggested.

'You don't know Iris. Once she shuts the door on someone' – he shook his head – 'it never opens again.'

Raising her glass, she gave him a slightly ironic look, a toast. 'So you're homeless, and I'm a widow.' She tipped the glass to her mouth and drank it down, spilling some of the vodka down her chin. She pulled up the neckline of her top to wipe her chin, lifting a breast against the thin fabric. 'Under the circumstances,' she said, 'I must say you don't look too broken up.'

'Yeah, huh?' He thought of saying the same thing to her.

She slid off the oil carton and leaned over his lap to get at the ice bucket, bracing herself with a hand on his thigh. 'I mean, six months without a drink, Sally, what exactly is the problem?' Her tank top fell away from her chest as she dropped a couple more ice cubes into her tumbler. A warm aroma rose from her body.

'Want me to get that?' he asked, turning his face away.

Retrieving the bottle, she uncapped it and began pouring. He could hear the liquid singing into the tumbler behind his ear, the ice cracking. He could smell the vodka. And Noel, leaning over him again to put the bottle back on ice, now he could smell the keen bite of her underarm.

'I should probably hit the road,' he said.

'I'll prove it to you,' she told him, straightening. Her leg remained pressed against his.

'Prove what?'

The glass rose between them, so close to his face that he could barely bring it into focus. She swirled the drink in little circles.

'That it's just a matter of perspective.' With that, she put the rim to her mouth. Staring at him, she slowly tipped the glass. The ice shifted. Her dark lips thickened and opened as she sucked the vodka into her mouth.

He lifted his hands. 'Uh, that's enough perspective for me,' he said with a nervous laugh. He moved his leg, wanting to get up, wanting to leave.

But her eyes narrowed, a challenging stare. And now, leaning into him, practically straddling his knee, she started moving the glass toward him. 'Hm?'

He felt his heart beating. But, resisting, he took hold of the glass and put his other hand on her hip, intending to move her back.

'Really, Noel, this is not good. I've got to go.'

She twisted the glass out of his hand and bore down on him with it. 'Uh-uh,' she scolded, like a mother administering medicine.

'Come on,' he laughed, weakening. 'You know I can't do this.' He turned his face to the side, but she found his mouth with the rim of the glass. 'Noel, stop, really—'

She gave him a flaccid smile and said simply, 'Tell me why.' Staring at him.

He stared back, heart thumping. She tipped the glass slightly, and the vodka touched his lip. Icy cold. Deadly. He kept his lips closed as he murmured an objection. She seemed aroused herself, almost hypnotized, the way she looked at him.

Then suddenly she stopped. A lightness came over her. 'See?' she said. 'Could an alcoholic resist that?' She smiled warmly at Sal as she began to lower the glass, and it was a powerful relief. But now he couldn't resist sucking a tiny stream of it.

'No, no,' she scolded, but she kept the tumbler at his lips, tipped.

The sensation was heart-stopping – the taste, the heat, the iciness; her smell, her heat on his leg. As he sucked a little more of it in, he gazed up at her, and now she was tipping the glass higher, watching him and making a humming sound, a soothing, motherly sound. Christ, it was like she was nursing him, and he became aware that she was moving her pelvis against his knee. It was far more than he could hope to resist. His mouth opened and he was drinking—

He pushed to his feet, pushing the glass away and sliding out from beneath her. She fell back against a stack of cartons. He didn't care. He just needed to get out of there.

'I can't do this,' he told her, backing away.

Standing there, disheveled, she looked stung.

'I can't,' he said again. 'Besides, I've got to go find a place to live.' He backed toward the main aisle of cartons. 'Are you gonna be okay?'

She didn't answer, just kept staring at him.

'Noel, I really have to go,' he said. 'I'll call you in the morning.' He turned to leave.

As if on cue, the telephone rang. Sal stopped, thinking it might be Iris, calling to take him back. Or Davey.

The phone rang again, but Noel paid no attention to it, just kept staring at him.

He said, 'Probably someone wondering if the store's going to open tomorrow.'

It rang again.

Noel looked at the telephone. Its second red button was flashing. 'No, that's upstairs,' she said. She leaned over the desk and pushed the button down.

'I've gotta go anyway.'

She raised a finger, stopping him, then picked up the phone. Her voice became instantly businesslike when she said hello. Then she scowled as she listened. 'Who were you trying to call?' she asked, then listened again, becoming more distracted. She hung up, then picked up the glass of vodka and walked past him, turned the corner around a pile of cartons.

He stayed where he was and waited a few seconds, but she didn't return. He called her name, but all he heard in response was Miles's soft and steady trumpet over an undertone of faraway thunder.

He followed where she had gone, around a pallet of stacked cartons to the main aisle that led into the store. He walked to the swinging door, looked through its window. 'Noel?'

He pushed on the door and emerged behind the meat counter. Inside, the store was a shade darker than the stockroom, and every bit as warm. Outside the two front windows (the only windows on this entire level), heat lightning continued to flutter, tossing shadows around. In that flickering light, Sal saw the glass of vodka on the lunch counter to his right. But no sign of Noel.

'Who called?' he asked.

When she answered, her voice came from one of the grocery aisles on the left. 'You didn't know I was an addict,' she said.

'What?'

She emerged from the aisles near the front of the store, lit for an instant by the flashing sky. 'Chocolate,' she said.

'Come on, chocolate.'

'The imported stuff,' she continued. 'Back before I knew you. I ate so much of it that I stopped eating everything else to keep from getting fat.'

'Noel, I doubt you were ever fat.'

She came toward him, slowly unwrapping a small package, six inches long. 'I couldn't get enough,' she said. 'The darkest, richest, most intoxicating chocolate I could get my hands on. Finally they put me in the hospital and got me into a twelve-step program.'

'I'm familiar with it.' He slid back onto a fountain stool three seats from where she had left the vodka, turned his back to the counter.

As she drew nearer, he could see that what she had in her hand was indeed a dark, thick bar of chocolate, about a half pound. 'They told me I could never eat it again. No candy, no cookies, no ice cream. Nothing. It's been five years and I haven't had a taste.'

'I'd say you were addicted,' he agreed.

'But I'm not like you. See, I don't isolate myself. I don't hide from it. I *surround* myself with it, the most expensive, the most intense chocolate I can find.' Standing in front of him, she waved the bar under his nose; its heady fragrance made him salivate. 'This is Caracas chocolate from Venezuela – I get it from an importer in Boston. There's a couple of people in Bar Harbor who buy it from me, they'll pay anything.' Now she began sniffing the chocolate, moaning as she did. Even in the dark, Sal could see that her eyes were losing focus. She seemed to float on her feet; her hip brushed his leg.

He turned on his stool away from her. He said, 'So why tempt yourself?'

She breathed a laugh. 'Temptation?' She reached around him, retrieved the glass of vodka and slid it along the counter until it touched his elbow. Then she stretched a knee up onto the stool beside him. 'That's what keeps us alive, Sally. Pure, uncut...' She pulled herself onto the counter, the backs of her legs squeaking on the Formica. Then she swung her body sideways until she was leaning back against the dessert display case in front of his face, her left hip touching his vodka glass. She gave the glass a nudge. 'Temptation.'

Demonstrating, she brought the bar of chocolate to her nose and inhaled deeply. 'God,' she breathed, 'I can actually feel my endorphins flowing.'

And he could already feel the vodka he had sipped, could taste it all around his mouth, could feel it flowing through his blood, working on his brain and body. 'At this point in my life,' he said, 'temptation is the one thing I don't need.'

He looked up at her and saw a dark smudge beside her lip where the chocolate had melted. She made a low sound in her chest, and her right leg reflexively rose in front of him, her silken inner thigh. He took a quick breath. Goose bumps danced up his sides.

'Sally, I'm serious,' she said. 'See how much you can take.'

Her voice was so soft, so weak, he wondered if he'd heard it at all. A bright light filled the store suddenly, turned shadows across the walls and then was gone – a pickup truck driving past, humming over the bridge, then turning left on the River Road. Noel hardly noticed. She was trembling, pulling the chocolate bar down her neck, actually painting it on her skin. She moaned loudly and then laughed, running the chocolate back over her cheek until it was at her mouth again, teasing her open lips. 'Go ahead,' she said, breathing harder. 'What've you got to lose?'

The ice cubes rattled inside his tumbler. He realized the glass was in his hand. His erection pressed against his trousers. What did he have to lose? Indeed.

'Sal?' She blurted his name suddenly, and with alarm. 'Oh God, Sal, I can't' – and all at once those dark lips closed around the end of the bar, the chocolate going softly inside.

Undone

'Noel, wait—'

Her knee kicked up, knocked against his wrist, splashing icy vodka over his hand, and then she turned away from him, lying on her side so that he could see the white cheeks of her buttocks, her dark panties pulled tight inside the cleavage. He could hear her lips working against the chocolate, could hear her swallowing as she murmured. He put a hand on her hip to stop her, and she moaned louder, opening that leg toward him. And now, in spite of himself, he was drinking the icy vodka, swallowing steadily – it was all he could do – and when the glass was empty he lowered his cold mouth to her humid thigh, pulling her roughly onto her back.

She made a noise – a protest – but her mouth was full and her sound was garbled. With his hand he opened her leg wider and then discovered her own hand there, three fingers working feverishly at herself. He pulled her hand away, took hold of the chocolate-sticky crotch of her silk panties and pulled them aside, her warm, liquid vulva squishing against his knuckles, then with his left hand he pulled her hips along the counter and lowered his own mouth to her flaccid lips, and God, the taste of her and Jesus, he looked up and beheld her there, propped against the display case, eyes closed, enraptured, her mouth working at that dark mass of chocolate, all the while roaring this loud, murderous ecstasy, and now Sal is reaching his left hand up under her top, up the length of her muscular, clammy stomach until he feels the firm swell of a breast, her nipple standing strong and hard, and he takes it between his thumb and forefinger and squeezes to soften it, and it makes her hips rise up, makes her clutch his head with her chocolate hand and grind her pubic bone into his jawbone, and now he's freeing his arm from her clothes, crawling up on the countertop, pulling her body beneath his own, and he's trying to kiss her dark bittersweet mouth, competing with her chocolate bar, and now they're both moaning in tongues of chocolate and saliva and it's like they're trying to swallow one another, and he's reaching under her, pulling her panties inside out – when more headlights flash across the store – and then they're falling off the counter—

He tries to catch her, tries to get his foot down and succeeds just enough so that when they hit the rubber mat they keep from separating. Their new bed is a cold cradle of hard rubber points, but he feels only an ecstatic sting on his side as he pulls her beneath him, and she squirms like a cat, delighting in the sparks, then wrestles him beneath her, working his trousers to his knees. He tries to toe them off the rest of the way, but she won't allow it, she's on him that fast, freeing his member from his underpants, her chocolate lips sucking down over the head and shaft, her fingers climbing his chest, nails singing his skin, and now he takes her under the arms and lifts her in the air, and her wet legs slide open around his hips, searching until they find what they want, precisely, perfectly – and then she stops—

poised . . .

He gasps.

Lightning flutters across the ceiling . . .

With a slowness that's the most exquisite torture, she lowers herself over him – an inch – just enough so that only his glans slips inside. And she stops again. Looking down at him hungrily, dark hair pasted over her forehead, dark lips in a lopsided near-smile, chocolate-smeared, engorged, slackly apart . . . she begins swallowing him inside her with a deliberateness that's reptilian. Staring. Staring. Shining.

There's no warning. The rush is immediate, tingling, overwhelming. He explodes, reaching for her, clutching the cheeks of her buttocks, spreading her apart and forcing himself deeper, entering her completely, pushing deeper still, ejaculating in colossal, heart-bursting spasms – three times, four times, five times, six times – straining as if every vein and artery is going to burst – until she cries out – seven times, eight times – the ceiling above them turning red ... redder ...

A car engine!

'*Somebody's here*—'

The knocking was tentative but persistent. Noel rose to her knees, twisted her denim skirt around, then wiped the chocolate from her face and neck with a towel that hung by the sink. Sal, on his back, hips raised, tried to zip his trousers over his erection.

'Stay down,' she whispered, and then she was gone, staying low, escaping down the length of the counter into the darkness.

From the stockroom he heard the music come on again – the same as before, Coltrane and Evans, smoky sax over a meditative piano – and then her bare feet padding back into the store, past the length of the counter. He heard the click of tumblers as she unlocked the door.

'Alston,' she said. Alston Bouchard. Sal wondered if the constable had seen his car down in back. After all his other transgressions, he did not need to be found here.

'Sorry I didn't hear you,' Noel said. 'It's so hot back there. I had the fan on, and the music.'

Sal saw her underwear on the floor beside him. He picked up the panties and bundled them softly in his hand as he heard Bouchard say, 'There's something I wanted to ...' A period of silence passed, and then the constable added, 'Should I come in, or do you want to ...' The man was more nervous than anybody his size had a right to be.

'No,' she said, 'come in, Alston, if you don't mind the dark. I'd put the lights on, but people would think we're open, and I've never been good at saying no.' The door hushed closed.

'Are Ellis's cows loose?' she asked. 'You're not usually out and about this late.'

Bouchard, his voice suddenly present, said, 'That was you I called then.'

'Oh,' she said, 'so that was you.'

'I thought I recognized your voice.'

'That's funny, because I thought it was you, too. But I didn't know why you'd be calling at this hour and not saying who it was. Would you like a Coke, Alston?'

'No, I'd have to pay' – Sal heard Bouchard slap the glass candy case that the cash register sat on – 'and where you've been closed, and the register's off...' More silence. Then, 'I guess you got two lines then,' he said. 'A separate phone line for your apartment upstairs.'

'The apartment, mm-hm. Do you want to sit, Alston? It seems like you're leading up to something.'

'No, I'll set when I get home. But you remember which line I called? The store or...'

Sal remembered. It was her upstairs line. But Noel seemed to have forgotten. 'I'm not sure, to tell you the truth. I just picked up when it rang.'

'Where?'

'In back.'

Bouchard cleared his throat. 'I don't suppose it'd be permissible if...' Sal could picture the apologetic turn of Bouchard's hand. 'The button'd still be pushed down prob'ly. I don't mean to be...'

'Alston, do you want to see my phone?'

'Well, not if—'

'It's just a little strange that you'd ask. But come on.'

Their footsteps moved through the store, the swinging door, and then their voices diminished into the stockroom. Presently Sal heard them returning, Bouchard saying, 'You didn't call anyone after I called you?'

The door swung open and they walked into the store again, stopping on the other side of the counter. 'Alston, this is all a little weird. You're not here because there's trouble with the phone lines.' Her tone was unabashedly patronizing.

Bouchard said, 'You'd just as well take a seat, Mrs Swift.'

'Alston, please just tell me what it is you have to say.'

'I'd still feel better,' he replied uncomfortably, 'if you'd set.'

Sal heard the small wheeze of a fountain stool as Noel complied. He could hear the constable breathing through his nose. 'Alston, what is it?'

'You know Eliot Wicker—'

'Of course.'

'Well, his body turned up today.' Bouchard made a soft grunt, or a cough, and then added, 'Passed on.'

There was a beat of silence. Then Sal heard Noel say, with no discernible emotion, 'Alston, that's terrible. Eliot, dead? How?'

'Won't know for sure until the autopsy. Got the medical examiner up there now. Killed, you'd have to say, by the looks of it.'

More silence. Sal heard Noel slide off the stool.

'Mrs Swift, I wouldn't get up just yet.'

'I'm okay, Alston.' She was walking toward the front door. 'Killed, like murdered?'

'I guess you were the last person he called.'

'Did he call me?'

Bouchard cleared his throat again. 'I went over there, to his place. When I pushed the redial button on his phone, it rang over here. That's how you happened to answer when I . . .'

'And you recognized my voice,' Noel said. 'That's very clever, Alston. I wouldn't have thought of that.'

'Just trying to...'

'But how did he – how was he—'

'Hard to say. But you don't recall him calling over here?'

Another period of silence. Sal heard a few deliberative footsteps. 'Did Eliot Wicker call me?' Noel said. 'Well, certainly for the funeral arrangements.'

'No, this would've been last night, after the funeral, after your reception. Otis Royal told me that Eliot called him about nine and told him to get the cemetery mowed today. The grass. So that means that Wicker had to call you afterwards. Sometime after nine.'

'God, let me think who I talked to ... after the reception. What I'm thinking, Alston, is that if he had tried to call me and my line was busy, my number would still be the last one his telephone remembers, wouldn't it?'

'I believe so.'

'Because, Alston, I'm sure I didn't talk to him last night. I mean, I don't know why he would want to call, unless to check up on me after the funeral. Maybe it's customary. Maybe he dialed my number by mistake and then hung up before the phone rang.'

'Maybe.'

'The phone company has records, don't they?'

'Not local calls,' Bouchard said. Then he cleared his throat again. 'I know you're closed up, Mrs Swift, but my flashlight died tonight, the batteries, 'course I'd pay you first thing in the morning, if it's not...'

'No trouble at all.'

He heard Bouchard walk toward the front of the store, stop, and then come back. 'Four ninety-seven, I think it says.'

'Pay me tomorrow, don't worry,' she said.

Sal heard the constable take a deep breath. 'Mrs Swift,' he said with palpable discomfort, 'I've just got two more things—'

'Oh, Alston, could it wait?'

'I'm just going to tell you both things before I go, once you set.'

Sal heard Noel sit down again, with a sigh. It was a nervous sound, cut with irritation. 'Alston, what?'

'Eliot Wicker's body,' Bouchard said carefully, 'was in your husband's grave. And your husband's body is missing.'

For a few moments neither of them spoke. Sal recalled the clipped conversation among the school board as he and Iris had entered; and later, the police car rushing into the cemetery.

'So,' Noel began, and then she stopped. 'Alston, I don't understand. Bobby's body – missing where?'

'These are the things I'm trying to determine. Like why he might have wanted you.'

'Who?'

'Eliot Wicker, I mean.'

'But I told you, I didn't talk to him.'

Sal didn't like the constable's insensitivity, or the way he seemed to be pressing her.

'But why he was trying to call you,' he said, and then the front door opened and he started to leave, his voice moving away. 'I'm just trying to figure these things...'

Noel stopped him. 'Alston, you must have some idea where Bobby is. His body—?' Sal could hear peepers singing down at the river.

'You didn't expect him to come here for anything.'

'Eliot? No, I told you that. But what was there – I mean, besides Eliot – in the grave? Just ... Eliot?'

Bouchard hesitated. Sal heard him breathing through his nose. 'Funny thing. Not *funny*, just...'

'Alston – What?'

A beat. Then: 'Well, the circumstances.'

'God.'

'Investigators are there now, medical examiner, whatnot, going over the crime scene. Probably a detective will be down to see you in the morning.'

'Thank you, Alston.' Sal heard the door close. Then open again.

'Mrs Swift, I should tell you also . . .' The constable sighed uncomfortably. 'The police notify insurance companies in a case like this, with unusual circumstances. Anything unusual they don't like to pay, not until things get resolved.'

There was a pause. Then Noel responded, 'I can understand that.'

'But you let me know if there's anything you think of . . .'

'I will, Alston. Thank you.'

Sal heard the door close again, and a moment later the car door closed and the engine started. Noel walked back toward the stockroom. 'Stay down,' she said. Red lights from Bouchard's taillights appeared, then the brighter red of his brake lights, and then he was gone, just the sound of his car going away.

Sal buttoned his trousers and made his way into the stockroom and down the aisle, where he found Noel standing by her desk, lost in thought. Miles's trumpet, barely audible, was picking out a deliberate, sultry melody. The fan was humming. Sal wasn't sure whether to touch her or not. He realized that he still had her red panties in his hand, and he didn't know what to do with them. What was equally on his mind was Eliot Wicker's death and Bobby's missing body. And the half bottle of Stoli on the desk – and how badly he wanted another drink.

'You have to go,' she said, turning toward him. Seeing her panties in his hand, she took them from him and set them on the desk. When she turned back to him again, it was with an odd, vulnerable look that he'd never seen from her before.

'Are you gonna be okay?' he asked her.

Undone

She shook her head, looking like she was about to cry.
'Oh, Sal, I don't know what you think of me,' she said,
'that maybe I should go around in a veil, that I'm selfish,
I'm self-centered, I'm vain ... I don't know what you think
of me.' She breathed a sigh that seemed filled with self-
abomination. 'You were his best friend,' she said. 'I know
he told you.'

'Told me. What?'

'He told you everything. He trusted you.' Noel's eyes were
all over Sal. 'The other night, when you were out together?'

Sal shook his head dumbly.

She looked away. 'Sal, I was leaving him.'

He stared at her, searching for words, but none came.

She met his eyes again and nodded her head, confirming
what she had said. 'We were getting divorced.'

Shaking his head in disbelief, Sal leaned back against the
support post. 'He didn't tell me.'

And there it was. He could have helped Bobby. He realized
that now. Under the bridge that night – *Sally, who do you
trust?* It was what Bobby had come to tell him, that she was
leaving him.

'Are you okay?' she asked.

'Yeah,' he answered, though it was a blatant lie.

'Come on,' she said, leading him around the wall of boxes.
At the main aisle, they walked through the semidarkness to
the back of the stockroom, where Sal had entered. Noel
opened the door and turned on the stairwell light, and they
descended the stairs in silence. At the landing they turned
down a few more stairs until they emerged in the back of the
garage, where the air was cooler and the room flickered with
lightning from outside.

Noel refrained from turning on the overhead fluorescents.
The stairwell shed enough light so that when they turned
around the partition they could see the cars: Noel's black

Volvo; Bobby's black Corvette on the other side. His old black Harley leaning on its kickstand behind the cars. The sight of the bike hit Sal like a dull shock, almost as if the machine were waiting for Bobby to return.

Noel seemed to sense it. 'He loved that thing,' she said, walking over to it, running her hand over the seat. Sal walked behind her. Another flash of lightning lit the room – flickered on and on, not wanting to die. She turned to him. 'He'd want you to have it,' she said, and she pressed a single key into Sal's hand. He looked at the key, took a sudden, reflexive breath. Moving away from her, he walked to the entry door, saying, 'I'll come back for it tomorrow.'

'Sal?'

He opened the door. She caught it.

'Sal, wait.'

He stood there shaking his head. 'I should never have come over here tonight,' he said.

'Take this,' she told him. He turned around and saw her taking a leather riding jacket off a hook. Bobby's. She draped the jacket over his arm. The leather was heavy. Its smell was Bobby's smell, and Sal felt another tug of sadness, of shame. 'Take it,' she said. 'It's going to storm tonight, and you may be sleeping in your car.'

He took the jacket from her and then saw the Stoli bottle in her other hand. 'You might need this too,' she said. 'It could be a long night.'

He shook his head. 'I don't need that,' he told him, as a long, distant thunder rolled overhead.

They looked out the door into the darkness. They could hear big drops of rain splashing lazily in her swimming pool. She took hold of his T-shirt, raised her face and kissed him on the mouth. He broke the kiss, his mind racing with misgiving. She kept hold of him.

'Sal?' she said softly.

He met her eyes longer than he had intended.

'Bobby's gone,' she said, and then he stepped out into the night.

7

The northwest corner of the cemetery was awash with lights: car headlights, portable floodlights, camera flashes – so much light that the lightning in the sky, which was becoming more frequent, might have gone unnoticed if not for the accompanying thunder.

TV news reporters and cameramen, along with print journalists, rimmed the yellow police tape that surrounded the empty grave, interviewing a large, steel-haired man in a cheap checkered blazer, a machine of a man. Inside the restricted area, two evidence techs in light blue lab jackets worked under a pair of tripod floods powered by the tall silver van parked nearby, the mobile crime lab. One man worked inside the grave; the other worked above, sifting the dirt through a wood-framed screen. Off to the side sat the mahogany casket, along with the scuba tanks and an assortment of grocery bags, pillboxes and tins.

The coroner's vehicle, a green Bronco emblazoned with the words STATE OF MAINE, was backed close to the grave with its liftback opened enough to allow the cameras a shot of the stuffed white plastic bag in the back, the undertaker's body. On the gravel drive to the left of the grave, parked behind the crime van, were two state police cruisers and a new, highly polished black Cherokee. A dozen other vehicles lined the road behind them, on down the hillside.

Alston Bouchard registered all of this as he wound up the terraces in his yellow Subaru wagon. When he spotted a space in the line of cars too small for a car to fit, he drove his car through and pulled onto the lawn. Some heads turned. He shut off his lights and engine.

The detective being interviewed was Murdoch, the troop sergeant from CID 3, out of Orono. Bouchard knew enough about Murdoch to know that he was here for the cameras. Somebody else would be leading the investigation. Bouchard's eyes caught another detective crossing to the grave site, a man in his thirties with dark hair and a neat mustache. A couple inches over six feet, he was dressed in a well-fitting beige suit, and he carried an instrument slung over his shoulder, a plastic box of some sort, same color as the suit. A computer, Bouchard guessed, or tape recorder.

The downpour started suddenly, as if the miles of clouds overhead had all opened at once. The rain was blinding. A floodlight flickered with surprise, the sergeant turned abruptly and marched off toward the cars, and the newspeople scurried for their vehicles. Activity at the grave hastened too. The two lab men quickly unfurled a blue tarpaulin over the hole, a trooper threw another tarp over the casket, and the lab men hurried their bags and boxes of evidence into the silver van.

The well-dressed detective who seemed to be in charge was in no such hurry. Pulling a blue poncho over his suit and hunching over the plastic box he wore (but otherwise ignoring the rain), he swung a leg over the barricade and went in close to the casket, raised a corner of the tarp, squatted down and ran his hand along its lid.

A trooper approached the detective then and pointed toward Bouchard's car. He was the on-duty officer who had initially responded to Bouchard's call, a young, close-shaven mastiff named Lemieux. Spotting the constable, the well-dressed detective rose to his feet and, with a casual stride, came over through the rain. Bouchard thought he saw a smile under the man's mustache as he opened the passenger door and bent to look in. A lightning bolt scratched the sky, followed by a whack of thunder. The detective didn't wince. The rain, incredibly, began falling harder.

'Detective Shepherd, state police,' he said. 'You are?'

'I made the call.'

Shepherd's smile broadened. 'The town constable.' He took a small notebook off the passenger seat and tossed it on the dash, then sat inside Bouchard's car. As he shut the car door, he opened his poncho, exposing the plastic box he wore. He released the strap, set the thing on his knees and flipped open its monitor lid. It beeped. A computer.

'Alston Bouchard,' the detective read. 'Mister Bouchard, are you aware that you single-handedly managed to contaminate this entire crime scene?'

Bouchard looked out at the tarpaulin fluttering against the wind. The trooper, Lemieux, had already chewed him out for digging up the body. But that was a sharp reprimand, from one ex-marine to another. It was deserved, and Bouchard had accepted it, despite the trooper's youth (and despite the fact that it was Desert Storm lecturing Vietnam). Shepherd's admonishment, on the other hand, was laced with civility, harder to take.

'For future reference,' the detective continued, 'keep this in mind: Every time you go someplace, you leave part of yourself. By the same token, when you return, you always bring something back.' Shepherd raised his eyebrows, studied Bouchard a moment to see if he understood, and then proceeded to take the constable's statement and enter it into the computer: the missing body, the found body, the heating pad hanging from the tree limb, the dead batteries inside the heating pad (Hi-Crown brand – which were stamped with the same expiration date as the Hi-Crown batteries that the Superette carried).

Bouchard gave the detective the new pack. He told the detective that he had last seen Eliot Wicker on the night of Bobby Swift's funeral, and that the last telephone call made from Wicker's house was to Noel Swift's apartment. When Bouchard explained about checking the redial function on Wicker's telephone, Shepherd stopped typing.

'Mister Bouchard, under what authority did you enter the premises of the deceased?'

'He was dead, and I'm the constable.'

Shepherd sat for a moment. Then he turned to look at Bouchard, who elaborated: 'I discovered a basement window which was unlocked. I thought there might be an intruder. So I went in.'

Shepherd shook his head. 'I see. And what besides the telephone did you contaminate at that scene?'

Bouchard, still holding the steering wheel, raised both index fingers. 'I used a handkerchief.'

'A list, please. You touched—'

'Telephone, with a handkerchief.'

'Telephone.' Shepherd entered the information.

'Doorknobs in the bedroom, bathroom. Toilet seat and flush handle in the bathroom. Downstairs in the funeral home, doorknobs, light switches, screwdriver . . .'

Shepherd drew a tight breath through his nose. 'Why the toilet seat and flush handle?'

'Just . . .' Bouchard's thumbs flicked out.

'You were looking for what? Blood? Hair? Semen?'

'I had to relieve myself.'

Shepherd stopped typing again. 'You continued utilizing a handkerchief?'

'Not on myself.'

Shepherd raised his face, uncertain if this nearsighted bear beside him was joking. 'Mister Bouchard, is there anything I should know about what you found in Mr Wicker's house?'

'His parking lot lights were off,' Bouchard answered. 'I found a wire in the wall switch disconnected.'

'What do you mean, disconnected?'

Bouchard looked at the detective. 'It had come apart.'

'I mean, did the wire become disconnected because of an electrical malfunction? Or is it your opinion that somebody disconnected it?'

Bouchard flicked his thick wrist. 'Ripped off, I'd say. Being that the terminal screw was tight and there were a couple of broken strands still fastened to it, I'd say somebody...' He snapped his wrist again.

'Motivation?'

'To make the parking lot dark.'

Shepherd paused. The rain beating against the windshield turned briefly to hail, then back to rain again, ice flakes washing down. Through the glass Bouchard could see Trooper Lemieux approaching Shepherd's door with something in his hand. The trooper knocked once on the window, rain splashing off his huge shoulders. Shepherd rolled the window down. 'Anything else?' Still addressing Bouchard.

'About a half hour ago I visited Noel Swift – the widow of the dead man whose body is missing – to find out why Eliot Wicker might have called her. She said he didn't call.'

Shepherd turned to Lemieux, seemingly unaware that the grim young ex-marine was now being pelted with hail.

'Sir, we found this in the woods.' He held the penlight in a handkerchief. 'The batteries are dead.'

'Depth?' Shepherd said.

'Sir?'

'In the woods. How deep?'

'On the surface. On the ground.'

'We're not communicating, Trooper. How far into the woods from the edge of the lawn?'

The hail came down harder. The trooper shouted as if to

keep from shivering. 'No more than fifteen feet. No less than twelve.'

Shepherd folded down the top of his computer, then he opened the car door. 'Constable, you've been a big help.' Pulling the poncho over his head and hunching over his computer, he ducked out the door, then turned back and added, 'But do me a favor. Leave the investigative work to the detectives, and I promise we'll be out of your town before you know it.' He threw the door shut, then he and the trooper headed for the silver van.

Bouchard leaned over, rolled down the passenger window and called out. 'The batteries in the flashlight—'

The trooper turned.

'Hi-Crown?'

Chain lightning webbed the sky, followed by a series of thunder. The trooper said something to Shepherd that appeared to be affirmative. Shepherd raised a hand, a wave.

'We'll sign you up at the academy, Constable.'

Noel waited until Sal drove away, and then she locked the door. Standing there in the dark, an undeniable heaviness had descended over the building, a disquieting silence. Sal had told her that the door had been unlocked when he'd arrived. Yet it was always kept locked. Had she unlocked it earlier when she went out? A fear came over her, a fear of carelessness, of things gone wrong. It made her feel terribly small in this dark little corner of the garage.

Bobby—

Had he escaped? Smashed out of his coffin and then burrowed his way up? She listened to the room around her ... much too quiet down here, even with the rain and wind and thunder. Had he gotten out somehow and taken his revenge on Wicker? She looked around the dark garage, from his low Corvette over to the door of his workshop and gym, to the

124

stairway partition, keeping her hand on the doorknob, ready to run out into the night if any shadow should jump. And then she stopped herself, forced the fear from her mind and formed a singular, comforting image: Bobby underground, closed in the casket, packed with almost five feet of earth on top of him. Tons of solid blackness. He could not have escaped.

Then where was his body? (And who had killed Eliot Wicker?)

Unless *someone else* had dug Bobby up. Wicker? No, Bobby would never have schemed with the likes of him . . .

Sal—

No, if Bobby had confided in Sal, and Sal knew Bobby was alive, he never would have made love to her. Unless—

An image invaded her thoughts: Bobby, teeth filled with gravel, laughing maniacally, clawing his blind way to the surface.

No! She needed to relax, to calm her mind.

Despite the heat, she thought of soaking in a hot, deep bath. And that's what she resolved to do, all she would allow herself to think about as she turned from the door and made her way around the partition, climbed up the stairs to the second-floor landing, where she stepped once again into the overwarm stockroom.

Turning off the stairwell light and then barring the heavy door behind her, she headed down the center aisle of cartons toward the green-lit ceiling, making the right turn to her desk. There was a wide oak door just beyond the desk that opened on her private stairway, and that was her singular focus now: her stairway, her apartment, her bath.

She unlocked the door and opened it, then flicked on the wall switch, lighting the lavish stairway from high above. Noel's staircase was undoubtedly the most expensive piece of carpentry in town: eighteen treads made of thick African zebrawood, four feet wide and highly polished. Railings of ebony gleamed like black glass as the stairway curved gracefully around to the left. The walls were papered in a rich jungle motif, a pattern of lush fern and fanleaf over smoky yellow.

After a year and a half in Maine, when Bobby still hadn't instigated the Plan, he had hired carpenters from Bangor to build the staircase for her – at a quarter the cost of the entire property. It was unabashed extravagance. After all, they already had two sets of stairs in the building: one in back (which wound two flights from the garage to the apartment's kitchen) and another in front (which led from behind the counter up to the living room). Noel's private staircase was her price for Bobby's procrastination. After a fourteen-hour workday in the store – hearing about this one's arthritis, this one's divorce, that one's delinquent twins – Noel would enter her staircase, shut the door behind her, and her world would be instantly transformed: rich, comfortable and quiet.

Now it was too quiet. Or not quiet enough. She held her breath, trying to *hear* – what? A breath not her own, the tick of a floor board, the rustle of a sleeve. But all she could hear was the humming of the condenser motors from the back of the store and the rain beating all around the building, crawling up the shingles. The steady collapsing of thunder could have been the footsteps of someone trudging across the floor above her, undead.

'*Don't.*'

She said it aloud to herself, and her own small voice chilled her. *Bobby was dead.* She had been there at the cemetery, removing the evidence at the same time she should have been digging him up. There wouldn't have been enough time for anyone to dig him up after she'd left. Neither had there been enough time before she had arrived – not under cover of darkness.

Bobby was dead.

She pulled the stairway door closed behind her, turned the

small lock in the center of the knob. She took a calming breath, then turned and looked up her zebra staircase, let its wild opulence soak into her. Holding the railing, she climbed slowly around to the top, thankful to see her sturdy apartment door closed. Yes, she was alone. *Bobby was dead.* There was no one but her in the building. She took the key out of her skirt pocket and unlocked the door. Pushed it open.

The hallway was dark, as it should have been. She could smell the flowers, but that didn't help. She reached around the jamb and flipped the switch, lighting the long corridor that connected the living room on her right to the kitchen on her left; the light also creeping a ways into the short hall that stretched out ahead of her to the bathroom and her bedroom.

Up here the rain on the roof sounded like the low buzzing of bees. She closed the door behind her, locked it, then turned left and went past the study into the kitchen. Even before she flicked on the overhead light she could see that the room appeared as she had left it this morning – her juice glass on the dish drainer, upside down. She checked the back door and found that it, too, was locked. As she had left it.

She went back down the hall to the living room. Crossed to the front windows and lowered the venetian blinds, then turned on the floor lamp. She checked the front door. Locked.

Back down the hallway, she turned into the wing that led into her bedroom, stopped to flick on the bathroom light and peek in. Her logic returning, she went to the bathtub and turned the faucet, dialed the control to hot. As water pounded in the tub, she walked into her bedroom, made her way to her bedside lamp and turned it on. Going to the window, she pulled down the blinds, then took her green silk chemise off the vanity chair. She glanced in the mirror, checking the reflection of the room behind her, the doorway – as if someone might be standing there.

She realized it was tiredness that made her imagination act

this way. She was exhausted – and wanted only to slide into her bath and quiet her overworked mind. She needed clarity.

She pulled off her top and tossed it into her straw laundry basket. She pinched the emerald studs off her ears and placed them on her vanity, then unzipped her denim skirt and dropped it to her ankles—

That's when she remembered her panties – she had left them on the desk in the stockroom. She thought of Bonnie True finding them in the morning and realized that she'd have to go back down and retrieve them.

She opened Bobby's dresser drawer and found his .22 revolver, the weapon he'd worn on his belt when he first opened the store. Then, pistol in hand, she went back down the corridor and opened the door to her staircase.

Her nakedness made her feel vulnerable, but the gun overcame that. Not that she was in danger, she told herself. It was playacting. So she turned on the overhead chandelier and aimed the pistol at the blind curve ahead of her, the maddening swirl of black-white-black, green on green. Playacting, she told herself, she would fire at the first thing that moved. The pounding of the bath water behind her diminished to a whisper as she descended the cool treads to the door. She turned the lock, pushed the door open.

Her shadow fell onto a wall of cardboard boxes in front of her. For a few moments she stood motionless in the doorway, her gun pointing out, her finger on the trigger . . . listening. The desk was located behind the boxes. Beyond the boxes, the rest of the stockroom hovered darkly, quietly. Hang the fear, she had the gun. Brazenly, she stepped out of the stairwell and walked around the boxes. Reaching the desk, she felt in the dark for the lamp, slid her hand along its base until she found the brass switch, and turned it on. Her heart jumped. Green light in her face, blackness all around . . .

. . . her panties were gone.

Goose bumps skittered up her arms. She picked up the lamp, held out her gun and turned a circle, tossing light around. She hoped to see the red silk on the floor – but there was too much darkness, too much quiet. She felt a fierce constriction, as if the world were suddenly pressing in all around her, and she was suddenly petrified of being there alone, sandwiched between two dark, wide-open floors. Dropping the lamp on the desk, she turned back toward the stairs, clutching the gun. In a blur she was back inside her staircase and the door was locked. Standing there with a foot on the bottom tread, pressing the pistol against her forehead, she hoped the cold steel would revive her logic. Then she remembered her bath and hurried up the stairs into the corridor, locking the stairway door behind her.

She walked across the hall into the wing, turned into the bathroom. The thick steam from the bath was brightened by the overhead light. She swatted the air with the pistol, exciting the vapor while she made her way to the tub, where she reached in and turned off the water. Standing in the cloud, with her naked back to the door, she searched her mind and tried to account for each moment. Maybe she hadn't left her underpants on the desk. Perhaps she had grabbed them on her way upstairs and simply forgotten in the confusion. After the news from Bouchard, anything was possible. A heavy boom shook the house – she spun around with the gun, facing the door. Then caught her breath. Only thunder.

Forgoing her bath, she walked out of the steam, closed the door behind her and made her way to her bedroom. Sleep, she told herself, pulling the bedcovers down. Sleep was what she needed. Still clutching the pistol, she closed the door and dragged over her vanity chair to prop under the doorknob, then balanced a delicate teardrop perfume bottle on top of the chair so it would fall if the door were disturbed. She got into bed and switched off the light. Then, in the dark, she turned onto her side, laid her head on the pillow and aimed the pistol at the door.

Detective Shepherd drove home to his empty Bangor condo under a violent drumming, a stampeding on the roof of his Cherokee. Lightning strobed continuously in the night, laying stark the lone houses and rocky fields along Route 1A. He reached over beside him, felt the heating pad on the seat. It was warm.

He had left Trooper Lemieux guarding the grave site overnight and another trooper keeping watch at Wicker's Funeral Home. The crime lab boys from Augusta – Percy and Esterbrook – had taken a motel room in Ellsworth. Murdoch, the troop sergeant, had given interviews to the media and then gone home. Two years from retirement, Murdoch had said that he wanted to take an active role in this case, which meant that he smelled good press, maybe a promotion and fatter pension. Murdoch.

Shepherd tossed the facts over in his mind. A missing body. An undertaker murdered and planted in the missing man's grave, holding a gun, wearing scuba tanks. An embalming tool found in the casket . . .

The detective's mind spiraled outward: dead penlight in the woods, dead heating pad hanging from a maple tree – same dead batteries: Hi-Crown, from the missing dead man's store, same expiration date. With new batteries, the penlight shone bright and the heating pad was plenty warm. He didn't ask himself why the things had been discarded. This early in the investigation, premature reasoning could get you lost.

Shepherd, who had the highest solve rate in his troop, concerned himself with facts. Fact: one good penlight found in the woods, twenty to twenty-five feet from the grave, batteries dead. Fact: one hunter's heating pad hanging from a maple branch ten feet high, ten feet from the grave, batteries dead.

With facts, you didn't need reason. Facts created their own reason. Given enough facts, the truth would narrow and steepen, like the lines on a statistician's chart. Enough facts, and the truth would tell itself.

King's Boarding House was a sprawling, three-story wooden structure (originally a farmhouse, later a nursing home), now a last refuge situated on a road that led out of Ellsworth's municipal district but not far enough to escape the slight congestion of the town. Over the century that had passed since the building's construction, a small neighborhood had pressed in around it, ramshackle and poor.

Now in its old age, its tin roofs spilling the rain, the heavy old building looked like it was weeping in the night. A wooden fence on the left separated it from the tenement building next door. On the right, a chain-link fence contained a cinder-block auto body shop whose back lot was packed with junkers. A glaring security lamp on a freestanding wooden pole threw bluish light across the bone-white face of the boarding house, saturating it with a moonlike wash and harsh shadows.

Sal pulled into the boarding house lot, swung right, nose to the wire fence. Only one other car was parked there. He stepped out into the downpour, grabbed the leather jacket off the passenger seat – and then he felt the bottle in the pocket. Noel had left it for him. Stuffing the jacket under his arm, he opened the back door and pulled out his suitcase, then walked to the front porch.

The woman who finally answered the doorbell looked to be in her eighties, wearing a bathrobe and knit sleeping cap. Peering out the screen door, she popped the door open and handed Sal a key. 'Twenty-one E,' she said. 'Right rear. See me in the morning.'

He found the door on the right side of the building, back

corner, out of range of the auto body security light. When he unlocked the exterior door, he entered a wallpapered stairwell that was overwarm and lit by a 100-watt bulb inside an antique wall fixture. Two white doors were situated on opposite sides of the stairwell. One had a black iron numeral 11 screwed to it; the other had a 12. Sal climbed the stairs and found an identical landing, with white doors numbered 21 and 22. He chose the one on the right, 21, looked for a lock, found none. He turned the glossy black knob and the door opened.

It was a kitchenette apartment with a studio couch against the right-hand wall. On the near side of the couch, a lamp stood on a low end table. Sal stepped in and found the lamp switch, turned it on, lighting the room. A black telephone and Bible shared the table with the lamp. He noticed a blonde wooden table in the corner of the room, on the other side of the couch. One wooden chair was pushed under the table. The only two windows in the room occupied the same wall, on either side of the couch. The windows were open six inches and propped on adjustable screens that did little to ventilate the room. In the terrible heat, the place smelled like its horsehair plaster had absorbed a century of piss, perspiration and medicinal vapors.

On the left-hand wall was a four-by-four closet made from birch paneling; beside it, a white three-drawer bureau. The closet had no door or curtain, just a pole with a single shelf above it. There was no television in the room, no radio. One framed picture hung on the wall above the couch – a sailing ship in a storm. On the far wall were two doorways. The one on the right led into a closet-sized kitchen, the one on the left, into a small bathroom.

Sal closed the door behind him, felt for a lock but found none. He carried his suitcase and jacket to the bureau, set both on top (hearing the knock of the vodka bottle), then went into the bathroom and urinated. He stripped off his wet clothes and hung them over two door hooks. Standing there undressed, sticky with chocolate and sweat, he could smell Noel on himself, and it made his heart beat. At the same time, a terrible longing was growing inside him, for Iris, for Davey. Images piled up: the cigarette-burned table, Davey practicing her piano, Iris curled on the couch studying...

He stepped into the shower, dialed the water to hot, as if to scald Noel's scent off of him. When he had dried off, he wandered back into the main room and found himself at the bureau, picking up Bobby's jacket, his hand going in the pocket.

Sally, who do you trust?

He lifted the bottle out, gazed at the orange-bordered label. So she had stuck it in the pocket anyway. He thought of Eliot Wicker, murdered. Bobby's body, stolen. Now he felt even more jittery, wished he had a TV or a book, to occupy his mind. He put the bottle down.

He walked over to the couch and sat, then stood up again; lifted the front of the couch until a hinged metal frame unfolded in three sections, covered with a thin mattress. A sheet and thin wool blanket were already wrapped tightly around it. As if he could sleep. More than anything, he realized, he needed to talk to Iris. Everything had happened so fast. He sat on the bed and lifted the receiver off the telephone, then set the phone down again.

He went back to the bureau and uncapped the bottle, imagined the vodka flowing through its clear neck and into his mouth. But instead of drinking, he brought the bottle to the window, pushed up the sash. The adjustable screen fell out and fluttered to the ground. He reached the bottle out the window and flung it. He heard a hard smash in the auto body junkyard.

Next he reached behind him, grabbed the Bible off the night table. PLACED BY THE GIDEONS, it said. He turned to the window and threw the book too, heard its good pages flutter as it left his hand. On the same impulse, he grabbed the telephone, swung around and chucked it into the night, but the wire snapped against the windowsill, and he heard the phone knock against the shingles below him.

He shut the window on the wire. Stood there feeling tense and hot. Ran his hands through his coarse hair and took a deep breath, let it out. Weather the storm. In the morning he'd buy a newspaper and look for a job, an apartment. He returned to the bureau and unlatched his suitcase, intending to put his clothes into the drawers. But something—

It confused him at first, slick and black and serpentine, the way it draped across his underpants. He took one end in his hand and lifted it. Delicate, long, and lacy – a black silk glove. He brought it to his nose, smelled it. Noel's.

He remembered the funeral, the way the black lace had hugged her forearm. But how the glove had gotten into his suitcase … He lifted it until he felt some resistance; that's when he saw that its fingers had been stuffed into the fly of his jockeys. He thought at first that Noel had put it there for him, like she had left him the bottle – but then he realized that she couldn't have. He had packed the suitcase at home and left it out in his car while he was upstairs with her. He pulled the glove out of the fly, his mind too dulled to make sense of it. When the smell of her perfume came to him again, he stopped wondering altogether. He brought the glove to his bed and shut off the lamp, then lay down uncovered in the dark, holding the glove on his chest, listening to the rain beating on the roof, the thunder playing off in the distance, unable to lose that brutal, gnawing emptiness, yet all the while basking in the glow of her scent.

Eliot Wicker was Gravity's first murder victim in forty years, and he not only made the front page of the *Ellsworth American* and every other newspaper in the state, but he was also the lead story on the morning news.

From the minute the Superette opened, the store filled with the cigarette smoke and chatter of men whose numbers rose and fell like the tides, conferring about Wicker's death, Bobby's disappearance, and the police interviews that were going on in town.

Sal sat near the end of the counter, working on his third cup of black coffee. Wearing his usual brown corduroy jacket over a plain black sweatshirt, he didn't quite fit in with the regulars, but that was nothing new. He staked his spot anyway and watched the people who came and went, looking for that one loaded glance that might tell him who had gotten into his car and slipped the glove in his suitcase.

Newspaper writers and news teams from two Bangor TV stations had been in and out since the store opened, talking to Bonnie True, asking for Noel, conducting interviews with anyone who would talk to them. Photographers stopped by periodically to take pictures outside the store and ask questions or directions to the cemetery or to Eliot Wicker's funeral home.

Detectives had already taken statements from a number of people – Wicker's neighbors and business associates, and anyone who frequented the Superette lunch counter in the afternoon, when Wicker took his tea. By nine in the morning Gravity, Maine, was teeming with intrigue, although not everyone was happy about it.

'Christ a'mighty,' complained Arthur Button (whose nickname was Belly), his 300 pounds sprawled over a fountain stool. 'Just because you're neighbor to a man don't mean you wanna kill him.'

'Don't feel bad,' Jerry Royal said, making a noisy entrance, 'I'm out of a job.'

A number of eyes fell on Jerry, who looked unusually spiffy

this morning, wearing green double knit pants and a blue striped shirt with a wide white collar, remnants of vagrant leisure suits. On top of it all, his hair, which normally resembled animal fur, was combed straight down to his eyebrows. With a tip of his nose, he signaled Bonnie for his coffee.

'Looks like ol' Mister Royal's set to go dancin today,' Belly said to him. The two men had been archrivals since third grade, and they missed no opportunity to taunt one another.

'I just got the third degree, that's all, which I passed it with flyin colors,' Jerry replied. 'They're workin on the old man now.' Waiting for his coffee, Jerry rubbed the counter clean with his shirtsleeve, looked over at Sal with a twinkle. 'There he is,' he said, apparently feeling some camaraderie with anyone in trouble.

Sal slid his empty mug forward on the counter, caught Bonnie's eye. He was thinking that the caffeine might help relieve the temptation he felt to grab a bottle and go back to his room. Actually, he had too much to do. For starters, he planned to get Bobby's motorcycle and take a long ride down to Augusta, where he would close out his teacher's retirement account; last he knew, he had about eighteen thousand dollars accumulated. If there was a waiting period, he'd get a cash advance on his Visa card. He'd keep some for spending money, job-hunting funds – the bulk he'd give to Iris.

'Motive, means and opportunity,' the man next to him said. Sal had never seen him before. A salesman, by the shirt and tie, by the build. Pod-shaped and slovenly, the man did paperwork while he ate, his elbows sprawled all over the counter. 'A competent detective'd break this case in a day,' he added with his mouth full, then turned to Sal and lowered his voice. 'You seen the *wife?*'

'She's out back with the insurance man,' Belly answered.

The salesman muttered to Sal through the side of his mouth, 'There's a surprise.'

Sal gave the guy a look, and he noticed Alston Bouchard standing by the door. The constable looked away as if he had been watching Sal. Sal recalled Bouchard's visit the night before, wondered for a moment if it was Bouchard who had put Noel's glove in his suitcase.

'Yeah, well, I got another theory,' said Belly Button, but no one paid attention until he lowered his voice and stole a furtive look at the stockroom door. 'You all knew Bobby,' he said. 'What if – I'm speculatin, of course – but what if Bobby was never actually dead? What if he's pullin a fast one?'

The others at the counter looked over at Belly while a country song came on the radio.

'Oh, I just imagine,' Jerry Royal said, riding him. 'How in the hell do you fit that big fat head of yours so far up your ass?' The others chortled.

'Laugh all you want,' Belly said. 'We're talking about Bobby Swift. I wouldn't put it past him.'

Behind the meat counter, the stockroom door swung open and Noel came through. A white-haired man, small and well-dressed, followed her into the store, and she walked briskly ahead, as if she were trying to get away from him. 'Certainly the last thing we want at this time is to complicate your misery,' the man was saying.

As she led him past the lunch counter to the front door, Detective Shepherd opened the door from the other side. 'So you call just as soon as you hear anything,' the insurance man said. 'Okay then?'

Noel did not respond, but focused her attention on Shepherd, and the older man turned awkwardly to leave. Shepherd let him walk under his arm.

'You must be Mrs Swift,' he said. The detective's sympathetic smile froze under the look she returned. What he failed to realize – what most men failed to realize – was that Noel Swift looked at nearly all men the same way. Whether they were fat, balding, arrogant, shy, too young, too old, too smart, too stupid, rich, or not so rich – her eyes bathed them, from head to toe and back again. For most men it was the sort of insomnia-provoking look they hadn't seen from a woman since they were twenty-five.

'Ask away,' Jerry said to the detective. 'Got half the town here now, you might get lucky.'

Shepherd ignored him.

'Any leads, Detective?' Belly Button asked.

'Just gathering facts at this point.' Shepherd gave the store a quick once-over, briefly running his eyes across Sal's. 'Is there someplace we could talk?' he said to Noel.

Without a word, she led him between the lunch counter and the candy case, then opened the door to the front stairs. Holding the door while he went up ahead of her, she glanced back and then went through. It was the kind of fleeting look that nobody in the place would have noticed, except Sal – full and right on target. He slid off his counter stool, stood and pulled two dollars from his pocket.

'If you're here for the motorcycle,' Bonnie said to him, and then nodded at the stockroom door, 'go on back, you know the way down.'

Sal tossed the bills on the counter. When he checked behind him, he saw that Alston Bouchard was watching him again.

Before Noel had unlocked her apartment door, the detective began his folksy interview: 'Smells like good coffee down there. I understand Eliot Wicker was a regular customer.'

'There are five or six of them,' she answered, pushing the

door open and letting him in. Shepherd squinted at the brightness, the morning sun shining through the front windows, lighting the jungle of vegetation in the room.

Noel stood behind him, her arms folded. As much as she had to hide, she felt relieved in a way to have the detective up here with her.

'This'll only take a minute,' he said. 'I just need to verify some facts.' He gestured to the couch and said, 'May I?' She nodded, and he walked over and sat down, set his computer on the coffee table beside a glass vase of red tulips.

He withdrew from his suit pocket a small photo in a plasticine holder and held it out to her. 'Ever see him in your store?' he asked. Noel came over and took it from him, a picture of a man who could have been anyone.

'Who is he?' she said.

Shepherd smiled pleasantly. 'Actually, I was hoping you could tell me.'

She handed back the photo. 'Detective Shepherd, do you suspect that I murdered Eliot Wicker?'

He scowled. 'Why would you ask that?' he asked, taking the plasticine by the edges and slipping it back in his pocket.

'You just fingerprinted me.' Her eyes remained on his, unflinching.

Shepherd winced. He had an expressive face, and he used it well. He took a breath as if to speak, then paused as Noel turned away from him, went to the front window and parted the curtains, allowing the full sunlight in.

He turned on the couch to face her. 'I want to be clear,' he began. 'We never suspect anyone until we've assembled and analyzed a preponderance of incriminating facts. At the same time, we cannot overlook anyone as a possibility: you, your customers, even your own town constable—'

'He suspects me.'

Shepherd smiled. 'To the novice, first clues can be difficult to forget.'

'Is that a computer?' she asked.

Shepherd opened the lid, and the monitor lit. He punched a couple of keys. 'Actually, it's a simple program I wrote myself. I feed it information, and it cross-references. If I want to check a name, or a word – like "batteries," for example' – he entered the word – 'see, two references already.' He looked up at her.

She looked right back at him. 'So it's a computer,' she repeated.

He smiled again.

He was single, she could tell by the careful way his dark mustache was groomed – a little overdone on looks. When he was younger he'd probably managed to bed every man-crazy girl who'd ever laid eyes on him, and some who weren't so crazy. But something in his face told her that his confidence had been uprooted. She turned away from him again, looked out the front window, down onto her parking lot.

'Mrs Swift, do you recall if Eliot Wicker telephoned you the night he was murdered? Speaking of first clues.'

Noel sighed, kept her back to him. 'Mr Wicker did not telephone me, despite what our local constable cares to believe.'

'I'll put down no. And, again, Mister Bouchard has nothing to do with this investigation. Were you home that night, to the best of your recollection?'

'Yes.'

'Was there anybody here with you who could verify that?'

Her face turned quickly, sideswiped by the sun.

Shepherd nodded contritely. 'Sorry,' he said. 'Sometimes my mouth works faster than my brain.'

He'd been hurt recently, Noel guessed, by a woman who had outgrown him.

140

'Did your husband have anybody who was mad at him, someone who might want to humiliate him?'

Noel shook her head. On a table under the window, beside a vase of gladiolas, stood a four-by-six photo in a plain silver frame. She picked up the picture and reached it halfway to Shepherd. He stretched his arm over the back of the couch to retrieve it.

'Everybody loved Bobby,' she said. 'That's him on the right.'

Shepherd examined the photo, a picture of Bobby and Sal standing beside an overturned wooden canoe, their arms around each other.

'Brothers?' Shepherd asked.

'Hm? No, that's Bobby's best friend, Sal Erickson. Sal lives in town.'

'He was downstairs at the counter when I came in.'

'Mm-hm.'

Shepherd looked at the picture, shook his head sadly. 'So young. How old was Bobby?'

'Thirty-three.'

'If you don't mind, I'd like to borrow this. It may help to identify your husband ... if the body turns up.'

Noel said nothing.

Shepherd laid the frame beside his computer. Hesitated a second, then said, 'I have to ask, I apologize. Any infidelities, either of you? Wondering who might want to embarrass him.'

Noel shook her head.

'What about Eliot Wicker – any enemies that you know of?'

She shrugged. 'One, apparently.' She turned to the window again and looked down at the lot, where Alston Bouchard was still talking to the insurance man.

'Your insurance agent?'

Noel turned. Shepherd's mustache straightened. 'We bump into each other from time to time. He probably came to tell you that they're withholding payment until the case is solved.'

'That's right.'

Shepherd showed her his sympathetic smile again. 'Insurance companies are wonderful, in theory.'

She watched him carefully. His identity was wrapped up in his work, she concluded. He was dangerous.

'While we're on the subject, do you know offhand how much Bobby's policy was worth? Again, I hate to ask, but we have to in cases like this.'

Noel turned back to the window. 'In cases like this?'

'I hate to ask.'

Down on the lot, the insurance man drove away, and Bouchard looked up at the window. 'Twenty-five thousand dollars,' she said, turning back to Shepherd.

A minute pause betrayed the detective's surprise. Typing the figure in his computer, he said, 'That's not very much.'

'Not enough for murder,' she answered, looking straight at him.

They videotaped everything. While Shepherd went through the kitchen, entering fact after fact into his computer, the detectives and lab men from Augusta pored over every inch of Eliot Wicker's home and business. With powders and lifters, they dusted doorknobs, drawer handles and tools. With a laser light and Luminol, they went over the upstairs floors and utensils, looking for blood that was both fresh and Wicker's type. The feeling was that Wicker may have been murdered at home by somebody he was familiar with, then transported to the cemetery later.

But no one said that, at least not to Shepherd. They were here to gather facts, not conjectures. Facts: the torn wire in the switch box, the scuba tanks strapped to Wicker's back, the penlight and heating pad, the dead batteries. Every piece of evidence labeled and boxed in the crime van, along with the plasticine envelope Noel had handled and similar envelopes that bore the fingerprints of everyone else Shepherd had interviewed so far.

The detective looked through the refrigerator, through the cupboards, through the dishwasher – and there he found something curious: a pair of champagne glasses, side by side. He removed them with his handkerchief. He recalled seeing an unfinished bottle of champagne in the refrigerator; he carefully took the bottle out and pulled the cork to check for carbonation. He put his nose to the lip and sniffed.

That's when Sergeant Murdoch came in from the dining room, smoking a cigarette. 'Wait'll you're off duty,' he said.

'Wicker lived alone,' Shepherd answered. 'Two champagne glasses suggests he had company.'

Murdoch snorted. 'You're the boss.' He ran the back of his hand across four black garments that hung on the wall. 'Snappy dressers, these morticians,' he said, poking a brown cap.

The only thing worse than having the sergeant along when you were leading an investigation was working for him every other day of the week. A twenty-year veteran of Chicago's finest, Murdoch had taken an early retirement in 1975 after receiving his second suspension for excessive force, and then moved to Maine, where he was hired as a sergeant because of his vast experience. From then on, there wasn't a detective in the CID who didn't look forward to the day that Sergeant Murdoch earned his second pension.

'I want to take an active role in this one,' he had told Shepherd. 'But I won't interfere. You're the primary. You give the orders, I'll do what I'm told.'

In the hour since he had arrived, Murdoch had spent

his time second-guessing Shepherd at every turn, second-guessing the lab men and generally hindering the investigation. 'Ask me, we're wasting time here,' he said to the detective now as he washed his cigarette down the kitchen sink. 'We should be out canvassing the townspeople, stimulating that little-known truth serum they call adrenaline.'

As Shepherd filled out an evidence tag and boxed the champagne glasses, the basement door opened, and Alston Bouchard came through, accompanied by Percy, the lab's fingerprint man. The constable had a grocery bag in his hand.

'Grizzly Adams,' Murdoch murmured, loud enough for Bouchard to hear.

While they watched, the constable walked over to the breakfast island, turned the bag upside down on the countertop, then lifted the bag, unveiling a can of Sprucewood Brewery pale ale, upside-down.

'Good morning, Constable,' Shepherd said, handing the finger-print tags to Murdoch for his initials. 'I see you have a can of beer.'

'It's from the back of the cooler,' Bouchard explained. 'In the store. I'd be interested to know if the fingerprints on it match the prints on the batteries or the diving tanks.'

Murdoch folded his arms in front of his chest, looked off at nobody in particular. 'This must be the local gendarme who was so much help at the crime scene.'

Bouchard said, 'Bobby Swift stocked the beer cooler, and Sprucewood doesn't sell that fast. The cans in back would still have his fingerprints.'

Shepherd took his pen from behind his ear and pulled the beer can toward himself. 'Bobby Swift's fingerprints. What are you conjecturing, Constable?'

Before Bouchard could answer – if he intended to at all – another of the lab men, Esterbrook, entered the kitchen from the hall. Tall and bent like an iced sapling, he wore latex gloves and a lab jacket, and he carried a slender green tank. 'This was under the bed,' he said, holding the tank carefully, as if it were some freakish infant.

'Green's oxygen,' Percy said. 'Probably did some welding.'

'Yeah, right, under his bed,' Murdoch answered.

Puzzled, Esterbrook said, 'It's full. Brand-new.'

'Any markings?' Shepherd asked. 'Company name?'

Percy shook his head.

'See if he's got any welding equipment downstairs.'

'He wasn't . . .' Bouchard said. His thick wrist rotated back and forth. 'A welder.'

'I didn't see any torches or rods,' Esterbrook said. 'We've been all around.'

'*It was under his bed!*' Murdoch told them, flabbergasted. 'Who welds in their bedroom? Jesus Christ, you country boys – he got off on it! *Think!*'

Sal logged almost three hundred miles on Bobby's Harley that first day, drove down to Augusta on Route 3, then up to Bangor on 95, across to Ellsworth and back to Gravity. It was a beautiful piece of machinery, a 1984 FXRT, basic black and chrome, tough and gutsy. With his inexperience and the frost heaves on the country roads, Sal took it slow going down. But coming back on the highway he averaged seventy-five, passing every car he encountered. At that speed the cold wind numbed his face, but Bobby's thick jacket kept his blood warm. He wore sunglasses more for the insects than the brightness. Racing across the spruce and birch plains, assailed by the season's first blackflies and every emerging springtime fragrance, he felt energized for the first time in days, momentarily liberated from his vodka cravings.

He got back into town in the late afternoon, drove slowly through the village, past the store and the firehouse and on to the health center, a facility housed in a former Baptist church.

Iris, standing behind the glassed-in counter, wearing a dark blue sweater over her uniform, didn't look up until Sal was halfway across the waiting room, and then she looked longer than she had intended. Other people in the waiting room seemed interested too. Gone was Sal's customary corduroy sportcoat, replaced by the leather jacket. In place of his corduroy slacks, he wore stiff black jeans and black, square-toed workboots. His hair was windblown from riding, his face dark and windburned. He didn't remove his shades until he reached the window.

'I didn't think you'd want me to come to the house,' he said, keeping his voice down. 'I brought something for you.'

'Sal, could we not do this here?' she replied. Her voice was as neutral as could be.

'It was that Librium,' he told her, just as matter-of-factly. 'I never would've taken a drink the other night if it wasn't for that.'

Iris looked past him. 'Eleanor?' she said, and an elderly woman rose out of her chair. 'Through that door, dear. Doctor Moody will see you.'

After the woman had walked out of the waiting room, Iris looked back at Sal, losing her smile.

'You're not going to give me a break, are you?' he said.

She replied evenly, 'Sal, I told you what I want.'

'You want me gone.'

She did not reply.

'Okay,' he said. He pulled a folded bank check out of his pocket, slid it through the opening in the glass. 'It's sixteen thousand dollars, my retirement, minus a couple of thousand to hold me over till I find a job.'

The check remained between them, untouched.

'Take it. I've got a call in to the teacher's placement office. They're sending me a list of openings.'

She sighed, lowered her voice. 'We can talk about this on

Sunday, when you come to get your things.' As she spoke, the phone rang, then stopped ringing, and presently a young woman in a white blouse and blue plaid skirt opened a door behind Iris. 'Mrs Potter, wondering about her mammogram,' she said.

'The lab hasn't called yet,' Iris told her. 'I'll check with them in a few minutes and get back to her.' She turned back to Sal, unflinching.

He looked through the glass at her. 'Iris, I'm not drinking,' he said. 'I'm over that.'

The way she looked at him, the way she sighed. She looked around behind her, then turned back to him. 'Sal, I went to the courthouse in Ellsworth this morning. I picked up the forms to start the proceedings.'

She avoided the word 'divorce,' but his heart fell anyway. He stood there nodding, knowing he should get out of there, when he heard the door open behind him and saw Iris's attention shift, her eyes brighten. He turned numbly to see Davey coming into the clinic, wearing her Gravity Bears T-shirt and oversized baseball cap, carrying her softball glove. When she saw Sal, she stared. The knees of her jeans were streaked with dirt, and her face was smudged.

Sal managed a smile, found his voice. 'Get a hit today?' He put his fists together.

She shrugged.

'You can sit down, love, I'll be a few more minutes,' Iris told her. 'We're going grocery shopping,' she said to Sal.

God, he wanted to go with them.

Davey walked to a section of the waiting room where there were toys on the carpet and a rack of children's books and magazines.

'Did you win?' Sal asked.

She nodded, not looking at him.

'Thata girl.' Feeling like a stranger.

He turned back to Iris, nudged the check through the opening in the window. 'Take it.'

Iris drew her hands back. 'Sal—'

He leaned closer to her and whispered, 'Do you know the things I've lost?' he said. 'Take the money. It means nothing to me.'

He turned away, back to Davey, who sat in a small plastic chair, her eyes pasted on a book. Sal could tell she wasn't reading. He noticed a man walk past the window over her shoulder. Sal recognized him, the detective who was investigating Eliot Wicker's murder. Sal went over to Davey and knelt in front of her, but she remained inside her book. He put his hands on her knees, rubbed the dirt off her jeans.

'I slid like you showed me,' she said, still not looking at him. Her voice was incredibly small, and it broke his heart.

'Oh,' he said in a low, hushed tone, 'I'm proud of you, honey.'

She lowered the book. Looked straight at him. 'Daddy, I want you to come home,' she said, utterly unconvinced that there could be any reason why they should be separated. It was inevitable, Sal knew, this confrontation, but he wasn't prepared just now.

'Honey—' He looked back as the detective came through the front door, glancing over. When Sal turned back to Davey, her eyes were full. He heard the detective at the check-in counter talking to Iris. He took Davey's hands in his, wiped dirt off her palm. 'Hug,' he said, but she wouldn't comply. He noticed, out in the parking lot, the yellow Subaru wagon beside his Harley, Alston Bouchard sitting behind the wheel, watching the clinic.

'Take me fishing,' Davey said.

'You want to go fishing?'

Her head went up and down.

Looking back, Sal saw the detective walking through a door

to the examination rooms. He wondered why. He reached his hands under Davey's arms and picked her up out of her chair as he rose to his feet. She seemed heavier than he remembered.

'Okay, I'll take you fishing,' he said. He looked outside again, Bouchard still there. 'I can't today because you're going with Mommy. But this weekend, Sunday, I'll take you down the pool. We'll catch us a stringer full of schoolies. Maybe a big Atlantic salmon.'

Davey heaved a sigh.

'Can I have a hug now?' he said.

She looked at him, her gray eyes glassy, a cheek already tear-stained, and he felt his heart plummet. He lifted the cap off her head, and she buried his face against him. He heard her book drop on the floor behind him. He spread the fingers of one hand across her back, from shoulder blade to shoulder blade. He could feel muscles there, strong, durable cords he had never noticed before. All the muscles she would need. She would grow up without him.

Inside the small examination room, Detective Shepherd entered three new facts into his computer. 'You were the attending physician who signed Bobby Swift's death certificate?' he asked Doc Moody.

'That's correct,' the young doctor said. In his early thirties and overworked like everyone else at the understaffed clinic, he was an hour behind schedule and due to go home in a half hour. He washed his hands while he talked and didn't offer Shepherd a seat.

'And you recommended that no autopsy be done.'

'An autopsy wasn't necessary, in my judgment. It was clearly an M.I. Mr Swift had a bad heart. He knew it, we knew it. Everybody in town knew it. And he continued to smoke a pack and a half a day.'

'You examined the body and you have no question he was dead.'

Doc Moody looked over at the detective. 'Of course not,' he said.

Shepherd nodded. 'A routine examination then. Nothing out of the ordinary?'

Moody pulled a paper cup from its dispenser and filled it with water. 'Detective, I hope you understand. Our office manager and head nurse has recently decided to become a single parent, she wants to leave at five o'clock this afternoon, and she means business.' He gave Shepherd the sort of smile that a doctor can afford and then said, 'The examination was by the book.' He drank the water down, then crumpled his cup and dropped it in the wastebasket. 'Anything else?'

Shepherd looked over the monitor screen. 'Not today,' he said. He turned off the computer and closed the lid, then returned the doctor's smile. 'See, I promised it'd be painless.'

8

The parking lot was dark. A moonlit fog had risen up from the river and drifted across the bridge, and for the past two hours peepers down at the river had blanketed the night with their shrill song. At nine o'clock Noel had shut off her parking lot light and dimmed the inside lights. Now it was quarter past. Sal sat on his motorcycle watching through the front window, waiting for Bonnie to leave – but the woman didn't seem to be in any hurry, standing there in her robin's egg uniform, talking to nobody while she scraped the grill clean.

And here sat Sal astride his Harley like some dark prince of the night, the collar of his leather jacket up around his ears. He hadn't shaved in a day, and the shadow of his beard darkened him even more. He steadied the beast between his legs as he watched Noel come into view from one of the grocery aisles, wearing this cool, sleeveless melon-green top over a short khaki skirt. She turned to speak to Bonnie—

'Can you drive?'

The voice deep in Sal's ear, he wheeled around. In the dark he could see only the wink of eyeglasses: Alston Bouchard – whose hand went to Sal's chest, just enough to ward off a rash response. The question remained. Could he drive?

'Why? You need a ride?'

'No, my car's over the firehouse. I just want you to get home safe.' Bouchard's thick lenses reflected the window light.

'I appreciate your concern,' Sal said to him. He got off his motorcycle, heeled down its kickstand and sat back against the seat. 'But I wasn't going home just yet.'

Bouchard peered at Sal through those glasses. He made a noise with his tongue, like he was cleaning his teeth. 'If I were you,' he said, 'I'd try to be realistic about the things I was risking.'

Sal studied the constable, as much as he could see him, and then the door opened and Bonnie came through. Stepping outside, she said goodnight to Noel and then turned to Sal and grabbed at her chest.

'Oh my dear God!'

'Bonnie, what?' Noel came to the door, a Pyrex coffee pot in her hand. When she saw Sal, her eyes sharpened – not conspicuously – more the way a cat becomes alert when something moves in the grass.

Bonnie left the doorway and walked across the parking lot, giving Sal one more look. 'Skulkin out here in the dark with his jacket on, you'll give someone heart failure,' she muttered. Reaching the hardtop, she turned right and then walked into the darkness. Bonnie and Herb True lived on the other side of the firehouse.

Bouchard turned to Noel. 'Didn't mean to startle you,' he said. 'I had a question, if you . . .' His hands moved inside his pockets.

Noel remained in the doorway, her bare legs set apart under her skirt. 'Guys, I'm so tired,' she said. 'Can it wait till morning?'

'It can wait,' Bouchard answered. 'But you remember the other night, after the funeral—?' He rocked from one foot to the other, as if he were about to turn and walk away – and then he sauntered over in front of her. 'Afterwards you had that little get-together upstairs . . .'

'I remember.'

'After everyone left, did you stay here or...' His pockets jumped.

She sighed. 'Alston, it's nice that you're trying to help, but wouldn't it be more effective if you worked with the police?'

Bouchard pulled a small notepad out of his pocket. 'Well, they go home every day at three-thirty, and I was just—'

'Really, I covered all of that with the detective this morning—'

'—wondering whether you stayed home the rest of the night, or maybe you went out for a drive...'

She closed her eyes. 'I told you, I have given all that information—'

'—being the night Eliot Wicker was killed—'

'*What are you accusing me of?*' She swung the coffee pot against the door frame, smashing it, then threw the handle at his feet. Sal pushed himself off his motorcycle. Bouchard stepped back. 'Not accusing, really, not trying to...'

Sal came over to Noel. 'I don't think he's accusing you—'

'*Everybody in this town is accusing me!*' she said, wheeling on him. '*You can't see that?*'

Bouchard backed toward the road. 'Anyway, you're upset and I'll let you alone now, but I'd think about' – he made a fist and turned it – 'locking your doors, at least until these things get...' He backed into the darkness the same way Bonnie had gone, and then his footsteps went sifting through the road sand.

'Accusing you of what?' Sal said to her.

She wouldn't look at him. He touched her arm again. She took a breath. Sal could tell she was listening to Bouchard's footsteps, and then so was he, relieved that the constable was gone. Presently a car door closed in the firehouse lot. The engine started and the headlights came on, then the small station wagon circled in the lot and came toward them. It passed the store slowly, hummed over the bridge. At the end of the road, it turned right. Sal waited until the sound of Bouchard's engine had faded.

'Accusing you of what?' he asked her again.

'Come out of the light,' Noel said, leading Sal past the windows, to the shadows where his motorcycle was parked. And there her hands went into his jacket pockets.

'What are people accusing you of?' he said, as he peered over her shoulder. His eyes sharpened. Down at the bridge—

'Sal, what?'

He stepped away from her.

Someone in the fog – a shape – sitting on the bridge rail.

'Wait a minute,' he told her, and he began walking toward the road, staring down at the fog.

'Where are you going?'

The figure seemed to stand, and then—

'Hey!'

Sal broke into a run, but now he wasn't sure what he was seeing, with the fog and the darkness and the vegetation surrounding the bridge. The closer to the bridge he got, the clearer he could see the bridge railing and only the bridge railing. Whoever had been there (if Sal had actually seen anybody) was gone.

He stopped at the head of the bridge and listened for footsteps running over pavement but heard only the loud river rushing below. He walked onto the steel grid work, looking out toward the end of the road, the streetlight on the corner, the window lights of the facing house. Nothing moved. No dogs barked. In fact, it occurred to Sal that, despite the river noise below his feet, the night had become noticeably quiet.

The peepers. Down on the river, the peepers had stopped. Someone was down there.

He ran to the end of the bridge, swung around the low

abutment and lowered himself down the steep, rocky furrow. He caught hold of a bunch of grass so he wouldn't fall, but when his foot could find nothing but a steep slide of gravel, he let go of the grass and slid the rest of the way on his hands and soles of his boots.

At the bottom, he stood perfectly quiet, turned his head to face downriver. He listened for footsteps, peered into the darkness for movement, but all he could hear was the river gurgling beside him like low laughter. All he could see were the hard, square shapes of the old bridge support standing out of the ground fog in front of him. He took two or three steps, until he came to the slab of concrete on which he and Bobby had sat the night before Bobby died. He stopped there, sensing something. A smell of fungus hit him, the dark odor of decay that misted up out of the rushing water. But it was more than the smell.

Something was happening.

He could feel it, a pressure mounting around his ears as if someone were creeping up behind him. He turned quickly, but saw no movement in the darkness. And now he wondered if the figure he had seen on the bridge was the thing Bobby had seen in the bog – or perhaps the thing the Passamaquoddies told about – how men were lured to the reversing falls and then haunted by their transgressions.

I trust Iris, he had told Bobby that night. *I trust myself*.

Motionless, he stared into the darkness, barely breathing. And then his eye caught a movement, a ghostly mist feathering its way up the river, coming steadily toward him . . .

He turned his head, saw the bridge looming solid and black above him, then looked downriver again, as the river mist softly blew apart.

Sally, who do you trust?

He turned and scrambled up the bank, clutched the bridge

support and pulled himself to his knees, started to get to his feet—

—Someone standing in the fog above him, a stiff, tense shadow.

'Sal?'

Noel spoke his name softly, but her urgency was unmistakable. 'Sal, you're scaring me. What's wrong?'

'Nothing,' he said, standing, putting his arm around her and leading her quickly over the grating. 'Nothing, it's my imagination,' he told her as they began mounting the hill. He thought of telling her about the glove in his suitcase but decided against it.

They walked into her parking lot again, keeping to the shadows. 'Sal, did you see something?' she said.

'I don't think so,' he answered. 'But I don't want you staying here alone tonight.'

'I'm having a security system installed tomorrow and all the locks changed.'

'Good,' he said, 'but tonight I think you should come with me.'

She stopped walking. When she spoke, it was in a frail voice, almost a whisper. 'Sally,' she said, 'I'm so scared.'

He turned to look at her and then they were kissing, her arms going around him. His heart started up, his breathing became charged. It was unreasonable, almost unreal, he thought, that he could be doing this or feeling like this while the rest of his life was falling apart, but with her lips against his, the heat of her body radiating through his leather jacket, the heat of her legs through his jeans, he felt overcome.

'I'll take my car,' she said, breaking the kiss, and even her breath on his neck stirred him. 'I don't want anyone to see you bringing me back here in the morning.'

In the next minute they were walking together through the store, through the stockroom, turning off lights, locking doors behind them, hurrying down the stairs into her garage. Noel turned the overhead lights on, the stairway lights off. She opened the garage door with an electric switch on the wall, then slid into her Volvo. Sal got in the passenger side. She started the car and backed out, then turned on the headlights as she activated the remote switch that lowered the garage door. He watched her legs move as she clutched and shifted into first, the Volvo crawling up the incline beside the building until they were in her parking lot again. She stopped her car beside his Harley.

'I'll follow you,' she said.

'It's right in town,' he told her, opening his door. 'Turn right at the river, at the lights—'

Her breath caught sharply, stopping him.

'Noel, what?' Seeing her eyes riveted on her rearview mirror, he turned.

OHW

The letters were backward on the rear window, finger-streaked through a film of dust, catching the moonlight.

'God,' Noel breathed.

'Hold on,' Sal told her, climbing out of the car, 'it's nothing,' and he went around the back to wipe the window with his hand. 'Probably some kids in a parking lot some-where—'

On the trunk, more words were smeared:

WANTS A CHOCOLATE KISS

'What is it?' she asked.

Sal stared, felt his legs weaken. 'Nothing,' he said again, even as he rubbed the trunk and window clean with his arm. He went back to the door. 'We're both a little shell-shocked,' he said. He locked the door before he shut it.

He swung a leg over his motorcycle and turned the key, gave the engine more throttle than it needed, feeling the shivering in his hands, trying to put out of his mind that on the other side of that storefront window was enough alcohol to stop his shivering for good, to warm him, to let him smile, to make him feel human again.

Noel followed him closely all the way to Ellsworth, making it hard for Sal to see anything but her headlights in his mirrors. When they had almost reached the boarding house, he waved her into the parking lot of the body shop so her car wouldn't be seen by the landlady (or anyone else), and then they walked quickly to the rear of his building. While he worked in the dark to insert his key in the lock, Noel kept her back to him, watching the street out in front, the starkly lit junkyard to her left, listening for any trace of furtive sound.

Sal threw the door open and they went into the bright stairwell, closed the door behind them. Noel gazed at the wallpaper, the light fixture, the enamel-white doors, and said quietly, 'You live in a museum.'

'You don't have to whisper, we're the only ones in the wing,' he said.

'I feel better whispering.'

'Up here,' he told her, and they took the creaking treads as softly as they could. At the landing, he went to his door and turned the black knob.

'There's no lock?' she said as he pushed the door open.

'The downstairs door locks,' he answered, going in. 'Wait here.'

With only the junkyard light through his windows lighting the room, he made his way to the bathroom, flicked on the light and looked inside, checked the space on the other side of the tub. 'If you need the john,' he said, coming back out and crossing to the opposite wall, verifying in a glance that the kitchen was empty.

'Somebody could be in one of the other apartments,' she said.

He smiled slightly, picked up one of the pair of wooden chairs from his table and carried it back to the entry door, wedged the top of the chair under the doorknob. 'We're safe now,' he said, joking, though his humor fell short of assuring even himself.

Behind him he heard the clatter of her lowering the window blinds. He walked around the bed to the other window, lowered those blinds too.

He took off his jacket. 'Listen,' he said quietly, 'who do you think had it in for Eliot Wicker?'

'Oh, Sal, I'd rather not discuss this now,' she told him.

He turned to toss the jacket on the bed and found her standing in front of him. Her arms went around his waist, her hands forced inside the back of his jeans. She kissed him open-mouthed, her fingertips clutching at his buttocks. His heart already drumming, Sal dropped the jacket on the floor. It was her fragrance, her wit, her confidence, her size and shape, the way she moved, the way she stood, the way she looked at him, the amount of pressure she exerted in holding him, the smell of her breath, the smell of her skin, the movement of her tongue, the way she pressed her body into his. And now they were about to sleep together, the two of them, warm and alone and naked through the long, dark night.

At the same time, Sal's head thrummed with misgiving: that in deepening his relationship with Noel, he was further distancing himself from Iris and Davey; that whoever had planted Noel's glove in his suitcase and written on her car window might well be the same one who had murdered Eliot Wicker. Equally unsettling was this vague notion that he knew something about Eliot Wicker that his mind was hiding from him, like a lost memory or a forgotten dream. It was almost as if he could solve the mystery if he could get his mind to cooperate. Pervading all these uncertainties was his alcohol craving, which by now had grown incessant, almost physical, like a buzzing inside him that he could not stop. As Noel's fingers worked around the front of his leather belt, she lifted her face to his.

'Stop thinking,' she told him.

He smiled. 'I don't think I can,' he said.

She pulled the belt through the buckle with a soft slap. As she stared at him, the leather came snakelike out of his jeans, one loop at a time. 'Then I'll have to make you,' she said, pushing him gently onto the bed.

Sal's chest jumped with a silent laugh as she crawled on top of him, laying him back.

'Wait, Noel,' he said. 'Hold on a minute—'

'I said stop thinking.'

'It's not that,' he told her, and then he breathed a sigh. 'I just don't know if I can do this sober.'

With his belt in her hands, she pushed his sweatshirt up to his chest, then bent to kiss his stomach, ran her lips up to his chest, sucked tenderly on his nipple. She stopped and looked up at him. Then, sitting up, she pulled her silk top up her stomach, past her breasts, over her head. Barechested, she looked down on him, eyes shining. Her nipples were dark and swollen. 'You don't think you can get drunk on me?' she asked.

Her hands flexed quickly, snapping the belt tightly between them.

He started to laugh. 'Noel, wait—'

She stretched the leather to his throat, pinning his head to the mattress. He took hold of her wrists.

'I don't think I heard you,' she said.

He turned his head slightly, to free his windpipe. She repositioned herself, staring down at him with the slightest of smiles, like he was something she had captured.

She lowered her face to his. 'You don't think I can get you

loaded?' she breathed, the belt cutting into his throat. She bent lower and touched his upper lip with the tip of her tongue.

He felt his face engorging as his heart pumped harder.

'Let go,' she breathed into his mouth. 'Let go of my wrists.' He felt her warmth moving slowly down his stomach. His erection throbbed, reached past the band of his shorts.

Leering at him, she slid her legs further down his body, smooth and humid, until the head of his erection was immersed fully in her heat. That's where she stopped. When she spoke again, her voice was little more than breathing: 'I said let go, Sally. You have to trust me.'

Watching her eyes, he made his fingers open. The belt tightened on his throat.

'Put your hands down.'

Her shining, throbbing eyes. The studied expression on her face. He lowered his elbows to the bed.

'All the way.'

Feeling like his face was going to burst, his hands slid to her thighs.

All at once she released the belt and plunged into him, her tongue entering his mouth, his tongue finding hers. He pulled her roughly over him, pulled her against him until she gasped, and then he rolled on top of her, all the while tearing at her underpants, throwing her skirt to her waist until she was fully, blissfully open, and then needing to open her more, to delve into the deepest part of her, to drink her in.

Their sex was breakneck and explosive, and over in minutes. As they lay there entwined, breathless in the dusky stillness of the room, Noel freed herself, then slithered across his body until their eyes were aligned, and their mouths, her hair draping like a curtain around his face. 'Now,' she said to him, 'tell me you're not wrecked.'

Detective Shepherd was roused by his telephone. He stabbed

in the dark to stop its ringing until he was awake enough to remember that there was no one else to awaken. He wasn't surprised to hear Murdoch on the other end.

'Are you screwing someone at the lab?' the sergeant said.

'What?' Four-thirty. Shepherd figured that someone had been murdered. But it wasn't his on-call week.

'We got your prints.'

Shepherd turned on the lamp. 'My prints – what do you mean, the Wicker case?'

'You must be blowing someone in Augusta. They stayed late, faxed in around ten last night. Dispatch just called me.'

'What prints? Where are you?' Shepherd grabbed the notepad he kept beside his bed; his pen. Time, date—

'The fingerprints on the beer can match the prints on the scuba tanks,' Murdoch answered. 'Plus they match the small oxygen tank we found under the bed, and the embalming tool, and every one of the batteries you sent down.'

'Wait a minute.' Shepherd stopped writing while he absorbed this. 'Bobby Swift, the missing corpse – his prints were on the beer can – on the scuba tanks too?'

'Yeah, and not only his. The undertaker's prints are on most of those same things – tanks, flashlight, embalming tool. Not the beer can, not the batteries.'

'But everything else.' Shepherd stepped off the wide bed and walked into the living room. 'Bobby Swift and Eliot Wicker,' he said. He lifted his computer out of his leather satchel, felt his heartbeat accelerating.

'Plus,' Murdoch said, 'they got Wicker's prints on one of those champagne glasses.'

'Yeah?' Shepherd returned to his bedroom, sat on the edge of the mattress and flipped open the lid of his computer. 'And Bobby Swift's on the other glass—?'

'Uh-uh.'

Shepherd stopped. 'Say that again.'

'Negative. Bobby Swift's prints aren't on the other glass – or the champagne bottle.'

'So whose prints are they?'

Murdoch didn't answer.

'Sarge, whose fingerprints are on the other glass?'

'What's your computer tell you?'

Shepherd sighed.

'Unidentified,' Murdoch said. 'No match.'

'Where are you?' Shepherd asked.

'In my car. I'll wait for you. Looks like we'll have to make some good old-fashioned human contact today.'

In the long, dead dark of morning, Sal opened his eyes. Flat on his back, not fully awake, he felt satiated and numb, completely at peace . . . But something about the silence, or the air pressure around his head, or the lack of air pressure – he knew that something had awakened him. He lay perfectly still, listening in the perfect darkness, the perfect stillness, and he became aware that someone was standing next to him, trying to remain just as still. Sal's heart started to beat. His urge to lunge into the darkness was tempered by a fear strong enough to keep him from even shifting his eyes. He did not alter his breathing. He knew precisely his situation: He was in his boarding room. Noel was in bed beside him. He was on the left side of the bed with his head toward the wall, and the lamp, which he wanted for a weapon, was on the other side of Noel. He listened for her breathing. He listened but could not hear her, could not hear a thing except the silent hum of pressure. Even outside the windows the town lay silent. He stopped his breath on an inhale, as subtly as he could. That's when he heard it – the bare rustle of cloth. He sprang out of the blankets, lurching across the bed for the lamp, flicking it on, lifting it by the base—

Noel—

Standing naked, holding his black jeans under her arm, his wallet in her hand. She squinted against the brightness, her orange hair scattered around her eyes. She pulled the jeans in front of her body, covering herself.

'What are you doing?' he whispered.

'What are you doing? You look like you want to kill me.'

He let out his breath. 'I must've had a nightmare,' he told her.

She pushed the wallet back in his jeans pocket. 'I stepped on your buckle coming back from the bathroom,' she said. 'When I picked up your pants, the wallet fell out.'

He stared; his belt was not in the pants.

'Or your zipper,' she said. 'I stepped on something sharp. Do you think I was stealing your money?'

'Of course not. Something woke me—'

'Hmm?' Her eyes sharpened. She let his jeans fall to the floor so she was completely uncovered. He stared. She lifted a knee onto the bed, stretched her other leg over his stomach. Straddling him, she lifted the lamp out of his hands, then slid up his chest to replace the lamp on the table. 'If you don't believe me'—

—'I believe you'—

—'maybe you'd better search me,' she said, and the room turned dark.

A locksmith from a company called Blue Fin Security Systems was already working on the front door of the Superette when the detectives came in. It was 6:50 in the morning. Besides Bonnie True, who was emptying the dishwasher, and her husband Herb, who was reading the morning paper while he waited for the coffee to finish perking, the locksmith was the only one in the store.

'I didn't think you boys hit the streets till eight,' Herb said to the detectives, 'when the donuts come in.'

Undone

'We wanted to catch Mrs Swift before she got too busy,' Shepherd replied.

'Won't catch her here,' Bonnie told them. 'She didn't spend the night on the premises. She's got 'em riggin the place with alarms and new locks from top to bottom, and I doubt she'll spend another night here till you people get things straightened out. I don't blame her. If it was me—'

'Where is she?' Murdoch interrupted. He bit a filter cigarette out of a pack of Winstons, crumpled the pack and dropped it on the counter.

Bonnie eyed the sergeant. 'Like I was about to say, it's none of my business. I only work for the woman.' She picked up the piece of trash and dropped it in a basket behind the counter.

Shepherd looked at his watch. 'I'm going to call,' he told Murdoch.

'We got a phone back here you're welcome to,' Bonnie said to Shepherd, 'the white one. Red's the fire phone, we like to keep it free in case—'

'We've got a phone,' Murdoch said, pushing the door open. Shepherd gave Bonnie a smile as he left the store, but she didn't smile back.

So orange. She rises, and the sheet slips down her back. The early morning air through the screen sends a chill across his chest as she rides him, dazzling – *orange* – their stomachs sliding together in their mixed perspiration. He is seeing her naked in the daylight for the first time, over and over, though they've been going at this for hours. Her breasts are white and slightly upturned, perfectly smooth. Her areolae are chestnut brown and goose-bumped, her nipples standing out pink and tender, stretching like buds to the dawn light . . . But her hair, *that orange*, fired by this sudden slice of sunlight. On and on she moves in this slow, steady union, while he tries to maintain his senses through the depths of his sexual inebriation: the exquisite warmth inside her, her acrid-sweet and secret smell; the smacking of their skin separating; the taste of her inner flesh still on his tongue, the deep, intoxicating fullness of her...

On and on she moves, her deep green eyes pinned on him, her mouth a slack, goading smile – like she's aroused by his oblivion. When she comes, he watches with a deeply subdued fascination. First she loses the smile; then her look becomes ravenous. Slowly she rises up, her back straightening, arching. Her puckered, hooded navel catches a pale shadow. And then one eye flashes sunlight, and it startles him – one ice-green jewel flashing over and over, orange hair wildly flaming, as she closes around him – *GREEN-ORANGE-GREEN-ORANGE-GREEN-ORANGE-GREEN*

From his Cherokee, Shepherd called his friend Phil Harwood in Augusta. The two men had gone through the police academy together and become close friends, competitive skirt-chasers, until Harwood got married and then spent a couple of years at the university to get his chemistry degree. Although the men never saw each other outside of work anymore, Harwood was still a valuable comrade at the crime lab, where evidence was backed up sometimes two and three weeks. Shepherd could usually get his stuff bumped to the front of the line if he asked. Like he had yesterday.

'Did I wake you up?' he said when Harwood answered. The car phone was on speaker while he booted up his computer.

'How are you?' Harwood replied, a measure of concern detectable in his voice. Murdoch smirked, looked out his side window.

'Going through some changes,' Shepherd said. 'Hey, thanks for getting the stuff done so quick.'

'I got more. Not official yet, but you're gonna like it. You know the corpse you dug up?'

'Wicker, right? The undertaker?'

'They'll be notifying you from the morgue that Mr Wicker died from suffocation – they found dirt in his mouth, trachea and lungs, even some in his stomach – he looked like he was trying to eat his way out.'

'Pleasant thought,' Shepherd said.

'It also appears that he was knocked unconscious just before he was buried.'

'Okay, that's what we thought,' Shepherd said, searching for his WICKER file. There followed a dramatic pause on Harwood's end, which Shepherd liked the sound of. 'What else, Phil, you got something?'

'The oxygen tank.'

'Yeah, what about it?'

'Just what I said. That's what he was brained with.'

'No kidding.'

'That's what I make of it. The same kind of tank you sent down.'

'Phil, not the one I sent down?'

'I don't think so. The green paint we took off his hair is an exact chemical match. But we would have seen a corresponding mark on the tank, some kind of hair imprint – and we didn't. This tank's shiny and new. Never been used for anything. Which means there must be another oxygen tank out there. Are you aware of another tank?'

Shepherd typed the information into his computer.

'Wait a minute,' the sergeant interrupted, 'what about the scuba tanks? This is Murdoch.'

'Scuba tanks? Why? They're a different color. Different paint altogether.'

'Alright, so we rule 'em out.'

'There's got to be another oxygen tank,' Harwood said.

'E-size, same kind as I've got here. That's what he was hit with.'

'Okay,' Shepherd said, 'so I'm looking for another oxygen tank. Phil, any way of determining where it was purchased?'

'Yellow Pages. Start calling. You have to sign for oxygen; even welders do. You got a name or two, anybody look good?'

'Yeah, maybe,' Shepherd said, then he thanked his friend and hung up. ROBERT SWIFT was the name he entered in his computer. For some reason, he also thought of Alston Bouchard at that moment, and he felt a twinge of anger, or something close to it.

Walt Moody opened his examination room door with his elbow while he glanced over his first patient's chart.

'Mrs Daoust,' he started to say, but then he saw Detective Shepherd sitting on his examination table in a beige jacket, his computer resting on his lap.

The doctor double-checked his chart.

'I told Mrs Daoust you'd be detained a minute,' Shepherd told him.

That's when the doctor understood the nature of the detective's visit. He raised his brow in question, not quite able to muster the level of informality he wanted.

Shepherd gave him a smile. 'Bobby Swift,' he said. 'I'm referring to your signature on his death certificate. I've got you down saying your examination was by the book.'

The young doctor blinked his eyes three times. Shepherd closed the door.

Murdoch bent low so his face filled the window. 'Would you be Mrs Erickson, by any chance?' he said through the opening in the glass.

Iris regarded him curiously. She assumed he was a detective, having seen him come in with Shepherd.

'Your husband,' Murdoch said, 'Salvator-ee? Somebody said he was a close personal friend of Robert and Noel Swift's.'

Iris studied the man. He had a large, unfriendly face and an intrusive manner that seemed to cloud the entire room. She noticed that a boy and his mother were sitting by the door, her eight o'clock, waiting to check in. The boy was coughing.

'Is there something I can help you with?' she said, straightening.

'That'd be your best bet,' Murdoch answered. 'I thought maybe you could tell us where we might find your husband this morning.'

'Excuse me,' Iris said, stepping to the side where she could see the boy's mother. 'Just bring him in the back,' she said. 'I'll weigh him in a sec.'

After the woman and boy had gone through the door, Iris told the sergeant quietly, 'My husband and I were recently separated.'

'Huh,' said Murdoch. 'See, that would be an answer if I had inquired about your marital status. But what I asked is where we might find him this morning. Actually, we need to speak with Noel Swift, and we thought your husband, being a close personal friend, might know where she spent the night.' His mouth opened again as if to say more, but then Iris realized that he was smiling.

The orgasm fires over and over. Like flames dancing under her skin, he's burning from the inside out. But he can't get at her with his arms shackled down, and she's not even close to stopping. She rides him resolutely, rising, rising, shaking him, knuckles hard on his collar bone—

'Hey!'

'Mr Erickson—'

'*What*—'

The man was pushing him down, another man holding his arms.

'Take it easy! *Take it easy!*'

Both on top of him – one was massive, gray-haired flattop, cheap checkered blazer, cigarette breath. 'Relax, Blacky, we got a couple of questions, *I said relax!*'

'Mr Erickson?'

The other one – younger, better dressed, dark mustache – Sal recognized Shepherd from the store, the clinic.

'Don't get cute,' the bulldog warned, releasing pressure from Sal's neck.

Sal sat up fast. 'What the fuck,' he said. 'Did I wake up in Mexico or what?' He looked around the room at the empty bathroom and kitchen, saw the chair returned to the table. Noel was gone, near as he could tell.

Flattop turned to the window and snapped the blinds up, flooding the room with sunshine. 'Your landlady let us in down below,' he said. 'You didn't answer your door, we thought you might need help.'

'Mr Erickson—?'

'What, for chrissake?'

Shepherd showed Sal his shield. 'I'm Detective Shepherd. This is Sergeant Murdoch. A couple of questions, if you don't mind.'

'Even if you do mind,' said Murdoch. He picked Sal's jeans and T-shirt off the floor and pitched them at Sal's chest. 'Somebody said you were a friend of Bobby Swift's. Maybe you can tell us where to find him.'

Sal stared at the sergeant. 'What?' he said.

'*What?*' the sergeant mocked. 'You heard me.'

Sal stepped out of bed and into the pants. 'You think I dug him up?' He snatched his T-shirt off the bed and pulled it over his head.

Murdoch stepped closer, squared his shoulders to Sal.

'Somebody told us you two were out gallivantin the night before he supposedly went to that big general store in the sky.'

'I don't know what you're talking about,' Sal told him. 'Bobby's dead. Back off.'

Shepherd bent down next to the bed, picked up Sal's wallet and handed it to him. 'We're actually looking for Mrs Swift,' he said, 'Noel. Thought maybe you could help us.'

Sal said nothing as he stuffed the wallet in his back pocket. He wondered why Noel had gone without saying good-bye.

'Whaddya, need a drink?' Murdoch said. 'Somebody said you got a problem.'

Sal looked him over. Than he sat on the edge of the bed again, and he shook his head. 'This is one crack investigation team, no shit. You want the person who killed Eliot Wicker and stole Bobby's body, right? You got no other suspects, so you start harassing the woman, the widow.'

'Mr Erickson—?' Shepherd pulled a wooden chair over, sat on the edge holding a small, plasticine-covered photo out to Sal. Before Sal could take it, Murdoch stepped between the two men, hovering over Sal. 'Maybe we don't think she comes across as your typical grieving widow, wise guy—'

Shepherd stood, palmed the sergeant's shoulder. 'Sorry to bother you, Mr Erickson. Sarge?'

Murdoch, however, was neither apologetic nor retreating. 'Like maybe we think there's something fishy when a man in his thirties supposedly drops dead and gets buried with no autopsy.'

'Yeah, yeah.'

'Sarge?' Shepherd took hold of the sergeant's arm, spoke calmly. 'That's enough.'

Murdoch knew it too, because he suddenly stopped talking and just nodded his head up and down at Sal, pink-cheeked.

Shepherd put the photo back in his pocket. 'So you don't know Noel's whereabouts?' he asked Sal.

'That's what I said,' Sal answered, still glaring at Murdoch. 'Come on, Sarge.'

'Wait a minute,' Sal told them, and then he addressed Shepherd. 'What the hell is he saying about Bobby?'

Murdoch reached inside his blazer, then stepped close to Sal and stuck a card in his T-shirt pocket. 'The name's Murdoch, Greaseball, and I'll tell you what I'm saying. From now on, I'm gonna be lookin up your asshole every move you make.' He flexed his thick neck a couple of times, then straightened and led Shepherd out the door.

Outside a Shop 'n' Save in Bangor, Noel made a long-distance call to Worcester. She wore dark sunglasses to hide her eyes and a hooded green sweatshirt over a kerchief to cover her hair. When the man answered the phone, she told him she was Brenda and gave him a phone number to call. She hung up, walked quickly to her car and drove out to the road, checked the lot behind her, checked left and right to make sure she hadn't been followed, then headed west on Broadway. After a mile she pulled into the small parking lot of a Trustworthy hardware store. She parked near the pay phone at the corner of the store, then waited in the car, surveying her surroundings. Only two vehicles sat in the lot, an old pickup truck and a maroon Toyota wagon, mid-'80s. Momentarily the telephone rang. She got out of the car and picked up. 'It's Brenda,' she said.

'Go ahead, Brenda.'

She turned her back to the brick wall so she could watch the parking lot. 'Does September thirty ring a bell?' she said.

The man on the other end paused for five full seconds, then said, 'Excuse me with that tone of voice, I know my business.

Is there something you want to alter regarding that date, or did you wish to cancel at this time?'

She pulled the phone cable to its limit trying to see around the front of the store, but it didn't reach far enough. 'Are you saying that one of your representatives wasn't here prematurely?'

'That is correct, Brenda.'

'Are you sure?'

'Hey, I haven't even put anyone on it yet, okay?'

Noel heard a door close, and then a man who looked to be in his seventies came around the corner carrying eight feet of plastic rain gutter under his arm. He walked past her and went to the pickup truck in the lot, set the gutter in the back.

Noel smiled. 'I need to cancel then. Somebody evidently got there first.'

Another pause. 'Happens,' the phone voice said.

The old man got in his truck and started it.

'We're all square, then?'

'That's correct. Your deposit covers eventualities such as this. So, maybe another time.'

'Another time,' she began, watching the truck pull out of the lot. 'Would it be possible to get same-day service?'

'Same day,' the man said. 'You realize in that case we have an escalating risk factor on our end, meaning the fee slides up a little, not much. Got a name, place of business, place of residence? Fax over a photo, we could begin the preliminary research.'

From Noel's right, a fortyish man in a knit cap rode silently around the front of the store on a mountain bike, braked at the curb by the phone. She smiled again. 'I'll let you know if I need you,' she said, and hung up the phone.

When the detectives returned to the barracks, Murdoch went over the day's log, checked in with the dispatcher and then went home. Shepherd got an egg salad sandwich and a black coffee from the vending machines and spent the rest of the afternoon with a stack of telephone books, calling every oxygen supplier in the state, asking the managers to go through their records for a two-year period and look for the names of Robert Swift or Eliot Wicker. Most of the people he talked to promised to have the records searched by the end of the following day; the others said they'd run it through their computers and call back within the hour if they found anything. Nobody called back. While Shepherd waited, he telephoned Alston Bouchard, but the constable didn't answer. He tried Noel Swift repeatedly, and Bonnie told him repeatedly that Noel still hadn't returned to the store. At six o'clock Shepherd shut off his computer and drove home.

The detective wasn't the only one trying to reach Noel. Sal had called her too, nearly every hour since morning, and he had visited the store three times. He was concerned about her disappearance, and concerned about the things the detectives had said. But it was more than that. With Iris and Davey and Bobby all suddenly gone from his life, his concern for Noel had turned to a steady fear, that he might lose her too.

At eight-twenty, when she still wasn't back and there was barely enough skylight left so he could see the road without his headlight, Sal rode slowly past Wicker's Funeral Home, checked his mirrors, then leaned the Harley hard into the turnoff and killed the engine. He dismounted the bike and pushed it into the brush so it was hidden from the road, took a penlight from his saddlebag and jammed it into his jacket pocket, then hiked up the hill through the woods.

At the rear corner of Wicker's property, which was surrounded by woods on three sides, Sal emerged from an orderly stand of white pine. The large white house sat giftwrapped with yellow police tape on a knoll facing the road. An attached four-car garage made an ell off the back, lining the left side of the driveway and parking lot.

Sal made his way to the rear of the breezeway, which connected the ell to the house. Colors had diminished with the daylight, and now everything lay quiet in the dusk. Sal had no intention of finessing the break-in. Pulling the police tape over his shoulder, he ducked under, then punched his elbow through a windowpane. The leather protected his arm.

He didn't know what he was looking for. All he knew was that somebody had murdered Eliot Wicker, and the police had made Noel their chief suspect. Wicker's was a good place to start.

What Sal knew about Wicker was what everybody knew – that the man had made a country fortune snatching up property from the estates of his recently deceased clients. So that's what Sal intended to search: Wicker's real estate files. He left the lights off, using his penlight to navigate through the house, eventually making his way downstairs, where he opened doors until he found the burgundy-carpeted office.

With his penlight in his teeth, he want through the Rolodex on the desk, but found mostly vendors: chemical companies, casket and headstone makers, a number of clergy, surveyors and attorneys. He turned his search to the file cabinet, where folders were arranged alphabetically – accounts of the deceased in the bottom two drawers, real estate files in the top two. He flipped through every file in all four drawers, one at a time, as the two casement windows at the ceiling slowly darkened over and his second set of penlight batteries died.

When he finished, he left the building through a door downstairs that opened onto the parking lot, feeling more perplexed than before he had come. Wicker had buried more than four hundred people in his years in town, and bought or sold nearly as much property. Almost anyone in Gravity could have murdered him with some degree of justification.

★ ★ ★

At 9:20, after Noel had returned to the store and Bonnie had finally left for home, the telephone rang. Noel turned off the outside lights, checked that the red alarm light was lit, then went behind the counter to answer. It was Sal calling.

'I'm at a gas station,' he said. 'They still haven't fixed my phone.'

'I was just going up to bed,' she told him.

There was a pause. 'I didn't know what happened to you this morning.'

'I needed to get away,' she said.

'I woke up and you were gone. I was a little concerned.'

Neither of them spoke for a moment.

'So,' Sal said, 'are we still friends?'

'If that's what you want to call it,' she answered.

'I was wondering' – another pause. 'Do you know if Bobby ever got involved in any of Eliot Wicker's real estate deals?'

For a second Noel kept silent. 'Why?'

'I don't know, I'm just – wondering. Listen, I don't particularly want to be alone tonight.'

'Oh, God, I know how you feel, Sal. But I really have to sleep. I didn't get much last night. Sleep, I mean,' she added dryly.

He laughed a little. 'Sure you're alright there?'

'They've been up here all day,' she said. 'They wired all the windows and doors. I'll sleep with a gun.'

'Yeah. Me too.'

'Mmm,' she purred, and she hung up. Then, turning on the light switch to the front stairway, turning off the store fluorescents, Noel opened the door and climbed the front stairs. It wasn't her usual way up, but tonight she didn't feel like going through the stockroom with its maze of shadowy passageways and cartons and corners. Unlocking the door at the top landing with her new key, she entered her living room

and closed the door behind her, set the new double locks –
latch bolt, dead bolt – then turned for the lamp and—

—Jerry Royal was there. Reclining in her small wicker
couch, a hardy grin on his face. Noel was startled by his
appearance; but it was his assurance that scared her – an
expression foreign to Jerry. He was drunk, she concluded,
and here to rape her. But something else told her it was more
than that. He turned on the reading lamp beside him.

'Din mean to scare you, Noel,' he said. His hair was wetted
and combed down to his eyebrows, like molded plastic. He
wore clean white overalls and no shirt, showing off his pink,
rounded shoulders. With a red neckerchief tied around his
neck, he looked as dapper as she'd ever seen him. What
worried her more was the piece of paper he held in his hand.
She guessed it was the source of his confidence.

'Jeez, you look like you seen a ghost,' he said.

'Jerry, you can't just come up here,' she replied. She
wanted to show him ire, not fear.

'You're right, I can't no more.' He opened his hand and
dangled a set of keys – Bobby's keys. 'So I bin up here all day,
waitin. Anybody ever teach you to vacuum under your bed?'
He dropped the keys on the coffee table in front of him.

Noel gazed placidly at him. 'Where did you get those?'

Jerry's craggy, weather-beaten smile bored into her. 'I
heard you down there the other night,' he said.

'I'm going to call the police,' she told him, and she walked
alongside a wooden curio of tribal artifacts, beyond his reach,
then turned down the hallway.

'"To whom it may concern,"' he began reading, '"I,
Gerald Christian Royal" – formal touch, make it legal – "do
testify that on May the twenty-fifth I was working at the
Wicker Funeral Home in Gravity, Maine, and I heard" – that
should be *overheard*, but what the fuck – "I heard Mr Eliot
Wicker having a conversation with Mr Robert Swift when

Robert Swift was supposed to be dead" – right to the point, see?'

Jerry paused; Noel's footsteps stopped in the hall. 'I guess that got her attention. Anyway – "I heard Robert Swift ask, 'What did she send this monkey suit for?' And Eliot Wicker said to keep his mouth shut because he was putting on the lip sealer, which seals the lips of the deceased. Only thing was, Bobby Swift was not deceased."'

Jerry looked up from his paper at the empty room and said, 'You callin 'em?' He smiled to himself, then found his place and resumed. '"So I and Otis Royal, my father, who personally don't know anything but that Robert Swift was dead like he supposed to be, dug the grave at Rest Awhile Cemetery, and after the funeral we set the casket in and filled in the hole like we always do. But I had my suspicions. I figured there was only one reason a man would let anyone bury him alive – to collect the life insurance, which they would split three ways – husband, wife and undertaker. I myself figured we could split it four ways.

'"So after the funeral, Noel Swift had a party, and when it got over I saw her getting into her Volvo car, which she told me she was going for a drive. So after she left I let myself back in with a set of spare keys that I borrowed from Robert Swift's workshop.

'"Up in the bedroom closet I found a suitcase packed with the clothes of Robert Swift, along with an airplane ticket and some other things, which I removed for the purpose of negotiating with husband and wife when they got back home. But then a half hour later Noel Swift drove back home alone, which wasn't enough time to dig up a grave. And that's when I thought of the other reason somebody might bury her husband. To get rid of him and collect the insurance herself."'

Reclining on the couch, Jerry looked up from his paper and

saw Noel watching him from the doorway. He gave her a cocky wag of his head. 'I bet never in a million years you thought you'd get caught by someone like me.' His lips flattened clownishly.

She brought the .22 up from behind her hip, aimed dead at that mouth.

'Whoa, copy, copy' – Jerry covered his face with one arm while he held the paper out to the side – 'just a Xerox copy, I thought I made that clear.' He gave a little nervous hoot. 'Jeezum, lady, you are a dangerous little thing. Slow down.'

But Noel kept the pistol aimed directly at those wet, elastic lips, certain that its report wouldn't sound any different to neighbors than a book falling (if anyone were awake to hear it at all).

'I got the original hid away someplace, which I'm not tellin you where, except it's in an envelope that says, "*To be opened in case Gerald C. Royal shows up missing or dead.*"' He gave a little head movement, conveying a reckless pride. 'Don't think I'm gonna underestimate you, girl. I've watched you work.'

Noel glared at him, wanting so badly to pull the trigger, as if by doing so she could be rid of this idiot complication. But she knew that she had to keep her head.

'Where is he?' she demanded. 'Where's Bobby?'

'Who, *Dale Newman*?' Jerry widened his eyes, demonstrating his knowledge, his power. 'You got me.'

'You killed Eliot Wicker,' she said.

He snorted, ridiculing her. 'Oh, as if,' he said. 'Right here I was, in this very house that night, with you. I saw Wicker come here, and I saw him go away again, some friggin ugly too. Whatever happened down there at that cemetery, I don't know any more'n you.'

She neither budged from the doorway nor lowered her gun. 'What do you want from me?' she said.

'Well' – his face jutting as if the answer should have been obvious – 'a little respect, for starters.'

Noel's expression didn't change.

'Meaning you could point that gun away from my head, bein as how, if you think about it, I got a gun pointed at you that'll take your own head off down to your knees, whether I'm dead or alive, personally speaking.'

But her revolver remained trained on his face. 'Tell me what you want,' she repeated.

He rocked his head back and forth to show that the conversation would not proceed until she had acceded to his first request.

She did so, finally, lowering the gun. But her icy glare persisted. 'I don't have any money,' she told him.

'Yeah, I heard. Friggin insurance companies, they got you comin and goin. Here I thought I was going to be a rich man, drive around town, "Hi, how y'doin?" Same with you, right?'

She sank to the floor, sliding down the corner of the curio. 'Jerry, just tell me what you want,' she said.

His protracted silence was all the answer she needed.

She looked up and saw it clearly in his face, that look of undisguised greed that men get when they imagine a woman is helpless. And then it began. He placed his letter on the coffee table and his voice took on a country-western softness. 'I got a little warm up here the other night, listening to you two down there, with all that chocolate business.' He put his hand deep inside a pocket of his overalls, moved it around, then slowly withdrew her red panties.

A wave of nausea gripped Noel. She raised the pistol again, squinted at him, catlike. 'I'd die first,' she said.

'*Daow!*' he said – an emphatic *no* – as he slid off the couch and sank to his hands and knees, the panties in his fist. 'Like in Cinderella, I'm Prince What's-his-name, come to put these back on you, see if they fit.' He started crawling toward her, his back huge and rounded, his pink shoulders flexing like a lion's. 'I got it all figured out,' he said.

She leaned back against the curio, pulled her knees underneath her, the revolver in both hands, aimed at the top of his head. As he came closer, his breathing became part of his voice.

'My word, look at them straps, *strings* is all you got there, strings holdin up them little titties.' That ragged grin again. 'Come on, Noel,' he said. 'You know you don't wanna kill me.'

Her head began to hum.

'Not with what I got on you.'

Jerry's right hand moved blindly through the air, he took hold of the pistol and lowered it to the floor. 'That's right,' he moaned, and then his raspy fingers slid the entire length of her arm to her shoulder, then headed south down her shoulder strap. 'Now let's just see what you're packin,' he breathed, his dry knuckles grazing the side of her breast.

Suddenly mindless, Noel lurched up, yanked the pistol from under her hip, and drove its muzzle straight against Jerry's cheekbone, under his eye.

Before he could pull his hand out of her top, she pulled the trigger, she couldn't stop herself, his head jerked back, but she stayed with him, on her knees now, forcing the barrel against his face, pulling the trigger again and again, the hammer making a lifeless clank,

a dead ring,

a toy sound—

He clutched her wrist, wrenched her arm powerfully so the back of her hand slammed against a shelf. With his other hand, Jerry fingered the small cut she had made on his cheek.

'Jeezum, Noel, take my fuckin eye out, why don't you!'

A quality in his voice told her that his pain was not only physical. His feelings had been hurt.

'It's not like I was friggin askin to marry you.' He let go of her wrist and felt under his eye. 'Jeez, you gotta think, girl. Number one, I been up here all day. You gotta *know* I'da took the shells outta that gun very first thing. I ain't dumb. Number two, you kill me, it's all over, the old man finds my letter, you spend the rest of your life in prison. Number three' – he fingered his cheekbone again, checking for blood – 'I'm gonna let this one go, but in the future, anything you do to me, I'll do back to you twice as bad. *Twice as bad*. Is that clear?' *Clee-uh.* He jabbed the floor with his finger. 'Now I got knowledge about something, and now the insurance part's all frigged up, and I deserve to get something outta this.'

Glaring at him, clenched with rage, Noel kept her voice remarkably even. 'And what you want is to rape me. Raping me is your life's ambition.'

'Well, maybe once, until you see how much fun it is.' He gave her a gawking, expectant look, waiting for a smile, but it didn't happen.

'You okay?'

She closed her eyes.

'You don't want to look at me, don't wanna talk, whatever, okay.'

She opened her eyes, gazed up at him.

A slow, bruised grin came over his face. 'That's more like it,' he said.

She sprang suddenly, swinging the revolver across her chest. He turned his head, but too late. The cylinder caught him above the ear, made a vicious pop.

'*Geee!*' he cried, pressing his head to his shoulder. As the gun came back the other way, the muzzle sideswiping his nose, he grabbed her throat, squeezing hard enough to slam her shoulders to the floor. With his other hand he tore the gun away from her and wrapped it in his fist like some primitive tool. He cocked his arm by his ear as if he were going to pulverize her face with the butt.

She glared up at him, eyes viciously narrowed.

'Go ahead, asshole,' she whispered. 'Make one fucking mark on me.'

Jerry's eyes opened wide, his lips puckered. He checked behind him for the hallway. Then he looked down at her again and two drops of blood fell from his nose onto her neck. He wiped his nose with the back of his hand. Repulsed, Noel nevertheless kept her steely eyes on him.

Jerry began bobbing his head. 'Don't worry,' he said. Still clutching her throat, he set the gun on the floor and slid it to the far wall. 'Don't worry,' he said again, 'you're gonna wish you didn't do that.' He released his grip on her throat by pushing himself to his feet. ''Cause tomorrow we're takin this up a notch, you and me.' He gave her a punctuation look, then backed into the hallway, where he turned and lumbered off between the walls to the kitchen, checking his wounds as he went. When he reached the kitchen, he turned back one more time and pointed at her. 'Fuckin feminist,' he said, 'you're in for one big surprise.'

9

Sal stood near the back of the store, looking over the videotape selection while he waited for the crowd to disperse. At ten to eight, when a couple of men paid for their coffee and headed off to work, it seemed like the others were getting set to go too.

That's when Jerry Royal walked in. He was carrying a brown bag, folded down tight. When he caught sight of Sal, the two men looked each other over – Sal in his black leather and boots, Jerry wearing magenta jeans and a green rayon shirt with a wide white collar. Although Jerry's raccoon hair was once again carefully combed, this morning a purple half-moon cupped his swollen left eye. He turned away from Sal and took a seat at the counter, between Herb True and Belly Button.

'Who'd you have a disagreement with?' Herb asked.

'Transmission,' Jerry answered.

His father Otis, at the end of the counter, said with low disapproval, 'Look of those dancin clothes, I'd guess a woman did the transmittin.'

'Ol' Mister Pink Pants,' Belly Button added with a chuckle.

Before Jerry could respond, Noel came through the stock-room door, carrying a small cardboard box of chewing gum. 'I'll start with a coffee this morning,' Jerry said to her. 'You can put it on my tab.'

Noel ignored him.

Sal came to the head of the grocery aisle hoping to catch Noel's eye, but she walked the length of the counter without looking his way either. Jerry seemed particularly interested in Noel's faded hiphugger jeans, tight in the thighs, worn through the knees, flared and flayed at the ankles.

'What's in the bag?' Belly Button asked him.

'Nothin 'at concerns you.'

'Pink pants,' Belly said again.

'You don't know your friggin colors,' Jerry answered, still watching Noel.

The bell on the door sounded, and Sal turned to see Alston Bouchard coming in. The Superette fell quiet, except for the creak of floorboards under the constable's feet.

'Coffee, Alston?' Noel asked.

'Just five on gas.'

'Coffee down here,' Jerry said, 'in case you forgot.'

Bouchard looked over at him, his gaze passing briefly over Sal and the other men, then returning to Noel as he flipped open the wallet. He dug out a ten and set it on the counter. As she rang it in, he said, 'Man named Dale Newman been in?'

Noel took a five out of the cash tray and held it out for Bouchard. 'Not that I know of.' To the others, she said, 'Dale Newman?'

The men at the counter looked at one another. Jerry nudged Herb. 'Ask what he looks like.'

Bouchard looked over at Jerry, then returned to Noel. 'No picture,' he said. He pulled a card out of his shirt pocket, light green, folded in half. He unfolded the card in front of Noel. 'Just this plane ticket. Looks like Mr Newman missed his flight Monday morning. Grand Cayman Island, his destination.'

Bouchard looked over at Sal again – at least that's the way it appeared to Sal – difficult though it was to see Bouchard's eyes through the glare on his glasses.

'I guess we can't help you,' Noel said, crouching behind the cash register to straighten something inside the candy case. Bouchard stepped back and looked through the glass.

'Monday being the day after Bobby's funeral, he was supposed to fly out of Logan Airport in Boston – Dale Newman, I mean. Maybe someone stopped by you didn't recognize—?' Bouchard knocked twice on the glass, self-consciously.

'Those detectives been in yet?' Jerry said. 'They'll prob'ly want to see that ticket.' He leaned over the counter, trying to get a look at Noel, almost like he was needling her. Sal wondered if it was because she hadn't brought him his coffee.

She stood up behind the candy counter, glanced back at Jerry as if she wondered the same thing. 'Alston, I know you're trying to help,' she said, 'but could you please work with the others?' The look she gave Bouchard conveyed more affection than she was used to showing.

He folded the ticket and tucked it away in his wallet. 'Just thought I'd check,' he said, turning for the door. 'Whoever this is, he missed his plane.'

Jerry said to Sal, 'Where'd he find the ticket, he say?'

Bouchard looked back at Jerry, not answering, then he opened the door.

Sal pushed off his stool, stepped back from the counter. 'Mr Bouchard,' he said. The other men at the counter turned to Sal. The constable stopped, the door in his hand.

'Mr Bouchard, you didn't say where you found that plane ticket.'

Bouchard nodded. 'I know I didn't,' he said, and he left.

As soon as the door closed, Noel slid the candy case shut, pitched the empty carton in the basket and walked the length of the counter, heading toward the stockroom. 'Jerry,' she said, pushing through the swinging door, 'do you have a minute? I need you to look at my car. It's skipping.'

Jerry cocked his head, as if deliberating. Then he dismounted the stool and patted down his hair. He tucked his
paper bag under his arm, looked over at Sal and said, 'I guess I
got the time.'

'We're not showing a Dale Newman in the whole state,' the
woman said over the phone.

'Is it possible the name is unlisted?' Sal asked her. Pen in
hand, he looked over Davey's social studies test on the kitchen
table, the word EXCELLENT red-penciled at the top of the
paper.

'Even if it were unlisted, it would still appear on the screen,'
the operator told him.

Sal thanked the woman and hung up the phone. He went to
the counter and filed through a stack of bills until he found one
from the electric company. He dialed the number listed.
Waiting for the phone to ring, he noticed Davey's bathrobe
hung on the bathroom doorknob, quilted, pink roses on blue.
He turned away before the pang gnawed deeper. When the
receptionist answered, he explained that the wrong electric bill
had ended up in his envelope. 'I got Dale Newman's,' he said.
'If you give me his address, I'll mail it to him.'

'His address should be on the bill,' she replied, 'right under
the name.'

'It's smudged,' Sal said.

The woman asked him to wait a minute. A few seconds later
she was back on the phone. 'We don't show a Dale Newman
anywhere in the state. Are you sure you're reading it right? D as
in dolphin?'

Sal hung up and then checked the Yellow Pages, under
AIRLINES.

'Don't talk,' Noel said. 'Just listen.'

Jerry shrugged his shoulders. 'No problem there.' He stood

at the bottom of the stairs in the garage, holding his paper bag under his folded arms.

'Get in,' she said.

'Yes, m'am.'

He stepped around her and ducked into the passenger side of her Volvo, found the lever under his seat and pushed the seat all the way back, stretching his legs. Noel got in the driver's side, started the car and let it idle fast.

She looked directly at him. 'Are you totally stupid?'

'I don't know,' he said. 'Am I?'

'Did you give that plane ticket to Bouchard?'

'I left it someplace where I thought he might find it. Like I promised, Noel, you take it up a notch, I take it up two. Now you wanna keep playin games, you best know I got enough to put you away for life.' He slipped his fingers inside the bag and pulled out a slim white box wrapped in cellophane. He nudged it toward her. 'Fanny Farmer,' he said.

She did not look at the chocolates. 'Jerry,' she said, 'you are risking your life – and mine – just to have sex with me.'

He shrugged. 'Not riskin *my* life.'

'Oh, yes, you are,' she answered solemnly, giving each word its full, ominous weight. 'Believe me, you are risking your life.'

Jerry gave it a moment's thought. 'So, you're risking your life *not* to have sex with me. I'd say that makes you the fool.' He set the box of chocolates on the dashboard in front of her. 'Mixed assortment,' he pointed out. There was a certain arousal in his eyes, slightly tempered by the knowledge that the garage was filling with carbon monoxide.

'Jerry, think about it.'

'Don't worry, I do.'

'Jerry, your *life*. Sex is not worth losing your life over.'

He snickered. 'Yeah. Maybe not your life, it ain't. Maybe Queen Elizabeth or what's-her-name, the president's wife, maybe not theirs. But hey, lady, look at my life. Whaddu I got to lose? A bunch of chickens and a new Chevy truck which you can't take that where I'm goin anyways. And you tell me gettin inside these hippie pants ain't worth a life like that?' He almost touched the low waist of her jeans but stopped short.

She turned away.

'That's not all I want, anyway,' he continued. 'I expect breakfast, lunch, dinner, whatnot, on the house, anytime I come in. Gas for my truck, free videos ... I figure that's fair.'

Noel closed her eyes. 'I can't believe this,' she whispered.

'I bet you can't,' he said. 'And here you prob'ly thought you were just about the slickest thing ever took a breath of air in this town. And I'm supposed to be so stupid. Well, now look where I got you, smarty.'

Noel looked away from him again, stared out her window into the garage, kept silent for a time. At last her chest heaved with a long sigh of surrender.

'Huh?'

She turned to face him, her eyes welled with defeat, and Jerry's heart nearly stopped. He regarded her recklessly.

'Not here,' she said. 'And not now.'

'You name the time and place, lady, I'll be there.'

She said, 'First I want you to tell me exactly what happened at the cemetery that night.'

'I already told you,' he said, 'I didn't have nothin to do with it, swear to God. For all I know, you and Bobby had it all planned to put the screws right back on Wicker.'

Noel stared at him.

'Give me the evil eye all you want, Noel, I'll tell you this: If Bobby's out there playin games, you best keep him way away from me. 'Cause that letter I wrote'll finish him in a heartbeat, same as you, I don't care what island you run to. And that goes for that other one you been cockteasin, my brother-in-law. Anyway, how do I know the two of you didn't cook up this whole thing from the start, and doublecross everybody?'

Noel's expression never changed. Keeping her eyes glued to Jerry, she said: 'I want you to stay away from Sal Erickson.'

Jerry studied her. 'Sounds like you got some plans for him yourself.'

Noel's eyes narrowed on Jerry so suddenly, so fiercely, that his hand reflexively went to the door handle.

'I said stay away from him.'

The black lab sat on the roadside, whining, as Shepherd peeled the prints off the mailbox. 'You're positive the ticket was inside,' the detective said. 'Folded like that?'

'Seven-thirty I found it,' Bouchard answered, 'when I got my mail.' He patted the dog, quieting him. His long house trailer sat across the road, twenty feet back from the tar. Behind the trailer a long, rocky hill rose, divided up the center by a pair of well-worn tire tracks. To the right of the road, the hill was white with blueberry blossoms that would be this year's crop; to the left, black with char from the biyearly torching.

'And something told you to take that plane ticket out, hold it in your hand, and bring it to the store to show your friends,' Murdoch said, standing off to the side drinking coffee from a thermos cup.

'The flight was the morning after Bobby Swift's funeral,' Bouchard answered. 'I thought it might be connected.'

Shepherd checked his watch. 'A lot of things happened the day after Bobby Swift's funeral,' he said.

'A lot of things happen every day,' Murdoch added. 'Doesn't mean they're linked up.'

'It was one way,' Bouchard said.

Shepherd looked over at him.

'The ticket,' Bouchard explained. 'Meaning he wasn't coming back.'

Murdoch, unimpressed, tossed the last of his coffee on the asphalt, splashing the dog. 'I'll be in the car,' he said. As he crossed the road toward the trailer, the lab barked at him.

'Katahdin, hush.'

Shepherd finished labeling his hinge-lifter, slipped it in his jacket pocket and started walking across the road. Bouchard and the dog walked behind him.

'You found Bobby Swift's fingerprints on those scuba tanks,' Bouchard said. If it was a question, it didn't sound like one. 'Eliot Wicker's too,' he added, 'if I'm not too far off.'

Shepherd stopped walking, turned and faced the constable, stared at him long enough to put both men on edge.

'Mr Bouchard, I don't know how that plane ticket ended up in your mailbox,' Shepherd said, 'or whether it means anything at all. But I would rather not see you again in connection with this investigation.'

With that, the detective turned away and walked to his Cherokee, where he ducked in behind the steering wheel and started the engine. Bouchard came a couple of steps closer. 'That coffin,' he said, 'the shape, I mean, inside – I'm guessing it was tore up some—?'

Shepherd shifted into reverse and backed around, ready to drive out. 'I may have to arrest you,' he said. 'I really may have to lock you up.' He began to pull out when a motorcycle came around the curve, cut in front of him and stopped. Shepherd hit the brakes just short of colliding with it.

Murdoch, recognizing Sal on the Harley, shifted heavily in his seat, muttering.

Sal clutched the bike around to Shepherd's window, shut it off. 'Dale Newman canceled his flight Sunday night at eight-fifteen,' he said to the detectives. 'I called Delta Airlines.'

'Night of the funeral,' Bouchard added from the other side of the vehicle.

'The original fucking Hardy Boys,' Murdoch said.

Sal took a piece of notepaper out of his jacket pocket. 'I couldn't get an address on him,' he continued. 'There was no refund because he didn't give enough notice. But I found out he bought the ticket through a travel agency' – he showed Shepherd the paper – 'Beliveau's, in Portland. He paid cash, last June the twenty-fourth.' Sal folded up the paper and offered it to Shepherd.

For a second or two, both detectives just stared at Sal from inside the Cherokee. Then Shepherd reached his hand out and took the paper.

'I'm just trying to find out what happened here,' Sal said. 'Maybe then you'll leave the woman alone.'

Murdoch opened his door, pushed himself out of the Cherokee so one foot was in the yard. He looked over the hood at Sal. 'Only thing you're gonna find out is how goddamn fast we lock you up next time you interfere in this investigation.' He kept on talking, but the rest of his words were drowned out when Sal started the Harley again, goosed the throttle and rode off.

Sal headed east from Bouchard's, veered right onto a dirt road that led through more blackened blueberry barrens, and then opened it up. Chased by a trail of sunlit dust, he let the wind beat his face while he tried to piece together the information: Somebody had murdered Eliot Wicker the night of Bobby's funeral. And somebody had stolen Bobby's body. And now a plane ticket turns up in town, belonging to Dale Newman, who should have been on his way to Grand Cayman Island the day after Bobby's funeral. Like everything's connected, everything's a clue. Sal tried to remember faces at the funeral, at the burial, at the reception in Noel's apartment, strange faces, but there were still many people who lived in Gravity that he didn't know. Almost anyone there could have been Dale Newman, and he wouldn't have known the difference. And even if this

Dale Newman were involved, even if he murdered Eliot
Wicker and buried him in Bobby's grave, then why would he
have removed Bobby's body?

In Sal's mind, nothing connected – not that his concentration was peak. In fact, he could think of nothing without Noel
invading his thoughts, so when the dirt road rejoined asphalt
he doubled back toward town and drove directly to the
Superette, unmindful that the store was busy with lunch
customers. He went inside and saw Noel making change at the
cash register. He never took his eyes off her as he approached
the register.

'Got a minute?' he said to her. He knew that the men beside
him were watching; wondered if they could read the look that
he and Noel exchanged.

'I'm busy right now,' she said, feigning disinterest.

'I just got pulled over,' he lied. 'The police want to see the
bike registration. I told them I'd get it from you and bring it to
the station.'

Noel gave him a momentary look. 'I'll check the desk out
back. Bonnie, can you manage for a few minutes?' She walked
past Bonnie, who was tending the grill, giving no indication
that Bonnie's answer would have made any difference. 'Through
here,' she said to Sal, throwing the stockroom door open.

He went in behind the meat counter, caught the door and
followed Noel down the dusky aisle between walls of cardboard boxes, gazing at her confident stride. At the first
intersection, she turned left around a pallet stacked high with
cartons of paper towels. He turned with her, caught her arm,
and immediately their mouths came together. He held her
neck, the back of her head; she ran her hands inside his open
jacket to the back of his jeans; he ran his hands down her sides
to the inch of her bare waist at the top of her hips; she kissed his
neck; he closed his eyes until the only thing that existed were
these two bodies, these two minds, these mouths and their own

labored breathing. They circled on the floor as if they were dancing, until she backed into her desk and knocked the telephone off the hook. Roused, they broke the kiss, still holding each other. 'What are we doing?' she breathed.

'Come for a ride,' he answered.

She shook her head, pushed his arms down. 'I can't,' she said, slipping his grasp. She bent to pick up the receiver. 'I have to get back in there, and you have to leave.'

Catching her by the hips, his hands slid up her sides, pulling her back and turning her to face him. 'Hire me,' he said. 'I'll live in the garage.'

Laughing, she looked down at the tail of his shirt that had come untucked. She pressed her body closer to his. 'You can't go out there like this,' she said. With the back of her hand, she pushed his shirt inside his jeans, down inside the waistband of his briefs, where her thumb brushed the face of his erection.

He gasped. She pulled her hand out slowly. 'Someone's going to see us,' she said. Looking toward the store, they could see the small, bright window of the swinging door.

'It's dark in here,' he said, holding her arms.

'Oh,' she shuddered, 'but we don't have time.'

'The way I feel, it won't take long.' Grinning, he reached down, found the button on her hiphuggers. She twisted her hips, laughing.

'God, have you always been this bad?'

He pulled her roughly back to him. 'Come on, we'll drive up the coast, rent a little place on the water.'

'Sal, we can't. The locals are ready to lynch me as it is.'

'Take your car. I'll meet you. I've gotta talk to you.'

She slipped away from him, backing toward the store, eyeing him with a fiercely seductive grin. 'Talk to me?'

'I found Dale Newman,' he told her.

She stopped, her smile frozen, her head cocked.

'The guy who lost the plane ticket,' he explained.

Facing him, she said nothing for a moment while her smile disappeared. She looked wounded – or angry – he couldn't tell.

'I found out where he bought the ticket,' Sal said to her.

She took a step toward him and then stopped, far enough so the distance was meaningful. 'Sal, don't you understand?' she said to him. 'Can't you see I am suffocating here? Everyplace I go, that's all I hear: Eliot Wicker, Bobby Swift, and somebody asking me where *I* was, what *I* was doing, who *I* was with. Sal, I feel like somebody's out there trying to make it look like I'm involved—'

'That's why I checked,' he said. 'I want it to stop. I want to find out what happened to Bobby.'

Eyes narrowed, she stepped closer. 'No,' she said, almost as if she were warning him. 'Sal, you need to stay out of this.' She reached out, put her hands in his jacket pockets and drew him in, drew the jacket around her. 'Sally, you're my escape, my way out of this insanity.' She lifted her face, lightly touching his body with her own, brushing his neck with her lips. 'And I don't ever want to lose you.'

And then she said nothing more, and neither did he, because the thought of losing her was far more than he could bear. So, holding her against him, hearing the low drone of conversations from the store, the clatter of silverware, the drone of country music too distant to distinguish, his lips parted against the side of her hair, breathing her fragrance in ... and he whispered a vow: 'I'm never going to lose you.'

When the detectives returned to the barracks, Shepherd shut himself inside an interrogation room with his computer and proceeded to telephone every one of the oxygen suppliers he had contacted the day before, with a new name to check: Dale Newman. After an hour of phone conversations and no luck, he heard the door open, and a shadow fell across his desk.

'A one-way ticket to an island somewhere, and you change

horses.' Murdoch leaning in the doorway. 'Don't you think it's a little suspicious that somebody gave it to us?'

Shepherd stopped dialing. 'I think it's connected.'

'And the murderer signed his real name for the oxygen tanks.'

'He signed some name. Sarge, you up for a little research?'

Murdoch turned his head to the side, unresponsive. Shepherd opened a manila folder, pulled out the photo of Bobby Swift and Sal Erickson and slid it to the edge of his desk. Murdoch stepped to the desk, turned the picture to face him. 'Fuckin greaseballs,' he said. 'I thought I left this shit back in Chicago.'

'I want facts on Bobby Swift,' Shepherd told him. 'Where he was born, where he went to school, who he worked for, what his hobbies were – everything he did after he learned to walk.'

The sergeant lowered his head; scratched at a spot on his crown with his little finger, same spot he always scratched when he wanted to show his skepticism.

'I want to get the lab boys back too,' Shepherd continued. 'I want a search warrant for the store, the apartment upstairs, the basement, garage and motor vehicles. The dumpster outside. I'm working up a list. We're looking for shoes – his or hers – so we can analyze any soil residue against the cemetery sample. We're looking for oxygen or scuba tanks or any other breathing apparatus, and I want to check the trash for discarded clothing.'

Murdoch snorted a laugh, shaking his head. 'No wonder it takes you guys so long,' he said. 'Analyze this, analyze that, Jesus Christ, find one speck of dust and analyze it a million different ways. Now you want a goddamn autobiography on this guy. That's what I mean, you go too far with this penny-ante stuff.'

Shepherd lowered the phone. 'Am I the primary on this case or not?'

'Your job isn't to tippy-toe around like you're Andy of

fucking Mayberry. Your job is to tear-ass through that town, scaring the shit out of as many people as you can until you make some sonovabitch talk!'

Shepherd hung up the phone, swiveled his chair to face the sergeant. 'Am I the primary?'

'If I say you are.'

'*Am I the primary?*'

The telephone buzzed. Shepherd picked up, snapped, '*What?*'

It was the receptionist from a Mid-Maine Supply in Belfast, about an hour down the coast. She'd just finished a computer search of their files and thought she'd found what Shepherd was looking for. He typed the information into his notebook computer as she spoke, then thanked the woman and hung up.

'What was that?'

Shepherd kept typing. 'Two oxygen tanks, size E, signed out last spring, May thirteen. The scuba tanks too. Same place, same date, same name.'

'Yeah?'

Shepherd said coolly, 'Dale Newman.'

'So, good. We find the asshole, we interrogate the shit out of him, we get a confession.'

Shepherd picked up the photo and held it out to Murdoch. 'I told you, Sarge, as long as I'm calling the shots, you're looking for Bobby Swift.'

The police tape was still in place, the back door window still broken. Sal reached through the hole and let himself in. If there had been any neighbors, his penlight beam would have been obvious. The house was dark, and there were no blinds on the windows. He knew he'd be arrested if he were caught here – and Noel would be furious with him – but the detectives seemed intent on hounding her until something better came up. Like maybe Dale Newman.

He went to the wall phone first, shone his light on a clipboard hanging beside it, a list of computer-printed phone numbers in alphabetical order. No Dale Newman listed, but Sal wasn't surprised. He figured that whatever connection existed between Eliot Wicker and Dale Newman – if any – he'd find it in the business files downstairs. He turned with his penlight toward the basement door—

Something stopped him.

He drew the light beam to his left, to a plain maple board attached to the wall, fitted with wooden pegs. A black nylon jacket hung from it. Sal ran the penlight beam to the left: black sportcoat; black hooded sweatshirt. Unused peg. Another peg . . . then—

A touring cap. He leaned toward the cap with the light, and the floor popped, startling him. He could feel his heart beating. Brown tweed. He reached out, lifted the cap off the peg . . . knew even before he turned it over and shined the light inside. PALMARY HATTERS, PROVIDENCE.

His.

He fit the cap on his head. Perfectly. He'd bought it ten years earlier when he was playing with Woody, wore it on stage, off stage, wore it all the time – until sometime last summer, sometime during the blur . . . when he had lost it . . .

—at Eliot Wicker's?

He heard a sound—

Bobby—

He wheeled around, the white door reflecting his penlight beam. He flicked the light off. Replayed the sound in his head, a sound that had no reason to be there. It had come from downstairs – a single muffled knock, like a door closing.

He stood in the blackness. For the first time he allowed the real possibility that Bobby was alive. If Bobby were alive, that would explain Wicker's murder. It would certainly explain how Bobby's body was missing. It would explain the glove in Sal's suitcase, the message on Noel's car window. A feeling rose up inside Sal, dark and aberrant, the likes of which he'd never known.

The sound came again, a soft drumming, almost as if it were calling him, daring him. He reached out and found the doorknob, turned it slowly so as not to disturb the latch. Deep inside, a voice counseled him to leave the dead man's house, go back through the woods, get on his motorcycle and go somewhere far away from town until he could make sense of all this—

but then the door was opening in his hand.

Feeling a movement of air rising over him, he listened again, wondering if the noise had been a mouse or a squirrel – or simply his afflicted imagination. But then he heard it again, plainer: a hard, dull knock, too heavy for a rodent. He determined that it was not directly below, but in one of Wicker's back rooms downstairs. He kept the penlight off. Holding the handrail, he descended the stairs slowly, silently. When he could feel the hard floor under his boot sole, he stopped again. The knocking seemed to come from his left, muffled enough so he could tell it was behind at least one wall. He turned on the penlight again, swept the beam quickly around the small room to ensure he was alone. He was. Only the furnace and water heater shared the space with him. He crept to the door that led into Wicker's office.

Standing at the door, he listened again to the noise – more of a rustling now – and guessed that it was coming not from this next room but from one further off. He doused the penlight anyway and turned the knob, pulled the door open. More darkness. But now the rustling sounded closer – and heavier – almost like someone was struggling.

Sal turned on his penlight, shot the beam left and right, lighting the plush burgundy carpet in front of his feet. He raised the beam to his left until he could see, twenty feet away, another door. He padded past the desk and file cabinets, his footsteps absorbed by the carpet. The nearer he got to the door, the clearer the rustling became. He took hold of the knob. Shut off the penlight. Stood in darkness, listening to the sounds. Point of no return, he said to himself, as if by going through the door, he was wandering into his own inexorable destruction—

—as if he hadn't opened that door already, some time ago. Now, finally, inevitably, he was going through.

The door hushed open and the noises stopped. He braced himself, lowered his shoulder, tensed his muscles. There was an odor in the room – carpeting, furniture—

A sudden loud knock startled him – and the rustling resumed, sounding like someone or something was trapped behind a wall. Then the noise stopped again. Sal stood in the thick of blackness, not moving. The room around him seemed to hold its breath, listening. Sal himself stopped breathing. He was afraid to even turn his head for fear that his collar would brush his neck. Then the knocking started again, seemingly oblivious to his presence, and in the knocking he could now detect a dull metallic ring.

He braced his thumb on the penlight switch, took a breath, readied himself. He turned on the light. The beam reflected off the end of a cherry casket ten feet in front of him. Sal swung the light around, saw three more caskets, each with its viewing lid opened, elevated knee-high on a platform that ran down the middle of the room, covered with burgundy cloaking. The rustling continued from the left, unmindful of his presence. He aimed his light in that direction, where more caskets were displayed along the wall, piggybacked on two levels, a row on the floor, another on a carpeted ledge. Under Sal's weak beam he could make out only one casket at a time, so he began crossing to the left, moving the light slowly ahead of him: buffed aluminum, red cherry wood, mahogany and lacquered pine, each viewing lid raised to reveal lush velvet and satin: white, deep blue, peach...

His light beam stopped on one casket just as the knocking started again. Dark, glossy mahogany. He stared. The casket was closed. Someone was inside.

He didn't stop to wonder who, or why, or whether he was in danger. He walked directly to the casket, took hold of the viewing lid, threw it up—

A light in his eyes blinded him, a hand from inside reached up, caught his wrist, pulled down powerfully. Sal pulled back, losing his penlight but twisting out of the grasp. In the same motion he grabbed the viewing lid with both hands and slammed it down, pressed it down with all his weight and muscle, heart pounding, while he tried to regain his bearings in the darkness, tried to calculate his way back through this series of rooms to the outside door.

Then, from inside the box, he heard a voice. 'Looks like I got your flashlight here...'

Bouchard—?

Sal released his weight from the casket, and the lid slowly lifted, throwing a spot of light at the ceiling. The light shifted as the constable grabbed the casket rails and pushed his shoulders up out of the viewing area, his torso following, sharply silhouetted. Something rang as he worked his hips out. Sal could see that a green cylindrical tank had fallen against a similar tank. Further inside the casket, where Bouchard's legs had been, Sal could make out a pair of scuba tanks. The light shifted again, and then in one extended motion, Alston Bouchard managed to push the rest of his body out, stepping onto the floor.

'If I'm not wrong,' the constable said, 'you were here yesterday too.' He walked past Sal, closed the door, and the room suddenly glared in light. As Sal's eyes adjusted,

Bouchard's hand turned the dimmer switch to a glow. No windows, Sal realized, the light was safe. But was he?

Bouchard tipped his John Deere cap and wiped his forehead with his sleeve. His cheeks were pink and moist, his glasses fogged.

'Somebody might think you're trying to cover something up,' he said to Sal, somewhat winded.

Sal would have laughed if not for the cap on his own head, and if the constable had not been blocking the door. 'They might wonder a tiny bit about you too,' he said.

Bouchard took off his glasses, wiped them on his shirt and gazed blindly at the floor until he replaced them. He walked past Sal to the casket, bent to retrieve the penlight from inside. Sal watched him carefully.

'Then again, it wouldn't make sense, you covering something up. Not when you just left your fingerprints all over.' He tossed the penlight to Sal, who one-handed it. 'My guess is you're here looking for information on Dale Newman, to keep Noel Swift out of trouble.' He gave Sal a long, magnified look.

'Whatever you say.'

'Then I'd say you're headed for your own trouble, quite a bit more of it than you suspect.'

Sal's chest jerked with a laugh. He was trying to show the constable disdain, but he knew it wasn't convincing.

Staring at him, Bouchard threw the lid closed. 'You'd best pay attention,' he said. 'A murder's been committed. Evidence turns up. Here, here, here' – Bouchard made a fist, thumped it three times on the polished wood – 'evidence incriminating one particular person.'

Sal folded his arms to watch, humoring the constable.

'See, what I'm afraid of – what if that particular person – the suspect – was to die in an accident ... or maybe commit suicide and leave a note?'

Sal nodded. 'I'll be sure to tell Noel you're concerned about her.'

Bouchard peered at him, his black eyes bulging. The fist opened, his short fingers spread apart. 'I'm saying, with enough evidence left behind and the suspect suddenly deceased—'

'Then the case is closed,' Sal said. 'The cops and the taxpayers catch a break, and everybody goes on their merry way.'

'Case closed,' the constable agreed. 'Only what if the suspect wasn't the guilty one? What if it was all a setup?'

Something about Bouchard's steadfast stare made Sal suddenly wary. He stared back, a spark of fear kindling. 'Are you telling me that Noel's life is in danger—?'

Bouchard shook his head. He spoke evenly. 'I'm talking about you.'

Sal raised his face.

'You got somewhere to go?' Bouchard said to him.

'What are you talking about?'

'Somewhere out of state, a good distance from her. That woman's a danger to you.'

Sal held the constable's stare another second. Then he smirked again, took his penlight out of his pocket and switched it on. He turned for the door. 'If you need me,' he said, 'I'll be around.'

'Mr Erickson—'

Sal turned the doorknob, with no intention of staying for more.

'Eventually somebody's going to want to know what you and Eliot Wicker were doing together in her apartment that night Mr Wicker got himself murdered.'

Sal froze, tried not to show it. Night of the funeral, night of his show ... that's where his memory stopped.

'I just don't know what you're going to tell them.'

Sal did not turn around to see if Bouchard was bluffing. He pulled his cap down snug on his head as he left the room.

'I'll tell them they're full of shit,' he said. 'Same as you.'

At nine-thirty Iris tucked Davey into bed – Sal's side – and lay with her through the tears. What Iris told her was that Daddy loves you, but Daddy has a problem, and sometimes he hurts people without meaning to. 'Daddy didn't hurt me,' Davey told her. 'You're the one that hurt me. You made him leave.'

That's the way they left it. When Iris awoke it was ten o'clock and Davey was asleep on her arm. She turned back the blanket, fit her hand under Davey's legs and brought her close, then lifted her off the mattress and carried her out of the room, across the landing and into her own room.

Now as she laid Davey in bed, a motorcycle passed the house. Davey's eyes opened, and her head snapped up. She stared, stark with fear.

'It's okay, love,' Iris whispered, kissing her forehead, pulling the covers to her chin. 'Everything's okay.'

Sal headed east, toward the coast. He didn't know where he was going. Not home, not to his room, not to Noel's – not just yet. Maybe down to Oyster Cove, maybe he'd stop at the fish pier and call her from the pay phone. And what would he say, that he'd been to Wicker's again? That he'd found his cap there? That Bouchard had told him to stay away from her, that his life was in danger? Or maybe he'd ask her directly whether he and Wicker had been in her apartment that night.

He veered right onto the Oyster Cove Road, where, a mile along, he noticed headlights in his mirror, following some distance behind. At the top of a long hill he opened it up, accelerated down the other side of the hill, then really goosed it going up the next, the Harley feeling weightless, pushing him back on the seat. His cap, stuffed in his jacket

pocket, pressed against his ribs. But how it had ended up at Wicker's—

It would have been last summer, when he was drinking hard – June, July, August – the months had vanished from his memory, swallowed by that impenetrable darkness (like the night Wicker was murdered). Still, if he had befriended Wicker during that time, or had just stopped by his house with Bobby one night, it stood to reason that he could have left his cap there.

Soaring over the top of another rise, he spotted the head-lights in his rearview again, gaining on him. He opened the throttle and shot down a long, winding decline, leaning hard against the curve, until near the bottom of the hill a yellow sign flew out of the lilacs: YIELD. Considering the late hour, Sal expected no traffic, thinking to join the main road on the fly. But he glanced over and saw headlights coming in from the left, seconds from where the two roads joined. He released the gas and squeezed the brake gently to create a moment's delay, but the brake lever snapped to his throttle grip, and the Harley sailed toward impact. He stomped his foot brake, his rear wheel locked, screeched, skated out to the left—

and he was falling, incredibly, falling into the path of the headlights, still holding on to the handlebars, laying the Harley down at fifty as if he and the bike were executing a perfect hook slide, sparks showering his hips and chest, the screeching of chrome over asphalt barely enough to drown out the screech of truck tires, as the headlights came at him, thoughtfully turned to low beam, GMC proudly affixed to the pickup's grill, Sal contemplating in this long swelling sequence that he was about to be crushed, and wondering just as clearly, *Who is doing this to me?*

When all motion finally ceased, Sal lay on his side in the oncoming lane, still holding the throttle, and his engine was

quiet. The front of the motorcycle protruded under the middle of the pickup truck, which was also at rest, its own front wheel up on a bank, its rear wheel touching Sal's front tire.

A man looked down at him from the truck window. 'You okay, Bud?'

'Is he okay?' a woman asked from inside the truck.

At that moment, the pickup and the man both became illuminated. Thick white beard. Leather cap. Sal turned his head, relieved that he could do so, and saw the car that had been following him stopped on the facing road. A skinny kid with long, stringy hair stood between the headlights, emergency flashers. 'Is he okay?' the kid said.

The truck driver opened his door and stepped out, his truck lifting an inch or two as he did so. 'Let's get you out of the road,' he said. 'Can you move?'

'Somebody call nine-eleven,' the woman passenger said.

'Turn on the flashers,' the man told her.

Sal raised himself onto his elbow. He felt a burning in his thigh, but he realized – gratefully – that his motorcycle had not fallen on top of him. He bent the leg, pulled it underneath him and raised himself to his knee. The leg trembled.

'Man, you are one lucky son of a bitch,' said the driver.

'Nice thing to say after you nearly killed the man,' said his wife.

'I had the right of way,' the driver replied.

'It was my fault,' Sal said. 'My front brake gave out.' He leaned on the bike to push himself up, then stood there unable to stop his shaking, looking down at himself in the orange flashing lights, amazed that the only damage seemed to be to the shoulder of his jacket. The leather was scraped dull – he scratched tiny pebbles out of it. His jeans were also torn along the outside of his thigh, where he could see raw red skin.

'You are one lucky son of a bitch,' the driver said again.

Indeed. Sal bent for the handlebars and hauled the bike out from under the truck, then strained to hoist it upright. The driver helped, pulling up on the seat. 'Don't look too bad,' he said. 'Got a peg snapped off, saddlebag ground down. Other than that—'

'Fluid,' the kid said. Sal looked over. The kid rose to his feet behind his car. 'There's a blotch of it over here.' He showed his hand, red in the taillights, then sniffed it. 'Brake fluid.'

'Right down here,' the truck driver said, feeling along the Harley's front wheel. 'See, your bleeder's loose. I can turn it with my fingers.'

Sal looked down.

'You ain't noticed your front brakes getting low?'

Sal shook his head.

'No shit, it's opened right up wide.' Now the driver looked up at Sal. 'Bleeders don't usually open up on their own,' he said. 'Not like this.'

The man's ominous tone sent a dull jolt through Sal.

'I don't know, man. You been sleepin in the wrong bed somewhere?'

'Complaint,' said Jerry Royal, signaling the waitress with a sluggish finger. His head was killing him. Worse than that, he felt like a flatlander, dressed like he was. Friggin blue shoes. He squashed out his cigarette and lit another.

Outside the window, nothing moved, everything was dark. The last window lights from the tenements across the street had gone out hours ago. Cars had long since stopped passing while he sat there waiting for her. Now he was the last customer in the place.

Noel had promised to meet him at eleven-thirty – not in town; not even in Ellsworth, where she was afraid they might be recognized – but fifty miles away, in Bangor, in this nowhere hotel, the Blue BelAir, off in some lost part of the city by the river.

Fuckin room had set him back forty-five dollars. Not to mention the new clothes he had bought at the L.L. Bean's outlet in Ellsworth. A hundred bucks to look like the store mannequin: turtleneck jersey with wide purple and white stripes. At L. L. Bean they didn't call it purple and white; they called it eggplant and oyster. They could have called them grape jam and chicken; he felt goddamned foolish dressed like that. White pants they called stone, with an elasticized waistband. And *reef runners* on his feet – soft nylon things with thin rubber soles, bright blue and black – they looked like friggin ballet slippers! But at thirty-two bucks, hey, compared to what they wanted for leather?

Fuckin buffalo wings was another seven bucks. *Buffalo wings*. Thirty more on rum Cokes, which left him a five-dollar bill, no gas in his truck and an hour's drive back to town. Four or five times he had climbed the stairs up to his room to see whether Noel was there; more often had checked at the lobby to see if she'd left a message for him, but there was not a word. And she had warned him not to call her. He did anyway, eventually – he called her – and he kept trying for over an hour, but all he got was a busy signal.

'The buffalo wings was bad,' he told the waitress when she finally made it over, 'what little there was of 'em. They gimme a wicked friggin headache.'

The girl had straight blonde hair and no makeup, the face of a ten-year-old, with freckles and full breasts. College girl from the university. He gave her a sorry look, imagining that she had her own room at the hotel and that she'd take him there and nurse him. Christ, the top two buttons of her blouse were already undone. Askin for it, that type. As horny as he'd made himself waiting for Noel, he was just the man to give it to her. He stretched his reef runners under the corner of the table so she could see. Mr L. L. Bean.

'I'm sorry you didn't like them,' she said. 'Would you like something else?'

He touched her ankle with his toe, and she moved her foot. 'Now that you ask,' he said, his voice sort of low in his throat, 'I might need a place to lay down later.' He was thinking that if she refused him, he might follow her home anyway.

'Did you want to speak to the manager, sir?'

'What for? I ain't gay. I mean you.'

She turned and walked to the bar, where she said something to the bartender, who looked over. Jerry put his hands on the table to push it away and almost tipped it over. He saved the table, but his glass tumbled onto the soft carpet, and two or three ice cubes skated away.

'Don't worry, I'm leavin,' he said. 'Long's you don't expect me to pay for buffalo parts that's about to poison me to death.'

Sal shut off the ignition as he turned onto the Village Road. He let the momentum carry him onto the bridge, where he eased on his foot brake and stopped, set his feet apart on the grating and balanced the bike between his legs. The river whispered below him, peepers chorusing off to his left. He looked up the hill at her building, darkened except for the two front windows in her upstairs apartment, wondering whether to go up there and ask her about what Bouchard had said – that he and Wicker had been together up there that night. And now Bouchard's telling him that someone was trying to pin Wicker's murder on *him*? He wondered, and not for the first time, if Bouchard himself had planted the cap, loosened the bleeder.

or Bobby

He decided to stay on the bridge for awhile, until her lights went out – and if he saw her pass by the window, he would go up. He would not ask about Wicker, not tell her about finding his cap or about his brakes failing. Not tonight anyway. He sat and watched her windows. Not a car passed. Five minutes went by, maybe ten, with no sign of her.

A chill rose off the water. Downriver, peepers sang anxiously. He lifted his collar, pulled his cap out of his pocket and fit it on his head. *Evidence turns up*, Bouchard had said.

He looked behind him into the darkness, thinking he had heard movement in the trees. But the river was too loud to distinguish any furtive sound. The river. Something about the river bothered him – its persistence, maybe – or indifference—

Evidence turns up.

Sins come back.

That's how the Passamaquoddies had put it. *Sins come back*. The legend was well known in town. In the spring of the year, when the river was still deathly cold, a young man would make his way to the reversing falls. He would sit alone on the sandbar between the river and the pool all night and wait. During the fifteen minutes when the incoming tidal waters made their noisy way over the rocks, defying gravity, the man would take off his clothes, walk into the water and lie on his back in the middle of the flow. It was believed that his past sins would ride in on the tidal waters and wash over him. If his transgressions were few, and if he were truly repentant, the spirits of his ancestors would protect him: he would survive the ordeal and emerge from the river absolved. But if his sins were many, or severe, in the morning his body would be found face-down in the pool.

Now the river rushed under Sal's feet, tearing into the black woods, and an acrid mist rose up through the grating, surrounding him. Downstream, peepers screamed. Above his head, a battery of clouds attacked the moon, further darkening the night. And then his uncooperative mind circled a darker notion. What if—

All at once the peepers stopped.

Someone was down there, down at the pool. Sal's fingers tensed on his handgrips. As he listened, the sound of the river washing over rocks began to sound like soft, secret laughter.

Sins come back.

The fear climbed into Sal's chest, and without another thought, he kicked the starter, engaged the gears, then pulled away, not looking back.

Everything was dark when Jerry left the hotel, everything black and still, as if the entire world were asleep. What he felt like doing was driving straight back to town, waking that smart bitch up and teaching her a good thing or two about keeping her word. But now, with her new locks on the doors and the whole building rigged with alarms – and Alston Bouchard and the detectives and god-knew-who-else keeping their eye on her – fat chance.

So now what? Randy as a three-balled bull in a henhouse, he walked alongside the brick building, looking over at the dark tenements across the street and wondering which one of those groundfloor windows opened onto a girl sleeping by herself.

He turned around the back of the building where the parking lot was even darker. Streetlights out too. Stupid fucking hotel with a pitch-black parking lot. He had gone to the front desk to get his money back for the room, but even that was closed up. So now what? Having forgotten where in the parking lot he had left his truck, he had to navigate his way around the other vehicles by lining up their shapes with the reflection of streetlights from across the wide river.

No one around. No lights for the customers. Good place to

get hurt, Jerry thought. Generate a little income. But then they'd say he was drunk – which he was. The bartender and waitress would testify to that. So, fuck 'em, he'd sue their asses too. Plump little thing dressed like that. Prancing around, waving her college butt in the air like a little white-tailed deer, bending over at the tables, giving everyone the tittie show.

Did you want to speak to the manager, sir?

Good place to get hurt, alright. It felt like the night was poised for it, the way his soft new shoes Indian-whispered over the asphalt. Very good place.

He found his truck where he'd left it four hours ago – when the lights were on and he had felt a whole lot better about things, all showered and shaved and dressed in his flatlander clothes – which no one in a million years would ever guess was him. He opened his door and pushed in behind the steering wheel, facing the hotel. Only the lounge windows were lit downstairs, however dimly. Bambi probably counting her five dollars in tips. Everything else was dark and done for the night.

It wouldn't be long, he thought. She'd come out feeling her way in the dark. See what she thinks of Mr L. L. Bean now, ripping off those college girl panties and stuffing them in that sassy little mouth while he teaches her something about customer service.

He stuck his key in the ignition, turned to accessory power. 'Ring of Fire,' by Johnny Cash, was on the radio. Country Gold. Jerry turned it up a little, to let her hear it when she came out, imagining it'd get her curious and she'd come over to investigate. A little louder, actually, in case she puts up a fight. He rolled down his window, slouched back, folded his arms, leaned the back of his head against the back window and set his eyes on the corner of the building, watching, waiting. His head against the window?

That's when he realized: his gun – his shotgun was gone!

The truck suddenly rocked, and before Jerry could wonder why, an oak log smashed through the glass behind him and struck the side of his face. Falling forward into the steering wheel, Jerry recoiled and started to turn, when the same log smashed through the window again, two gloved hands following in the shower of glass. Jerry tried to duck, but in the same instant he felt a fierce constriction around his throat. His head snapped back into the broken window. Stiff shards snapped against the top of his head. But his throat! He gagged, groped for the constriction and felt absolutely nothing except the fabric of his turtleneck jersey.

He reached behind his neck, felt the gloved hands, hard as knots, twisting around each other. That's when he found the wire, tight and thick, like fence wire. He realized he was being killed. He shot his elbow back, it struck the cab. He wanted to fit his head back through the broken window, to relieve the pressure, but whoever held the wire was pulling much too hard, and he couldn't bend his head to get it through.

Then he was aware of something hard and cold pressing against his cheekbone – someone standing outside his door. The man spoke in a low, almost comforting voice through Jerry's open window. 'Okay, my friend,' he said, 'you've got ten seconds to save your life, and I'll tell you how.'

Friend? Jerry made a gagging sound down in his throat below the wire to show that he understood. The man reached in across Jerry's chest, turned the radio louder, Johnny Cash boomin on 'bout how it burns, burns, burns. Fuckin' A.

'I can either shoot you right here through the ear, or my colleague behind you can give this piano cord one more good twist, which is the way we prefer it. Less noisy, no mess. You, on the other hand, would probably rather take the slug. Less pain and suffering.'

The man in the back of Jerry's truck gave a sharp grunt, the wire tightened unbelievably, the knuckles digging into the nape of Jerry's neck. Jerry's butt came off the seat. His legs straightened and his feet pressed the brake to the floor. He picked at the wire with his fingers, but as thick as his turtleneck was, he couldn't get his nails under it.

'Of course, we could also let you go. I'm guessing that's the option you'd prefer, am I correct?'

Jerry made a clipped, strangling sound, his eyes swelling, ready to blow.

'That's what I thought. Okay then, I'm going to ask you one question. Accordingly, you'll have one chance to answer.'

'*And only one,*' said the man in the back of the truck, his mouth practically touching Jerry's ear, his voice higher-pitched and much less comforting.

'Ready for your question?'

Jerry stomped the brake twice.

'Now, we know that you recently wrote a letter; and, furthermore, that you are now using that letter for the purpose of blackmail. See, we all know that for a fact. But what only you know, and what we *need* to know, is exactly where you hid that letter. So now you tell us.'

'And then we'll let you go,' said the voice in his ear.

Again Jerry stomped twice.

'I think he's going to tell us,' said the man with the gun.

'Hands on the wheel,' said the man with the wire.

'Put your hands on the wheel,' repeated the man with the gun.

Jerry reached out, took hold of the steering wheel, his throat wrung with wire, his face bulging.

'Now my colleague is going to release a little tension from your throat in order for you to give us your answer,' said the gunman.

'However,' added the wireman, 'if you give the wrong

answer, or if you take your hands off the wheel or otherwise piss us off, I'm gonna slice through your freakin neck like a piece of provolone. And then he's going to shoot you through the eyes.'

'Are you ready to give us your answer?'

Jerry stomped the brake three times.

'I think he's ready.'

'Okay then,' said the wireman, and he shoved his fists alongside Jerry's neck, releasing the garrote from his neck. Jerry sucked in a harsh whistle of wind, and it caught in his throat, choking him.

'That happens,' said the gunman. 'Take your time.'

Jerry gagged, felt almost like he was going to be sick. The muzzle of the pistol poked his ear.

'Okay, friend, now tell us where you hid that letter.'

Jerry gasped, shut his eyes.

'Tell us now.'

Jerry strained for a breath, filled his lungs. 'Friggin liars,' he whispered. 'You won't kill me unless I *do* tell you!'

Immediately the fists punched into the back of his head again, and the wire snapped against his throat – except this time the wire caught his skin above the turtleneck material, above his Adam's apple, and Jerry rose off his seat, strangling. His fingers went to his neck, trying to pick at the garrote.

'Hands on the wheel!'

Incredibly, the wire tightened, slicing into his flesh. Jerry's knees pummeled the bottom of the dash.

'*On the wheel!*'

Obediently, Jerry grabbed the steering wheel, pulling and pushing on it so hard that its shape began to change. For several seconds while he strangled, nobody spoke, except for Johnny Cash, that is, boomin and burnin, until all of a sudden the radio went quiet.

Then the softer, more reasoned voice of the gunman.

'Okay, my friend. Now I'll have to introduce a rider to our first rule, and that is, if you don't answer our question correctly this time, then you will be tortured until you do.'

'Tell him about the eyes,' said Wireman.

'Now, you called us liars, and I have to say I take personal umbrage at that remark. I gave you my word as a gentleman, and I give you my word again: You tell us where you hid that letter, and we will let you go.'

'Tell him about the eyes,' Wireman said again.

Jerry made a choking sound deep in his diaphragm.

Wireman pushed his face into the broken rear window, close to Jerry's ear. 'See the way your eyes are poking out right now,' he said, 'like a couple of ripe olives? If I wanted to, I could just dig in with my thumbnail and pop that one right out.'

Jerry could not even blink. Now Gunman leaned further in the side window. The muzzle of his pistol pressed hard against Jerry's cheekbone.

'Okay, Jerry, tell us where you hid the letter.'

'The eyes go first,' said Wireman. 'Then the ears, the tongue – we snip them off with pruning shears – then your thumbs. And that fuckin hurts.'

'Jerry, tell us where you put that letter and we'll let you go. Now, we know it's not in your truck, because we've been all through your truck.'

'So then we deduced that you must have hidden the letter in your house. Is that right? Is that where the letter is?'

Jerry forced a grunt, stamped on the brake.

'Was that a yes, in your house?' asked Gunman. 'Loosen up,' he said to Wireman, and the wire suddenly relaxed, peeling out of Jerry's flesh, the man's fists separating behind Jerry's neck and pushing up under the ears, giving the wire an inch of slack.

Jerry made a strangling sound as he gasped for air.

'Just shake your fucking head,' Wireman said. 'Did you say yes, it's in the house?'

Jerry took another breath, let it out noisily. He lowered his head.

'Wait a minute, he's trying to talk,' Gunman said to his partner.

Jerry took another breath, then raised his face, sat up straight.

'*Pigfucker!*' he rasped, and then with a grunt, he lurched forward, caught the wire against his turtleneck, and pulled against the steering wheel as hard as he could, throwing his big shoulders powerfully forward, dragging Wireman's arms through the rear window clean to the shoulders. In the same motion, Jerry grabbed the wrist that held the gun and pulled the gunman's arm deep into the truck. Then, jerking back again, he created enough slack in the wire to grab it with his right hand, and before Wireman could uncoil the wire from his gloved hands, Jerry pushed the wire forward with all his might, hauling Wireman's head and shoulders through the broken window until Gunman's pistol and Wireman's face were touching.

'*Look out!*' shouted Wireman. Jerry slammed the gun barrel down on his temple, hard enough to make him grunt, but not hard enough to knock him out. Adrenaline surged. Gunman's left fist came searching through the open window, punching at Jerry's face, and Jerry warded off the blows with his left shoulder, while Wireman desperately worked his wrists, trying to unwind the wire. To slow down Gunman, Jerry forced his pistol hand up against the windshield, making it necessary for Gunman to cross his punches over, effectively disarming him. To slow down Wireman, Jerry kicked his right knee up and caught the man's jaw, making a loud *clack*. Wireman cursed, seemed to get stronger. His wrist swiveled and suddenly came free of the wire. Just as fast, Jerry let go of the wire, got his hand around Wireman's neck, thumb hard in his gullet. Wireman threw his left elbow back, connected with Jerry's chest. Jerry retaliated by shoving Wireman's face straight down as his knee came straight up, caught him square. Wireman's head snapped back, as if off its hinges. Jerry kicked again, needlessly – the man was out – but Jerry's knee connected anyway and his foot kicked the dash, the keys gouging his toe knuckle through his nylon shoes. The shoes showed him the way out.

Leaning hard to his left, still clutching Gunman's gun hand and Wireman's neck, Jerry angled his foot upward so the key pressed into his toes. While Gunman continued to throw rapid but powerless punches, Jerry squeezed his first two toes together, caught the tip of the key and twisted his foot, leaned hard to the right, taking Gunman's arm and Wireman's head with him.

The engine turned, started. Jerry reached his left foot to the gas pedal and stomped it. The engine roared. He banged into gear with Wireman's face, and the truck shot forward. Gunman cried out, became an anchor, his body turning backwards. Jerry suddenly let the gun hand fall away as he grabbed the wheel and cut left. The truck jumped. Jerry braked. A gurgling scream came from behind him. Shifting with his knee, Jerry banged into reverse and kicked the gas. The truck shot back, met instant resistance. Jerry braked again. The cry strangled under the truck. Deftly, Jerry toed the accelerator and brake in tandem, and the back of his truck climbed.

Still holding Wireman by the throat, Jerry jammed the gearshift into park and threw his door open. Wireman, emitting a pinched, squeaking sound, started moving an arm. Jerry rammed his head into the doorjamb; Wireman's body once again fell limp. Jerry staggered out, hauling the unconscious man behind him; knees and toes tearing through the

broken rear window, then bouncing out the door and onto
the pavement. Gunman, pinned face-down under the rear
wheel, moaned painfully. Jerry spotted the man's pistol lying
on the asphalt beside him. He gave it a kick, sent it spinning
underneath a van beside them. Then he dropped Wireman in
a heap.

Gunman groaned. 'Oh, man, get it off. I can't feel my
legs.'

Jerry bent over him. 'This is a brand new Chevy half-ton,'
he rasped.

Gunman breathed loudly.

'Now you best tell me what you did with my shotgun, or
next I'm gonna drive it straight over the top of your head.'

'Oh, listen,' Gunman whispered, 'we only wanted to shake
you up a little—'

At Jerry's feet, Wireman stirred, sounded like a dog
whimpering in his sleep. He pulled his knees up, looked like
he was thinking about crawling under the truck. Jerry placed
his reef runner on his hip, pushing him over onto his side.

'And you,' he said, 'trying to cut off my head—'

He bent down, grabbed Wireman behind his knees, turning the short man onto his back.

'Oh,' Wireman said, protecting his head with both arms.

It was a wrestling move. Jerry had seen it hundreds of times
before, never had a chance to use it himself. Now, locking
Wireman's knees in his arms, lifting the man's hips off the
pavement, he jerked back and turned to his left, sweeping the
man's head and shoulders into the air.

'Oh,' Wireman moaned.

Jerry, leaning back, swinging Wireman by the legs, made a
full revolution and then stepped toward his truck. The sudden bang of skull against tailgate stopped his motion. He
dropped the man in a motionless pile behind the truck.

'I swear,' Gunman said, 'we were gonna let you go.'

Jerry reached over the side rail, felt among the logs, chain saw, gas can, toolbox, empty beer cans, until he found his shotgun. He lifted it out.

'Honest to God, we never killed anybody in our life—'

Jerry slammed the shotgun butt down between the man's shoulder blades.

'*Huh!*' Gunman said.

Jerry leaned into his truck and set the shotgun in its rack, where it belonged. 'You tell her she's paying for the damage to my truck,' he rasped as he stepped in behind the wheel and Gunman groaned. 'And another thing,' he said, shutting his door. 'Tell her I get the friggin hint.' He punched into drive, hit the accelerator and heard a vicious screech, leaving one strip of rubber on his way out.

At midnight Iris finished folding the laundry and turned off the television. The days without Sal were full and hectic and long – endless, with work and study and house chores and tending to Davey. Evenings were the worst, after Davey went to bed, closed up in her hollow, unforgiving house with no other adult to talk to. So she did homework until after midnight, when she was finally tired enough to sleep, and then she went into the bathroom, where she washed and brushed, and finally she climbed up to her bedroom. She took off her jeans and hung them in the closet; took off her jersey and her bra and was setting her alarm clock when she became aware that a low rumbling had just stopped outside the house. When she heard the squeal of the kitchen door, she pulled on her nightshirt and hurried out of her room onto the landing. By the time she had reached the stairs, Sal was down at the bottom, looking up. Iris's finger went to her lips, silencing him before he could speak. She tiptoed across the landing and pulled Davey's door closed, then went down the stairs, feeling self-conscious about her bare legs. She walked around him into the kitchen, directly to the door, intending to see him out. She did not want a conversation.

'I know it's late,' Sal said to her.

'We'll have to figure something out,' she told him, opening the door. 'You can't just come over because you have a key.'

'Iris, I need to ask you—'

'Can it wait till Sunday?'

'*I need to ask you.*'

'Shh,' she said. The sharpness of his voice, the look on his face. Iris stiffened.

He folded his arms, looked awkward doing so, as if he didn't know what to say now that he had her attention; or else he didn't know how to stand in his own kitchen anymore. 'I found my hat,' he said. 'Remember I couldn't find my hat?'

The wall clock whirred between them. She looked at him. *Ask.*

'What I wanted to say – I'm trying to remember – Eliot Wicker, was I a friend of his or – an acquaintance – like maybe back in the summer? I'm a little blocked.'

'I don't know what you did last summer.'

He nodded contritely. 'The other night – after my show – do you know what time I came home?'

She sighed. 'Sal, the end of this conversation is you promising to never drink again and asking to come back – and me having to refuse.' She punctuated her statement with her eyes, so soft and gray behind her specs, yet so unyielding.

He shook his head staunchly. 'Iris, I have not been drinking,' he said. 'I'm telling you, I'm over that.'

'Are you over *her?*' Iris glared for an instant, then shut her eyes, wishing she could erase that. Unable, she took a stiff breath, let it out and moved to the door. 'You have to go.'

'Iris, I need to know,' he said. 'I need to know this.'

Her eyes suddenly focused beyond him. He knew that Davey was there. He turned and saw her staring from the bottom of the stairs.

Iris moved quickly. 'Love, please go back up to bed. Daddy will come see you on Sunday.'

But Davey was not retreating. Iris turned on the stairway light, then bent and grazed Davey's head with her lips, saying to her, 'Daddy's just leaving now.'

'Go ahead, hon,' Sal said. 'Day after tomorrow.' Managing a smile, he made a casting motion.

Davey continued to stare, adamant.

He went to her, stepped around Iris and let Davey's hair slide through his fingers. He leaned over and kissed her on the cheek, then knelt beside her and put his arms around her warm back and held her. He wanted to tell her, too, that he was sober and that he would remain so. But the look Davey gave him made him feel like his chest was collapsing. 'Day after tomorrow,' he said again—

All at once Davey's face shone brilliantly, and a colossal boom rocked the house.

Iris cried out. Davey sat hard on the stairs. 'Jesus!' Sal said, capturing his daughter in his arms, covering her.

'It's on fire,' Iris said.

Sal looked back. Through the lace curtains at the bottom of the stairs, he could see that the garage attached to her father's house across the street was fully engulfed.

'I'll call the fire department!' Sal said, releasing Davey and pushing past Iris, turning the corner into the kitchen.

Iris pulled the curtains back and stared. Already the right side of the house was ignited, flames jumping up the sky blue shingles.

In the kitchen, Sal turned on the table light and hit the FIRE button on the automatic dialer. The phone rang three times before it was answered.

'Fire department,' the sleepy voice answered on the other end. Noel.

'It's Sal.'

'Hi. You're on the fire phone, you know.'

'There's a fire,' he said. 'My father-in-law's house, across the street. Royals'.'

There was a pause, and then Noel asked dryly, 'Where are you?'

He tried to decipher her tone. Concerned? Curious? No, she sounded almost casual. He glanced back and saw Iris in the doorway, watching him. The window curtain flickered wildly behind her.

'It's going up fast,' he said into the phone. 'Hurry up, I'm going over to try to get them out.'

'Be careful,' Noel told him, and he hung up. The siren began wailing in the village before he was out the door.

In the living room, Davey moved back to the third step. Iris came and stood in front of her, watching out the window as Sal ran across the street toward the conflagration. Chickens, dancing in the driveway, scattered from him as he bounded through them, shielding his face from the heat. Thirty feet from the house, he was driven back.

Already the fire had worked its way to the front door. The window on the right was pulsing in flames, and black smoke shot out the peak vents both left and right.

Iris could feel the heat through the window glass. And now, beneath the wailing of the firehouse siren and the hard crackling of flames, she detected a dull, steady pounding, like someone beating a drum out of rhythm.

In seconds, flames were surging out all the windows, black smoke pumping into the sky, her father's house roaring like a waterfall. Above the roar, she could hear high-pitched squealing, loud popping, glass breaking. To the right of the house,

Sal stripped off his leather jacket. Holding it in front of his face, he seemed to wade into the flames.

'Mommy?' Davey cried.

Iris peered into the fire, trying to see where he had gone, trying to see also if her father or brother had escaped. But all she saw was the white chest freezer on the knoll in back, lit up brilliantly, the blue gospel bus just beyond, the random trail of junk cars and snowmobiles dancing in the firelight. Besides the scurrying chickens, there was no sign of life, not even Sal; just the flames eating up the shingles, slapping at the eaves in a solid sheet, hollowing out the house. Already its flimsy skeleton was evident, compliantly holding up the flames. In the village the siren wailed on. Iris realized that the pounding had stopped.

'Mommy, I'm afraid,' Davey said.

Iris hardened herself with rationalization: If they had gotten out, they were saved; if not, they were already dead. There was nothing she could do. 'Feel,' she said.

Davey reached out and touched the window glass, then pulled her hand away, giving her mother a look of horror. All at once, as they both watched, the garage across the street fell in with mocking slowness, taking with it the attached right wall of the tinder house. The roof dropped four feet at the corner, nodding. Waves of sparks bellowed into the sky.

'I want Daddy to come back,' Davey said, her voice shaking.

The siren of a fire engine suddenly distinguished itself from the firehouse alarm and the crackling of flames. Headlights cut through the smoke.

'Here they come,' Iris said as the fire truck pulled up, red lights flashing.

'I don't see Daddy.'

A smaller fire truck came up behind. Iris watched a man

jump out and grab a black coat off the side. Now cars and pickup trucks began converging from both directions, men in black fire coats hauling the fire hose from the bigger truck.

Another siren screamed in from the right, and a rescue van came in behind it, yellow lights flashing. Men ran shouting, pulling on gear, carrying axes, shovels, portable water tanks. Martha Abraham hurried down the road in her bathrobe, taking flash photos with a pocket camera. A man and woman from the rescue van hurried past her with a stretcher. Another man, adjacent to the back corner of the house, began wheeling his arm, hailing the stretcher-bearers.

'I don't see Daddy,' Davey said again.

The shouting suddenly intensified as a diesel engine raced. The men holding the fire hose planted themselves, and a thick cord of water exploded from the hose. The instant the water hit the house, the entire front wall fell in and the roof collapsed in a dense, loud wall of smoke and sparks. Through the rolling black cloud, suddenly Sal appeared, circling around the back of the ruins, laden with a hulking body in his arms.

Davey pressed her face close to the window. 'That's him! That's Daddy!'

As Sal struggled away from the fire, he was pursued by a concentration of men in fire gear, their faces concealed by breathing masks attached to their helmets. Four of them bore the empty stretcher.

It was her father in Sal's arms, Iris could tell by the shape, and she wondered how Sal could possibly lift him. A uniformed woman hurried alongside Sal, holding a mask to Otis's face.

Davey looked fearfully up at Iris. 'Is he dead?' she asked.

'I don't know,' Iris answered. The deeper truth was – and this hardened her more – she did not actually care.

At the road, Sal transferred Otis to the stretcher. As rescue workers wheeled him into the ambulance, two other men tried to attend to Sal. One was Herb True, the fire chief, who looked like he wanted Sal to get in the ambulance too. The other tried to put a mask to Sal's face. But Sal waved them both off, trudging heavily through the smoke and headlights. Giving up, Herb signaled the ambulance driver. A woman climbed into the back with Otis and closed the door, and the vehicle took off with lights flashing.

Iris watched out the warm window. Sal's face was blackened, and smoke rose off his back and shoulders. He stood there balancing himself on the roadside, and then he looked across the road at his house, at the front window, where his wife and daughter were watching him. Iris closed the curtains.

An hour later, the last three firefighters quietly wound the hose onto the truck. Only the small pumper remained in the Royals' driveway, ostensibly to prevent the fire from reigniting. But with the ground saturated from the recent rain and the barrage of water from the trucks – and nothing left of the structure but the four corner cinder blocks that had been its foundation – there was little chance of a fire spreading. The main reason the men stayed was to wait for Jerry to come home.

At two o'clock he did, a chill wind whipping through the broken glass behind his head, his neck raw and burning from the necklacing he'd received, his brain racing with the plans he had for Noel Swift. Fifty feet from the destruction, he hit the brakes.

His house was gone.

Gaping out his windshield, a wave of light-headedness overtook him. Where he'd once had a home and a bed, a TV and VCR and recliner, now only a heap of black rubble remained, surrounded by his stony, junk-strewn land.

'Oh boy,' he said.

The fire truck's headlights illuminated his bathtub, sink and toilet clustered together in the ashes, gleaming white. His stove and refrigerator. Worthless survivors, like the chickens that wandered in the road, dazed and homeless; the blue gospel bus; the old chest freezer up on the rise—

'Oh boy,' he said again.

He pulled the truck to the foot of his driveway, shifted into park and left the motor idling as he stepped tentatively onto the road. The freezer, up in the new grass, shone in the pumper's headlights as if it were on stage.

'Jerry?' It was Herb True, heading him off.

'Where's my house?' Jerry said.

Herb's voice was unusually somber. 'We got him outta there,' he said, shaking his head sadly.

Blood turned icy in Jerry's arms; his face grew hot.

'They took him to Downeast. Sal Erickson pulled him out. He'd got himself trapped in the bathroom and punched his way through the medicine cabinet. Must've took it for a window. He drove that sucker right through the side of the house, but then he got stuck halfway out. He's burnt up pretty bad.'

Jerry continued walking up his driveway, twenty feet of gravel that led nowhere. He looked up at his freezer again. 'So what am I gonna do now?' he rasped. 'I suppose the power's out.'

'You want,' Herb said, 'we can offload your frozen goods. Probably room at the Superette, if Noel doesn't mind.'

Jerry stared at the freezer for a second. Then he looked straight at Herb.

'Jerry, you got a place to stay?' The voice came from inside the fire truck. Alston Bouchard.

Jerry ignored him, turned and walked down his driveway.

'Jerry, you okay?' Herb called. Jerry didn't answer. He got

in his pickup truck, circled around and was driving away even before he shut his door.

'Downeast Memorial!' Herb called to him. 'Check the emergency ward.'

Sal sat on his bed and ran a B-flat blues scale up and down, turned it into a rough *Misterioso*. His breath was tight, his lungs gnashing each time he drew a breath. He played because he couldn't sleep, he couldn't go home, couldn't talk to Noel, couldn't take a drink ... because he couldn't fathom his own thoughts. So he played on, grateful there were no neighbors to disturb. His face was parched, red and swollen, and his eyes burned so badly that he kept them closed. Even after showering and tossing his clothes out the window, he continued to smell smoke with every breath. But he played on, hoping to remember.

He thought of Avery Bingstream, the school principal, his arm in a cast. Sal was told that he had pitched the principal off the stage and broken his arm. He recalled nothing of it, not a glimpse. Sober, he never would have harmed the man, who was decent and sincere and gentle. But, blinded by vodka, he had assaulted Avery Bingstream with no apparent reason or remorse.

That same night, Eliot Wicker had been bludgeoned and buried alive. And now Bouchard was telling him that he and Wicker had been together an hour or two earlier. So where was the night hiding? Somewhere deep in his memory, walled over by this narcosis, this uncooperative mind.

He set the trombone on the bed, leaned over to the telephone and called Rhode Island directory assistance, got his parents' phone number. He dialed, then lay on his back while he listened to the phone ring.

'It's Sal,' he said when his father answered.

At first there was no response.

'It's Salvatore, I'm up in Maine.'

Another pause. 'How are you?' his father said, although he didn't sound like he wanted to know.

'I've been teaching school. Eight years. What are you doing? You retired?'

'I was just sleeping. It's very late.'

'You still carving decoys?'

Sal waited while the big man cleared his throat. 'Some.'

I saved a man's life tonight, what do you think of that?

'How's Mom?'

No response.

'I want to talk to Mom.'

'I got her in a home.'

In a home. 'I want to talk to her about Anthony – about the day he drowned.'

Another pause.

'There's no point now.'

'No, there is. I want to get something straight.'

'It's in the past—'

'*Yeah?*' The word came out in a laugh. 'Maybe *your* past.'

His father responded, 'We can't change what's in the past.'

'I didn't tell him to go out on the ice, you know. Do you think I did? Do you think I pushed him in?'

'Why don't you call back another time when you're feeling better—'

'No, why don't you tell me what you think I did that day, because my memory's shot, and I'm never gonna feel any better than I do right now. I saved a man's life tonight, Dad, what do you think of that? I'm a goddamn hero tonight.'

The phone clicked dead.

Up in his boarding room, Sal laid his arm over his eyes, still holding the phone. He pictured the old house, his mother standing by the back door, looking out the window; the ruffled, red-checkered curtains, the sunny little porch filled with grocery bags of apples ... and nobody speaking. He reached over and replaced the receiver in its cradle. Chuckled once, bitterly. *In the past.* He turned over, moving slowly at first. Then, in a blur, he lunged across the bed, toppling the night table and telephone, until he was on his feet, his fist arcing toward the wall, the framed print of a four-masted ship in the storm.

Darkness covered the town, a steady, solemn quiet. Up at the village, only the fire station remained lit, one of its garage doors opened on the empty bay, while two cars waited outside for the pumper's return. A hundred feet back, the Superette stood closed and dark.

Even Jerry's truck was quiet as it swung down the driveway. Headlights off, engine off, his tires barely humming. He braked without a sound and then quietly opened the door. Up on the road he heard the fire truck drive past; he watched its lights flutter over the treetops, from left to right.

Smart bitch, she had hired the hit men, and then she'd set the fire, any fool could figure that. Lured him up to Bangor to have him killed and then burnt him out to destroy his blackmail letter. Smart bitch, high time somebody took some of that smart out of her. He stepped quietly onto the driveway and moved to the door in his soft new shoes, with barely a hush. He didn't have her new keys, but a locked door or an alarm wasn't about to stop him now. He took hold of the doorknob—

To his surprise, it clicked open. Smart bitch, so she burnt his letter. Too smart for her own good – she forgot to lock her own door. What did she think, that he was too stupid to figure it out?

The shadow that rose in front of him was about to answer his question when a voice behind him yelled, '*Jerry!*'

Startled, he spun, and a pistol shot fired. Jerry jumped clear. A second shot rang—

'*That's enough!*' the other man yelled, standing beside the door, his back pressed to the wall. 'That's enough!' he yelled again.

A light came on inside the garage, flooding out the open door. The man standing against the wall was Alston Bouchard. '*Don't you shoot me!*' he said.

'Alston, is that you?' Noel's voice, from inside.

'It's me.'

'He was breaking in.'

'I know.'

Jerry lay flat against the garage door, his heart pounding. He ran his hand up his shoulder to the right side of his face, feeling for blood. He had *heard* the bullet zing past his ear.

'Jerry, you alright?' Bouchard asked him.

'*Jerry?*' Noel said, stepping outside. 'Jerry Royal?'

Jerry raised his arm, felt the torn elbow of his new jersey. 'Fuckin A,' he whispered.

'You were breaking in, Jerry,' Bouchard told him. 'She's got a right to protect her property.'

'Jerry, what were you thinking?' Noel said from the doorway, the revolver in her hand. 'I could have killed you.'

Bouchard looked down at him, also waiting for an answer.

Jerry raised himself to his elbows, weighted by a weakness that approached nausea. Oh, she's suckered him good.

'In case you didn't know,' he rasped, 'I just lost my house! What happened to neighbors helpin neighbors?' He pulled himself to a sitting position, where the faint window light illuminated the glistening raw line on his neck, as well as the dried blood on the turtleneck and shoulder of his jersey. Another blotch marked the knee of his right trouser leg. He looked like he'd just finished a session with his chickens.

'Jerry, what happened to your neck?' Bouchard said.

Undone

Seeing how far he was from the door, Jerry realized he had jumped a good ten feet in the air. 'Cut myself shaving,' he answered as he struggled to his feet, leaning on the building for support.

Testing his legs, which were still shaky, he looked back at the door. 'Fuckin blue shoes,' he said with some amazement, thinking for the second time tonight that the reef runners had saved his life. He brushed the seat of his trousers and turned to his truck, and that's when he saw the bullet hole in the door. His shoulders dropped.

'Jerry, you really have to be more careful,' Noel said. 'You can't just go opening people's doors.'

Jerry wandered to his vehicle, touched the bullet hole. He looked at his shotgun hanging from his broken back window, considered pulling it out and blasting her Volvo. He would have, too, if Bouchard hadn't been standing there.

'You got somewhere to go?' the constable asked him.

'*Yes.*' Jerry twisted the word into two syllables, even with his raspy voice. 'Won't be the first time I slept in this thing.' He got in his truck and slammed the door; threw his elbow out the open window, then said, 'Alston, where'd you come from, anyways?'

'I was down your place with the fire truck,' Bouchard answered.

'What *used to be* my place,' Jerry corrected him, glaring at a vague area between Bouchard and Noel.

'Followed you down here to see if you had somewhere to spend the night...'

'Yeah, well.' Jerry started the pickup, gunned it some, then gunned it some more just for the barking it made. 'Brand-new truck,' he said, disgusted.

'Jerry, I'm sorry,' Noel said. 'I'll call my insurance company in the morning.'

He hit the gas and pulled the truck straight for her –

stopped with a chirp of rubber – jammed into reverse and shot back into the tulips that bordered her swimming pool.

Bouchard started toward him. 'Jerry, you need to calm down.'

Giving Noel another look, Jerry gunned it good, flinging a few pounds of topsoil and whole, flattened flowers into the chlorinated water. When his tires hit the asphalt, they gave a generous screech, and he shot up the hill and was gone.

After the sound of his engine trailed away, Noel breathed a sigh. 'Thank God you were here, Alston. I'm so jittery, I might've killed him.' She looked down at the pistol in her hand as if the thought had just occurred. 'Oh, no, am I in trouble?'

'Nope,' he answered, 'you've got a right to protect your place.'

'He was trying to break in.'

'I saw that.' Bouchard sniffed. 'Funny, though...'

'What?'

'Well, why you'd turn your burglar alarm off.'

'I didn't *turn* it off,' she told him. 'I still don't know how to program it – God, you need a degree in engineering.'

Bouchard stood there, saying nothing. With his hands hidden in his pockets, all dressed in black, it was hard to see him.

'Alston, where's your car?' Noel asked.

'Over the firehouse. But the other thing I'm wondering ... Why you were...' He gestured toward the garage, but she couldn't see.

'Excuse me?'

'Downstairs in the dark.'

She folded her arms, the .22 still in her hand. 'Alston—'

'I don't mean to...' He rubbed his hands together, then shoved them back in his pockets. 'It's just that it's late, and all your lights were off...'

'I've become an extremely light sleeper these past few days,' she said. 'I heard the truck pull in and I came down.'

She heard keys jangle in Bouchard's pockets, and she figured he was just about finished. 'Home all night, were you?'

'Alston—'

'It was you that took the fire call—?'

'That's right. Sal Erickson made the call from his house, I answered the fire phone, and then I sounded the alarm. Are you finished interrogating me now?'

For a few moments there was only silence, and she thought he wasn't going to answer her. Then she saw the moonlight glint across his glasses. 'Yup,' he said, and he turned and walked up the hill.

10

Dressed in his new, torn, bloodstained jersey and trousers, and wearing his lucky blue shoes, Jerry Royal sat on his chest freezer and watched while the woman poked through the blackened remains of his garage. She wore a plain blue sweatshirt with no insignia, no badge. Her trousers, however, were uniform: black with shiny black piping. She held a leash in her hand, with a German shepherd on the other end, sniffing at the ashes. They had positioned themselves this way – Jerry on his freezer, the woman and dog in the rubble – for almost two hours. She was big-boned and meticulous. He liked the way her butt filled her trousers.

'Find anything?' he called over, as he had from time to time. This time the woman was bent over, talking to her dog, and she did not hear. Down past her, beyond the slab, Jerry caught sight of Sal walking up the driveway; Jerry shielded his eyes from the sun and made out that his brother-in-law was carrying a cardboard box.

'I brought you some clothes,' Sal said as he came closer.

Jerry gestured to the collection of boxes and bags strewn around the freezer. 'People been bringin me things all morning. Two cases of Coke, you name it, toaster, electric lamp, FM radio – and me without electricity. Christ, I got more fuckin cookies than you wanna know.'

Sal shrugged. 'People like to help.'

Jerry threw his arms up. 'So how 'bout someone bringin me a new house! I mean, cookies, really.' He took the box of clothes from Sal and bounced it in his hands, gauging its weight as if he were making a trade. 'Kind've on the musty side,' he said, then dropped the box down beside the others.

Sal looked at Jerry's bloodstained turtleneck. 'They've been in my garage,' he said. His right hand ached from punching his wall. His face and arms were red from the fire, and his eyes still burned.

'How come you keep 'em out in your garage?' Jerry said. 'You got an attic over there.'

'Iris doesn't like the attic.'

Jerry sniffed. 'She don't like the attic.'

'How's your dad?' Sal asked.

'Perfectly good storage space, but she don't like the attic. So your clothes get musty. That's women for you.'

'What happened to your neck?' Sal asked him.

'Nothing,' Jerry answered, 'I cut myself.' He turned abruptly to the fire investigator. 'Anyways, you can rule me out,' he called. 'I was fifty miles away, up in Bangor with a dozen witnesses, in case you got any ideas.' He gave Sal a small, triumphant nod and said, 'Government woman.'

The woman didn't turn. 'I'm not looking for suspects at this time, Mister Royal, just a point of origin and probable cause. Kaiser seems to think accelerants were involved. It was definitely a hot fire.'

Jerry looked at Sal again. 'You need a uniform to tell that?'

Sal kept his eyes on Jerry's neck.

'She prob'ly told you about last night.'

'Who?'

'Who do you think?' Jerry replied. 'Noel. I go down there to see if I can use her freezer and she takes a shot at me. Pops my friggin truck. Wasn't for Alston, I'd be a dead man right now.'

Still picking through the rubbish, the fire inspector asked,
'Mr Royal, did you work on motors out here?'

'Chain saws, snowmobiles, you name it, I fix it.'

'You used gasoline or some other solvent—?'

Jerry didn't respond.

She stood up, turned to look at him. 'Gasoline to clean with
– in uncovered containers?'

'Nope.'

She lifted a blackened coffee can so he could see. 'Like
this?'

'Can't prove it by me.'

'It's not a crime,' she said. 'Definitely not smart, but not
against the law. Besides, fuel alone does not a fire make.
You also need ignition, something to start the flame. Did
you have an electric lamp on the workbench, a droplight of
some kind?'

'What?'

'You were raising chickens in here, by the looks of it –
hatching chicks?'

'I was hatchin 'em out in a box.'

'And you used the droplight to keep them warm—?'

Jerry raised his face.

'It's not the first fire that's started this way, Mr Royal. You
have a dog, maybe?'

'Not anymore.'

'They'll get after the chicks, disrupt the light. They could've
easily knocked over the can of gasoline. Then again, it could've
been anything, raccoon, fisher, cat—'

Jerry leaned forward in disbelief. 'You sayin animals burnt
me out?'

'Then again, it could've been one of the chicks themselves.'

'Oh yeah,' Jerry said as he slid off the freezer. 'Some chick
alright.' Sal gave him a curious look.

'People are always surprised,' the investigator said. 'That's why we say, "Keep gasoline in covered containers."' She pushed her notepad in her top pocket, over a breast. Just like that. Then she gave her leash a tug, and the dog followed her out of the ruins.

'Well, thank you, Mrs Smoky the Bear,' Jerry muttered, walking toward the blue gospel bus, which sat on a slight rise off to the right.

Sal watched the fire investigator get into her car and drive away. When he turned back to look for Jerry, he saw a green seat fly out of the gospel bus and land on top of two similar seats. Piled around the seats was an assortment of engine parts and several bulging trash bags; a television, a wooden door.

Sal walked to the bus, climbed the two steps and looked inside, down the gray corridor. Ratchet in hand, Jerry was bent over one of four remaining seats, unbolting its base.

'I wanted to ask you,' Sal said.

'I'm right here.'

'Blueberry Blossom Night—'

Jerry stopped working; he turned his head to the side. 'What about it?'

'I'm trying to remember. Did I see you that night?'

Jerry rose to his feet. 'Maybe you did, maybe you didn't. Maybe you tell me.'

Sal shook his head, wondering if the reaction was just Jerry's normal guardedness. 'I can't remember,' Sal told him. Considering the ordeal Jerry had been through over the past twelve hours, Sal decided not to push it any further. 'What about Alston Bouchard?' Sal said.

'What about him?'

'You think he's on the level?'

Jerry bounced the ratchet in his hand. 'The things you can count on in this life: shit happens, women'll fuck you up, and Alston Bouchard is on the level.'

Sal chuckled, although the implications of Bouchard's levelness were less than comforting. 'Just thought I'd ask,' he said, and he backed down a step, preparing to leave.

'Ol' Mr Do-good,' Jerry continued, bending to his task again, 'and look what good it does. Nothin to his name but a fifteen-year-old Jap car that shoulda been scrapped the day it left the boat and a piece of land no bigger than that fallin-apart trailer parked on it.'

'He's got land,' Sal said. 'What about those hills behind him?'

'Not his land,' Jerry said. 'Used to be. Prob'ly a thousand acres that family owned, at least until Alston's mother died.'

'What happened?' Sal said.

'Lost it, I don't know, ten, fifteen years ago. Eliot Wicker took it over.'

Sal stopped his descent, took hold of the railing. 'Wicker took it?'

'Well, bought it, technically. But he bought it right, part in trade for the funeral, part for the back taxes the old lady owed. Hey, those days everybody was losin their blueberry land to the big growers or the developers, take your pick. Wicker had the old house bulldozed down and then put the land up for sale in some New York magazine for a half million dollars, which no one in their right mind's gonna pay that. But he sat on it, every year leased it back to Alston for the berries. That's how he paid for his New York advertising. Charged Alston more than the berries were worth.'

Sal thought back to the business files he had searched at Wicker's house, wondered how he had missed that transaction. 'Was his mother's name Bouchard?'

Jerry shook his head. 'Blackstone. The old lady married again after Alston's father died. Indian fella from Canada, name of Blackstone. Only lasted a couple of years himself.

Died of cancer, they said, but most people figure Indian, prob'ly drank himself to death.'

Sal nodded.

'Lotsa stories,' Jerry said, turning back to his work. 'Lotsa stories.'

'Just thought I'd ask,' Sal said, turning out the door.

'No harm in askin,' Jerry answered.

The Silver Bullet was all the advertising the Superette needed. With the mobile crime lab parked in the lot, the store stayed crowded all day, filled with curious townspeople lingering over coffee or ice cream, or stopping for gasoline they didn't need, watching as men in blue lab jackets carried paper bags and boxes out to the van.

It seemed like everyone had a theory, or at least a notion, about the mystery. Now, with Shepherd upstairs questioning Noel for the second time, the lunch counter crowd was busily and quietly reassessing.

The whispered consensus, at least among those who had known Bobby Swift, was that Bobby had pulled off a one-in-a-million scam and was basking in the sun somewhere waiting for Noel to join him.

'Get real,' the potato chip man said. 'It's your classic cover-up job. She poisons him for the insurance, and the undertaker discovers it during the embalming. He tries to blackmail her, she does him in, and then she buries the husband's body out in the blueberry fields to hide the evidence.'

'Really,' Bonnie said as she flipped bacon and burgers, 'don't you people have better things to do?'

'I say it's your classic makeup job,' argued Herb, her husband.

Down the length of the counter, heads turned.

Tamping cherry tobacco in the bowl of his pipe, Herb

242

explained, 'I think Bobby came back to take his revenge for Wicker's makeup job.' The others made noises of approval.

'Not funny,' Bonnie said.

'I don't hear anyone laughing,' Herb replied.

Shepherd prided himself on his interviewing style. He never bullied, never threatened, never accused. He liked to think that he made friends with the people he talked to, even those from whom he secured confessions. Indeed, most of his suspects would eventually grow so rattled over the course of an investigation that they were actually relieved to finally be able to confess to him. He liked it that way. He liked the psychology of it.

Settling his long frame on Noel's couch, he eased into a conversation about the weather, the blackflies, the tourists, as if this were nothing but a social call: 'Once April rolls around, they come from everywhere – Japan, France, Australia – and now the Cayman Islands. You know, until this plane ticket showed up, I didn't even know where the Cayman Islands were.'

Noel sat curled like a cat on the other side of the couch, her green cotton shift pulled tight over her legs, waiting him out.

'From what I hear,' he said, 'Grand Cayman has the best diving in the world.'

Noel unfolded herself from the couch and got to her feet. She stretched, then walked away. 'You like Gnawi?' she asked, crossing to the wall shelves, where she turned on her stereo.

'Hm?'

'The Gnawa people, from Marrakesh.' She punched a couple of buttons and an eruption of drumming started, dark, humid and hypnotic. Noel turned up the bass, moved her knees with the beat. She came back to the couch and stood there, still moving, looking down at Shepherd as a chorus of chanting joined in.

'Detective, we both know scuba tanks were found on Eliot Wicker's body. And you obviously think the plane ticket to Grand Cayman Island is significant. Please don't patronize me.'

He smiled. 'I'll try to be more direct. Was Bobby a scuba diver?'

She bent to sit down again, and her shift fell away from her body, revealing a fleeting view of her breasts. 'Bobby, a skin diver?' She sat cross-legged, pulled a lime-green pillow between her legs. 'Maybe before I knew him. He did everything else. Skydived, raced motorcycles. When we got married I made him stop.' A smirk escaped her, self-deprecating. 'I didn't want to lose him.'

That's when he saw it – the eyes – always watch the eyes. And hers had just watered over. He softened his approach, took his fingers off the keyboard and leaned back against the couch arm. 'You never did tell me how you guys met.'

Noel fingered a lock of hair off her cheekbone. 'I didn't think it would cast any light on Eliot Wicker's murder.'

He shrugged. 'Probably not. Just curious.'

'I quit college,' she said, 'and then I started modeling in Boston. His ultralight company contracted with the agency.'

'Hm?' The chanting made it hard to hear.

'Ultralights,' she explained, 'one-person airplanes. You don't see them much anymore.'

'You said you modeled.'

'They put me on the dunes in Truro, in a black leather one-piece and an apple-green crash helmet that showed just my eyes. It was Bobby's idea. I think he was after the S-and-M market.' She gave Shepherd a sharp look.

He pretended not to notice. 'So he wrote the ads, he flew the things, I imagine he got down in the trenches and helped put them together too.'

'That sounds like Bobby. But I wouldn't know. I never got involved in his business.'

Shepherd nodded thoughtfully and was about to respond when a loud knock overpowered the drumming.

Noel turned to the door without expression, and before she could get up to answer the knocking, the door opened and Sergeant Murdoch was standing there.

Shepherd rose from the couch, setting his computer on the coffee table. He glanced at her stereo system as he went to the door, wishing the music were softer, or different. 'You got something?' he asked the sergeant.

Murdoch looked around the room.

Shepherd stepped into the stairway with him and pulled the door closed. The drumming seemed to throb against the wood.

'Sounds like you're having a meaningful interview in there,' Murdoch said.

'What've you got?'

'Nothing,' Murdoch answered cryptically.

Shepherd waited.

'Two million bucks.'

Shepherd studied the sergeant, who pulled a narrow pair of reading glasses from inside his blazer. When he had adjusted them on his nose, he withdrew a document from the same pocket and carefully unfolded it, a fax printout.

'Robert Swift,' Murdoch read, 'three-million-dollar business loan from River City Savings and Loan, Fall River, Massachusetts, January third, nineteen eighty-eight. One year later he files for bankruptcy after defaulting on his loan. Brought to trial in nineteen ninety, found guilty of tax fraud and falsifying receipts to obtain the loan. Three years probation and a hundred-twenty hours' public service.'

'Yeah? What about the money?'

Murdoch glanced over his reading glasses, then continued. 'Loan officer Charles J. Mariotta, the bank employee who made the loan, convicted on the same charges – falsifying records and tax fraud. But get this – fourteen years in prison.' Murdoch removed the glasses. 'Mariotta's doin time, and there's two million dollars unaccounted for. The government bailed out the bank.'

Shepherd leaned back against the wall, felt the drums beating in synch with his heart.

'Two million bucks,' Murdoch said again, self-congratulating.

Shepherd made a fist, whispered, 'We got him.'

Murdoch took off his glasses and slipped them back inside his blazer. 'I went through Boston and Providence. Providence came through.'

Shepherd took the fax from him. He looked at it a second, then said very quietly, 'I'm not gonna let on to her. I'll ask her a few more questions, then head back to the barracks, start a search in the Caymans for Bobby Swift – or Dale Newman, if that's his alias. He'll never see it coming.'

Murdoch was already shaking his head. 'Nobody gets jack shit outta that place. Boggs even tried Interpol, but they kicked it back. The case isn't *advanced* enough.' Murdoch looked almost happy about it.

'How advanced do they want? We've got enough to charge him and bring him back. The fact that he's even alive is insurance fraud, to begin with. Incontestable.'

Murdoch, still shaking his head. 'We're gonna have to get it from her. She's an accomplice. Got to be.'

Shepherd paused, seeing the challenge in Murdoch's expression. 'What if Dale Newman wasn't Bobby Swift's alias but actually a third accomplice? He didn't use his plane ticket because Swift got rid of him the same night he did the undertaker. I say we try the Cayman people again, find

Bobby Swift. He's a sure thing. And that's where the money is.'

Murdoch gave a futile but satisfied shrug. 'It's not our country, not our rules.' He nodded toward the drumming. 'Let's go back in there and double-team her. Tell her what we've got, I'll promise her thirty years in Thomaston, she'll give him up in a minute.'

Shaking his head, Shepherd reached for the door, giving the impression of blocking it. 'She's too smart for that.'

Murdoch snorted. 'Jeez, I hate to offend, but from what I hear, you haven't had much luck with smart women.'

Shepherd gave him an indulgent nod. 'I'll let you know if I need you,' he said.

'It's against the rules to screw it out of 'em, you know.'

Shepherd looked at him, didn't respond.

Murdoch snickered, then said, 'I'm going down for a bite to eat.' He began a slow, cocksure descent down the stairs, then stopped, as Shepherd knew he would. 'Don't get too cute in there,' he said. 'I wouldn't want to have to take over the investigation.'

Noel was standing at the front window when Shepherd came back into the apartment. He closed the door and walked straight to the stereo receiver, turned down the volume.

'Good news?' she said, though she seemed mildly distracted by something outside.

Shepherd returned to the couch, took the computer off the coffee table and returned it to his lap. He folded his hands over the keyboard, looked over to her.

'See, Noel,' he said, 'what's weird about the Caymans – their crazy confidentiality laws. Six hundred banks on those little islands. Twenty-four hundred corporations and trusts, with a mandatory three-year prison sentence for anyone who divulges information about any depositor.'

'Tax haven for the ruling class,' Noel said, returning to the couch and sitting down beside him. 'You'd think we'd wise up.'

'Except in drug cases. Then our two governments have what's called reciprocity, which means they'll cooperate. Murder cases too.'

'This is a murder case,' she said indifferently. 'Call them.'

Shepherd looked at her. He reclined on the couch, folded his arms confidently and didn't take his eyes off her. 'Noel, we found Bobby's two million dollars.'

Her eyes narrowed on him. 'What?'

He laughed effortlessly. 'Come on, Noel, now you're patronizing me.'

Her back straightened. '*What two million dollars?*'

'Noel, you have to admit—'

'*Nothing!*' In a single motion she was on her feet, glaring down at him fiercely. 'You come into my home and my business, degrade me in front of the entire town, and now you tell me that my husband was hiding two million dollars from me – while you sit there so smug and superior so you can watch my reaction—'

'Noel, I don't enjoy this any more than—'

'Do you want a fucking reaction?'

She grabbed a cut-glass vase of tulips off the coffee table and hurled it past his head.

When the upstairs window blew out, Sal was filling his gas tank, waiting for the detectives to leave. Window glass, green water and red tulips rained down the front of the store. Percy the fingerprint man, on his way to the lab van with a cardboard box, ducked under the flying debris, then hurried back inside the store. In a matter of seconds Noel charged out the front door. She headed directly for the gas pumps, pinning Sal with a secretive stare. Over her shoulder she carried a large, red leather handbag. Behind her, the door swung open and Shepherd came out. It was easy to see by the way he followed her that the detective had been the cause of her wrath.

'Ask me if I want to take a ride,' she said to Sal when she reached the gas island. A bottle neck protruded from the top of her bag, its top sealed – Stoli vodka.

As Shepherd came closer, Sal leaned his hand against the gas pump, a barricade to keep the detective away from her.

'Noel, just five minutes more and we'll be through,' the detective was saying.

Now Murdoch came out of the store too, eating a hot dog, sauntering toward the island, looking pleased. 'Everything under control, detective?' he said.

Noel narrowed her eyes at Sal, cuing him. But he concentrated on the pump, stopping the gas at five dollars and replacing the nozzle in its cradle. He screwed on his gas cap, still feeling her stare. He turned and looked at her, full on.

'Would you please get me away from here,' she said to him. She was not asking.

'Get on,' he told her. He flipped open a saddlebag and she stuffed her handbag in.

'Mr Erickson,' Shepherd said, 'where are you heading today?'

Sal took off his leather jacket and handed it to Noel.

'Hey,' Murdoch said, showing Sal the pâté of hot dog and bun on his tongue, 'you were asked a question.'

Noel shoved her arms into the heavy jacket, said to Sal, 'They think Bobby and Eliot Wicker staged Bobby's death. And then Bobby murdered Eliot—'

'Nobody said that,' Shepherd corrected.

'Is that what happened?' Murdoch asked her.

—'and now Bobby's supposedly living on Grand Cayman Island with two million dollars—'

'Could be ten by now, with interest,' Murdoch said. 'You tell us.'

Shepherd held up a hand. 'Hold on,' he told his sergeant, then turned again to Noel and said, 'I do apologize if I offended you—'

Murdoch snorted a laugh.

'—but we have made no such inferences in this case. We are simply following leads and asking pertinent questions, same as you would do in our position.'

Their attention was momentarily drawn to Alston Bouchard, who came driving into the lot, directly to the island. His black lab was riding shotgun.

'If you're here for gas,' Shepherd told him, 'I suggest you go somewhere else.'

Sal looked over at Bouchard, made eye contact, then swung a boot over the Harley seat and turned the key. 'Let's go,' he said to Noel.

Murdoch moved in from the side, puffing up his chest. 'We'll tell you when she's ready, smart-ass.'

'Noel, it really is in your best interest to cooperate,' Shepherd said. 'Five minutes, no more.' He held up five fingers, gave her a look that was just short of pleading.

Ignoring him, she zipped the leather jacket, then stretched a long bare leg over the Harley, her short skirt notwithstanding, settling in behind Sal, high on the queen seat. Sal pressed the starter and the engine rumbled to life.

'Mr Erickson,' Shepherd said, 'you didn't tell us where you were going.'

Sal checked behind him, ready to pull out.

Murdoch said, 'Yeah, where's that smart mouth of yours now?'

Sal shifted into first, gave the throttle a turn and roared out of the lot, Noel's arms wrapped around his chest.

* * *

As the sound of the motorcycle got lost in the bright afternoon, Murdoch turned to Shepherd and said, 'I'll tell you right now, I don't like that greaseball.'

'Hard to tell,' Shepherd replied.

Behind them, Alston Bouchard cleared his throat. 'Bobby Swift you're looking for, if I'm not wrong.'

Paying no attention to him, Shepherd took a felt-tipped marker out of his pocket and inscribed a wide circle on the window of the gas pump, where he had seen Sal lean his hand. 'Make sure nobody touches this,' he said to Murdoch, and then he walked into the store. In a minute, Detective Percy accompanied Shepherd back out to the gas island, carrying a black attaché case. As Bouchard and the detectives looked on, Percy opened his case and brought out a small plastic container the size of a spice tin. He opened the box and carefully poured iron shavings into a cupped piece of paper. As he held the paper up to the pump window and gently blew the fine powder over the glass, Bouchard opened his car door and stepped out, held the visor of his cap to block the sun.

'That casket they buried Bobby Swift in,' he said. 'I imagine if Bobby was still alive, if somebody had dug him up, then that casket'd be in pretty good shape. Inside, I mean.'

Roundly ignoring him, Shepherd watched as Percy waved a small magnetic wand over the face of the gasoline window, and uncommitted iron powder rose, gradually revealing four fingers and a thumb. 'Nice,' Percy said.

Shepherd bent over, picked an evidence tag out of the black case and handed the tag to Murdoch. 'Initial this for him,' he said, walking away. 'I'm going back inside.'

'Detective Shepherd, I'm talking to you,' Bouchard said.

Shepherd turned his head as he continued walking. 'You're interfering in my case, Mr Bouchard—'

'*My town!*' Bouchard declared, pointing a finger at the

asphalt under his feet. '*This is my town.*' The depth of his voice stopped Shepherd like a wall, and the detective turned. Or perhaps it was the depth of the constable's conviction. It *was* his town, and he was its protector, and Shepherd understood at that moment that nothing he could do, short of arresting the constable, would alter that fact.

The two men stood ten feet apart, glaring at one another. The fingerprint man stopped writing. Murdoch moved in beside Shepherd, wiping his mouth with his handkerchief. Two or three customers stepped out of the store to watch.

But when Bouchard approached the detective and spoke again, it was too quiet for anyone else to hear. 'You seem to think that Bobby Swift is alive, don't you?'

Just as quietly, Shepherd responded, 'I take it you don't.'

'I believe things'd be considerably quieter if he was,' Bouchard said.

Shepherd nodded again. Pretended to mull it over. 'That's an interesting theory, Constable. Except for one thing: The inside of Bobby Swift's casket is good as new.'

He gave Bouchard a sustained look, then added, 'I know if I lost my life trapped in a casket, fighting for my last breath of oxygen, I might do a little damage.' He turned back to the store and started walking. 'Have a nice day,' he said.

SUGAR COATED PUFFS OF CORN! Davey brought the bag of yellow cereal into the living room with her and settled into her beanbag chair in front of the television. Some Saturday afternoon movie about a creature that looked like a giant lizard devouring Tokyo pedestrians, although you never actually saw the eating part, you only saw the shadow fall over the person about to be eaten, and then you heard him scream. Other than that, only bowling, golf and a gardening show were on, so she watched the monster movie and ate the sugar puffs out of the bag and tried to keep her mind from wishing that her father was there. When she heard the screen door open, she jumped out of the beanbag and ran into the kitchen, thinking it was he.

But it was her uncle standing between the doors. Uncle Jerry – though she had never called him that, never actually spoken to him at all. She unlocked the inner door before she thought about what she was doing, and then wished that she hadn't.

'Gawd, I didn't expect a grown-up girl,' Jerry said, his blue eyes traveling down to her red sneakers and back up again. 'Look at the size of you!'

'My mother's delivering a baby,' she said to him, staying in the doorway. Davey knew she should have said that her mother was upstairs taking a nap, but she figured it was obvious that her mother's car was gone.

'Anyways,' Jerry said, lowering his voice as if he were about to share a secret with her, 'I bet you don't even recognize me.' He was bending toward her, and his breath smelled strong, like a bunch of onions gone bad. He had a brown bloodstain on his jersey.

'Yes, I do,' she told him.

'Hah? You know your Uncle Jerry? Hey, we're lettin the blackflies in.' She stepped back as he squeezed in, and the screen door shushed closed behind him. He looked around the room, over her head. Blackflies don't come in, she thought.

'Same table,' he said, walking across the kitchen. 'Same chairs, cupboards.' He opened one, swung it back and forth. 'Different squeak.' He had something on the seat of his pants that looked like he had sat on a fat spider; gum or tar.

He walked out of the kitchen toward the living room, stopped at the stairs and looked out the front window, ducking under a heavy, hanging planter pot. 'You see the fire last night?' he said.

Davey nodded. She noticed the charred blue reef runners on his feet. She wondered if she should tell him that she was sorry about his house burning down, the way adults console one another.

He took hold of the rail. 'Yup,' he said, starting up the stairs, the narrow risers creaking under his weight, 'same old everything.' His dialect reminded her of Mr Walker, the school custodian, and Mr Philbrook, one of the older bus drivers. It was a friendly, country sound. But she wasn't sure she liked him going up the stairs like that. She followed a few treads behind.

'My mother'll be home pretty soon,' she said, trying to be hospitable about it.

'My old bedroom too,' he said. 'Prob'ly you got it now.'

The top of the stairs led onto the landing, a scuffed pine floor, wide boards, with knee-high wall storage on the facing wall; bins for doors. To the left and right of the landing were the two bedrooms, the master bedroom on the left, hers on the right. As Davey mounted the landing, she could see Jerry looking into hers.

'There it is,' he said. 'Right over there, my bed, under the window.'

Davey didn't come any closer. 'I thought that used to be my mother's room.'

'Both of ours. We slept together when we was kids – same bed even, but ol' mother put an end to that just 'bout the time it got interesting.' He turned his head, giving her a strange grin.

'Do you remember your mother?' Davey asked, changing the subject.

Jerry came back onto the landing, looked up at the ceiling, at the square, hatch cover made of gray shiplap boards and a black iron handle. ''Course I do. I was fifteen when she got killed. I almost bought the farm myself that night. Frigged up my leg for life.'

'My mother said she was mean.'

Jerry doubled his chin. 'Mean?' He snorted like a horse. 'That woman didn't have a mean bone in her body. *Mean?* I can't believe your mother said that. Christ, the ol' lady thought the sun rose and set over that girl. Always buyin her new clothes, settin up with her, readin books. I got stuck with the old man. With Mother, you was always safe, no matter what stupid thing you did. Never holler, never hit, never so much as look at you cross-eyed. Mean? I'd say *your* mother's got her memory banks screwed up.' He looked up at the hatch again, and his raw, red-lined throat poked out of his turtleneck. 'I can't believe that one. Mean.' He looked down at Davey, gave her a quick nod of his head. 'Ever go up?'

Davey shrugged.

'What, you never been up?'

A black handle in the ceiling. That's all the attic had ever been. A handle and a warning. Now, the way he was talking, the prospect of going up excited Davey a little. She shook her head.

'Whoa. How about your mother or dad, they ever go up?'

'My mother said it wasn't safe.'

'Well, by the Christ, what kind of horseshit is she feedin you over here?' He reached up and gave the handle a tug. A cloud of dust fell over them like a blizzard, while a gray wooden ladder jumped out of the dark and unfolded noisily from the hatch's underside. Jerry pulled on the ladder, and a second ladder unfolded from it, skreaking as it unfolded a third time, until the whole thing extended to the floor, like steep, narrow stairs. He put his blue shoe on the bottom rung and pushed, and the ladder snapped in place, straightening.

'Really, you never been up?'

Through the dust that continued to cloud the opening, Davey could see only darkness.

Jerry took hold of the rails as if he were about to climb up, then he turned to her. 'What'd she tell you 'bout it?'

Davey shrugged. 'I'd fall through—?'

He grinned, eyes sparkling. 'She said *that*?' He had a boyish, playful nature that Davey kind of liked. 'Well, then' – he swung off the ladder with one arm and put his hand on her lower back – 'you're in for a treat.'

Davey hesitated.

He gave her a dumb look, like a clown trying to be sad.

'Think about it. If it wunt safe, I wouldn't go up myself, and I'm about two hundred somethin pounds heavier'n you.' He nudged her. 'Come on. You got adult supervision.'

Davey knew that he could have tossed her into the attic with the one hand if he wanted to. But his touch was feathery light. And she really liked his shoes. She gave a moment's thought to her dress, that she should be more modest about going up a ladder with a dress on, ahead of a man. But he was her uncle.

'Here you go, little boost-up,' he said, taking her under the arms and lifting her up to the second rung, his hands so big that his fingertips touched one another across her chest. 'Nothin to be afraid of. Christ, couple years you'll be coming up all the time with your boyfriends.'

Something about that remark unsettled her a little. Maybe it was the way his voice had softened. 'Gaw'head. I'm right behind you.' She took another step until her head was level with the hatch. The first thing she noticed was the smell: dusty and wooden, like the inside of an old cupboard.

'You got a boyfriend yet?' That voice again. Davey felt the ladder sink as he stepped onto it, and she grabbed the rails, startled. 'Prob'ly still too young for that.' He took another step, and the ladder creaked. 'Not you, I mean the boys. Girls develop earlier, they just don't talk about it all over the place like boys do.'

Now she could feel his breath on the back of her leg. 'All girls got thoughts. Nothin to be ashamed of.'

She didn't like him so close, didn't like what he was talking about, didn't like the darkness above her, or him below—

'I want to go down now,' she blurted.

'*Daow!*' he said. 'Turn on the light, the string by your head. Gaw'head, I'm right here.'

Davey reached up, felt the hot air above her head, waved her hand around – and then she felt it, a little bead on the end of the string, it bounced out of her hand, then bounced off her wrist as it swung back again. She caught hold and pulled. The bulb flashed on above her, illuminating the reddish ceiling rafters, reddish chimney and darkness beyond. Davey's face at floor level, she stared up at the room and all its contents: a green carousel clothesline on its side – like a giant spider web – a brown kitchen chair, a dark chest of drawers, a dark bass fiddle leaning on the wall, a white wedding gown on a dress form, a dirty mattress beside it . . .

'Go on up,' he said.

Suddenly the attic felt terribly unsafe – scary – like the kind of place that would harbor ghosts. Davey shrank back, but Jerry held his hand on her bottom, squeezed her a little. 'That's it,' he said softly. 'I got you.'

'I want to go down,' she told him, lowering all her weight onto his hand, willing to fall if she had to. In fact, if she weren't on the ladder, she would have been running away from him as fast as she could.

'Easy does it, sweetheart,' he said. 'You don't want to go up, that's okay.'

He swung back, giving her just enough room to squeeze past him, and she spiderlegged down the ladder, barely touching the treads with her feet. When she reached the landing, she wiped her eyes.

Jerry looked back at her. 'I'm just goin up for a sec,' he said. 'But one thing.'

She looked up at him.

'Swear to keep a secret?' He was hanging off the ladder like an orangutan.

She nodded, barely.

'I'm hidin something up here that only you know about. Swear to keep a secret?'

He reached into his back pocket and pulled out a white envelope so she could see.

'Swear to keep a secret?' he said again.

She nodded again.

'Just in case anything ever happens to me – that means if I turn up missing or dead – then you tell your mother this is up here. There's somebody evil who wants to do something to me. This is my protection.'

He looked down at her in a way that made Davey's insides shiver.

'But if you tell anybody about it *before* I'm dead – then somebody's gonna come over here and do something to you. And your mother too. And anybody else who knows.'

Davey stared, stunned with fear.

'Swear to keep a secret?'

She made a small, dry noise of consent.

'You got to say it.'

'I swear.'

He went up.

Noel's legs, pink from the wind, pressed in around Sal's hips. Her arms wrapped around his chest. He turned his head and shouted at the wind, 'What two million dollars? What are they talking about?'

'Just go!' she shouted back. 'They're crazy!' He goosed the throttle, and they flew up a long hill.

'Why do they think Bobby's alive?'

'Go!'

Heading down the coast, they tore through quiet towns already populated with license plates from other states: black on white, white on green, yellow on blue: the first wave of tourists, idle retirees up for a taste of the rugged and quaint working coast.

And here came Sal and Noel – he, unshaven in black jeans and T-shirt; she, in black leather over a short cotton shift; both of them sticky with the salt and spring-flowered air, racing down the highway with no destination except getting away. When Sal saw the turnoff to Blue Hill, he took it. Noel leaned with him. It was an aggressive ride, soaring up and down the blueberry hills. Every now and then the ocean would rise in the distance, flat and silvery, broken by strands of islands. Sal felt edgy and unclear, but he was glad to have her holding him.

Coming down a long hill, he shouted, 'They say anything about Bouchard?'

'What about Bouchard?'

'Anything!'

'I don't want to talk about it!' she said, her hands crawling up his chest. 'Let's find an island somewhere – we'll never go back!'

He shouted sideways at the wind: 'What about me? They say anything about me?'

'Just forget it!' she shouted at him.

'Noel, I have to know!'

He pulled back the throttle some more. The speedometer jumped past seventy. They ripped through the wind. 'My brakes let go last night,' he yelled back at her. 'I think somebody opened the bleeders.'

'I think you're paranoid!'

He pulled back the throttle some more, to see what her reaction would be.

She pressed her mouth to his ear. 'Are they okay now?' she said.

'Yeah!'

'Good. Go faster.'

Cresting another hill, the Harley whipped over the top just under eighty. A white Saab suddenly appeared in front of them – with a pickup truck coming at them in the other lane. Sal didn't brake. He leaned left and shot into the oncoming lane, passed the Saab in an instant then swerved back just as the truck tore past, dust flying, horn blaring.

His jaw clenched tight, Sal kept his eyes peeled on the distance. *I think somebody's trying to pin this on me.* But he refrained from saying that to her.

'What happened with Jerry Royal last night?' he yelled.

'He's an imbecile!' she yelled back. 'He tried to break into my garage, and I shot at him.'

'I'll be sure to knock next time I come over.'

They screamed down the hill, the speedometer needle shivering past eighty. Approaching the bottom, he backed off as he leaned into a long leftward curve, then started up another hill. She nuzzled his ear with her warm mouth, her voice like low cooing. 'Let's find the most expensive hotel on the coast,' she said, her breath warming him. 'We'll pretend it's our last night on earth. We'll do things to each other that no one's ever done.'

The Harley dipped left, right, tore through the road sand. He straightened, easing back the throttle.

'We'll be animals,' she breathed. 'We'll be cannibals. We'll devour each other.' Her lips closed around his ear; he felt her tongue move inside. 'We'll feed each other poison. We'll eat orchids till we piss purple.'

Now her fingers were sliding to his belt. He was there
already, straining to get out. She unbuckled him, unzipped
him, then slid her fingers down the front of his jeans, took a
rough hold of him. 'Or maybe we'll find a lovers' leap,' she
said.

'You wanna jump?'

Still in his ear, still in his pants, she said, 'No. I think we
should throw each other off.'

He opened the throttle as she worked him over ... 75 ...
80 ... 85 ... all the while finding it more and more difficult
to ignore what Bouchard had told him the night before: *That
woman is a danger to you.*

Pulling into her driveway, Iris got out of the car and bent to
give Davey a kiss. 'Trudy has a baby brother,' she said. 'What
are you doing out here, hon?'

Davey shrugged. But the look on her face—

Behind them the screen door opened, and Iris turned.
Reflexively, she reared back.

Jerry held up his hands. 'Don't worry, I didn't steal anything, if that's what you're thinkin.'

It took a moment before Iris found her voice. 'Why is he
here?' she asked Davey.

'You're not exactly talking about a dog, you know,' Jerry
said. 'I come over for some water.' He looked right at Davey,
who averted her eyes.

Iris kept a firm hold on Davey's shoulder. Davey squirmed,
letting her mother know she was hurting her, but Iris wasn't
paying attention.

'The other thing,' Jerry said. 'I'm off the booze now, same
as the old man. So, whatever, I guess we can all be family
again. I didn't know what you wanted to do about him, the
house and all. We got no insurance.'

Iris glared.

Michael Kimball

'Well, hey. Sorry if almost burnin to death and losin everything we had puts you out.'

'Don't you come over here,' Iris said to him, her voice low in her chest, nearly trembling.

Jerry rocked his head. 'Well, there's a loving daughter for you. A real fine example you set.' He gave Iris a long distasteful look as he walked past her. Then, at the foot of the driveway, he turned once more. 'And that's another thing – your memory's all frigged up when it comes to Momma. She spoiled you rotten and you know she did. Which is why today you can't keep a man.'

They sat looking out the tall, multipaned window, the only two customers in a cozy dining room with crème fraîche wall and three antique oak tables. The moon, oblong and pale hung over the ocean like a stopped pendulum. A Beethoven quartet soothed through the inn, buoyed by the hush o breaking waves, crème d'Atlantique spraying over the jagged rocks. Through the flames of a double sided fireplace, Sa could see another couple in the adjacent room. They looked like lawyers or doctors, well-dressed, sitting close, talking intimately, exquisitely secure at their table.

Sal, in his T-shirt, and Noel, in her work dress, sat just a close, their bare arms touching, not saying a word. Bathed in the heat of the applewood fire, they spread chocolate butter on warm baguette and sucked smoked oysters from the half shell. Noel drank sixty-dollar Merlot. Sal drank seltzer with lime wedge. He had charged three hundred dollars on hi Visa card for a corner room upstairs, which they had yet to see. He glanced at Noel.

What two million dollars?

Sucking chocolate butter from her thumb, Noel returned secret look, as if she knew what he was thinking. But then h was thinking something else.

262

'You're eating chocolate,' he said.

She answered by sticking her wet thumb into the small crock and bringing it out again, crowned with a wad of silky chocolate. Still watching him, she brought the thumb to her mouth and slowly sucked the chocolate off. 'That's not all I'm eating tonight,' she said.

Their waiter appeared then, a portly, balding man in a white dinner jacket, carrying a second appetizer, a pâté of rabbit, along with a Stoli martini for Sal, straight up.

'I ordered it when you were in the bathroom,' Noel told him, touching his leg under the cloth. 'What I want to do to you up there, you're going to need it.'

'More baguette?' the waiter asked, his continental accent betrayed by a tinge of *mow-ah*.

Moving her fingers up the inner seam of Sal's jeans, Noel slid the basket toward the waiter, who thanked her and started to walk away.

'Wait a minute,' Sal said. The waiter stopped. Still holding Noel's gaze, Sal found his martini and held it up for the man. 'I promised Davey I'd take her fishing tomorrow,' he said, as the waiter took the drink and left the table.

'Fishing,' Noel said dryly. 'I'm hot just thinking about it.'

He smiled a little, distantly, and her eyes narrowed with impatience. 'Sal, where are you?' she said.

He looked at her. 'The night Eliot Wicker was murdered—'

She shook her head slowly, resolutely.

'Noel, I have to know. I was with him that night – in your apartment – wasn't I?'

By her silence, he guessed it was true.

'*I have to know.*'

As he watched, the candle flame liquefied in her eyes. When she spoke, her voice was almost fearful. '*You can't know*,' she said, and he realized in that long, floating instant that, indeed, Noel was afraid. For him.

His own fear burgeoned, pressed out against his chest. He took a deep breath, then whispered, 'Tell me.'

She checked the door to her right, looked through the flames at the couple in the next room, then turned back to him. 'You were all fucked up,' she said. 'Acting insane.'

He nodded.

'You couldn't go home. I was trying to sober you up.'

'What about Wicker?'

She paused.

'*Tell me.*'

'*I don't know.* He just barged in. I thought he was there for me – he'd made a couple of passes at me after the funeral. But—'

'What?'

'The look on his face when he saw you—' Noel lowered her eyes.

Sal took hold of her wrist. 'What kind of look?'

Noel shook her head. 'You said something to him I didn't hear, or I didn't understand – but it meant something, I could see the way you were looking at him. And then you left. Afterwards, Eliot stuck around making small talk, just long enough to watch you walk down the road. Then he left too.'

'That was it?'

She took another drink of wine.

'What time did I leave?'

'Sal, don't ask me any more.'

'Which way did I go?'

She turned toward the fire.

He moved his chair closer to hers. 'Last summer,' he said, 'I was working at the store, spending time with Bobby. We were both drinking too much. Did Wicker ever come over?'

'Every day,' she said, 'for coffee.'

'After hours, I mean.'

'After hours I don't know. You and Bobby didn't always stick around. Why are you looking at me like that? Sal, would you please have a drink and stop—'

'What they said about Bobby – that he faked his death—'

'*I don't know!*' She tried to pull out of his grasp, but he held tight. In the adjoining room, the other couple looked over. Sal, nonplussed, released her. Most of a minute passed while they sat, not speaking.

'I think I want you to take me home,' she said.

He met her eyes.

'Noel, if you were involved in this,' he said to her, 'would you tell me?'

She responded by matching his steady gaze. 'If I were involved in this,' she replied, 'I would not tell you.'

He stared at her.

'But I'm not involved in this,' she said. Then she leaned into him, opened her mouth and pressed it gently to his. He breathed in her chocolate, her smoked oysters, her apricot, her Merlot, he melted under the assault of her intoxicating tongue. He wanted to consume her, wanted to stop his racing brain, wanted to hold back time. Indeed, he wanted nothing short of oblivion with her. And he had an idea that oblivion wasn't far off.

The blinds drawn, the doors locked, Davey was finally asleep. Iris sat near the top of the stairs, level with the landing, staring at the footprints in the dust, going this way, going that way, like the primitive grounds of some ritualistic dance. Except no music came to mind. No ideas connected. Only the vague, leaden notion that her mother was watching ... always watching.

'*Why did you let him in here?*' she had yelled at Davey (and she never yelled at Davey). She didn't even give Davey a chance to explain. '*That's why we have rules!*' She slammed a cupboard door. It bounced back, and a jar of honey fell onto the counter and broke with a thud, lost its shape slowly.

'He just wanted some water,' Davey said in a small voice. 'You never, *never—*'

Davey stormed up the stairs in tears. Iris paced a few times, slapped the cupboard door again, waiting to discharge, and finally got a trash bag to put the mess in. She was aware that she had overreacted, but she had to make Davey understand. Understand what? The rules. The Ice Queen rules. Steps to take with an alcoholic family. One: she had discarded her husband. Two: she had watched her father burn without a tear. Three: she had turned her brother away when he needed water. All with perfect composure. Screaming at Davey was the sum total of her emotional involvement.

Iris scraped the honey and broken glass off the counter with a spatula, pulled it into the trash bag, tied the bag in a knot and set it by the door, then scrubbed the counter with a warm sponge, scrubbed the woodwork, wiping everything clean. Calm again, intending to go upstairs and apologize to Davey, she had stopped at the landing ... and that's when she saw the footprints.

Monster footprints, flat-footed prints circling in the dust like the feet of some big, lummoxy, goat-headed creature, while smaller sneaker treads moved tentatively on their toes. A fierce shiver started inside Iris, goose bumps skittering up her sides. Another spasm started her head shaking, a wordless, mindless refusal. It was a relief at first, the head shaking, but then when she wanted to stop, she found she could not. A noise escaped her, like a child's cry. She clamped down on it, terrified of losing control, forced the impulse down, and went crawling through the footprints, smearing them as she went, decimating them with her hands (angel wings, angel wings), keeping it down, blanking her mind, keeping it down, wiping everything clean.

Back in their room, a new fire crackled in the fireplace. Their bed was an antique four-poster, with a green silk canopy and green silk sheets. Two heart-shaped chocolates wrapped in red foil had been left for them, one on each of their pillows. The window was open just enough so they could hear the ocean, the surf charging against the rocks at long, lazy intervals. Sal sat at the foot of the bed, head down, leaning over his knees, listening to the fire, to the waves. Behind him, Noel crawled around the mattress like a cat, coming to him and finally pulling herself up his shoulders, her knees at the small of his back. He could hear her breathing, could hear the flames devouring the birch logs. She ran her fingers upward from his neck into his hair. Her thumbs pressed into the soft spot behind his skull, and then her hands moved warmly down his shoulders and biceps, her fingers finding their way up inside his T-shirt sleeves, her thumbs searching the dark humidity of his underarms. She pressed her face against his back and she moaned, as her hands moved down his chest to his stomach and then rose again inside his shirt.

She kissed his neck above the neckline, ran her palms up the flat of his stomach to his warm chest, softly covered with hair. She raised herself higher, pressed her body hot against his back and kissed his jaw below his ear. The dark shadow of his beard had grown through the day, and he considered how it must have felt against her cheek (like Bobby's face would have felt).

'God, can you stop thinking?' she said, and rolled away from him.

He took a breath and let it out. He looked back at her. Now she was lying on her side, back to him, facing the pillows. He lay down behind her, put his arm around her. Her breathing was slow and steady. He ran his fingertips over her skin, from her ear down to her neck, until goose bumps rose on her. With one finger, he lightly stroked her lips. With his thumb, he lightly traced her jawline. He breathed in her complex aroma. Her chest moved evenly as he caressed her, and then he pulled her shift down to her shoulders until it restrained her arms. Her breathing intensified. His hand went round to her chest, felt heat rising from her shallow cleavage, the top of her dress confining her. With his thumb, he forced the top button through its buttonhole. With his other hand he reached down to her thigh, then up under her dress. He bunched her panties in one hand and pulled them down to her knees. She began to turn, but he stopped her, held her shoulder down while he rose over her. He forced his knee between her legs. Unbuckling his belt, the leather tip flicked the back of her thigh and he heard her catch her breath.

He lowered his face to her ear. 'Is the temptation hard to resist, Noel?' he breathed.

'What?' she said, not moving.

'Those chocolates in front of you.'

Neither of them moved for a few seconds. 'What are you accusing me of?' she said.

Still holding her down, he whispered, 'I did not do this.'

She paused. 'Okay,' she replied, not looking at him.

He leaned down harder, gazing at her perfect ear, her perfect jaw, her supple, white neck – and he was swept with a sudden urge to take her by the throat.

He fell away from her, turned onto his back. Breathing. Listening to her breathe. Listening to the ocean, which sounded more like machinery now than a rhythm of waves.

'What is wrong with you?' she said, an edge to her voice. 'I said I believe you.'

He sat up, pushed himself off the bed. 'I'm going,' he told

her, taking his jacket off the chair. 'I'm going fishing with my daughter.'

She snickered.

'Do you want a ride?'

'Go,' she answered. 'Fishing.'

He took his keys off the vanity and went out the door.

Jerry Royal sat at his plywood table, his head thrown back against the window, a six-inch TV throwing bluish light on his face. Half awake, half asleep, he didn't hear the motorcycle pull into his driveway. But the instant his bus door squealed open, he was on his feet. 'Come on in,' he said, registering Sal, 'pull into a chair, my head's asleep.'

It was hot inside the bus. The power company had constructed a temporary pole at the end of the driveway, from which Jerry ran a long orange extension cord. Besides the TV and table lamp, he was powering a four-foot space heater that faced the table.

Jerry rubbed the back of his head briskly, trying to drive some feeling back in. 'Friggin bus,' he said. 'Thirty-whatever years old, prime of life, livin in a friggin gospel bus.'

He sat down again at his table. The plywood was propped on sawhorses, between the two facing bus seats. The Styrofoam cooler sat in the aisle beside the table. Empty cola cans littered the floor. Sal stepped carefully over the cans, noticed the muzzle of Jerry's shotgun sticking up behind the seat.

'Warm enough in here,' Sal said.

'Day at the beach,' Jerry answered, working his head around. 'She called you, huh?'

'Who?' Sal remained standing.

Jerry searched Sal's face. Than he gestured toward the road with his head. 'I figured my sister called to tell you I was over there today.'

'Nope.'

'Huh,' Jerry said. 'Well, I was. Great state of affairs when a man loses his house and all his worldly possessions and can't even go to his own flesh and blood for help.'

Sal sat down on a corner of the seat opposite Jerry. He rubbed the plywood with his palm, gathering grains of salt. 'I was thinking about that fire you had,' he began.

'Worst thing that ever happened to me.'

'I mean afterwards, why you didn't go over to see Iris last night, instead of Noel Swift.'

Jerry shrugged. 'Shoulda, woulda, coulda, hey. So I misjudged a woman. Wasn't the first time, and it sure the fuck won't be the last. Don't worry, I know where I'm not wanted. Matter of fact, I'm makin a list.'

Sal looked at him for a few seconds, then stood up from the table.

'You look worse than I do,' Jerry said. He reached into his cooler, took out a fresh can of cola and popped it open. 'You oughta try this stuff – caffeine. Keeps you alert.' He slapped at the back of his head. 'Lotta good it did. Friggin pins and needles, my head's still asleep.' He was still slapping his head when Sal left the bus.

11

Sunday morning the sky was white, and the forecast called for rain, yet the Superette was busier than usual. At noon, when Noel walked through the front door carrying her red handbag, Bonnie True was at the cash register selling beer and prewrapped grinders to a couple of fishermen, while Chad worked behind the meat counter preparing more sandwiches, and Erica made ice cream sundaes for the fishermen's sons.

Bonnie thought it peculiar that Noel came in the front rather than from downstairs, especially since everyone in the store could see that she had arrived in the back of a taxi (and she had left the day before on the back of Sal's Harley). 'How are you?' Bonnie said to her, but Noel went in behind the counter and up the stairs without answering. Bonnie gave the fishermen their change, then locked the register. 'Chad, mind the money,' she said, as she opened the door. Climbing to the landing, she spotted Noel sitting at the top of the stairs. 'I've been wondering when it was going to get to you,' Bonnie said.

In the living room, on the wicker couch, Noel bared her soul. Sal had been Bobby's best friend since they were boys, she explained. 'When Bobby died, he was wonderful, he took care of everything. And afterwards, the way he'd call and come over, to make sure I was alright. And then last night ...' She shook her head, unable to continue.

'Take your time,' Bonnie said.

Noel inhaled shakily, then let it out. 'After the detectives were here—'

'—I know—'

'—With all their questions, I was feeling—'

'—*pent up*. My God, who wouldn't!'

'I needed to get away. And then he was here. He offered me a ride. We ended up on Deer Isle. At the Urchin Inn.'

Bonnie nodded sagely. 'Mm-hmm.'

'I know I should have suspected. I was just so—'

'*Desperate*. You just don't *know* when you're in mourning.'

'He started drinking at dinner, and then after . . .' Noel stopped abruptly and just stared at her fingers, eyes glistening. 'I feel like such a jerk.'

Bonnie stroked her hand. 'Oh, I could see it from the start,' she said, 'the way he's been coming around. Like the friggin fox to the henhouse.'

Sal gathered the fishing rods and boat net from the garage and leaned them against the car. Dandelions blossomed around the tires of his car. He glanced across the street, where Jerry Royal was tending a fire inside his chest freezer, stirring up thick gray smoke with a flattened aluminum curtain rod. Gray clouds were lowering, keeping the smoke from rising.

'Ready, Freddie?' Davey said.

'Hmm?'

'To fish.' Davey opened the plastic bag of seaweed and bloodworms that Sal had brought. Blackflies swarmed around her head. Sal took a small bottle of fly dope out of his fishing vest. 'Hold still,' he told her, while he doused his hand and rubbed it gently behind her ears.

'I hate that smell,' she said.

'They'll be worse by the river.'

The back door opened, and Iris came out carrying a heavy cardboard box, duct-taped shut. She was wearing a flannel shirt and old jeans. She brought the box into the garage without a glance at Sal.

'We'll be back in an hour or two,' he told her, 'if you want to talk then.'

Walking back into the house, Iris gave him a look, not unfriendly but somehow detached, as if she hadn't heard him. Watching after she'd gone, Sal took the fishing rods off his car. 'Ready,' he said, and Davey took the lead across the road, joining the path that ran alongside the Royals' property.

'What are you defrosting over there?' Sal called over to Jerry. Standing in the smoke of his freezer, Jerry raised his nose, a hello.

'I heard your uncle was over yesterday,' Sal said to Davey. She kept her eyes on the path. She didn't mention Jerry's secret letter. Nor did she mention the fact that Iris had been up all night long washing and waxing all the floors in the house.

At the end of the field the path divided; one branch led straight down to the reversing falls, where the state had once maintained a picnic area complete with a barbecue grill, trash barrel and a sign that explained the tidal phenomenon and the Indian legend. The rightward branch, which Sal and Davey took, led through a stand of pines, then down a rocky bank to the fishing pool.

Their timing was perfect. The tide was in, and the pool was wide, dark and deep, the falls having reversed some hours earlier. By September the water here would be filled with spawning Atlantic salmon, the surface a carpet of red backs you could practically walk on. This time of year the pool was a feeding hole for schoolies – striped bass that hunted upriver with the tides.

Sal stepped down to his fishing rock, a wide slab of granite that overhung the pool. He took off his vest and made a cushion on the rock for Davey. Directly to their right, where the pool formed a small cove, river junk accumulated – plastic bottles and bags, hunks of Styrofoam and other floating things – everything that the last few tides had returned upriver and not taken back again. It was Sal's custom to bring a couple of trash bags with him when he came fishing; he'd scoop the stuff into the bags and bring it home to throw away. (Iris would jokingly refer to the debris as his 'plastic fish,' since Sal kept none of the real fish he caught.) Today he hadn't brought the bags.

When Davey was settled on the rock, Sal pulled out her line and set to baiting her hook with a fat, eight-inch worm. Davey turned her head when it started to curl. 'Hold still, hon, so you don't hook me,' Sal told her. When he was through, he released the line and wiped his fingers on the rock. The pretzeling worm swung out over the water, rocked by the counter-swinging of the red and white plastic bobber above it.

'Poor wormy,' Davey said.

Sal reached for her pole again, saying, 'You watch while I cast.'

'No, I want to,' Davey replied, already rearing her pole back, holding on with both hands.

'You don't know how.'

'Yes, Shannon's father showed me last summer. Remember?'

Sal plainly didn't. 'Just watch out for the trees behind us.'

Davey swung the rod two-handed, and the bobber slapped the water about four feet out, sending out wide, concentric waves.

'Want to try again?' Sal said, but Davey turned away from him, watching her bobber as it drifted slowly toward the bottles on their right.

Sal stripped his own line, tied on a rusty rat, then added a splitshot two feet up the line. He knew the whereabouts of all the submerged rocks, where the smart feeders would be hiding – one rock in particular – about thirty feet out. He gauged its location and then cast side-arm, easily. The tiny lead weight kissed the surface about ten feet upcurrent from the center of the pool, sending out narrow rings to the grassy sandbar that formed the opposite bank. The fly hugged the surface for a second, then sank, and Sal's line began drifting. He caught the line in the first joint of his index finger.

By now Davey's bobber was off to the right, in the thick of the bottles and bags and Styrofoam. 'If you leave your line there, hon, you might catch a plastic bass, but that's all.'

Davey gave him a dour look, then returned to her bobber again, apparently satisfied with its position (Iris's independence – he loved it in Davey). 'Maybe I'll catch this tube of hair goop for you,' she said, her bobber bumping up against a floating yellow-and-blue tube. 'Then you can get all dressed up and bring Mommy some flowers and propose to her again.' She started reeling in, trying to hook the tube.

Sal forced a gentle smile. 'I don't think hair goop'll work, hon.'

Suddenly she stopped. 'Daddy, I got one!'

He looked. She lifted her rod in the air so its tip bent down, but it didn't play. Her bobber hung in the air three inches above the cans and bottles, caught. 'Plastic bass!' she cried, as she let the bobber pull back down. Eyes wide, teasing him, she yanked up on the rod, making the bobber tremble, while the cover of river trash rocked in the turbulence she had created.

Then his own fly was hit. He jerked his arm, set the hook. 'Wait a minute, Davey, I got one,' he said. 'Real bass.'

It felt good, the way the underwater tugging shook his wrist. A healthy striper, to be sure, six, maybe seven pounds. He let the fish run toward the river, his drag *wheeing* as the line ran out. He saw that Davey was still holding her line taut beside him.

He glanced down at her. 'Don't force it, hon. I'll help you in a minute.'

Davey returned a terrified stare.

'That's just my drag releasing,' he explained, 'so my line doesn't break.'

But she continued to stare up at him, tears filling her eyes. 'Davey, what is it?'

He looked down her line, past her bobber to the floating litter, where her worm had hooked a piece of tweed – a jacket sleeve—

a green hand—

a rose tattoo—

Bobby.

'All my life,' Sal said to the detective. Then he tipped the bottle to his lips again. 'Since I was thirteen or fourteen, I don't remember. We went to high school together.'

Down in the water, two scuba divers turned cranelike amidst the river debris, their backs flat to the surface, poring over the muddy bottom of the pool. Up in the field behind them, reporters and cameramen had gathered, kept out of sight by crime-scene tape and the two state troopers who had responded to Sal's call. The medical examiner was on his way.

Detective Shepherd, writing in a notepad, leaned his foot on the bare limb of a deadfall that lay alongside the path. Sal faced away from the river, kept his legs spread for balance. Behind him he could hear the river gurgling beyond the pool, where Bobby's body lay face up on the fishing rock beside Davey's rod like some grotesque trophy, still hooked in the cuff. Murdoch walked slowly along the bank, video-taping the scene.

'Then you'd characterize yourself as a close friend,' Shepherd said, keeping his voice low in consideration of the reporters.

'*Best* friend,' Sal replied. 'They moved up here because of me.' He put the bottle to his mouth again and drank slowly, to make the vodka last. As much as he'd already consumed, he still couldn't look at the body. Bobby's arms inside his jacket sleeves had puffed up like knockwurst. But it was the face that got to Sal: green as the pines above him; cheeks bloated like they'd burst; and the lips, partially disintegrated, were pursed in a gruesome whistle.

'And you're absolutely sure that's him?'

Sal snorted.

Down by the water, Murdoch said, 'Just answer the question, tough guy. Yes or no.'

Sal said, without turning, 'It's Bobby Swift. That's the suit he was wearing when he was buried, that's his tattoo. What do you guys need, a name tag?'

Murdoch sauntered up the bank and stopped within reach of Sal. 'Actually, we got a name tag,' he said. 'Wanna see?' He reached a waterlogged wallet in front of Sal's face. When he flipped the wallet open, a white card showed through a fogged plasticine window. 'But it's not Bobby Swift.'

'It says his name is Dale Newman,' Shepherd said.

The name careened through Sal's mind. He turned toward the river, looked down at the body and swayed a bit.

'Nice friend, you don't know his name,' Murdoch said, giving Sal a come-and-get-it grin.

Sal returned a look that said he was more than ready to oblige.

'Which way to the swimmin hole?' a voice called. Behind the men, Dr Franklin Cafferty, deputy medical examiner for the area, came marching over the bank, carrying a black case.

'Down there,' Murdoch told him, and Cafferty charged past them to the corpse, never slowing. The doctor was a paunchy man with thick glasses and white hair combed stiffly over the top of his head. 'Whadda we got,' he called back, 'creature from the black lagoon?'

'Doctor, there are reporters up there,' Shepherd told him.

Snapping on a pair of latex gloves, Cafferty knelt on the rock beside the body. 'Goddamn human blowfish,' he said, just as loud.

'This gentleman's daughter landed him about an hour ago,' Murdoch explained, flipping a glance at Sal.

Shepherd added, 'We think he might've been buried at the local cemetery last week.'

'Ah, the missing corpse, I heard about you.' Cafferty lifted the green face toward his own. Brownish water ran out of the nostrils. 'What were they using for bait?' he said to no one in particular.

Shepherd turned away. 'Doctor, I'd like your opinion on how long he's been dead. Any way of estimating?'

Cafferty shook his head. 'Not until we get him in the lab. I *can* tell you that his body hasn't been in the river any more than twenty-four hours – if that.'

Murdoch folded his arms, gave Shepherd a satisfied look. 'A third accomplice – just like I've been telling you. Had to be three of them.'

Sal stiffened; weaved dizzily, brushing against the sergeant.

'Have another drink,' Murdoch told him, moving down the bank.

'*Foul!*' Cafferty honked. 'Oh, there's some nasty business afoot.'

'Doctor, they can hear you up there.'

Cafferty turned Bobby's bloated face toward the men. 'See, they prettied him up, but that's about it.'

Shepherd took a couple of steps closer. 'What do you mean?'

'You gentlemen ever hear of embalming?' Cafferty squinted up at the detectives, angling his head to focus through his trifocals. 'This man still has his own blood in his veins.'

Up on the path, Sal turned away again. He felt a drop of rain on his arm, and then two more drops, but it meant nothing. The meaning of the doctor's words dangled out of reach.

Murdoch walked down to the doctor. 'That's been my theory all along,' he said. 'The guy fakes dead, they bury him with some oxygen tanks, the undertaker comes back at night and digs him up, and, whammo – now it's the undertaker underground. Perfect crime, right? But then, just when the trusting husband is about to split the country and start a new life—' Murdoch pointed at Shepherd. 'Poison. I'll bet you a ten-spot she slipped him something.'

'You lose!' Cafferty chimed, deriding him. 'Think, man! The lips. The lips!' He sank his index finger knuckle-deep through the hole in Bobby's mouth, then flicked his finger out again with a sickening pop. 'Hah? How long you think Mister Whistle went around like this? You think he drank the poison through a straw?'

The doctor pushed an eyelid open. 'See, you got petechiae here.' He leaned back so Murdoch could see. 'Red-eye, broken blood vessels – a condition consistent with strangling or suffocation. But there's no hemorrhaging around the neck.' He looked back at both detectives. 'I'd say you got yourselves a little insurance scam that went south.'

'Are you saying he died in his casket?' Shepherd said.

'Of course he did. You want my professional estimation? I'd say this poor bastard got taken for a whale of a ride.'

The rain started falling harder.

Cafferty said, 'I'd better wrap him up and take him along. Don't want him getting wet.'

Gesturing toward the divers in the pool, he said to Murdoch, 'I don't know what you expect to find in there. There's no weapon. He was already dead. They just dumped the corpse here to get rid of it.'

Shepherd stared. Standing there in the rain for another second or two, he turned toward the field, and a scowl came over him. 'Son of a bitch,' he said softly.

Murdoch looked over at him.

Sal stood unsteadily on the path. Despite all that he'd drunk – most of the liter in less than two hours – his entire body was racked with trembling. He spun around and made for the field.

Murdoch called after him, 'Hey, Greaseball, where do you think you're going?'

Sal kept walking.

Iris stood in the rain at the edge of the road, having forgotten why she was there. Davey was upstairs in her bedroom. Sal was on his way to the store. Iris herself was dressed in a flannel shirt. The back of her hand was spattered white. The rain did not affect the spatters. She did not know how long she had been standing here – a few seconds, a minute, or an hour. Looking off toward the village, she could no longer see Sal. Rainwater ran down her face. Her shoulders were drenched.

It was the house, her own hollow house – the reason she was out here. She had felt it as soon as she'd caught sight of Sal marching past – this vague, utterly ridiculous (yet utterly persistent) notion that – somehow – the house was her mother, and it was watching her; the vague fear that she had finally and inescapably been wrenched from her sanity. Yes, everything was perfectly, swimmingly, vague – except her paralysis. Standing here in plain view of every car that drove past, she felt so conspicuous, like a fawn pinned by headlights.

She could not remember why she had come out here, or what she had been doing before. Working? Studying? Cooking dinner? By the paint on her hand, it might have seemed reasonable to assume that she had been painting, but she made no such connection. It was as if her mind had shut down. Rainwater ran down off her nose. A welling rose up in her chest.

She thought of Davey up in her room, turning pages of a

book she had read dozens of times. The welling grew. Iris swallowed it, and she swallowed again. She refused to acknowledge the house, hollow, cold and unforgiving. Instead, she watched the rainwater gather in the ditch by the side of the road and go running off toward the village.

Presently, she became aware of a car in front of her, a silver car, idling. She could see the bottom of the car at the top of her vision, but she refused to look up. She could tell that the driver was watching her.

'Mrs Erickson?' A woman's voice.

Iris flinched.

In her mind, she turned and walked calmly back into her house. In reality, she remained stuck in this spot. She couldn't even get her mind to move.

'Mrs Erickson, are you okay?'

Iris heard the car door open, the footsteps approach—

'Mrs Erickson?'

—and then the hands on her, first on her arm, then on her back. 'Mrs Erickson, are you alright?' Warm, dry hands.

Iris looked at the woman. She shuddered—

'Helen Swan,' the woman said.

A rich tremor swept through Iris. She let out a low, tremulous sound.

'Is everything okay?'

Iris closed her eyes. The hand on her back, the woman's voice, felt so soothing. 'No,' she whispered. God, her own voice – what a relief to hear it. Goose bumps coursed over her arms, and she realized how cold she was. She spoke again. 'I can't go in my own house.'

'Are you locked out?'

Iris shook her head and almost laughed at herself, but now she was crying. 'I just can't go in.'

'That's okay,' the older woman said, holding her a little more firmly. 'Are you alone?'

Iris took a breath, let it out. 'Davey's inside. My daughter.'

The woman's arm wrapped around her shoulder, turned her gently around. 'Is that Davey in the window?'

Iris looked up, saw Davey's face behind the glass. The relief was overwhelming. Recognition of the woman came to her in a flood. Helen Swan, the school board chairperson who had caught her in a lie, who had fired Sal – Helen Swan, she remembered, was a retired psychologist or psychiatrist from New Jersey who had moved to Maine after her husband had died. And here was stalwart Iris, clutching the woman dearly in her own front yard, with Davey and the hollow house and God knew how many other people watching.

And it felt so good.

'I was painting the ceiling,' Iris told her. 'I think I painted my whole house today.' She laughed in amazement, closing her eyes, tears running with the rain. She wiped her forehead with her arm, and then she cried harder.

'That's okay,' Helen said. 'Let's go in and get you into some dry clothes.' Helen had the most soothing voice; Iris took hold of her arm, and they started walking.

The Stoli bottle, not quite empty, stood centered on the roof of Murdoch's black Mercury where a police light might have been.

Murdoch batted the bottle onto the side of the road, where the glass shattered. He walked up to Shepherd's Cherokee, bent to look in the window. Inside, Shepherd held his telephone to his ear. 'That son of a bitch,' the detective said, setting the phone back in its cradle. 'He knows.'

''Course he knows,' said Murdoch, his blazer absorbing the rain. 'He's screwin her, of course he knows.'

'Not him,' Shepherd said. 'I mean Bouchard, the constable.'

'Yeah? Knows what?'

Shepherd switched off the phone. 'About Bobby Swift's casket. Why it wasn't torn apart.'

'Because they whacked him before they buried him.'

'No. Those scuba tanks were empty – he was down there breathing. Till he ran out of air.'

Murdoch gave it a moment's thought and then looked in the window. 'I'd say it's time we interviewed your lady friend.'

'Nope.' Shepherd started the engine. 'I think it's time to interrogate her.'

Sal reached the store just ahead of the detectives. Too drunk to run, barely able to walk, his mind spun with fragments: Bobby, buried alive; his green, whistling face; Dale Newman; Eliot Wicker. Sal pulled the front door open and walked in. Jerry, eating beans and franks at the counter, turned a full circle on his fountain stool, watching as Sal strode toward the back. 'She already knows,' he said.

From the register, Bonnie sang, 'She certainly doesn't need to see *you*.'

Sal ignored them both and pushed in behind the meat counter.

'Chad—'

Chad followed after him. 'Mr Erickson, you can't go back here.' Sal banged through the door without slowing, navigating down the middle aisle of cartons until he turned to her desk, then around another stack of cartons, and—

Noel was there.

Sal leaned against a support post to steady himself, while he tried to focus on her, to wring some understanding from the look she was giving him, that slack, knowing smile. He stepped away from the post, spreading his legs for balance.

'I did not do this,' he said, his words emerging slow and deliberate.

Standing in the open doorway, she wore a plain green dress,

while zebra-striped stairs rose madly around her head. 'Why do you keep telling me?' she said.

He took a step toward her. 'Because it had to be one of us. You or me.'

She stood there, not answering, seeming to float above him.

Behind him, the voices, the footsteps, came fast.

Noel pulled the door closed behind her, leaned back against it. That look—

Bonnie and Chad appeared first, sweeping around the wall of cartons. 'Here he is,' Bonnie said. The detectives came around them.

Shepherd dropped a hand by his hip, to calm things. 'Do me a favor, folks. Go on back to work now.'

Neither Bonnie nor Chad retreated. Shepherd took a step closer to Noel, ignoring Sal. 'Want to take a ride?' he said.

She smiled disdainfully. 'You're arresting me?'

'Not arresting. Just going somewhere to talk.'

Murdoch stepped toward Sal. 'You got a hearing problem, Greaseball? You were told to leave.'

Slowly Sal turned to face the sergeant, who happily moved in closer. 'What, you got something smart to say to me?' Murdoch said. 'Go find a bottle and crawl back in your hole.'

Their eyes clashed.

Murdoch's mouth opened. He puffed himself up and folded his big arms, his smile curling downward. 'Real bosom buddies,' he said. 'Oh yeah, I can see the way you ran over here – oh yeah, I can see how you're real broke up—'

Sal jumped him, slammed his shoulder into the sergeant's gut and drove him to the door. Unfazed, Murdoch's grin never left his face while he rabbit-punched at Sal's kidneys. But his angle was off, and the blows had no effect. So he leaned his weight down on Sal's back, wrapped his arms around his chest and pulled up with a grunt, lifting Sal's feet off the floor. The men stumbled in a circle. Cartons toppled.

Now Shepherd came in from the right. 'Get his legs!' Murdoch barked. Like noseguards, the two men captured Sal, hauling him through a wall of boxes, four-foot cartons of toilet paper avalanching down. As the men tumbled, Sal threw an elbow and extricated himself, a perfect fullback scramble. In the same blurring motion he executed a full-force roundhouse right that caught Murdoch squarely on the neck, just below the ear. The big man staggered a few steps back, then went heavily over a box. Sal spun to face Shepherd, expecting another attack.

He didn't see Alston Bouchard beside him until the constable's fist connected with the side of his jaw. Sal's heels and toes pivoted beneath him as he fought for balance. Instinctively he turned and raised his guard. Bouchard's second punch shot under his defense, slammed into his chest like the butt end of an oak log. Sal reeled backward into the support post. Struggling with consciousness, he slumped there, out on his feet.

Shepherd fell upon him instantly, held him against the post as he pulled the cuffs from his pouch. Bouchard was there too, holding Sal under the arms to keep him from falling, as Shepherd snapped a cuff on Sal's wrist.

'He's not resisting now, Detective,' Bouchard said.

'Yeah?' Shepherd pulled the cuffed wrist behind Sal's back, reached for Sal's other arm.

'I mean, I'd just as soon take him with me,' Bouchard continued, 'get him out of your way.'

Shepherd gave the constable a look, wishing they were alone so he could find out exactly what Bouchard knew about the casket.

'He just needs to sleep it off.'

Shepherd also wanted to get Noel out of there before Murdoch came to and could interfere any more. And he certainly didn't want to leave Sal alone with Murdoch.

'You got what you came for,' Bouchard persisted.

Already the sergeant was pulling himself onto the desk chair, however groggily. Shepherd turned to Bouchard again, pulled the cuff off Sal's wrist. 'Before I change my mind,' he said, nodding toward the front door.

As Bouchard led Sal away, Murdoch pushed to his feet, held onto the desk for balance. 'What's this? Where's he going?'

Shepherd waved them off. 'He's not worth it, let him go.'

It was like telling a pit bull to leave fresh kill. 'You gotta be kiddin me, you cut him loose—?'

'You okay?' Shepherd asked.

''Course I'm okay!' Murdoch stepped forward and bent for his handcuffs, missed the first try, rocked back on his feet. 'Goddamn blood pressure medicine.'

Shepherd nodded to Noel, and they began walking toward the aisle. 'Catch your breath, Sarge,' the detective said. 'Have a coffee or something. I'll see you back at the station.'

Noel's interrogation took place in the August Tea House, a Chinese restaurant in Ellsworth. Shepherd chose the restaurant because it was poorly attended and because he knew Murdoch would never find them there. They sat in the rear of the dining room, in a corner booth. Shepherd had given the maître d' a five-dollar tip and asked him not to seat anybody near them. He ordered appetizers for them both while Noel excused herself and went to find the bathroom. When she returned, Shepherd's notebook computer was opened on the table in front of him. He poured a cup of green tea and passed it to her. She ignored it.

'Okay,' he said, 'let's start with Bobby's business.'

'Bobby's business.'

Shepherd punched a couple of keys and looked down at the monitor. 'After Bobby left the navy, he started a skydiving school outside Providence. Sold the business in 1988 to a group of his former students, then started manufacturing and flying ultralight airplanes.' Shepherd looked up from the computer. 'Bobby liked to take chances.'

'A lot of people fly, Detective.'

'But a three-million-dollar business loan – that takes courage. Especially when it's illegal.'

Noel stared across the table, stone-faced. 'I told you, Bobby was his father's son.'

'Meaning—'

'Meaning when it comes to business, the less the woman knows, the better off she is.'

'Yet you strike me as so modern.' Their eyes remained locked.

'Bobby took on the world every day,' she said, 'and he seemed to be winning. That's all I needed to know. I had my own life.'

Shepherd stroked his mustache with the side of his finger. Watching for signs – dry mouth, restlessness, flushed face, preoccupation with the time – he saw none. Not taking his eyes off her, he recited from memory: 'Charles J. Mariotta, the bank officer who okayed Bobby's loan. Mariotta was sentenced to fourteen years in prison. Bobby, who testified against him, got community service and probation. Not to mention over two million dollars that was never recovered.'

'And I've told you I don't know anything about that money.'

She took a sip of her water. Shepherd watched her swallow. Started to push.

'I don't imagine Charles was too happy with the arrangement. Bobby gets a slap on the wrist, Charlie gets fourteen years. Charlie? Chuck?'

She narrowed her eyes.

'Do you know when Charles Mariotta gets out of prison?'

'You said he was sentenced to fourteen years.'

'Next month, after seven years. A reasonable person might assume he'd want to speak with Bobby about that missing money. Dead's a good way to disappear.' He folded his hands on the table as the waitress arrived with their spring rolls, set them down, then went quickly away.

'This is what I think,' Shepherd continued. 'Charlie Mariotta made Bobby Swift a three-million-dollar bank loan to start a business. In exchange for the loan, which wasn't entirely aboveboard in the first place, Bobby agreed to cut Charlie in on a share of the company's profits – definitely against the law. That much is indisputable.'

'According to you.'

'And a jury and a judge. Noel—'

She refused to acquiesce, even on this point, but Shepherd wasn't waiting.

'Bobby gets his loan, he starts his company, it's the '80s, money's making money, and Bobby gets rich. That's when you come into the story. You meet this daring young millionaire, you fall in love, you get married. Then the economy bottoms out. The business turns sour. You get this idea, this brainstorm.'

Noel sighed.

'You, plural – you and Bobby. First he stashes a couple million bucks in an offshore account, let's say in the Cayman Islands, where it can't be traced.'

'I must say, the story improves with time,' Noel said, picking up a spring roll.

'It's a joint account or trust – maybe a corporation – with two partners, Bobby Swift and Dale Newman. See, *New-man?* I like it when they give you clues. Anyway, the brainstorm: you move to some little backwater town in Maine, strike up a deal with the local undertaker—'

'Too greasy,' Noel said, setting the spring roll down.

'One day in June a man named Dale Newman walks into a supply house in Belfast, picks up a set of scuba tanks and a couple of oxygen tanks. A year later Bobby Swift dies. There's a funeral, and he's buried. Next day, lo and behold, Mr Dale Newman arrives on Cayman Island and begins living the life of Riley. At least that was the plan. Bobby's plan.'

Noel reclined slightly in the booth. Her eyes, candlelit, glinted with ridicule.

Shepherd stole a glance around the dining room and then leaned forward, leveling his gaze. 'You let him die, Noel. You and Wicker were supposed to dig him up, and you let him suffocate down there.'

Now Noel leaned forward and leveled her own gaze. 'Detective, are you aware that you're accusing me of *not* doing something?'

Once again the waitress interrupted them with food, three covered stainless steel bowls balanced on one arm. In turn, she set each one down and uncovered it for their approval. Shepherd thanked her, and she went away.

Noel looked across the table at Shepherd with something akin to pity. 'Please continue, Detective. I'm dying to hear your theory on why I put scuba tanks on Eliot Wicker and buried him alive in Bobby's grave, with a gun in his hand. Or why I threw a heating pad in a tree—?'

'To make it look like Bobby did it.'

She nodded gravely, with rich sarcasm. 'Bobby would have done that. And then I spread more clues around – I put a plane ticket in Alston Bouchard's mailbox. I dumped my husband's body in the river a quarter-mile from home. Detective, has it crossed your mind that someone might be trying to make me look guilty?'

The candle on their table flickered.

Shepherd shook his head. 'I'll be honest with you,' he said.

'I've thought about this and I've thought about this, and for the life of me, I can't think of a single scenario in which you would not be involved.'

Her eyes flitted past him with a quick glimmer of relief. He turned.

'Detective,' the man behind him said, offering his hand.

'Do you know my attorney?' Noel said. 'Hal Jones, this is Detective Shepherd.'

'We've met,' Shepherd said.

'He was handling my divorce,' she added as she swiped her purse off the seat and slid out of the booth.

Shepherd pushed awkwardly to his feet while his mind grasped for clarity: *divorce?*

'How's it going, Detective?' the lawyer said with a slight, superior smile.

'How are you?' Shepherd replied, trying not to show his anxiety at the turnabout.

Noel started toward the door.

Shepherd grabbed his jacket from the booth. 'Wait a minute, I'll take you home.'

She kept walking.

'I'll take her,' the attorney said. Jones was a heavy man, in his early forties, with thick brown hair, wire glasses and a drooping mustache. He wore a gray suit, twice as rich as anything in Shepherd's wardrobe. 'Listen,' he said, friendly enough, 'from now on, why don't we make sure I'm present if you plan to question my client?'

Shepherd felt disheveled, blindsided. He smoothed his jacket sleeve.

'It's a strange one,' the attorney said with a laugh. 'Noel's been filling me in: the fake death, the missing money, and now her husband's body. Definitely strange.' He picked a cloth napkin off the table and handed it to Shepherd, nodding to a spot of tea on his pocket. 'I'm telling you this as a favor,

Detective. Maybe it'll save you some time. She really was divorcing her husband.'

Shepherd rubbed the napkin on his jacket. 'I appreciate that,' he said, not entirely sincere.

'She was determined not to leave empty-handed. The business, the property, future profits of the store, you name it – their savings and investments – half would have gone to her. I have a list of their assets. If Noel Swift had known about two million dollars, believe me, it would've been on that list.'

Shepherd tossed the napkin on the table, then looked back toward the door.

'If anybody had a motivation for a faked death and disappearance, it was Bobby Swift, to keep that money away from Noel.'

Shepherd nodded. Never saw it coming.

When the detective returned home, there were two phone messages for him to call Murdoch at the barracks. 'I'll be waiting,' the sergeant said, sounding displeased. Shepherd telephoned him before he removed his jacket.

'I got a call from your lady's attorney a while ago,' Murdoch said to him. 'Did you have a date with her tonight?'

Shepherd's ears hummed.

'Take her home and screw her or what?'

'I interrogated her. It was time to eat, so we went to a restaurant. You know the way I work.'

'Yeah, meanwhile I'm back at the station with my thumb up my ass, waiting for you.'

'There's a new wrinkle, Sarge. Bobby Swift had reason to hide the money from her. She was divorcing him.'

'I know that,' Murdoch said. 'The lawyer and me had a long talk. For curiosity's sake, I'll tell you something else. She's going on a little vacation the day after tomorrow. A two-week cruise out of Tampa.'

'Shit.'

'Figure she's gonna boogie?'

Shepherd sighed, pulled his computer across the counter and flipped the lid open. 'We'll check it out.'

'Already did. Delta confirmed a round-trip flight from Bangor to Tampa and back again. She's down for ten days on Tampa Bay Cruise Lines.'

'She could connect to the Caymans.'

'Oh, you don't think she'd do that,' Murdoch said.

Shepherd waited, typing the words DELTA, TAMPA BAY.

'I had it checked out,' the sergeant continued. 'The boat doesn't go there, and nobody by the name of Noel Swift or Noel anybody is flying Cayman Airways in the next two weeks.'

'How about Dale Newman?'

Murdoch chuckled softly. 'Jeez, you know, I thought of that too.'

'So?'

'So nothing. No Dale Newman, no Newman Dale. What I need to know is whether or not you have anything to keep her here, solid enough to convince the A.G.'s office.'

Shepherd told him, 'I don't have it.'

'That's what I thought,' Murdoch said. 'So write up what you do have and leave it on my desk in the morning.'

'Wait a minute—' Shepherd looked up from the computer. 'What are you saying? You're not taking over this case—?'

'Can't be helped.'

'Sarge, I'm almost there. Look, you're right about the third accomplice. No way around it. Maybe it's her, maybe it's not. We've got to get through the Caymans, to see the names on that account. It's clearly a murder case, they'll waive their confidentiality laws.'

'I'll take that under advisement,' Murdoch replied. Shepherd

could hear the nasty smile in his voice, and that's when he
realized—

Murdoch had planned this from the start, taking over in the
final round. High-visibility case, possible promotion before
retirement, something to fatten his second pension.

'You're not taking over this case,' Shepherd said again.

'Sorry, it's not my decision,' Murdoch replied. 'It's Boggs.
You embarrassed the lieutenant. The media's all over him,
and he wants this put to rest. See, once again, *Andy of
Mayberry* has led you astray.'

Murdoch hung up the telephone and pressed back in his
chair, his upper body stiffened by the cumbersome brace
that fixed his neck to his shoulders. He lifted the remote
control off his desk, aimed it at the VCR that sat on a cart
in front of his desk, and thumbed the button that said
SLOW. The television screen flickered on a scene. A black
sportcoat hanging on a wall. Slowly the angle panned across
the dark fabric to a black hooded sweatshirt; then up the
sweatshirt until Eliot Wicker's wooden coat rack was visible,
a plain flat board attached to a white plaster wall. Continuing
rightward to an unused wooden peg ... and then to the
cap, black against the white wall. PAUSE. The image froze
on the cap.

Murdoch leaned forward, reached over his desk to the
television and turned up the brightness until the black light-
ened to brown, and a tweed pattern became apparent. He slid
the photo under the desk lamp, the picture of Bobby Swift
and Sal Erickson, shoved a magnifying glass over it and
moved his shoulders until one face rose out of the frame,
looking out from under the cap.

Sal opened his eyes, tried again to raise his arm, but it was
caught. He tried to shake it free, heard a jangle – and then

something dug into his wrist – something cold. He reached with his free hand, found that he was attached to the iron bed frame—

Handcuffed.

'Hey – *Hey!*'

Outside the door a light came on, dimly illuminating the room. Footsteps approached, and then another light came on, much brighter, and a figure appeared in the doorway. Alston Bouchard. A big black dog beside him.

'What the hell is this?' Sal said.

'You've got to get sober,' the dark man answered in a low voice.

A throbbing pain flared through Sal's jaw, rifled across his head. A blur of recollection, nothing clear. (The green hand rising out of the pool ... Noel rising in front of the zebra stairs ...)

'Go back to sleep, best thing.'

'Where is she? I need to talk to her.'

'Home, I'd imagine, this hour.'

Sal jangled his wrist again. He sat up on the mattress and pulled against the cuff. 'What are you doing? Get me off this thing!'

The dog started to bark, rapid-fire explosions. 'Katahdin, stop,' Bouchard said, and the dog whined. Sal dragged the handcuff up the frame until it snagged. He rolled off the bed and planted his feet on the floor.

Bouchard closed the door, pulled a wooden chair over in front of it and sat down. The black dog pressed against his knee, whining nervously. 'You've got to get sober,' he said again. 'There's a pan on the floor for you. Don't step in it.'

'I'll tear this goddamn bed apart!'

Bouchard replied, without emotion, 'You'll try, prob'ly.'

Sal rose to his feet, toppling the mattress and blankets, lifting the bed frame halfway up the wall.

'Get some sleep,' Bouchard said to Sal, 'best thing.'

Sal jerked his arm, and the bed frame jumped off the floor and came down again.

'I'd appreciate it if you wouldn't tear apart my room,' Bouchard told him.

Sal stood there defiantly, sweat-soaked. The windows were closed, the room airless. He fixed Bouchard in his vision. 'I got the hat,' he said. 'My hat that you left at Wicker's.'

Bouchard leaned forward and tossed the blanket over the mattress. 'I saw your hat at Wicker's,' he said. 'I didn't put it there. You didn't either. I've got a good idea who did.'

Sal watched him warily.

'Get some sleep,' Bouchard told him again. 'We'll talk in the morning.' He reached for the lamp on the bureau and turned it off.

Sal stood in the darkness for another minute, then lowered the bed frame to the floor, slumping to his knees on the mattress. He exhaled heavily. 'You can't keep me here,' he said.

'Got to,' Bouchard replied.

Jerry peered through the garage window as he leaned on the service bell. Shortly, a light emerged from the stairway, and then Noel came down, wearing a long dark sweatshirt that reached to the middle of her thighs. Jerry moved over to the entrance door and pressed his face against the window. He shone a flashlight on Noel as she came closer, on her legs. When she opened the door, she stepped back, making room for him to enter the garage. He checked her hands before he did, made sure they were empty.

'Busy day,' he said, 'down the falls.'

She shut the door behind him. 'Come out of the light,' she said, and she walked around the cars to the back of the garage, where it was darker. He followed warily, shining his flashlight up and down the back of her, exceedingly alert from the volume of caffeine he'd consumed over the past forty hours. Lucky shoes or not, he knew enough to watch her.

'So they found Bobby in the river,' he said. 'Staties, reporters, detectives, the whole nine yards.'

He rocked his head while he watched for her reaction. But she gave him none. Her eyes remained steady. In fact, she was looking at him with a kind of piqued interest, as if there were something about him tonight that fascinated her.

'Jerry, I want you to know that I had nothing to do with that fire.'

He studied her suspiciously for a second. Then his eyes rolled. 'Oh, yeah, well! Pretty big coincidence, then, if you ask me.'

'Shh.'

He whispered forcefully. 'You get me down to Bangor where I almost get my head cut off, then my house burns down. Next thing you know, you put a bullet in my new truck try'na blow me away. Oh yeah, big coincidence, really.'

'I didn't know it was you breaking in. I didn't know who it was.'

Jerry fluttered his lips. 'Just like a woman. I take it up one notch with the plane ticket, and then you take it up twenty-five, burnin down my house and almost gettin me murdered.' He glared, his caffeinated eyes glinting hard. 'I'm right on top of this, Noel. Right on top.'

'Jerry, I'm telling you the truth.'

'Yup, yup, yup.'

'I admit I asked a friend of mine to talk to you about that letter you wrote—'

'Talk, oh yes.'

She inched closer to him. 'But I swear, I don't know anything about that fire.'

'Yup.'

'I was the one who answered the fire phone, how could I have set the fire?' She gave him a look that caught him off guard, her eyes sponge-bathing him.

Jerry leaned back against the Volvo, his own eyes focusing in the vicinity of her hips. 'Well, anyway, they got the dead body now.'

She touched the sleeve of his shirt. 'Is this new?'

Jerry studied her. 'I gotta say, Noel, you don't seem too friggin concerned.'

She laid those eyes on him again. 'Should I be?'

He tipped his head. 'Well, it's not gonna take a brain scientist to figure out that Bobby was buried alive. For starters.'

'Mm-hmm.'

'Alright then,' he said, making his point. It felt good to be in control. The truth was, Jerry was feeling less in control by the minute. Even now, the way Noel gazed at him with that half smile, he felt more like he was being stalked.

'Jerry, I want you to understand something,' she said. 'I didn't kill my husband. Eliot Wicker killed Bobby. And now Eliot Wicker is dead.' She lowered her voice so softly that even if someone else were in the garage with them, he mightn't have heard her. 'And we both know who killed Wicker.'

Jerry's chin doubled, ready to laugh it off. At the same time, his stomach percolated.

'Jerry, it's obvious from your letter that you dug up Bobby's body to blackmail Eliot Wicker—'

'Wrong, wrong—'

'—and then you murdered Wicker.'

'*Wrong!*'

'It's completely obvious. Anyone who read that letter would know exactly what you did.'

Jerry's heel began tapping on the concrete floor. He

glanced back at the door, then returned his gaze to her, amazed at how small she was, and how dangerous.

'In the first place,' he said, 'the only reason I dug Bobby up was to save his dumb ass once I figured out that you and Wicker were just gonna leave him down there. Then, alright, *then* I figured since I was too late and he was dead already, and I had the inside information, why not? So I removed his body for safekeeping.'

'And then you murdered Wicker.'

'*No.*' He widened his eyes to make his point. 'I came back here to make a deal with the both of you, but then you went and invited Sal Erickson up – and the next thing I know, here comes Wicker up to see you, and five minutes later there he goes again, spittin and sputterin all the way down to the cemetery, where he digs up the grave and gets even madder when he sees the body's missin. And that's when I went over to make my deal. But Wicker, dumb shit, he pulls a gun on me – which is why I say, self-defense all the way. No question about it.'

'Jerry, you buried him alive.'

'Yeah, well. Not on purpose. He got hit on the head with an oxygen tank, and then he wasn't breathing. Looked dead to me; turns out I only stunned him. Anyway, he got his justice, even if it wasn't from a judge.'

Noel sighed. 'Jerry, you told me that you didn't know anything about Wicker's death, or who took Bobby's body. You lied to me.'

'Oh! Well! Excuse me, Mrs George Washington!'

Noel smiled calmly. 'Jerry, you know we're going to have to be honest with each other now that we're in this together.' She moved closer to him, her eyes *shining*. 'We are in this together, aren't we, Jerry?'

He rocked his head skeptically, but inside his lucky shoes, his toes clenched hard.

Noel's eyes lowered to his chest. 'I really did want to meet you in Bangor, Jerry. I really did. But how could I? You know how I'm being watched.'

Stunned, he folded his arms; looked at her as a dog might look at a grasshopper: playful, distrusting.

'Jerry, I'm serious. You have this *quality* – earthy, physical ... Do you know what that does to a woman? I feel an animal attraction for you that's – overpowering.'

He felt his trousers tightening.

She gazed at him hungrily, laid her hand on his chest. Then, as if rousted from her fantasy, she spun away from him. 'God, I must be crazy,' she said. 'We can't do this here.'

'No, upstairs,' he said. 'You got a back door up there. Christ, you got three doors. Don't, uh, don't—'

She turned back, silencing him. 'First of all, Jerry, I need to know that you trust me.'

He expelled a column of air, mocking her. But it was easy to see he was transfixed.

'Jerry, you have all the power,' she murmured.

He snorted bitterly. 'That's what I thought.'

'I'm serious. You have the one thing that can save us both. And the thing that can destroy us.'

Jerry was listening; he was also preoccupied with her offer. 'We could go up now,' he said. 'Two in the morning, who's gonna know?'

Her eyes bored into him. 'The oxygen, Jerry.'

'Yeah, no problem. What?'

'When the other two oxygen tanks are found,' she said, 'we'll both be in the clear.'

He tossed his head up and down, eyes bulging. 'Oh, yes, M'am. Like I'm going to give 'em the murder weapon. I just imagine, really!'

She wouldn't stop staring at him. 'Jerry, those oxygen tanks can't be traced to you. Just wipe them off.'

He folded his arms, tapped his heel on the floor. 'You tell me how those tanks are supposed to save us.'

She breathed an exasperated sigh. 'I can see this isn't going to work between us.'

'I'm only askin a question.' He tapped his heel faster.

Now she refused to even meet his eyes.

'Alright, so what about the other thing, the thing that'll destroy us?'

Her words came out cold as polished steel: 'Your letter.'

He folded his arms, folded his face into a scornful mask, once again showing his power.

'Jerry, you are going to have to trust me.'

'Oh, yes, M'am. Trust you?'

'Just like I have to trust you.'

He gawked. 'How the hell do you have to trust me?'

'You say there's only one letter. How do I know there aren't two letters? Or three?'

Jerry flattened his lips. 'I ain't numb, Noel. I don't want that letter found, no more'n you do. There's only the one, and I got it hid in a place where you'll never find it.'

'Jerry, even one letter isn't very smart.'

'Oh, no. That letter's only keeping you from killing me.'

She pinned him with her eyes. 'No, Jerry. It's keeping me from fucking you.'

His knees loosened. He leaned back on the Volvo and peered at her, squinted at her as if he were looking into the sun. Then he slid off the car and moved around her to the outside door.

'That,' he said, 'that right there?' He shuddered as he turned the knob. 'That's what I call head games.'

Halfway to morning, Sal jumped awake.

'*Holy shit!* Bobby, you okay?'

Bouchard left the light off. 'I'm okay,' he answered.

'Oh, man, it's cold. Fuckin whose idea was this?'

Bouchard reached down, felt Sal's arm, taut and trembling; felt the blanket in a humid pile beside him. He tossed the blanket over Sal's back.

'Thanks, man.'

'Yup.'

'Bobby, you sure you're okay?'

'Yup.'

Twenty minutes later, Sal spoke again. 'Anthony, time to go home.'

'Yup.'

'Come on, brother.'

'Yup.'

12

A t seven in the morning, when Jerry came into the store, the counter was deserted and Noel was working alone. Jerry had on a short-sleeved madras shirt, a pair of Sal's old khaki pants and his own lucky shoes.

'How about a cup of instant for starters?' he said to Noel. 'Then I guess a stack of pancakes, a half pound of bacon, one of those blueberry muffins toasted, and three eggs, sunny and runny.'

He unscrewed the lid off the big mayonnaise jar beside the register, the one that read: DONATIONS FOR OTIS AND JERRY ROYAL, and emptied the money onto the counter: eighty cents more than the five-dollar bill he had left as bait. 'Thanks, everyone,' he said. He put the five in his pocket, returned the change into the jar and closed the cover. He swung a leg over the stool and started drumming on the counter while he watched Noel break his eggs onto the grill.

'Guess you're the talk of the town today,' he said. His eggs sizzled.

'Word does get around,' Noel replied. Provincialism aside, the extent to which townspeople avoided the Superette this morning surprised even her. Sure, the usuals had all stopped in at the usual time – for gas, or the newspaper, a jug of milk or a loaf of bread – but nobody had sat down for coffee. In fact, even Bonnie had called in sick. A few had mentioned hearing that Herb and Bonnie were going to mind the store while Noel went away on a cruise; a couple of people told Noel, in nice ways, that she should stay longer. That, precisely, was her plan.

She poured Jerry's hot water, set a spoon and the instant coffee in front of him, and then watched as he stirred six teaspoons of granules into the cup. 'I'm on a caffeine diet,' he explained. 'Wicked buzzed, wicked buzzed.' As he poured sugar in, he said without looking up, 'I took care of it, thought you'd oughta know.'

'The letter?' she asked.

He swallowed the coffee, shook his head. 'Oxygen tanks.'

She blinked once, slowly, like an owl.

'Figured with you leavin on your cruise tomorrow,' he said, a shoulder twitching.

'You figured what?'

He swung off his stool, grabbed a ballpoint pen off the cash register. 'Well, I give up certain things, and tonight you go ahead with – your animal attraction, whatever, and I don't get my head bashed in this time.' He underlined the word DONATIONS on the mayonnaise jar, scratching the pen back and forth. 'Better watch my eggs,' he told her. 'Crispy they're no good.'

'Jerry,' she said. 'The letter.'

'I know, the letter for *all-the-way*. But I'm just sayin, okay, up-to-that-point for the oxygen tanks. Preview of coming attractions.'

The scolding, teasing look she gave him made his stomach buzz. 'Where are they?' she said.

'Really, watch my eggs.'

'Jerry, where did you put the tanks?'

Under the word DONATIONS, he wrote PLEASE HELP HIM, but the curve of the jar made his writing a childish scrawl. He looked up at her with a caffeine gleam in his eye.

'You'll find out.'

In Belly Button's backyard, as it turned out. Belly and his wife, both devout Catholics – Jerry had left them a surprise: one tank, propped on an overturned pail, rested against the crotch of their ceramic garden Jesus, like a bright green erection. The Virgin Mary got the other.

The voice on the telephone was British in tone, spiced with West Indian staccato. 'As I explained to your commander, Detective, we have no taxes here in the Caymans; therefore, no tax fraud.' The sentence ended with a lilting brogue that Shepherd found particularly annoying.

'And I'm explaining to you,' he replied, 'that this is not a tax fraud case, but an advanced-stage murder investigation.' He sat on the dispatch desk in the troop barracks, waiting for a reply that turned out to be silence. Seven-thirty in the morning, a half hour before duty, he was the only one on the floor besides Stacy Myotte, the dispatcher, who sat behind the desk buttoning his back pocket for him.

'We have a corpse,' he went on. 'We know that the victim was planning to relocate to your island under an alias, Dale Newman, and that approximately two million dollars of our government's money has been deposited in one of your banks.'

'I see,' the official said. Shepherd slid off the desk and paced toward the wall until Stacy grabbed the phone to keep it from pulling off the desk. He stopped and came back.

'We also know for a fact that the funds are most likely in a joint account, or trust, in the names of Robert Swift, Dale Newman, and a third name – which is the purpose of this inquiry, to verify the identity of the third party, who happens to be our chief suspect.'

'I see,' the Cayman official said again, which Shepherd took as a hopeful sign until the man elaborated. 'If, as you say, your investigation is in an advanced stage, Detective, then surely you must already know the identity of your chief suspect.'

Shepherd turned a circle. Stacy tugged him back.

When he looked up, he saw Sergeant Murdoch walking through the front door. A thick white neck brace holding Murdoch's chin in the air made it necessary for the big man to turn his entire upper body in order to spot Shepherd, and when he did, he came over.

'Look, all we want is a name. I'm asking for a simple professional courtesy.'

'What's he doing?' Murdoch asked the dispatcher, but then another phone line rang before she could reply. She went to a desk on the opposite wall to take the call. Murdoch turned 180 degrees to watch her walk away.

Shepherd covered the phone. 'I'm on my own time here, Sarge.'

'Do you have a confession?' asked the official on the phone. 'Or perhaps the testimony of an accomplice?'

'I told you,' Shepherd said, 'the two accomplices are deceased. They've been murdered. That's why we need the third name.'

The islander cleared his throat. 'I see.'

While Shepherd waited for the bureaucratic kiss-off, he saw Stacy summon Murdoch to the other phone.

'When you have indicted your suspect,' said the Cayman official, 'I have every confidence that we will be able to verify a name for you. Now, was there anything else I might be able to help you with this morning?'

'Yeah,' Shepherd said, 'you could change your goddamned laws.' He slammed the phone down just as Lieutenant Boggs came through the outer door.

Boggs, a tall, white-haired man, was wearing his gray suit, which meant either television cameras would be in today or he was speaking at another Rotary Club meeting. When he spotted Shepherd, he came directly toward him, saying, 'I've got the media coming in this morning, Detective. I want to tell them we're making progress.'

At the other desk, Murdoch hung up the telephone and walked a bisecting route, cutting the lieutenant off. 'I'll be filling you in,' the sergeant said, gesturing in the direction of Boggs's office.

Shepherd cut in. 'Lieutenant, I'd like to speak to you about taking me off the Gravity case.'

Boggs studied Shepherd for a moment. 'Detective, are you saying that you'd like to be taken off the case?'

Confused, Shepherd turned to Murdoch, who abruptly said to the lieutenant, 'I was going to explain that this morning. Last night I made the decision to take charge of this case myself. It's my professional opinion that Detective Shepherd has made some errors of judgment.'

'That's bullshit,' Shepherd said.

Boggs cleared his throat, looked pointedly at Shepherd, then down at the floor. But it was to Murdoch that he finally spoke. 'Sergeant, I don't know what the hell is going on here, but in a few hours I'm going on the noontime news. I plan to announce that our investigation is going forward, that we're examining evidence, conducting interviews, and that an arrest is imminent.' He scowled at Murdoch, then nodded toward the corridor. 'My office,' he said, then started walking.

When he was out of earshot, Murdoch handed Shepherd a note.

'You got your oxygen tanks,' he said. 'Two oxygen tanks turned up in somebody's backyard.'

'Wait a minute. Why two? We're only missing one.'

'That's what I want you to find out,' Murdoch told him. 'Run the tanks down to Augusta and have your friend check 'em out.'

'Wait a minute, you want me down in Augusta? Can't you send somebody else? She's only going to be here one more day.'

Murdoch turned his body toward the corridor to check for Boggs. Then, turning back to Shepherd, he added, 'That's why I want you in Augusta.'

When Sal awoke, it was with a sense of despair that felt bottomless. No longer handcuffed, he found himself sprawled on the floor beside the mattress, feeling like every nerve ending was exposed. His face, in particular, ached from ear to ear. The act of breathing hurt his chest. The sun shone bright on the window shades, and the room was already too warm . . .

. . . and Bobby was dead. Sal knew that now, without doubt. Likewise, there was no question that his separation from Iris and Davey was real. Tears burned in his eyes. He felt profoundly, desperately alone.

Images flitted through his mind (the green hand rose out of the river trash, repeatedly) and musical riffs played on and on. Alcohol withdrawal, he knew the symptoms well, the constant tremors. He felt like someone was pumping trash amphetamines into his veins, like he needed to run a twenty-six-mile marathon at a flat-out dash. Trouble was, he lacked the desire to even get off the bed. He saw no reason to take another breath.

He looked up at Bouchard, slouched asleep in his wooden chair, backed against the door. The bearded man's eyes were closed, his thick glasses halfway down his nose, a paperback book opened in his hand. On the bureau beside him, the lamp was still lit. A black-haired girl, about eighteen, full-faced and very pretty, smiled out of a framed photo, a sparkle in her dark brown eyes.

'I know what Eliot Wicker did to you,' Sal said. His voice was raspy.

Bouchard stirred, closed his book. He straightened his glasses, pulled himself upright.

'I know what Eliot Wicker did to you,' Sal said again.

Bouchard cleared his throat. 'Didn't do anything to me,' he said quietly. 'Eliot Wicker was just being himself. Wasn't his fault that I lost my family's land. I'd lost everything else, it was just a matter of time.'

Sal stared at him for a number of seconds, then looked back to the picture of the girl on the bureau, realized it was Bouchard's daughter.

'What the hell are you,' he said, 'the A.A. secret police?'

'Fourteen years it's got me through.'

Sal sat up quickly. A rush of dizziness swept over him. 'I've gotta go,' he said.

Bouchard perched his hands on his knees, ready to stand. 'You're not ready, my opinion.'

'Yeah?' Sal studied him, realized that the constable's resolve was as strong as his own. 'Save your breath, I know the program, and it's not for me, okay? Step two: *Came to believe in a power greater than ourselves*. See, that doesn't work for me. I don't believe in myths. I had a drinking problem, so I stopped drinking. That's logic, not magic.'

The men locked eyes.

'I liken it to the geese,' Bouchard said.

Sal scratched at his whiskers. 'Geese—?'

'You take a flock of geese in the air,' Bouchard said. 'When one gets shot or gets sick and falls to the ground, two others'll fly down and stay with him till he dies or gets back to health. They don't know why they do it. They just do. Keeps the flock going, what I say.'

Sal's head throbbed. He leaned forward on the mattress, Bouchard's slow, deliberate speech only intensifying his anxiety.

'Same thing with people, what I've found,' Bouchard

continued. 'I've been the same place you are, pretty much. Finally came the day I sawed the barrel off my shotgun and headed up that hill back here. When I got to the top, I heard a truck coming up. See, no one ever came up that hill unless it was the berry crews, in August. This was October. Turned out to be Barlow, the beekeeper I get my hives from. He asked me what I was hunting. I told him Canada geese. He said he found that peculiar, considering I'd chained my dog down here with enough food and water to keep him alive for a week. He took the gun away from me, brought me down to a meeting, and then he kept going with me every night for three months. He told me some time later he never knew why he came over that day, he just woke up and decided to take a drive.'

Sal took a breath. 'You ever hear the term "captive audience"?'

Leaning forward in his chair, Bouchard fixed Sal in his thick lenses. 'You might be a captured audience, Mister. And you may think this is all a myth. But when you're in need of help, I suggest you keep your eyes wide open, 'cause someone'll be there – every time. You just got to be smart enough to know who it is – and who it isn't.' Bouchard rose off his chair, dropping his book on the floor. Then, as if embarrassed by his outburst, he opened the door to leave the room, saying, 'I'll make us something to eat.'

Murdoch took the boarding house stairs as quietly as his 300 pounds would allow, and the old oak boards cooperated with barely a groan. Less than agile with his weight, his age and his stiff neck, Murdoch wasn't that concerned with agility. He had the element of surprise on his side. He also had his Combat Commander, a particularly convincing .45 automatic that he had yet to use in the Pine Tree State. He didn't knock, didn't even bother to listen at the door, but just turned the knob and walked straight in, his .45 swinging from wall to wall and back again.

That's when his cell phone trilled. He reached back and closed the door behind him, then took the phone off his belt, unfolded it, and answered. 'Yuh.'

'I'm in Augusta with the tanks,' Shepherd told him. 'They finished with the Bobby Swift corpse this morning and they're confirming that he suffocated – probably in his casket, since there's no dirt or water in his lungs. They think he was probably kept frozen till he was dumped in the river.'

'Okay, that's good,' Murdoch said, reaching his hand in the pocket of Sal's sportcoat, feeling along the lining.

While Shepherd talked, his friend Phil Harwood stood at the end of a long table, examining one of the oxygen tanks under a close, bright light. Two rows of tagged grocery bags and cardboard boxes of various sizes lay scattered around his feet, backlogged evidence from other cases.

'It still doesn't seem right,' Shepherd continued, 'the casket unmarked like it is – that he'd just give up and go to sleep.'

'Well, you keep working on it,' Murdoch said. For the second time, the response seemed too civil for Murdoch. Or too cocky, given the urgency of the investigation, with Noel about to bolt.

'Sarge, has anything come in that I should know about?' Shepherd asked.

'Like what?'

'I don't know. I get the feeling we're working at cross-purposes here.'

'You feel that way, huh?' Murdoch replied, pushing his fingers inside one of Sal's sneakers, feeling around.

'Sarge, we need to get together if we're going to keep her from getting on that plane.'

'No question about it.'

'The other thing,' Shepherd said. 'Those oxygen tanks I just brought down? They've identified marks on one of them that probably correspond with Wicker's hair, where he was struck. The paint's an exact match.'

'Any fingerprints on the tank?' Murdoch asked.

'Only from the man who found the tanks in his yard. They were wiped down before he handled them.'

'Uh-huh.'

'Sarge, I'm going to stop in Belfast on my way back, check out the place where Swift bought the tanks. Only two were signed for, now we've got three. I think this might be the anomaly we've been looking for.'

'That sounds like an anomaly to me. Let me know what you find out.'

Way too cocky.

'Where are you?' Shepherd asked.

'In my car, going down to Pat's for lunch,' Murdoch answered.

Just then the chemist gave a whistle. Shepherd looked up to see him shaking his head. With plain satisfaction, Harwood held a scalpel up for Shepherd to see, a speck of green paint on its tip. 'Hold on, Sarge,' Shepherd said into the phone, then covered the mouthpiece.

'Blue,' the chemist said. 'Under the green paint. The tank's blue. Somebody painted green over it.'

'So, blue – what's the significance?'

'It's not oxygen. Oxygen's green.'

'What's blue?'

His friend smiled. 'Nitrous oxide.'

'Nitrous—?'

'Laughing gas.'

Shepherd stared at Harwood. He uncovered the phone. 'Sarge, I'll call you from Belfast.'

'Yeah, what's up?'

'I'm going to check on that anomaly,' he answered, then hung up.

They sat at the kitchen table over two bowls of corn chowder. Although Sal was anything but hungry, he tried not to let on. In his bowl, a kernel of corn moved through the broth, seemingly under its own strength. The Formica pattern swirled dizzily under his arms. Finally he put down his spoon and got to his feet. 'I gotta go,' he said.

Bouchard pushed his chair back an inch or two, enough to prevent Sal from getting to the door. 'You best get some strength first, my opinion.'

'You're entitled to your opinion,' Sal replied, as he pushed for the door.

Bouchard rose to his feet, blocking the path.

Sal grabbed his shirt to pull him out of the way. 'This is not your concern!' he growled. The dog jumped up, barking.

Bouchard, shorter than Sal by an inch but broader all around, took hold of Sal's arms and swung him into the middle of the room, upending a chair.

'You've got to face this!' he said. 'It's already cost you your home, your career—'

Sal lunged to his right, slipping Bouchard's grasp, but the constable caught him again and drove him hard into the counter.

'Your wife,' he said.

Sal closed his eyes.

'Your little girl—'

'*Yeah!*' Sal drove his elbow into Bouchard's chest. In the next instant, his arm was locked behind his back, his cheek pressed against the cupboard.

'See, I don't understand that logic,' Bouchard said in his ear, 'why anyone would give all that up.'

The dog barked. 'Lay down,' Bouchard told him.

He held onto Sal for a few more moments, then loosened his grip. 'Don't you know,' he said, 'that you're being set up for a murder? A murder you had nothing to do with.'

Sal leaned against the counter. 'You don't know what I did,' he said quietly. 'You don't know anything about me.'

'You got drunk,' Bouchard answered. '*You got drunk*. That's what you did.'

Sal closed his eyes, haunted.

'Noel Swift murdered her husband, as far as I can figure. They were supposed to dig him up, her and Eliot Wicker – but they left him. Killed him for a pile of money stashed in some foreign bank account. And then when things went wrong, she set you up to look guilty.'

Sal shook his head. 'Noel would not do that,' he said. 'Not to Bobby. Not to me.'

'Did you?'

'What?' Sal turned, faced Bouchard.

'Help kill him.'

'Bobby was my best friend.'

'Being his best friend doesn't help.'

Bouchard reached into his back pocket and withdrew a piece of paper, ledger green.

'See, it was someone who cared for him that let him die.' As he unfolded the paper to show Sal, the dog suddenly snapped toward the door and barked – twice, like gunshots.

'Stop!' Bouchard said. He leaned back to look out the low casement window. As the black car crept over the gravel, he folded the paper and stuck it back in his pocket. 'Go in the back and shut the door,' he told Sal, bending to pick up the chair.

'What's that paper?' Sal asked.

A car door closed outside. Bouchard went to the table, grabbed one of the soup bowls and spoons, opened a cupboard and set them inside. A maroon-and-orange checkered blazer

314

strode past the window. Bouchard shot Sal a look, the urgency of which sent Sal backing into the hall as if he'd been shoved.

The dog barked again. Bouchard allowed it to continue.

Sal closed the bedroom door just as he heard Murdoch's voice in the kitchen say, 'Mind if I come in? I didn't think so.' The storm door banged shut.

Shepherd drove north to Belfast, to the company where the two oxygen tanks had been purchased twelve months earlier. But after telling the counterman what he was looking for, he was told that the tank of nitrous couldn't have been bought there.

'Congress says it's a classified hallucinogenic,' said the counterman, an elfish sort of person with a gray beard and light blue, twinkling eyes. 'Christ, you need a special license just to transport the shit.'

'You mean even if I worked for a dentist, I couldn't come down here and pick up a tank of nitrous oxide?'

The small man shook his head. He lifted a thick three-ring notebook from behind the counter and slapped it on the countertop. 'We deliver to dentists' and doctors' offices all over the midcoast area. After we drop it off, who knows? Anybody could've slipped it out. They inhale the shit for recreation, some of 'em. Which is why you need a license.'

Shepherd nodded. The facts told the tale: Bobby Swift had purchased two oxygen tanks to stash in the casket with him. Before the burial, Wicker had replaced one of the tanks with the disguised nitrous – and hidden the oxygen tank under his bed. Therefore, it had to have been either Wicker or Bobby's other accomplice who had signed for the nitrous. Someone with access to a dentist or doctor.

'Could a funeral director sign for nitrous oxide?' Shepherd asked.

'What the hell for?' the counterman said. 'Yeah, right, that'd be one fucked-up funeral.' His laugh sounded like he was choking.

Shepherd opened the book and ran his eye down the signatures on the first page. He knew he wasn't looking for Dale Newman, since Newman was an alias for Bobby Swift, and it was Swift the nitrous had been used against. He was convinced that it wasn't Wicker who had signed for the nitrous. Everything he had learned about the players told him that Wicker would have limited his involvement to the masquerade funeral. No, whoever had procured the nitrous would have been the same person who ended up double-crossing both Bobby and Wicker – someone who had Bobby's trust – the third accomplice.

And Noel still seemed likely, her divorce plans notwithstanding. Of course, the divorce could have been a ruse – Shepherd had suspected that the moment he'd heard it. On the other hand, if she had truly planned to divorce Bobby, then suspicion fell to Bobby's next closest confidant, Sal Erickson. Except something about the man didn't fit; he didn't seem cool enough – or ambitious enough – to have carried out such a deceit. And Noel seemed so perfect.

Ignoring the dog, the sergeant walked stiffly past Bouchard until he was in the center of the kitchen. 'I'm not one to waste time,' he said. With his neck brace, he couldn't move his head without moving his whole body, so he turned a half circle and then stepped to the left in order to look down the hall. 'My colleague Detective Shepherd is down in Belfast right now, at a place called Mid-Maine Supply. Why? Because Mid-Maine Supply sells oxygen – and two oxygen tanks were signed for last spring by a Mr Dale Newman, whose plane ticket ended up in your mailbox, and whose body we fished out of the river yesterday. You ever been in jail yourself, Constable?'

Bouchard leaned back against the sink with his arms folded and his dog pressed against his leg.

'Because now we have a third oxygen tank and, frankly, I get the feeling you know why.'

Bouchard blinked.

Murdoch turned his body and peered down the hall again, at the closed door. 'You don't mind if I have a look around your home,' he said.

'I don't believe that'd be proper,' Bouchard answered. 'Not without a search warrant.'

Murdoch bent his knees, getting a lower angle on Bouchard. 'I like to see a man's eyes when I question him. Are you serious about the search warrant?'

'You got a question,' Bouchard told him, 'I suggest you ask it.'

Murdoch snickered. 'Oh, I've got a lot of questions, Mr Magoo. Number one, I've been trying to locate that olive-complected gentleman you absconded with yesterday – the one I was about to arrest – and now nobody seems to know his whereabouts. He didn't sleep in his room last night. His car and motorcycle are both parked in his yard, but his wife and daughter swear they haven't seen him since yesterday.' Murdoch walked to the table and sniffed the air. 'You probably know that the young widow he's taken up with is heading down to Tampa tomorrow for a little cruise.'

Bouchard studied Murdoch to see if he was bluffing.

The sergeant shrugged, as well as he could manage. 'What's the matter, you think he might be going with her? You can see how that would set you up for a little aiding and abetting charge, can't you?'

Bouchard scratched under the dog's ear.

'Your choice, Sparky, you can talk to me here, or we can take a drive.'

Bouchard stood for a second or two, then he stepped to the

door and pushed it open. He felt a draft push past his neck, outward.

Murdoch said, 'You trying to tell me something, or just letting more insects in?'

Bouchard replied, 'We're going for a drive, Sergeant Murdoch, as far as I can tell. I don't have any answers for you.'

Murdoch chuckled.

The door remained open.

'Oh, you fuckin country boys,' the sergeant said, stopping beside Bouchard. 'You live in one of these submarines and you think you own a piece of the pie.' He stepped onto the porch, jiggled the railing pointedly. As he sauntered down the steps and to his car, he stopped to look in each of the trailer's windows he passed. Then, stooping to direct his rear end onto his car seat, he looked at Bouchard and said, 'I'll be taking a personal interest in your career, Constable.'

The minute Murdoch's car pulled onto the road, Bouchard went back inside. Locking the kitchen door, he walked down the hall, grabbed the doorknob and pushed. A breeze blew through the open window.

Detective Shepherd sat at a small reception table in the lobby of Mid-Maine Supply and opened another notebook. He had been there for two hours, poring over eighteen months of medical receipts, occasionally entering a name into his computer, checking for – what? Names that were signed only once in a particular office? Signatures that seemed forced?

'Any luck?' the counterman asked, as he had done every few minutes.

'We're narrowing it down,' Shepherd replied again, as he had replied every time. He was relieved when the telephone rang and the man had to go back behind the counter to answer it.

'He's here, but he's not looking for oxygen,' Shepherd heard the counterman say.

'Is that for me?'

'Nitrous oxide,' the man answered. 'Laughing gas.'

Shepherd pushed away from the table and held his hand out for the telephone, trying to stop the man from saying more.

'Not yet, but he still hasn't gone through the ice-cream accounts.'

'What ice-cream accounts?' Shepherd said. Apparently the caller had asked the same question, because the counterman began answering them both.

'Whipped cream,' he said. 'They use nitrous as a propellant in whipped cream dispensers – it doesn't leave a taste.'

'Let me have the phone,' Shepherd said.

'Hold on, he wants to talk to you himself.' The small man handed over the telephone, saying, 'It's Sergeant Murdoch.'

Shepherd lifted the phone to his ear. 'Yeah, Sarge, I was just gonna call.' Shepherd listened for some nasty witticism; instead, he got the dial tone.

He handed the phone back to the counterman, who said to him, 'I'll tell you right now, ice cream's gonna be harder to track down, being as how the drivers can pick it up right here.'

Shepherd scowled at him. 'Are you telling me a dentist can't transport nitrous oxide, but an ice-cream driver can?'

'Don't ask me,' the counterman said. 'Freakin Congress.'

At the public telephone inside the school lobby, the phone book lay opened to the Yellow Pages – ICE CREAM MANUFACTURERS. Charlie Walker, the custodian, closed the book and slid it on the shelf. 'Don't worry, I'll put it back,' he muttered, glaring out the glass doors at the Harley rumbling out of the parking lot. 'Friggin wino.'

Sal headed for Ellsworth on the Cooper Road, a winding

logging road that crossed the Maine Central Railroad tracks
four miles out of Gravity. When he reached the crossing, Sal
pulled the Harley onto the tracks and headed west, toward
town. Knowing that Murdoch was searching for him, he
thought it best to avoid being seen until he could figure out
what was going on. He kept the bike between the rails, taking it
slow at first, bouncing over the ties and sliding where the gravel
was deep. But as he considered the implications of nitrous
oxide, he gradually increased his speed, all the while keeping
an eye on his rearview, afraid that he wouldn't hear over his
own engine if a train were to come up behind him. However,
his fear of being rear-ended by a lumber-loaded freighter only
approximated the fear he felt knowing that Noel was getting on
an airplane in the morning.

Behind the meat counter in the empty store, the door opened,
and Noel backed through, carrying two bundled trash bags.
She was wearing a faded green SAVE A TREE – KILL A
LOGGER T-shirt; a green kerchief, banded around her head,
was darkened with her perspiration. When she turned, she saw
Detective Shepherd standing by the counter. She ignored him.

Shepherd raised his hands in mock surrender. 'No questions, I promise,' he said.

She set the bags on the floor, then stood and wiped her face
with her forearm, giving him a droll glance.

He added, a bit contritely, 'I feel a person should apologize
when he's wrong.'

She walked around behind the counter and washed her
hands in the sink. 'I find it hard to believe that you're here to
apologize.'

He sat down on a counter stool. 'No, you're right. Actually,
I've always had a weakness for a good hot fudge sundae.
Homemade ice cream, the sign says. Do you make your own?'

'We buy it locally.'

'Oh, where?'

She turned and gave him a look.

'I can't help it, it's in my blood.'

Her expression turned slightly cynical. 'What flavor?' She lifted the scoop out of its cradle.

'Vanilla, chocolate, coffee, whatever's handy,' he replied, 'as long as you load it up with whipped cream.'

She bent low into the freezer. When she straightened, two mounds of pistachio ice cream sat side by side in the bowl.

'Busy packing for your cruise, or just spring cleaning?' he asked. 'The way your dumpster's heaped over, someone might think you were moving out.'

Lifting a lid off a tub, Noel ladled on the hot fudge sauce slowly. 'I buy my ice cream from Windswept Farms. It's on the island. Nuts?'

'No, thanks. Just the whipped cream.'

Noel opened the refrigerator and took out a stainless steel canister, about eight inches high. There was no label on it, no printing. She shook the can, tipped it upside down, slid her thumb down the nozzle, and pushed. A thick cloud mounded up over the ice cream.

'Keep it coming,' he said.

'I thought you'd get a thrill.'

He chuckled. 'It really is amazing how so much whipped cream can come out of such a small can. How do they do that?'

She set his sundae in front of him. 'You'll have to ask Stan the ice-cream man.'

'Stan the ice-cream man.' Shepherd stirred the whipped cream into the ice cream. 'Stan a friend of yours?'

'Oh, absolutely. Stan tells me about the weather and I agree with him. Of course we don't enjoy the sort of rapport that you and I have. But if you take him to dinner sometime and astound him with your investigative prowess, I'm sure he'll tell you how whipped cream comes out of a can.'

Shepherd allowed a penitent smile. 'Noel, if I had known about the divorce, things would have gone differently.' He took a bite of ice cream, tasted it, swallowed. 'While we're on the subject, do you know if Bobby ever told anyone you were leaving him?'

She watched him.

'See, people are different. Man and woman split up – that's tough, emotionally. A lot of guys'd have a friend or somebody close they could confide in.' He stirred the sundae some more. 'The thing is, I haven't been able to find anyone who knew about you and Bobby. Except your lawyer.'

She seemed to smile at Shepherd. 'Who did you confide in, Detective?'

His spoon stopped.

'You hear things in a place like this,' she continued. 'From what I've heard, she got her doctorate degree and left you with the condo. She sounds like a very intelligent, independent woman.'

He acquiesced with a nod. 'That's a fair assessment.'

Noel turned her back to him, casually toweled off the butcher block. 'I only mention it because Mr Jones, my attorney, thinks it may explain your aggression toward me.'

'That's what he thinks, huh?' Shepherd put down his spoon and wiped his mouth with a napkin. 'Listen, before I go, you don't have the phone number of Windswept Farms, do you?'

'Right here,' she answered, nodding to a clipboard that hung beside the wall phone.

'May I?' he said.

'Please.' She folded her arms, sat back against the ice-cream freezer to watch.

He brought his sundae behind the counter and dialed. The man who answered the phone identified himself as Fuzzy O'Coin. As soon as Shepherd introduced himself, the man sighed impatiently. 'We buy our nitrous oxide from Ellsworth Oxy-Acetylene, I just got finished telling your Sergeant Murdoch, thank you very much—'

Shepherd looked over at Noel: 'Has Murdoch been in here?' he asked. She shook her head. 'Has he called?' Again no.

'—I'm sorry, but are you people charging Stanley with a crime?'

'Mr O'Coin, I just want to know if Stanley is the one who signs for shipments of nitrous oxide.' Shepherd kept his eye on Noel.

'What shipments? Stanley picks it up when he's out on deliveries, when we need it, which isn't often.'

'How does he do that?'

'How does he do what? He picks up the full tanks and turns in the empties and signs a book. It's not complicated, Detective.'

'Just like that.'

'Of course, we had to get a license from the FDA, swearing that we were a manufacturer of ice cream and would never use the nitrous for enjoyment. Heaven forbid people should actually *enjoy* themselves.'

While Fuzzy fumed, Shepherd traded another glance with Noel. She seemed to take pleasure in his side of the conversation.

'Mr O'Coin, has Stanley lost that license in the past year? Physically, I mean, has he reported it missing, so that you've had to apply for another one?'

There was a brief pause, and then Fuzzy said, 'You *have* heard of the pursuit of happiness, Detective. It's one of our fundamental rights, you know.'

Shepherd smiled. 'I'll take that as a yes. When did he lose it, do you remember?'

'A year ago, I suppose. My God, crime of the century. Somewhere someone is laughing illegally.'

'Mr O'Coin?'

'*What?*'

'Have a nice day.'

Sal found the oxy-acetylene company in Ellsworth, on a back road that wound through an industrial complex of low, flat-roofed structures that looked like they had been built in a week. Framed by withering potted birches, the orange entrance door led into a small lobby that contained two orange plastic chairs and a collection of *Small Business* magazines fanned neatly on a table. Behind a high orange counter, a young receptionist with piles of blonde hair stopped typing and said, 'Can I help you?'

Sal picked the business card out of his T-shirt pocket and slid it across the counter. 'Sergeant Murdoch,' he said, keeping his eye on her. 'State Police.'

Behind her, a door swung open and a man in a blue suit came through, about forty-five, with round wire-frame glasses, thinning brown hair and a scruffy, reddish beard. 'Now what?' he complained. 'The other guy was in when? Saturday afternoon—?' Redbeard looked at the receptionist, who confirmed eagerly. 'Saturday afternoon.'

'What guy?' Sal asked.

'I don't know. Vice squad, by the looks of him. Scruffy, like you. Black beard, Coke-bottle glasses.'

Bouchard.

Sal's insides clenched. 'What was he looking for?'

'Ask him. He looked through the nitrous book for about ten minutes and then he took off.'

'Yeah, what book is that?'

The man answered by tossing an opened three-ring notebook on the counter in front of Sal. The pages that stared up at him were ledger green.

'Would you like to sit down?' said the woman with the hair, but Sal was already out the door.

Undone

* * *

Driving to Ellsworth, Shepherd set the blue flasher on his roof. He wanted to reach the company before it closed – and before Murdoch beat him there. He could feel things coming together rapidly. Like maybe last spring Stan the ice-cream man had stepped away from his truck and someone had grabbed his nitrous license. Shepherd figured that Murdoch had already reached the same conclusion. As he crossed the town line into Ellsworth, the sergeant came over the radio.

'Pick up,' Murdoch squawked. 'You pick up.'

Shepherd left the mike in its cradle.

'Listen to me. We just got another call from the lady's lawyer. They're filing harassment charges. Are you listening? Because you're not only off this case, wise guy, but the next case you're gonna get is a good case of assburn from riding the dispatch desk. You hear that, Mister Dick? Your shift is over.'

Shepherd snatched the microphone, pushed the trigger. 'I'll file with the union, Sarge, I'm telling you now.'

'*Fuck your union!* What are you trying to pull?'

'I'm in Ellsworth,' Shepherd said. 'I'll be there in a minute.'

'Be where?'

'The acetylene place!'

'What acetylene place?'

Shepherd looked at his radio.

'*What acetylene place?*' Murdoch barked.

Shepherd switched him off.

He reached the building in slightly more than a minute, at twenty to five. When he showed his badge over the counter, Redbeard flipped his ballpoint pen into the air. 'Jesus Christ, can't you guys get together?'

'Excuse me?'

325

'I'm just saying – One comes in Saturday, two today? No wonder we can't pay our goddamn taxes.' He slid the notebook in front of Shepherd. 'Knock yourself out, we close in fifteen minutes.' He opened a side door and disappeared into the warehouse.

Shepherd looked at the receptionist. She smiled.

'He mentioned somebody else—?'

She described Alston Bouchard first, which did not surprise Shepherd.

'Who was in today?' he said, as he opened the book.

'Undercover,' the receptionist said. 'He just left a few minutes ago. On a Harley.'

Shepherd looked up from the book. 'What did he want?'

'To see the book.'

'These detectives,' Shepherd said, 'did they show you their shields?'

She scowled apologetically. 'When somebody says they're a detective, I guess you don't ask.'

He nodded. 'How about when somebody wants to pick up a tank of nitrous oxide, do you check their licenses?'

She hunched her shoulders. 'Always. Until I get to know them.'

He began turning pages again. 'You make them sign the book?'

She nodded. 'Always.'

He fanned the pages back to May of the previous year, when the oxygen tanks had been bought. From there he started flipping forward. 'How about the driver from Windswept Farms?'

'That'd be Stan. He's wicked nice.'

'Do you remember anybody else from that company ever coming in? Maybe last summer—?'

She hunched her shoulders again. 'I only just started in January.'

Shepherd stopped on June 25. Turned back a page, to June 23. The missing page had been ripped at the perforation; specks of paper still clung to the tear.

Shepherd closed the book and walked around the counter, a heady sensation coming over him. It was a feeling he loved, the rush of facts converging. With a quick thank-you to the receptionist, he threw open the door and walked quietly to his Cherokee, where he sat inside and turned on his computer. *Search*, he instructed the machine: *Bouchard*.

Sal muscled the Harley up the rocky farm road, the low sun on his back. After finding Bouchard's house trailer empty and the Subaru parked in front, he decided to try the hill. Muscling the Harley up the rock-packed earth that bisected the blueberry hill, halfway up he saw a blue farm truck pulled off to the right, near a birch windbreak. As he drew nearer, he made out Bouchard on the other side of the truck, wearing gray overalls, a corduroy shirt buttoned to the neck and high rubber boots.

Sal pulled up to the farm truck and shut off the engine. Bouchard kept his back to Sal as he worked over a stack of four white boxes sitting on a wooden pallet. Dark shadows breathed around the boxes like a moving storm cloud. Sal could hear the low, sonorous humming of bees.

'Don't worry,' Bouchard said, 'they wouldn't be worried about you.'

Sal could see a bunch of the honeybees crawling on Bouchard's arm.

'I'd pull that motorcycle behind the truck,' Bouchard said as he lifted the lid off one of the hives and shook the bees off his hand. 'Lay it down in the grass.'

'You took that receipt from the acetylene place,' Sal told him. 'I want to know why.'

Bouchard replaced the lid carefully, then took off his

gloves, tossed them in the open window of the farm truck and started walking up the hill. He shook more bees off his arm

Sal stayed where he was, watching. He noticed Bouchard's dog for the first time, sitting nervously in the road about fifty feet ahead. He hadn't seen the black dog at first, blending as it did with the burned-over land to the left. But now the dog rose, wagging its tail, anticipating his master.

'I want an answer,' Sal said.

Bouchard kept walking.

The computer!

The revelation hit Shepherd a minute too late, as the employees were filing out of the building. Spotting the young receptionist, the detective opened his car door. 'Excuse me, he said.

She glanced over, smiled.

'The information in the receipt book – you enter it in you computer—?'

She thought about the question and nodded. 'Uh-huh.'

'Including the person who signed for it?'

'I knew it!' a voice said – Redbeard, coming out the door 'No way. My kid's got a ball game. Come back in the morning.' He locked the door behind him.

'It'll only take a minute,' Shepherd said. 'I need one name off your computer. One minute.'

'I don't mind staying with him,' the receptionist volun teered. 'I can lock up.'

Before Redbeard could respond, their attention turned to the parking lot entrance, where a black, unmarked Mercury had turned in from the street, its blue dash light flashing.

'Here we go,' Redbeard said, and he tossed his keys to the receptionist. 'Just remember,' he said to Shepherd, 'w cooperated.'

Murdoch pulled the sedan to the front of the building and

pushed himself out the door like something robotic. Falling in
step behind Shepherd and the receptionist, he said, 'I'll take
over from here. Whadda we got?'

Shepherd led the way into the lobby and around the
counter without responding, walked directly to the receptionist's desk, where he turned on her computer. He leaned
over the monitor, reading the on-screen menu. 'June twenty-
fourth, last year,' he said to the receptionist as she came
around beside him.

'The third oxygen tank,' Murdoch said to him. 'You got a
name?'

Shepherd looked up at him curiously.

'Let me take a wild guess,' Murdoch continued. There was
a light, superior quality in the sergeant's voice that Shepherd
could not resist shooting down.

He reached behind the computer monitor and shut it off.
'It's not oxygen we're looking for,' he said.

Murdoch chuckled. 'Whatever,' he replied. 'Your buddy at
the crime lab called a while ago. They got a print match on
that other champagne glass from the undertaker's house.'

'Yeah?' Shepherd said, studying the sergeant, who was
happily hoarding the information.

Murdoch folded his arms. 'You want to work for me on
this case?'

Shepherd glared at him.

Murdoch, no less smug: 'I need to know that we're com-
patible. Which means no union horseshit, pardon my French,'
he added, for the receptionist's sake.

Shepherd continued glaring, fighting the impulse to haul
off on Murdoch's pink, jeering face. Instead, he flicked on the
monitor again.

The receptionist punched a couple of keys. 'Six-twenty-
four,' she said. 'Want the name?'

'I already know the name,' Murdoch answered, turning his

body and heading for the door. 'You want to be in on the apprehension,' he said to Shepherd, 'I suggest you follow me.'

From the top of Blueberry Hill, the ocean spread flat and silvery against the eastern sky, its dark strands of islands floating like clouds; while off to the west a lone white steeple rose out of the greenery. Just beyond the top of the hill, where the field road ended, the entire ground was black all the way to a low stone wall that rimmed the field and kept back the woods that led down the northern slope.

When the two men reached the stone wall, Bouchard stepped over and pushed his hand into a pocket of his overalls. Sal tensed on the near side of the wall, wondering if he was about to see a gun. But it was the green receipt that Bouchard pulled out. 'See, they let him go easy,' the constable said.

Sal stepped over the wall, took the paper from Bouchard and unfolded it. The page was divided in fourths – four separate receipts, four signatures. One jumped off the page: *Salvatore W. Erickson.*

'Is that your handwriting?'

Sal stared. His chest expanded.

'A year ago you presented your ice-cream manufacturer's license to a clerk at Ellsworth Oxy-Acetylene and signed out a small tank of nitrous oxide. That's what this means.'

The paper shivered in Sal's hand. 'What license?' he said.

'You were drinking heavy back then, most likely. Last June?'

Salvatore W. Erickson. Sal stared at the signature, but it made no sense.

'I think she had you drive into town and pick up the tank for her. Had you show the license and sign for it. You were drunk.'

Undone

Sal shook his head. The rest of his body was shaking on its own. He eyed the wooded hillside, ready to bolt.

'She knew you wouldn't remember.'

On the other side of the wall, the black lab looked up, grinning nervously. Suddenly the dog's ears perked; he turned to face the gravel road, which fell out of sight about fifty feet away. Bouchard looked that way too, then said to Sal with sudden, uncommon urgency, 'Go into the woods.'

'What?'

'Go now.' Bouchard tapped the receipt page. 'There'll be more.'

Sal stared at him.

'She had a contingency plan, in case something went wrong. The way I see it, you.'

The dog took three steps onto the road and stopped. An explosive bark froze Sal, and then the dog barreled up the road in a cloud. Engines sounded, climbing up the other side.

'They're coming for me,' Bouchard said. 'They won't know you're here. Now go into the woods. There's a path to my sister's house. Tell her I sent you.'

'Wait a minute,' Sal said.

Bouchard pulled him toward an old, spreading oak that was part of the wall. *'You've got to get hid!'* Transmissions whined like insects. 'She's smarter than you. And she's been planning this too long.'

Sal held back, resisting.

'Either that or you did it. You and Bobby and Wicker together. Then you double-crossed them both and set her up. That's the way she's made it look.'

Sal stared at him.

'Where were you the night of Bobby's funeral?'

'I don't know!'

Bouchard grabbed him, swung him around the back of the

oak tree, and spoke directly into his face. '*It doesn't matter.*
The only way you're not guilty is if you were there digging
him up. Anyplace else, you murdered him.'

Sal stood frozen, incapable of absorbing what he was being
told. The engines grew louder.

'You stay away from her,' Bouchard warned in a low voice.
'She'll kill you. It'll be self-defense, and she'll go free.' He
took the receipt page from Sal, stuffed it in Sal's shirt pocket.
Then he pressed a set of keys into Sal's hand.

'Remember, she's not perfect.'

'*What?*'

Unzipping his fly, Bouchard climbed over the stone wall.
Sal heard him pissing on the front of the tree. Suddenly the
engines got louder, tires grabbing gravel and rock. Sal's heart
pumped another shot of adrenaline. Then car doors opened
and closed. Sal stared at the keys in his hand. The first voice
he heard made him cringe.

'Destroying more evidence, Mister Magoo?'

Behind the tree, Sal clenched every muscle in his body,
trying not to breathe.

'I was relieving myself,' Bouchard answered, walking away
from the tree.

A different voice, coming closer: 'You have someone who
can take care of your dog, Mr Bouchard?'

'My sister lives over on the next hill.'

'Save yourself the trouble,' Murdoch said. 'Tell us where
to find Sacco and Vanzetti.'

'Salvatore Erickson,' Shepherd said. 'You know who we're
talking about.'

Sal's stomach floated up.

'And turn over the evidence you took. Hindering the
apprehension: that's time, you know.'

'I don't believe I have any evidence.'

'Mr Bouchard, you're protecting a felony suspect.'

'You're looking for the wrong person,' Bouchard said. 'Sal Erickson was set up.'

'We've got a dozen witnesses who place your buddy out on a drunken rampage the night Eliot Wicker was murdered. Half a dozen who put him with Bobby Swift the night before Mr Swift *passed on*.'

'The facts are there,' Shepherd said. 'Bobby Swift wanted to disappear. He needed the undertaker to bury him. And he needed someone he could trust to dig him up – his best friend.'

'And then the best friend does 'em both.' Murdoch hawked a laugh.

'Noel Swift planted the evidence against him,' Bouchard said. 'And she's leaving in the morning.'

'We're well aware of her travel plans, Mr Bouchard. As far as the Constitution is concerned, she has a right to take her vacation.'

'She won't be back,' Bouchard told them, 'and you'll have an innocent man in custody.'

'I'm sorry, Constable, the facts don't support your theory. We have videotape of Erickson's cap at Eliot Wicker's house, his prints on a champagne glass and bottle over there. He and Wicker were going to split Bobby Swift's Cayman money – at least that's what Mr Wicker thought.'

Bouchard's voice again: 'I know these people, Detective. Sal Erickson is a good man. He was Bobby Swift's friend.'

Murdoch smirked. 'I've never yet seen a man double-crossed by his enemy.'

Goose bumps tingled over Sal's arms. He pressed against the back of the tree.

'Why do you suppose he'd leave his fingerprints at the victim's house?' Bouchard said. 'Or sign his own name on the receipt?'

Murdoch answered, thick with satisfaction: 'Guy kills his

best friend and then diddles the widow. I don't know, maybe
he's feeling a little guilty and he wants to be punished. I'll tell
you what. Detective Shepherd is our resident psychologist.
Why don't you take a ride with him, and you can discuss your
theories while he reads you your rights. Or save yourself the
trouble and give up the greaseball.'

Bouchard remained silent.

'That's actually good,' Murdoch said. 'I was hoping you
wouldn't cooperate. Detective, take Ray Charles for a ride
and introduce him to the inside of the county jail. I'm going
down to say hello to some of the townspeople.'

As Sal heard the footsteps scratching away on the hardpack,
he heard Murdoch say, 'Put the nips on him, detective. This
ain't a joyride.' The footsteps stopped, replaced by the metallic jangle of handcuffs – and Shepherd's attempts to lighten
the circumstance.

'One thing I can say for you, Mr Bouchard, I respect your
loyalty.'

'I'm trying to do my job,' Bouchard answered. 'Seems all
you want is a closed case.'

'Not at all. We're entirely directed by the evidence.'

'You know he's not guilty.'

'I think we can prove he did it.'

'You know he didn't do it.'

'We can prove he's guilty, then!' Shepherd snapped. 'Either
way.'

The footsteps started up again, and then a car door
slammed shut. Another car door closed, and then another.
The engines started up again, revved, and then the vehicles
drove over the rocks and gravel and were gone. Sal remained
motionless behind the tree, his body quivering, his mind
racing with confusion, while overhead a flock of swallows
darted about, chittering madly.

13

Sal waited until dusk settled before coming off the hill. Knowing that Murdoch and other police would be patrolling the town for him, he took Bouchard's prescription sunglasses off the constable's dashboard, popped out the lenses with his thumb and fit the frames on his face. He pulled one of Bouchard's caps over his brow and drove the Subaru toward the coast. He had no idea where he was going. The fuel gauge registered a quarter tank. He had less than eighty dollars in his pockets; and even though his Visa and ATM cards were in his wallet, he had no doubt the police would have traces on them by now. He wasn't going far.

All he really wanted was to be in his own warm living room again, sitting on the couch with Iris on one side and Davey on the other. He knew the police would have already been there. He wondered what they had told Iris, wondered what she believed, and what she chose to tell Davey.

He felt the paper in his shirt pocket, took it out and turned on the interior light. *Salvatore W. Erickson.* QUANTITY ONE, NITROUS OXIDE, RECEIVED BY . . . Not a forgery, but his actual signature. According to the date, he had signed for the tank almost a year ago, beginning of summer, right after school got out. He was drinking heavily then, he and Bobby both, going to ball games and bars. He could remember only isolated patches of those months, nothing of a plan with Bobby and Wicker.

He did remember the day Bobby died: jogging to the store; the way Wicker went speeding past ... and at the funeral, thinking it strange that Bobby was wearing a wrist-watch ... The signs were there, now that he had an idea what they meant. And then the reception at Noel's – when the wall went up, when he'd started drinking again. He remembered the way Noel had come up behind him with the drink in her hand ...

wearing her gloves ...

The champagne glass—

He pulled off the road about a mile outside of town, in the Oyster Cove Post Office.

She'd planted the glass at Wicker's. Same time she'd planted his cap. Sal felt a terrible sinking in his chest. Simultaneously, an irrepressible need arose in him to see her, to confront her. But he couldn't go over there, not if Bouchard was right—

And Bouchard was right. Sal could deny it no longer.

He wheeled the Subaru around the parking lot and turned back toward Gravity. He avoided the main road, cut back into town on a dirt road that wound through miles of disused blueberry flats and woods. The road would eventually join the River Road, a hundred feet from Sal's house.

You stay away from her.

Going home. He would see Iris and Davey. Profess his innocence to Iris, kiss Davey goodnight, and then ... play it by ear. Maybe borrow some money from Iris and try to make New Brunswick. Or maybe he'd call the police and give himself up, trust his fate to the courts.

There'll be more evidence against you. She's been planning this too long.

He imagined going over there – if he could get past the

police. There were two ways in: through the store or through the garage. He'd wait until just before dawn, when he was sure she was asleep. He'd get inside the garage, then sneak up the stairs, catch her in her bedroom. Force her to confess.

She'll kill you. It'll be self-defense, and she'll go free.

Headlights flashed in his rearview, and his heart jumped. He hit the gas, and the Subaru rattled over the washboard road, its back end sliding out. Behind him, the headlights kept pace. When the blueberry flats ended, the road climbed into the woods and turned to the left. He took the curve and lost the headlights momentarily, but as soon as the road straightened again, the woods in his rearview lit bright green. He went faster, even though he knew he couldn't outrun whoever was following him, with the road so rutted and full of curves. As he watched the mirror, the headlights shot over a rise, nailing him.

The woods in front came up too fast to negotiate. Sal stomped the brakes, and the car swerved to a stop, its right wheels halfway up the bank, its grill two feet from a thick birch. Suddenly the Subaru's interior brightened. Bright lights off his mirror blinded him. He leaned across the passenger seat, took hold of the door handle, ready to bolt.

The approaching vehicle slowed, pulled alongside. With his hand on the door handle, Sal pretended to be searching through his glove compartment. He waved them on, as he imagined Bouchard might, subtly, his arm blocking his face. He heard a sharp roar, and the vehicle shot around him, coming to the road's end just ahead – a Jeep, full of kids. They screeched their tires as they swung out onto the River Road. Sal watched the taillights flicker through the trees and then disappear.

He turned the key, and the Subaru started again. He backed off the banking, then pulled slowly to the stop sign. Looked right and left and saw no other vehicles on the road. He thought of leaving the Subaru where it was and making his way to his house through the woods – sneak in the back door. But Bouchard's car would be spotted in minutes – it would be obvious where Sal had gone. No, he had to ditch the car someplace where he could buy more time. He pulled onto the road and drove past his house slowly – Iris's car and his own, parked side by side; lights on in the living room; he could make out the stairs and the hanging plant through the big front window, as if nothing in the world were wrong. But there was no sign of Iris or Davey, no sign of life. He wondered if they were in on the plan to capture him.

Up ahead, headlights turned toward him from the village. As the vehicle passed slowly under the streetlight, Sal saw the light rack on the roof, saw two heads in the cruiser. State troopers – Sal hoped they wouldn't recognize Bouchard's car. He adjusted his cap, put both hands on the wheel, steadied his foot on the accelerator. As the cruiser approached, he brought his fist to his mouth, pretending to cough, and then he watched his sideview to make sure the car's brake lights didn't flash.

At the Village Road he turned left, drove over the bridge, stayed in second gear up the short hill, and then he was passing the store. He saw two cars in the lot and a pickup truck at the pumps. He didn't want to look in the windows, didn't want the temptation, but he shot a glance just the same. A man at the cash register, but that's all he saw. A hundred feet past the store he checked the mirror to make sure he wasn't being followed, then he doused his headlights and pulled a hard left into the firehouse lot.

Several other vehicles were parked there. The garage doors were opened on the town's two pumpers – the monthly meeting of the volunteers. Sal tucked the Subaru beside a panel truck, slipped out the door and disappeared behind the wooden building.

Undone

Keeping to the tree line, he made his way back toward the bridge, running across Herb and Bonnie True's backyard, then veering a ways into the woods to avoid the lights that reached across the road from the Superette. Stopping behind an old pine, he couldn't resist looking for her again; but all he saw were a couple of people through the front windows and one outside pumping gas, none of them Noel. He started moving again to the next tree – and that's when he spotted her. Upstairs, in her living room window. He stepped out from behind the tree and watched as she stood behind the glass – almost like she knew he was out there. Like she was waiting for him. And then her arm went up, and the blinds came down.

All at once headlights shot over his head, and a car engine roared. Sal dropped to the ground. The black sedan tore up Noel's driveway, then cut across the parking lot. With equal urgency, another car suddenly shot up from the River Road, headlights flashing. Sal raised himself on his forearms. It was Shepherd's Cherokee. Both vehicles converged on the firehouse at once, blue lights flashing. At the same time, the store opened up and three men ran diagonally across the road toward the police lights; they didn't appear to be cops themselves. Now the sound of a police radio cut through the air, and Sal knew it wouldn't be long before they'd be coming his way.

He needed to get across the bridge in order to reach the path to the river – which meant he needed to get out to the road – either that or swim, and the river was much too cold, especially when he might be outside for hours in the cold night air.

Staying behind the trees, he made his way to the high river-bank, where he stopped for only a second. Down below, the water was fairly loud – a good sign, if he could judge by the volume – it meant the river was running fast – low tide – and the pool would be traversable. But along with the river sounds, he heard a change in the men's voices at the firehouse. They were starting to move.

He checked to make sure no more cars were coming, and then he ran along the riverbank straight to the bridge, where he ducked behind the low concrete abutment. He looked up the road, where, against the lights of the firehouse, he could see heads moving down, flashlights painting the asphalt. Staying close to the ground, he crawled around the abutment and was about to run across the bridge when headlights swung in off the River Road. Sal pulled behind the concrete again and dropped to his knees.

To his left, he heard the voices getting closer. To his right, the car was approaching dangerously slowly. He lay flat on the gravel, perpendicular to the road. Keep breathing, he told himself, keep moving. He thought of Iris and Davey, steeled his nerves. He shifted to his right until he hit the edge of the bank – a steep fall here, fifteen feet to concrete and rocks. He looked down, thinking if he jumped out far enough, he might make the water, but it was only two or three feet deep. He looked across the span and saw the bright light moving along the opposite bank, dancing across the greenery, then flooding out over the river. Now he heard the tires humming over the steel grating, the engine moving closer to his ear. To his left, the men walking down from the firehouse were almost on top of him. He pressed his cheek to the sand, held his breath. He saw the spotlight touch his left boot. It lingered for a moment and then moved away into the grass as the car passed, its headlights glaring on the men walking down. A rush of urgency overcame Sal. He jumped up into the red glow of taillights while the search party was blinded by headlights, and ran low along the bridge to the other side, where he swung around the abutment and was hidden again. With no thought of safety, he dropped into the darkness, sliding down the steep path on his ands and the soles of his boots. He landed painfully, his right foot twisting against the base of a sapling, and he hobbled to keep from falling.

Despite the pain and the darkness, he immediately resumed his escape, keeping the river noise at his right, climbing over concrete and rocks with diminishing regard for his safety. Behind him, the men mounted the bridge and walked noisily across, shining flashlights down. Sal ducked behind a block, watched the light beams crisscross around him. Then they moved on. He got up and continued making his way downriver.

As his eyes became accustomed to the moonless night, the river began to show itself more clearly on his right, a dim sparkling under the deepening yet still luminous sky. Ahead in the darkness of land, peepers chorused in rapt oblivion. Sal kept to the path as the bank inclined, increasing his pace. But, approaching the pool, a sense of foreboding came over him, far heavier than the danger he was in. He stopped walking. He thought it might be a sixth sense at first, a warning. Then he feared it was something far more ominous.

He stood frozen at the edge of the pool – a tidal bog now, keening with peepers. The entire cove was still, the shallow water taking on the misted sheen of buffed aluminum, broken only by the black shapes of exposed rocks and tussocks – his stepping stones. Sal had crossed the bog dozens of times, knew the way by heart: nine or ten steps to the other side, his fishing rock—

He heard a scratch. He spun around. Heads ducked behind trees, shadows tossed about. *Sins come back.* He closed his eyes, focused his hearing, trying to distinguish any sound other than the flowing water and beckoning tree frogs. And now he could hear whispers . . . the rustle of leaves . . . sounds, he told himself, that, like the visions, were merely the by-products of his poisoned imagination. He took a deep breath, let it out.

He opened his eyes again, focused on the bog. Peepers screeched on, unwary of his presence. He looked out and visualized his way across: three staggered rocks and then a wide tussock; then three quick steps – rock, tussock, rock – a short hop to a double tussock; and then the final leap to his fishing rock—

Bobby's hand, reaching up.

Sal refused the image. Iris and Davey, he thought, Iris and Davey – he pictured their faces as he lowered himself down the bank and made the first two rocks in two steps. Arms spread for balance, he did not allow himself to think of anything but the next rock – a flat two-footer about three feet away. He took a deep breath, let it out. *Iris and Davey*. He threw himself at it, landed with his left foot, then brought his right to join it. His sense of balance helped center him. The next step was a couple of feet to his right, a high, wide tussock. Despite his shaking legs, Sal stepped onto it gingerly. The tussock wobbled, but he worked his arms and stayed with it. Balance. In the past, he would offer his sense of balance to Iris as proof that he was not an alcoholic. I never left my feet, he'd tell her, and it was always true – he could sleep standing. Now he shut off his mind again, became automatic. The next three stepping stones were clustered together, right, left, right. And that's how he stepped – right, left, right – until he was standing on a smooth, humpbacked rock, with only two steps to go.

Mentally he prepared to make the jump – first the twin tussocks that stood out of the mist four feet away – then a quick leap to his fishing rock. The fear bubbled to the surface unexpectedly.

Silence.

He realized that the peepers had stopped.

It was as if the bog itself were holding its breath, while the river on the other side of the sandbar continued its malignant whispering. Sal refused to listen. He looked out to his fishing

ock, and then beyond, up the rocky bank to the pines.
Shadows were everywhere now, shadows crouching behind
shadows, shadows walking the tree line ... Sal lowered his
eyes, focused only on the distance to the tussocks and not
beyond. He knew what was there: his fishing rock, and nothing
more.

He would make the leap and then leap again and not stop for
anything, not look back. He'd run up the path through the
woods and into the field, where he would see his house. He
would run across the road and let himself in the back door. He
would see Iris and Davey—

He let go, threw himself at the tussocks and landed on his
left foot, with which he intended to push himself off again.
Instead, the tussocks gave way. Arms outstretched, Sal started
to fall, reaching for the rock—

but there were arms below him—

reaching out of the mist—

He slammed down into three inches of water, shattering his
own image, then scrambled out of the muck and was racing
across the rock, over an upward ledge, breaking through thick
dead pine boughs into the field, where he could see his lights
across the road, his house—

A beam of light shot toward him—

He threw himself to the ground, flattened himself.

Like a lighthouse beacon, the searchlight brushed the tops of
the grass as the patrol car crawled along the road. Panting, Sal
stayed down, listened to the car go away. Then he pushed
himself to his hands and knees. The *clatch* of a shotgun stopped
his heart—

But it was a voice, not a gunshot, that he heard next.

Terry Royal sauntered out of the pines with the gun under his
arm, a cigarette in his mouth.

'Yeah, one day you're the town singin teacher, next thing

you know you're a hundred-eighty-pound Caucasian male.' A
three-pack of cans hung from Jerry's belt.

'Shh,' Sal said. 'They're looking for me.'

'No shit, they been goin by your house every other minute.
got 'em on the radio. They want you bad, man. What for?'

'They think I killed Bobby.'

Jerry stared at Sal through the darkness.

'Eliot Wicker too.'

'Whoa!' It was a cheer, but the way Sal looked up at him
Jerry turned the sound into a sinus-clearing hawk, which he
spat into the grass. 'No, that's bad, really,' he said. There wa
only one thing that made Jerry happier than seeing someone
else in trouble, and that was when someone else was in troubl
for something he did. He flipped his cigarette into the air an
turned back to the pines. 'Come on, I got a good place,' h
said, and he proceeded to lead Sal to a hollow in the trees
where an old flatbed truck was sunk in the ground to its axles
its plank bed overlooking a carpet of flattened cans and half
planted bottles.

'I been up keepin watch,' Jerry explained as he boosted
himself onto the truck's bed. 'Break the Guinness record fo
not sleepin – three days and nights now. But they think you
killed Bobby, no shit.' Jerry acted unnaturally agitated, patting
the truck bed beside him, inviting Sal to sit. 'It's a good place
'cause you're hid up here, but you can still see the road, see a
around, in case anyone's got ideas.' He fished a cigarette out o
his shirt pocket, snapped fire from his plastic lighter. The flame
shivered as he drew. 'Want one? Want one of these?' Holding
up a can of cola.

Sal shook his head.

'No, but many's the time I come out here to sort things out,
Jerry continued.

Without a doubt, Jerry had his own sorting out to do. For i
Noel had indeed fixed things so that Sal Erickson was about to

344

pay for their crimes, then Jerry was free and clear, just as Noel
had promised. Except—

the one thing that could destroy them both—

'This is like a nightmare,' Sal said.

'Hey, tell me about it.'

That fucking letter, again and again. How many times today
had Jerry volleyed that thing back and forth, and for how many
sleepless nights? Noel was right: It wouldn't take a genius to
figure out that the person who wrote the letter was the same
person who had killed Wicker. Bottom line: He could leave the
letter hidden in the attic where it might remain until he died –
of natural causes (as long as he could count on the little girl not
to get nosy . . . fat chance). On the other hand, he could destroy
the letter and then have sex with Noel – and hope she didn't kill
him afterwards. Real fat chance.

'They found my fingerprints in Wicker's house,' Sal said.
'My hat was there.'

Sex. Always sex that confounded things. Even as Sal talked,
Jerry couldn't help picturing Noel naked in her bathtub,
nipples like twin pink pacifiers. 'So, fingerprints,' Jerry said,
cigarette smoke closing his eye. 'Hard to argue with fingerprints.'

'But I didn't know Wicker,' Sal told him. 'I never visited
him. I never even talked to him until the day Bobby died.'

Then again he could lie about it. That was always Jerry's first
inclination anyway. He could tell Noel that he had destroyed
the letter when actually he hadn't. No. That would be double
jeopardy. Because not only would the letter still be around for
somebody to find, but Noel would think she had nothing to
lose by killing him.

'So maybe you'd oughta give yourself up,' Jerry said. 'Sign a
confession. They'll prob'ly go easier on you.'

'I'm not confessing to something I didn't do.'

Or he could go ahead and destroy the letter – but not tell

Noel about it . . . No, that was even worse. Then he'd not only be out the sex, but if she did kill him, he wouldn't be able to get her back.

'No way I would've done that to Bobby,' Sal said. 'He was my best friend.'

Jerry dragged ponderously – the cigarette glowed. *I feel an animal attraction for you that's overpowering.* Over and over he heard those words: *animal attraction.* Now she was crawling up the aisle of his gospel bus in a leopard-skin corset and a Cat Woman mask . . . Disgusted, Jerry flipped his cigarette into one of the cans.

'Battle of the sexes,' he said. 'I'll tell you, just once in my life I'd like to find a woman I could trust.'

The words died in the pines, but a reverberation came at Sal with the impact of a slap—

Trust with your life.

Bobby had said the same thing by the river – the night before he had faked his death. It's what Bobby had come to tell him – not that Noel was divorcing him – but that she was about to bury him alive. And he was having second thoughts.

'You alright?' Jerry said. 'Hey—' He poked Sal's arm. 'Christ, don't have a conniption fit on me.'

Sal continued staring at him. Like the perfect break shot, balls began dropping into every hole.

He remembered what Bouchard had told him:

She's not perfect.

'Jerry,' said Sal.

'I'm right here.'

Still staring at him, Sal asked, 'How is it you think that fire started?'

Sal watched as Jerry pulled a cigarette out of his pack, tamped it rapidly on the truck bed. 'What fire we talkin about?'

'I mean, how do you figure your house caught fire that night you were up in Bangor?'

Jerry stuck the cigarette in his mouth, dug his lighter out of his pocket. 'You heard the lady – somethin got in after my chicks.'

'Is that what you think?'

Jerry lit the cigarette, kept the flame going so he could see Sal's face and Sal could see his.

'What I think? I wouldn't get any ideas, that's what I think.'

Sal slid off the truck, took a couple of steps toward the field, stared through the trees at the lights of his house. When he turned around again, Jerry had his shotgun propped under his arm, aimed at Sal's stomach.

Sal stood there, suddenly too sure of himself to feel threatened. 'What are you going to do, Jerry?' he said, in a way that could only be taken as admonishment, a warning.

Jerry's cigarette head brightened. The shotgun didn't move.

'You gonna shoot me?'

Jerry blew the smoke out his nose, and it billowed around his head. 'I guess I'm waitin to see which way this conversation goes.'

'I need your truck,' Sal told him.

'Whoa.'

'Just for an hour.'

Breathing loudly through his nose, Jerry kept his gun trained on Sal. 'That truck, you know – only thing I got anymore with any sentimental value. That and this gun.'

'One hour.'

'Sure, that's what you say now. How do I know you're not gonna—' Jerry stopped, stared off into the darkness, then dragged on his cigarette, transfixed. He set the shotgun noisily onto the bed and stepped down, kicking noisily through the cans. Then he turned back to Sal. 'What the hell,' he said, reaching into his pocket. He came out with a rabbit's foot, a single key hanging from it.

The suddenness of his change might have alerted Sal under different circumstances. But not now, with everything falling.

Dangling the key between them, Jerry said, 'Your car's across the way. You best gimme your own keys in case, you know, an emergency pops up.'

As Sal reached into his pocket, Jerry peeked through the trees at the window lights across the road. 'Be gentle with her,' he said, making the exchange. 'She's barely broke in.'

It was a couple of state troopers, Lemieux and Rolley, out patrolling the roads in search of Sal, who were dispatched to the gospel bus, but Murdoch and Shepherd, having heard the call on their separate radios, got there first.

Jerry had phoned the police from Mrs Abraham's house and reported that his truck had just been stolen with two loaded .38s in the glove compartment, thinking it the perfect brilliant strategy to seal Sal's fate and win favor with Noel. The detectives questioned Jerry for only as long as it took to get the year, make and model, and then they dispersed.

A general broadcast went out across the state, but, with few exceptions, nobody's routine was radically altered. In Bangor, a trooper pulled into a truck stop at the entrance of Route 95 and watched the passing traffic. Guards at the border crossings into Canada were faxed a description of Sal and of Jerry's truck. Troopers patrolling the southbound highways were similarly alerted. The on-duty deputy from the county sheriff's department made a couple of extra passes through Gravity when he did his rounds. In the long run, a stolen truck in Gravity didn't count for more than a stolen vehicle anywhere else, even if the suspect was armed and wanted for questioning in a murder investigation.

For their part, neither Murdoch nor Shepherd believed that

Sal Erickson was looking to get far. After briefing Lemieux and Rolley, the four officers divided the town in thirds and went off in three vehicles, scouring fire roads, farm roads and woods roads, aiming their searchlights behind every garage and barn and lobster shack for Jerry Royal's truck.

Sergeant Murdoch, a year from his second retirement, was fiercely determined to make the collar. Equal in his motivation was his animosity for Sal and his particular hunger to exact payback for the damage to his neck. He wanted this one bad. However, not bad enough to drive into the cemetery, which he had passed once heading out of town and once again heading back in. If he had driven through those iron gates and followed the drive up the terraces to the northeast corner, he would have found Jerry Royal's new Chevy truck parked up against the woods, beside Bobby Swift's grave.

Had he seen the truck, he might have also noticed a thread of cigarette smoke curling out the top of the window. A careful investigator might have wondered about the length of rope that led out of the same window and extended down into the gas tank. He might have noticed that the end of the rope inside the cab seemed to be coiled on a pile of newspapers and rags underneath the ashtray, or detected the smoldering cigarette balanced on the edge of the ashtray. He certainly would have smelled the gasoline fumes. Calculating that such an un-attended cigarette would burn itself past the balance point in five to seven minutes and then fall into the gasoline-soaked trash, the detective also would have calculated that by the time the fire worked its way down the rope and the gas tank exploded, the man who had planted this diversion would be eight to fifteen minutes away.

Minute by minute, another hour passed. Iris lay relentlessly in the dark, physically exhausted and emotionally drained, but not tired enough to sleep. Even though the upstairs was warm and stuffy, the constant passing of patrol cars had made sleeping impossible with the windows open, so she had closed them. But it did little good.

At midnight, when a car stopped outside the house again, its radio barking, Davey came into Iris's bedroom. 'Did they find Daddy?' she asked. Iris lifted the sheet, and Davey climbed in. 'Go to sleep, love,' her mother told her. 'Daddy will be okay.'

Five minutes later Davey was asleep again, breathing deeply. Outside, the last quarter moon was just rising in the sky, while peepers chirred hypnotically down at the river. Any other night, the moon and the breathing and the peepers would have put Iris to sleep. Tonight they only added to the nerve-racking inertia she felt.

To soothe herself, she thought of Helen Swan. She pictured Helen smiling. It was a particular smile Helen had given her the last time they'd talked, in response to Iris's maintaining that she didn't feel especially upset about Sal's leaving – or about her father's house burning. She had told Helen that she simply was not an emotional person. That's when Helen had smiled. Helen always seemed to know more than Iris was telling her.

Iris turned over in bed, covered her ear with her arm and tried to occupy her mind with practical things: whether to go through a realtor or advertise the house herself; whether or not to repaper Davey's bedroom. Or to paint the ceiling over the upstairs landing. Something needed to be done, that's how she felt.

Because it was the house that was keeping her awake after all, and not the heat, or the passing cars, or the peepers, or the moon or Davey's breathing. Ever since the fire, ever since Jerry had been inside the house – her mother's house—

Iris sat up in bed. Something needed to be done.

Boxes were packed. Doors were locked. Her father was in the burn ward at Downeast Memorial. Sal was wanted for murder. The peepers chirred. The moon rose. Davey breathed in and out, in and out . . .

Iris found her glasses and put them on, took the flashlight from her nightstand, slipped out from under the sheet in her jersey and underpants, and padded out of her room. Crossing the polished landing, intending to go downstairs for a cup of tea, she became suddenly conscious – not of the dark, but—

above her

—the attic.

Iris was suddenly, keenly, aware of that musty, wooden room above her, that somehow – somehow her mother was up there, looming over the house, hollow and heartless, always and forever, watching.

She swept the flashlight beam slowly up the wall, across the white ceiling . . .

Ridiculous!

She knew what Helen would say, so soothing in her abject rationality: 'Do you really believe that if you went up into your attic you would find your mother?'

Iris stood there enraptured by her own silence, hearing another car passing outside.

Going up?

The fear solidified in her, made her almost afraid to move. She stared up at the hatch, the black handle.

'It's only a room,' Helen would have said, smiling. 'What are you afraid you'll find?'

Without knowing what she was about to do, Iris stepped softly across the landing and pulled her bedroom door closed, silently turning the latch to keep from waking Davey. Then she returned to the landing, aiming her flashlight up again. The hatch wasn't two feet over her head. She'd never been tall enough; now she simply reached up. Resisting the impulse to pull her fingers from the cold black handle – *How many more years?* Helen would have said. *How much longer do you want to feel this way?* Iris wrapped her fingers around the handle and gave a tug, just enough to feel it give. She knew precisely how the ladder would unfold.

By road, the village was a mile from the cemetery, half that distance if one could fly. The way Sal ran down the road, he might as well have flown. After leaving Jerry's cigarette burning in the truck's ashtray, he took off down the terraces at a dead-on sprint and didn't miss a beat as he flew out of the gates and hit the asphalt. Just after midnight, the only cars he was likely to encounter would be the police looking for him, so he watched for lights in front and behind as he ran, ready to ditch for cover. At the end of the Townhouse Road he turned onto the River Road, actually picking up speed in his work boots. He made the village in under five minutes.

As he approached the lone streetlight at the corner of the Village Road, he spotted car lights and abruptly cut into the pines. The headlights were coming slowly up the road from his house. He was sure that the police were also watching the store, which was directly uphill from where he stood – across the river and through two hundred feet of woods. Laboring to catch his breath, he did not stop but plowed purposefully through the trees, his elbows around his ears to protect his face from the branches. He knew the river at low tide wouldn't be much more than three feet deep, even though it was fully thirty feet across and frigid. Not taking the time to reconsider – not even removing his pants and boots – he walked steadily down the bank and plunged in. The water was far colder than he'd imagined, its iciness burning him as he stumbled through a current that grew stronger as it deepened, climbing to his hips.

Emerging on the opposite bank, Sal pushed immediately up the hill, his noisy steps through the thicket barely covered by the running water behind him. As the hill leveled off in a stand of scrub fir and wild blueberry vines, Sal could see Noel's upstairs lights. Ahead and to the left, four windows were lit on the side of her apartment – her living room, bedroom and kitchen. He veered further to the right, putting more distance between himself and the building. When vines gave way to lawn and he was at the back of her property, he crouched in the shadows to wait, deeply winded.

He looked up at her kitchen windows for a few moments but saw no movement there. The second floor – store and stockroom – had no windows in the back or sides. Down at ground level, the garage was dark, and her driveway was vacant. Her backyard was rectangular and deep, ornamented with four ancient apple trees that became defined only at the tops, where their branches twisted against the sky. Resisting the temptation to move ahead, Sal stayed put fifty feet behind her swimming pool, deeply inhaling the chlorinated air while he waited. Only when he felt the chill from his wet pants did he begin to consider his various mistakes in coming.

Jerry snored deeply, his shotgun aimed at the door. Between snores he listened. When he was satisfied that the sound he had heard was only a skunk or raccoon rummaging through his stuff outside, he laid the gun back on the table and concentrated on the TV again. He kept the volume down so he could listen for the distant volley of gunshots, the signal that he and Noel were home free.

It was a thirty-minute commercial, some busty woman spray-painting a man's bald spot black while the audience applauded. 'Oh, I imagine,' Jerry muttered. Worse than wrasslin, how people could believe that shit. He drank the rest of his cola and flung the can over his shoulder into the back of the bus.

Jerry was beyond sleep now, way beyond, in some other state of consciousness. Not that he needed to sleep, anyway. He had convinced himself that he remembered a Bible story about Jesus going forty days and forty nights without sleep, to prove a point. Either that or it had something to do with a woman.

Animal attraction.

Jerry's brain brimmed with visions of Noel, his stomach buzzing as though a little motor were going inside. He didn't know what the hell endorphins were, but his sure as hell were boiling over tonight. He reached into his cooler for another cola, popped it, and drank it down till his eyes watered.

Closed his eyes and listened once again for those gunshots, and then he started thinking of last night for the hundredth time. See, it could have gone like this: He goes over there, down in back where it's dark, and he rings her doorbell, then stands and waits all shaved and washed. She comes down the stairs into the garage. In the darkness he can barely make her out – until she emerges into a square of moonlight, and then he sees that she's wearing this sleeveless white undershirt and nothing else. Little red chipmunk fur between her legs. She comes to the door slowly, giving him that animal attraction look. She reaches for the doorknob ... but then she hesitates ... looking up at him, teasing. Testing. They both know what she wants.

And so he gives it to her – he raises the letter to the window. She looks. With his other hand, he snaps a spark from his lighter, but he stops short of letting the flame lick the letter, teasing her right back.

The way her lips part...

Then he does it, touches the tip of the flame to the paper. Her green eyes flare as the fire climbs higher, digesting his story. Her nipples swell, dark fetching knobs under her T-shirt. And then that crooked little half-smile appears. The flame climbs around Jerry's wrist, but he doesn't mind the heat, because it's making her hot, because she's right now crossing her arms in front of her and peeling that T-shirt slowly

up her chest, it catches on her nipples, and her little tits flip
when they're freed. Just like that. Totally naked now, bathed in
the orange light of his dying flame, she reaches down for the
lock. He hears a *click*.

He tries the door—

Wait – not the lock—

—a gun! She swings back, punches the revolver through the
glass, aimed dead at his face—

He jumps – bangs his knee on his table.

Fuckin letter.

Jerry drained his cola, slammed the can on the table, pushed
to his feet and headed up the aisle to the front. Only thing
about drinkin this much, you sure had to piss every other
minute.

The hot cedar smell came over Iris, and with it, the first flood
of weakness. She pulled herself to a higher rung, rising into
darkness, instinctively reaching her right hand over her head,
circling around the string until she hit the metal bead. She
fingered the tiny bellshaped thing, wrapped the string once
around the knuckle of her index finger and gave a tug, hoping
the light wouldn't go on. But it did.

click

Brown. Red-brown, yellow-brown, dry-brown rafters crossing overhead, brown roof descending to the two-foot kneewall
on both sides. Brown chimney in the center of the room, a
vertical fissure snaking down the old bricks. To Iris's left, a
wooden chair lay on the floorboards – glossy brown – her
mother's kitchen chair. Under the eaves, Jerry's bass fiddle.
Iris felt a shaking in her legs, but she kept her perch with her
arms, viewing the left side of the room from floor level. A
clothesline on its side, the carousel kind – meant nothing to
her. But the cedar chest ... She remembered a wool coat
inside, burgundy, with a gray fur collar – her grandmother's.

And the cream-colored hat she used to wear when she was four years old, five and six, playing dress-up with her mother—

(No, she was ten, in her Girl Scout uniform. Her brother was seventeen, goat-scented farm boy with whiskers on his chin and dog pads on his palms ... and her mother...)

Iris's heart pounded.

She took a breath. Turned her head to the right and saw the big footprints heading straight through the dust. She gripped the hatch frame to keep from falling...

The mattress, striped and stained, flat on the floor. A small sound came from Iris's chest, like a child's cry.

But there was something else. Standing over the head of the mattress. The wire dress form. Hollow. Fitted with a white wedding dress. Her mother's.

14

Jerry stood on the doorstep of his bus, trying to piss into the small riverbed he had created over the past three days and nights, but he overshot the mark and hit a box of dishes. Never easy aiming with a hard-on.

One thing for sure. Just like the old man liked to say, all that blood rushin down to his manhood away from his brain, the thing was gonna get him killed one day. Old man might've been right too. With Noel keeping him awake with all this animal attraction bullshit, he couldn't force a clear thought if his life depended on it. And for once in his life, it did.

When he had finished urinating, he decided that since the thing was in his hand, he'd might as well take care of business and clear his head. Because even if he and Noel got away with this, and Sal Erickson got himself killed in a shoot-out with the cops so that everyone in the world figured he had it coming—

Jerry still needed to hang onto that letter, no matter how many animal attraction looks she gave him. If he had to jack off every fifteen minutes to stay alive, then by God he'd do it and no one was around to tell him otherwise.

'You got that right,' he said, already in motion.

He leaned his head back against the mirror of his bus, looked up at the darkness and started the fantasies rolling, when off in the distance there came a resounding boom that echoed across the sky for a number of seconds. Not the volley of gunshots he had expected to hear, Jerry thought to himself, but then he thought no more about it, because at that moment he was seeing a light that he shouldn't have seen.

He stared across the road at the old family house, the odd, dim illumination high on the gable end. In fact, Jerry wasn't sure that the light wasn't just another one of Noel's tricks on his imagination, so he stepped down from the bus, still masturbating, and walked down to his driveway until—

the attic vent—

Noel! he thought. *She'd found it!*

He turned and hurried back to the bus, stuffing himself into a fly that was way too tight and seemed to have a million teeth. The blood raced back through his veins, engorging his brain now, until at last he knew exactly what he needed to do to stop this chattering once and for all.

On her knees beside the wedding dress, Iris let herself cry. Softly, like a cleansing summer rain. In one way, it was fascinating what her mind had done with its memories. In that way, she marveled how it had protected her, drawing curtains over the reality of her younger life, masking events with bits of dreamlike imagery. The hollow dress form had become her mother, formless and heartless, the specter who looked on scornfully yet silent, always without objection. Yes, Iris had enough appreciation of psychology to be fascinated—

But in another way, she could only begin to fathom what her brother had cost her. The years of pervasive, unfocused shame; the isolation. The way she had become, herself, like the dress form, silent, scornful, hollow. Her brother had even robbed her of her mother's memory.

How many times? Once? Twice? It seemed it must have become a routine occurrence. After school; while their father was down at the clam flats, or tinkering outside with his truck, or sitting downstairs with his bottle and his gospel music.

Up.

Up was the word Jerry had used. *Ready to go up? Time to go up.* Iris's chest heaved. She let the tears flow.

She thought of Davey, realized that she must have been Davey's age when it started. She thought of Sal, imagined how their lives might have been different. She thought of her father and how his alcoholism (and his own pain) had prevented him from protecting her. She thought of his courage in finally getting sober, and his desperate, naive attempts to win her back, and how he never stopped trying. She cried harder when she realized how successfully she had thwarted him. The tears burned. The tears felt wonderful.

She wiped her eyes, then reached out to touch the silk. In fleeting glimpses she envisioned her mother: laughing, trying to pour milk over her Cheerios on the bus . . .

This—

is a dress form.

This—

my mother's wedding dress.

This—

She heard the floor creak behind her. Thinking it was Davey, she wiped her eyes before she turned.

'Mommy?'

It was Davey, pulling herself up through the hatch, testing her weight on the floor, walking tentatively ahead in her calico nightie. Iris gazed at her daughter as she came barefoot over the loose and dust-covered pine boards.

'I thought you said it was dangerous up here.'

Seeing that her mother had been crying, Davey came directly to Iris and wrapped her arms around her, fit her warm cheek against Iris's neck. Inexplicably, Iris felt a sudden welling of joy, and she almost burst out laughing. But, afraid she might become hysterical, she restrained herself. She breathed deeply the warm cedar air.

'I'm remembering things, love,' she said.

'Bad things?'

'Mm-hm. And some very good.'

Iris reached out and brushed dust off the silk sleeve. 'This was your grandma's wedding dress,' she explained. Neither of them looked back toward the hatch, or they might have seen that the landing light had come on below.

'Maybe it'll be yours someday.' (As her mother used to say to her.)

Iris lifted the sleeve again, and the corner of an envelope poked out between the breasts. Davey spotted it, reached to tuck it back.

Swear to keep a secret?

'Love, what was that?'

Iris unfastened a button, pulled the envelope out – TO BE OPENED ONLY IF GERALD CHRISTIAN ROYAL TURNS UP MISSING OR DEAD. Curious, Iris turned the envelope over, pushed her thumb under the flap and tore it open—

But the look on Davey's face.

'Love, what?'

Davey stared past her mother, terrified. Iris turned. Her heart lurched.

Jerry was peeking over the hatchway.

Shivering from the cold, Sal crouched at the edge of the woods. Listening to a car crawl up the road in front of the store, he saw Noel's building outlined with light, first left, then right. He watched, he waited, he listened.

When the explosion finally sounded, distant as it was, Sal tensed. A dog started barking nearby, but then the dog stopped, and everything once again became quiet and dark, deceptively so. The swimming pool rolled the low moon gently over its surface, chlorine wafting into the air.

Abandoning caution, Sal rose to his feet and began approaching the pool. All at once a man charged out from around the right corner of the building. Sal stopped, braced to break for the woods, but the man showed no sign of seeing him. Instead, the man ran up the driveway, speaking anxiously into a handheld radio. Sal remained motionless while he heard a car's engine start and the car speed off. Simultaneously, up at the firehouse, the fire siren began to wail.

Beneath the din of the fire alarm, Sal walked deliberately around the pool, pulling his T-shirt over his head and wrapping the cloth tight around his fist. Approaching the garage, he stopped in front of the door and tried to see through the window. But all he saw was his own black reflection in front of the moon-shredded water, while apple branches behind his head grappled for the sky. Nothing was innocent anymore.

He punched his wadded fist through the glass, and the pane shattered on the concrete floor like hundreds of bells ringing. But under the wailing siren, Sal was confident that the breaking glass wouldn't be heard. He reached in with his left hand to turn the lock – and found that the door had been left unlocked. Not stopping to wonder why, he pulled the door open and stood there in absolute blackness. He shook the shirt off his hand and dropped it on the floor, then waded into the dark. He reached out with his hands, felt her car with his left. He moved two steps to his right until he could tell that the stairway wall, the half partition, was getting closer – he could sense the change in air pressure. His right hand confirmed his suspicion. He hoped his senses were keen enough to also register someone hiding behind a corner.

When he reached the end of the partition, he turned around it and looked up into more darkness. Again, he could feel a difference in air movement. He could also hear cool saxophone notes rolling like water down the stairwell. Suddenly he hadn't a shred of hope that Bouchard had been wrong about Noel.

She was in the building waiting for him, drawing him in. He realized that by causing the diversion that had drawn the cops away, he had inadvertently served them both. With no witnesses, with the broken window, she could eliminate him and nobody alive could call it an ambush.

He knew that the staircase ahead of him reached a landing and then turned to the right. He took the treads as quietly as his waterlogged boots and jeans would allow, the pants chafing, the wet leather squeaking traitorously with each step. Holding the right handrail, he waved his left hand in front of him to feel the wall at the head of the turn – or to ward off an attack. However, before his fingers touched the facing wall, the change in pressure told him that the right-hand wall had disappeared. And then his toe kicked an angled tread. He swiped the air in front of him and turned right.

From here he was able to make out dim light above the top step. Here, too, the jazz sounded clearer – Coltrane and Miles – like the last time he'd climbed these stairs. Three steps up, he was able to see the origin of the light, a line of it leaking under the stockroom door. He kept his eye on the line and counted his steps as he climbed, thinking that if the door suddenly swung open, he'd know how many steps down before the turn. At the same time, he knew that the nearer he climbed to the door, the less chance he'd have to make that turn.

He knew that she was expecting him, that's why the door had been unlocked and the music left on. He guessed that the stockroom door was also unlocked. He knew that she had a gun.

Very quietly he stepped onto the landing and stood there in front of the door, listening to the steady trumpet, considering his options. Push the door open and stand there looking down those dusky aisles of boxes. That's where she'd be waiting for him – somewhere among the boxes. To his left, another flight of stairs rose eight or ten steps to a wide landing on the southeast corner of the building, where they turned one hundred and eighty degrees for the final ascent to the back door of her apartment.

Sal reached out and touched the stockroom door. It pushed open without a sound, exposing him. He looked in at the shapes, the long, shadowy aisles. Somewhere to the right of the room's center, over her desk, a soft spot of light shone on the ceiling, as Miles blew a doleful line. 'So What' was the name of the tune.

This was where she wanted him.

What he wanted was upstairs.

He broke left, found the handrail and took the stairs at a run, making no effort to disguise his footsteps. He reached the first landing, swung around the partition and continued up. He ran to the top, found the doorknob, turned it and rammed his bare shoulder into the door. Bouncing off, he threw himself at the door again. Now he heard Noel's footsteps drumming across the apartment from the left. Again he drove his shoulder into the wood. It answered with a *crack* but didn't give. He lined up and rammed it again. This time the crack was sharp, startlingly so, and he fell back, catching the handrail to keep from falling.

He noticed two things simultaneously, without realizing they were connected. His left shoulder burned from the impact; and a tiny dot of light shone through the door, off-center. His hand went to his shoulder, felt the wet flap of flesh, the hot cavity – just as another *crack* sounded, and another lighthole appeared, lower, more centered. She was shooting at him!

Had he kept his head, he would have dropped to the floor and rolled down the stairs. But, enraged, he turned his right shoulder to the door and threw himself again. Another *crack!* another hole, and he was stung in the forehead by a shard of oak. He lined up again, gave a long, painful shout and sprang at the wood, splintering the jamb.

Stumbling into her kitchen, he was blinded by the light, but Noel came into focus fast, sprawled on the floor in front of him against the legs of an overturned chair, her arms stretched between her own legs, a black revolver aimed at his midsection.

'Oh, God,' she said, 'I didn't know it was you.' But she didn't lower the gun. Her jeans were bright red, and she wore a black leotard top.

'They said you were dangerous,' she said.

He stared at her. Shirtless, he could feel his blood running warmly under his arm, down his ribs, but he hardly noticed it, struck by the set of her face, the way her finger locked around the trigger.

'You did just break down my door. What was I supposed to do?'

He stepped toward her. Her aim rose to his chest. He stopped. She said, 'I do have to protect myself, you know.' Leaning on the overturned chair, she pulled herself to her knees, then to her feet, keeping the gun on him.

He shook his head at her, showing his confidence. 'You're not going to shoot me, Noel.' He took another step, and she stepped back, keeping the gun on him. 'It's too intimate this way. It's not your style. Through the door, that's different.' She backed around the stove, into the hallway, while he slowly pursued her. 'Like leaving someone in a box underground. No, face to face, you don't have the stomach for it.'

The look of assurance that came over her easily outmatched his own, and he knew it was a mistake to have challenged her. She stopped backing and smiled. He stopped coming forward, while his blood gathered at the waistband of his jeans.

'For what it's worth,' Noel began, 'I don't think people will judge you harshly. Two lives for two million dollars? I think people will say you knew the value of life.'

Her eyes lowered to his chest. Her aim followed. Her finger tensed.

'You should've known the river,' he said.

Noel balked, just for an instant, looked up at him again.

'The reversing falls,' Sal explained, trying not to sound desperate (though he knew he was only buying seconds). He took another step toward her. Although her expression showed no flagging, she stepped back.

'I'm talking about things someone might throw in the river, thinking they'll wash down to the ocean.'

Noel's mouth became cocky, that goading, off-centered smirk.

'I don't think you want to pull that trigger,' he said. 'You know you made a mistake.'

She brushed up against the bookcase on the left wall.

'See, unless you time it right, things you throw in the river don't have time to make it down to the ocean. They come back.'

He took another step, approaching the bookcase – the reason he had come here.

'What I can't figure out is why you burned down Jerry's house. I know you did it, Noel.'

Her pistol swung up and she fired. He saw the flash, felt the percussion slap his face, but the bullet missed him, banged off the stove in the kitchen. Ears ringing from the shot, Sal came forward again, trying to hide the shaking in his legs. When he was even with the bookcase, he took his eyes off her and looked down at the spines.

'See, I remember that book. You said it was for burning down billboards, though. Not houses.' He reached into the case, flipping the books, one by one, onto the floor, looking for the right one.

Keeping the gun on him, Noel reached behind her and pulled open the door to her zebra stairway. 'Actually, I don't know what book you're talking about,' she said, backing through in such a way that Sal should have been alerted, the way she burrowed into the landing so that her arm was the last thing through the door, her arm and the hand holding the gun.

He looked up, too late.

The cylinder twitched—

He dived across the hall, slamming the door against her arm. The shot fired over his back, and she screamed and fired again. Denying the pain in his shoulder, Sal reached up and grabbed the barrel with his left hand while he forced the door open with his knee. But she jerked away, and his shoulder snapped in fiery pain. She swung the revolver down at his face—

He lunged, caught her by the legs, and they fell, tumbling down step after zebra-striped step, both grappling for the gun. When they slammed against the bottom door, Sal threw himself on top of her, crossed his right arm over her throat and caught the small barrel striving for his head. He forced it down, twisting her wrist until the muzzle pressed against her own chin.

'Go ahead,' he whispered, 'pull the trigger. We were gonna do each other anyway, remember? You do me, I do you. Yeah, let's do that.'

Her green eyes drilled into him. With her free hand she tore at his face, his eyes. He twisted his head away, and her knee swung up, thumped his back. He hardly felt it.

'You tell me!' he whispered. The pistol inched down to her throat. But her eyes on him never flickered.

'Tell me what you've done!'

Upstairs, footsteps suddenly thundered down the hall, then down the stairs. Then a voice:

'*Get down!*'

Sal turned halfway, saw the large figure at the curve in the stairs, unevenly crouched, taking two-handed aim – Murdoch.

'*Your legs! Your legs down!*'

'Tell him, Noel!'

'*Get your legs down!*'

'Confess what you did!'

Glaring at Sal, she smiled. Stopped kicking and lowered her legs to the floor. Smiled. Sal jumped at the door—

a shot exploded.

—turned the knob and ran, breaking through rows of cartons, stumbling, racing through the dark, tripping over corners of pallets, careening off shelves. He heard another gunshot as he banged through the swinging door into a blinding, flashing blue light. Ran at the locked door – bounded off and turned – grabbed a bubble-gum dispenser in the crook of his good arm and swung it into the window, bringing the plate glass down in solid, chiming sheets. He leaped through and charged off in the darkness.

'Real smart,' Jerry said, pulling himself onto the attic floor.

Iris didn't understand the look on his face, why he had the shotgun, or why he was here. She figured he was drunk, and part of the manhunt for Sal – out to make a name for himself. But he seemed strangely agitated, almost afraid – dangerously so. She held onto the envelope and kept her hand on Davey's shoulder.

'Jerry,' she said (it was the first time she had spoken his name as an adult), 'I've been remembering things.'

With a sudden jerk of his arm, he cocked the shotgun, the metallic clatch loud, brutal. 'You stay put,' he told her. His face was drained, his eyes haunted. He held out a hand and said, 'Have her bring it over.'

Before Iris realized what he was talking about, Davey took the envelope from her hand.

'Davey, no—' Iris grabbed Davey's arm.

'Don't worry, I'm not gonna do anything. Just have her bring it to me.'

Iris's gaze turned fiery. 'Do you?'

'Me, what?'

'Remember.' Her voice rang like steel. '*What you did to me up here.*'

He contemplated. 'So? Growin boy, that's all that was.'

'No. No, Jerry. You were seventeen. I was ten. You were my brother.'

'Hey' – he waved the shotgun at Davey's bare feet.

Iris started toward him. '*You get that—*'

He swung the gun at Iris, stopping her. His eyes sparkled. '*Jerry, what are you doing?*'

'It's not anybody's fault,' he said, his voice tight and fast. 'Just have her bring the letter and I'll be on my way. Nobody's gonna get hurt.'

'Jerry, I don't know what's in this envelope, and I don't care.'

'Yeah, another woman speaks.' He glared from one to the other, preoccupied, electrified. Then he jerked the shotgun toward the mattress. 'Okay, get down on the bed.'

Davey looked up at her mother, quivering.

'Both of yuhs!' He swung the shotgun back and forth. 'Now! On the bed!'

Iris went cold. 'Love, go downstairs,' she said to Davey.

Jerry stepped in front of the hatchway and took square aim at Iris. 'I'll kill your mother! I'll kill you both, I'm all fucked up!'

'*No, you will not!*'

'*Lay down!*' He stamped his foot on a loose board.

Davey shivered quietly, her eyes wide and wet. Iris hugged her to her side, unable to stop her own trembling. 'Jerry, what's the matter with you?'

'Nothin. I got put in this position by dishonest people. Now lay down on your bellies.' His aim lowered to their feet again.

'*Jerry, what are you doing?*'

He raised the gun back to Iris's chest, and she saw a look come over him that she recognized with horror – a sudden blankness, a detachment from reality. She knew at that moment he was going to kill them both.

'Jerry,' she said. Kneeling on the mattress, she took the envelope from Davey's hand. 'Please. Let Davey go. Whatever it is—'

'Get down on your bellies. Don't make a big deal of it. Nobody's gonna get hurt.'

Davey squeezed Iris's hand. They both knew he was lying.

'Just get down and stop the noise so I can think a minute. Faces down.'

Iris took Davey around the waist. 'It's okay, love,' she whispered, unable to control her own shaking. Together they lay down on the dusty, must-scented mattress. Iris put her arm around Davey, hugged her tightly.

'And I don't want to see any eyes.'

His footsteps approached softly as he talked. Iris pulled Davey's head underneath her own. 'Curl up in a ball,' she whispered, and Davey did.

'Like I said, it's nobody fault—' His sooty blue reef runners stopped beside Iris's face.

Her voice quivered. 'Jerry, you're scaring us.'

'Just close your eyes, I'm gonna take the letter and then I'm gonna go, let bygones be bygones. Just close your eyes.'

She felt the gun barrel rest against the side of her back as he snatched the envelope from her hand. Then the barrel lifted. She heard him take a single step back. Then the snap of a cigarette lighter ... and silence. She opened an eye and turned her head just enough to see the flame climb the corner of the envelope. His shotgun, held under his arm, was aimed vaguely at her legs. She thought about lunging for it. It was her only hope.

'See, that's your problem,' Jerry said, rotating the paper so

369

the flame climbed to the opposite corner. 'You just can't do what a man tells you. It's your own fault, if you hadna been so friggin nosy—'

A creak of wood alerted them. Jerry dropped the envelope, wheeled toward the hatch – a head and shoulder poking up—

'*Freeze, greaseball!*'

Both men fired in a flourish, and Davey screamed. At the hatch there was a spray of white and red, as Murdoch's big head riveted back and plunged from sight, the body cracking once off the ladder, then knocking heavily on the landing below.

Iris pulled Davey beneath her and held her tighter, thinking wildly that if she squeezed hard enough, it would stop both of them from shaking.

Confounded, Jerry turned back toward them, his knee buckling. He staggered a little, clutching his forearm to his stomach, the muzzle of his shotgun scraping over the floorboards. Then he turned his gaze back to the hatch, where white fragments of neck brace were scattered like bloody chicken feathers.

'Oh great,' he strained. 'I suppose this is my fault.'

He lifted his arm from his stomach, saw a solid spot of darkness, and then a thick drop of blood blossomed on his lucky shoe. 'Yeah, just great,' he said. 'Now I'm friggin gut-shot.'

A metallic *pop* alerted him – from the darkness at the back of the room. He snapped his head toward the sound. Thinking it was Noel, he looked down for his burning letter and moved to drag a reef runner over it, to put the fire out. But he was unsteady and slow, and the last corner of the envelope was already folding over, blackening. To his surprise, the voice that came from high on the gable wall was a man's.

'Jerry, what are you doing down there?'

He squinted up at the darkness.

'Daddy?' Davey cried.

Jerry regained his footing. 'No shit, that *is* you.'

'Daddy?'

'I thought you prob'ly bought the farm,' Jerry said.

High on the gable end of the house, Sal stood on the third highest rung of the ladder, two rungs above the danger zone, bracing himself with one hand holding the small wooden frame that surrounded the attic vent. Because of his wounded shoulder, Sal's left hand could only rest against the shingles beside his leg.

'Iris, Davey, are you okay?'

'Daddy?'

'It's okay, hon,' Sal told her. 'Jerry, let them down so we can talk.'

Through the vent screen, Sal could see Jerry silhouetted to the left of the chimney, bent heavily over his shotgun. A finger of smoke was all that remained of the paper by his feet. To the left of Jerry, Iris and Davey lay huddled on the mattress.

'Iris, are you alright?' he called.

'Yes.'

'Jerry, what are you doing? What's that you burned?'

Down in the attic Jerry looked up for the voice, but the chimney threw a black shadow over the middle of the wall where the vent was located. Making a quick, painful grunt, Jerry rocked back on his heels and hoisted his shotgun up under his arm.

'Put that down, Jerry,' Sal told him. 'I've got a gun up here.'

'What, you up on a ladder or something? I can't even see where you are.' Stealthily, Jerry secured the butt of the shotgun under his arm.

'I'll shoot you!' Sal cried.

'I'm already shot up pretty friggin good. Can't hardly feel it ... bleedin like a bastard, though.' Leaning over the barrel, Jerry cocked his gun.

'You let them go, Jerry!'

'You got my truck out there? I'm gonna need some wheels, man.'

'*Let them go!*'

Jerry squeezed his eyes closed. 'Whoa,' he said, 'blackin out here.' As he wavered, his gun hitched up another two inches, until it was nearly level with Sal's position. 'Hey, no shit, I think I'm blackin out, really—'

Slower than he intended, Jerry jerked the barrel and fired a tremendous boom, knocking himself to the floor.

Through the screen, Sal saw the muzzle explode. In the same instant the top corner of the vent frame blew apart, and Sal fell back off the ladder. Catching his right foot between the rungs, his body went down backwards, slammed against the ladder. He hung by his instep.

Sal's right hand found the rail by his thigh, then a rung. Pocket change dropped out of his pants onto his chest and chin. He heard Davey call for him. Holding his weight with his right arm, he let go of the ladder with his foot. His hip scraped down the rungs until he caught a toehold again, and then he righted himself. He climbed back to the top. At the blown-out corner of the vent, the screen flopped over, so now Sal was able to push his hand inside and catch the interior wallboards.

Down in the attic Jerry was just pushing himself off the floor, using his gun as a crutch.

Sal's voice came down from the darkness. 'Tell me what you burned, Jerry. That paper you burned.'

Hunched over his gun, Jerry's reef runner slid through his blood, and he almost went down again. His velour jersey hung heavily.

'You knew about her, didn't you, Jerry? You knew what she did.'

Jerry fit his fingers around the gun stock.

372

'Answer me, Jerry. That paper you burned. You had something on her.'

With a grunt, Jerry lifted the shotgun off the floor.

'Leave it!' Sal said.

'Don't get excited,' Jerry answered, 'it's for self-protection.' His body swayed noticeably; blood transferred from his thumb into the grain of the stock. He took an uncertain step to the right.

'I think she's got something on you too, Jerry. That's why you didn't turn her in after she burned down your house. That's why you're up here now.'

'Wait a minute,' Jerry said. 'I can't hear you.' He took another step, until Sal realized what he was doing – trying to get behind the chimney.

'Don't screw around, Jerry!'

Looking through the screen, Sal saw a sudden, quiet flash, and then darkness overtook the room. Aware that Jerry had popped the lightbulb, Sal leaned to his left, trying to see around the chimney, afraid that Jerry might be making his way downstairs and would have him trapped on the ladder. But as Sal's eyes adjusted to the dark, he saw light glowing out of the hatch from the landing below, vaguely outlining the lower half of the chimney. And then the chimney sprouted an elbow.

'Daddy, get down!'

The elbow jerked, the shotgun cocked.

'Jerry, we don't have to do this!'

'That's alright,' Jerry answered. 'You say you got a gun up there, let 'er rip.' He shuffled slowly out to the left until he was clearly silhouetted by the hatch light. Wavering there, he spread his legs and lifted his arm off his side. 'Gawhead, man, I'll give you first shot.'

'Jerry, listen. She made a mistake.'

'Okay,' Jerry said. Then, as if he were setting up for target practice, he painstakingly raised the shotgun into position, fit his jawbone against the stock, tried to steady the gun while he sighted down the barrel. 'You best take your shot,' he said. 'It's not like I got all night.'

'She screwed up, Jerry.'

As Jerry's sights shivered over the vent, his target slowly materialized: a little piece of metallic sky outlining Sal's head and shoulder.

'*Daddy, get down!*'

Jerry snickered weakly. 'More or less like a raccoon up a tree,' he said, as his finger curled around the trigger. 'Lookin at the situation, man down here bleedin half to death, I guess we're gonna have to call this one self-defens—'

Jerry saw it too late, swooping up at him—

a ghost in a white wedding dress, headless, hollow—

—solid.

The impact knocked him off his feet, and he sat inside the rising light of the open hatch. His head knocked off the wood frame, his butt scuttered down the ladder rungs, flipping him over in the air so that when he landed, his shotgun muzzle hit the floor and the gun exploded, the butt recoiling into the full weight of his falling body, snapping his right-side ribs like kindling.

On the landing beside him, Sergeant Murdoch lay mortally wounded in his checkered blazer, gaping dark-eyed like a jacked buck, blood pooling from his open neck.

His own wounds notwithstanding, Jerry rolled to his feet, shotgun in hand, eyes flaring. Whether he was escaping the ghost or just anxious to tree Sal, he swung around the banister and started down. But at the head of the stairs his lucky shoe skated over the polished floor, and his upper body, weighted by the shotgun, started down ahead of his legs. Jerry's disconnected feet drummed down the treads to keep up, faster and faster. But his plummeting torso went faster still. He saw the window curtain at the bottom of the stairs fly up at him like another ghost, and he put out his shotgun to stop it. The barrel broke the window first, his head knocked off the planter pot then shattered more glass, and then the white curtain caught his face and hung his body and shotgun out the smashed window like a June bug snagged in a spiderweb—

Immediately a pair of headlights swung at him, flashing bright. Then a spotlight. Then a second car roared up alongside, blue light strobing, car doors opening, someone shouting, '*Drop the gun! Drop the gun!*'

But Jerry, caught in the curtain, could not comply. To make matters worse, his warm shoe was sliding back, while his shotgun pulled him forward. The curtain rod bowed, the nylon stretched.

'*Drop it now!*'

His blood-soaked jersey pulled up slowly, his glistening torso poised over the jagged glass in the bottom frame. Worst part was, he lacked the strength to resist.

'*Drop it or I'll shoot you!*'

He lacked the strength to even voice an objection. He saw a figure with a rifle run around the side of the house. He felt a point of window glass poke into his stomach. But, pressed against the curtain, Jerry could not release ballast.

Then two shots barked off behind him. It felt like a finger tapping him on the back – *tap, tap* – followed by the curious sensation that he was deflating. He managed to turn his head to the side, enough to see Murdoch lying red and shiny at the top of the stairs, death mask gaping, his .45 on its side in his hand, glaring down. As Jerry watched, the muzzle barked, and another round punched through his shoulder. Then, for better or worse, the curtain rod snapped free, and the plant pot smashed down on Jerry's back, driving him down on the glass.

He slumped over the sill like a waterlogged rug. Lying there, gazing at the shrubs swallowing his shotgun, imagining that the dark liquid running down the curtain was cola . . .

'*Don't move,*' he heard in the retreating distance. '*Don't you move.*'

Jerry managed a flick of his wrist, a final defiance. Then he let go.

15

While Sergeant Murdoch and Jerry Royal were rushed to Downeast Memorial and issued death certificates, and evidence technicians from the local CID drove to Gravity to take videotape and blood samples from the Ericksons' attic, landing and living room, Iris telephoned Helen Swan.

In four minutes Helen was there in her bathrobe to take Iris and Davey back to her house. When she knocked at the back door, however, Iris and Davey were sitting at the kitchen table with Detective Shepherd. Davey drank a glass of orange juice, while Troopers Lemieux and Rolley stood at the sink looking on. It was one-thirty in the morning. Shepherd asked Helen if she'd please wait in her car for a minute while they finished up.

Iris had told the detective about Jerry burning the envelope, but she said she did not know the contents of the letter inside. Davey told about the day Jerry had secreted the letter in the attic, but neither did she know what was in the letter, only that Jerry had told her it was keeping him alive. They both told about Jerry shooting Murdoch in the hatchway, about Sal appearing at the attic vent, and the things he had said to Jerry. Shepherd tape-recorded the interview, and at various, seemingly random, times he would ask them to repeat Sal's words.

When Iris recalled that Sal had warned Jerry that he had a

gun, Rolley and Lemieux exchanged a look that didn't escape any of them, least of all Davey.

'Wait outside for me,' Shepherd told the troopers at that point. When they left, he said to Iris, 'But you're saying he never fired the gun?' and she affirmed. In three different ways he asked where they thought Sal might have gone, but each time neither had an answer. '"She screwed up, she made a mistake," you're sure those were the words he used?' Shepherd asked. Iris nodded. Davey looked down at the table, afraid that she had already unwittingly given the police more than enough information to help them arrest her father.

Shepherd shut off the tape recorder, gave Iris a sympathetic smile, Davey a pat on the knee. 'Why don't you go with your friend now and try to get some sleep,' he told them. 'We should be out of here in a few hours.'

When he walked them out to Helen's car, he saw Trooper Lemieux sitting in the cruiser with the door open, his feet out on the lawn, his service piece in his hand, checking his clip. Rolley was standing beside him.

Shepherd left Iris and walked immediately to the troopers. 'Don't do that here,' he said in a low voice.

Lemieux snapped the clip back in the pistol, lifted himself out of the car and holstered the weapon. 'Think we should call in for the dogs?' he said.

Shepherd looked at him, waited for Helen to drive away. After she did, Shepherd said to both troopers, 'No dogs. No canvassing. No guns.'

'She said he was armed, Detective.'

Shepherd looked at them both. 'Listen to me,' he said. 'We're not chasing a cop-killer here. The man who shot Sergeant Murdoch is on his way to the morgue. The man we're looking for is a suspect in a separate crime. You need to disassociate the two.'

Lemieux shifted nervously against the car, stole a glance at Rolley.

'I want you two to split up. Stick to the roads and stay in your vehicles. Rolley, you take Murdoch's car. Keep an eye on the store, go down her driveway from time to time and check the back. You see anything suspicious, you're on the radio to me.'

Shepherd turned to Lemieux. 'You, I want on the telephone.' He reached inside his suitcoat and dug a wallet out of his pocket. 'I found this under the ladder in back, along with some change and a fair amount of blood.'

He flipped Sal's wallet open and squeezed the sides to get at the cards beneath the driver's license. Shuffling through them, he pulled out a card and handed it to Lemieux. 'Blue Cross. Get this number and his description out to all ERs within a two-hour drive.' Shepherd sifted through some more cards and pulled out a Visa card. 'He's gonna need money. He may call to report his credit card stolen and try to get some money wired. You get to them first.' He pulled out another card, AAA. 'He might try to get cash out of these people, or else a loaner car. Call them.' He shuffled through the cards to the bottom of the stack, and then he stopped, separating one from the others. He looked closer.

'What's that?' Lemieux said. 'Another driver's license?'

Shepherd angled the card toward the light. 'From Rhode Island,' he said. Sal's photo was on it. But the name beside the picture—

Shepherd looked up.

Dale Newman.

'Alright, let's go,' he said, sticking the license back in with the other cards. 'Stay in your cars, is that clear?' He addressed the question to Lemieux as he jammed the cards back in the wallet.

'Yes, sir.'

'I don't think he'll come back here, knowing that we're looking for him. The main thing is, I don't want him going anywhere near Noel Swift. She's leaving tomorrow, and he may go over there again to try and stop her.'

'If he tries?' Lemieux said.

The detective nodded. 'Then I guess we're going to have to stop him.'

Shepherd waited until the troopers drove away. Then he went to his Cherokee, checked the clip of his own service piece and holstered it. With the night growing colder, he put on his jacket and zipped it, then walked out behind the house, where he had seen fresh blood on the rungs of the ladder and a sizable puddle in the grass.

He shone his flashlight around and saw another drop not five feet away, and then another in line with it, heading toward the road. The arrival route, Shepherd reasoned. Sal would have escaped the other way, probably around the garden and into the woods in back.

Shepherd returned to the ladder, then walked toward the garden. Ten feet out, as he suspected, he spotted a red drop on a blade of grass to his right. He looked back at the ladder and lined up the drops: heading toward the garage. The next blood drop wasn't for thirty feet, but it led behind the garage. Shepherd walked around the other side and discovered, at the front corner, blotted droppings in the sand the size of a tea rose. He figured that Sal had waited there while the police were engaged with Jerry. Given the activity that had centered around the front of the house thereafter, he guessed that Sal must have headed to the left, keeping the garage between himself and the house. He shone the light off into a thicket of young red pines and spotted the crimson glistening on the fine needles about five feet off the ground; he deduced by the height that Sal was bleeding from his left shoulder, chest.

He pushed through the trees, staying to his right to avoid getting blood on himself. It was like tracking a wounded deer in November, he thought, half expecting to find Sal lying dazed and panting inside the thicket. But than he saw a red smear on a branch to his right, and he stopped. Backed up a step. Sal had turned ninety degrees here, toward the road. Shepherd pushed through another fifteen feet of pines and then was in thick new grass that bordered the drainage ditch alongside the road. Another drop of blood had caught the far side of the ditch.

Shepherd stepped across to the asphalt and toed a line in the sand that pointed to the last blood drop. He imagined Sal would have run across the road here, and he looked out into the dark field, thinking it strange that Sal would have come out in the open so close to his house, unless he'd had a particular destination.

He walked into the road, moving his light slowly over the weeds and blueberry vines on the other side, from right to left and back again, and there he detected a slight depression in the ground cover, recently trodden upon. He joined the path and followed it for about fifty feet, where it cut abruptly to the right. When Shepherd turned that way, he knew where Sal had headed: to a light source that he realized was the open door of Jerry Royal's bus.

Trusting his suspicions, Shepherd doused his flashlight and stepped quietly over the vines until he reached the Royals' cluttered yard. Coming up quietly behind the burned remains of the house, Shepherd unsnapped his holster and fit his hand over the cold butt. He stopped and listened. Except for the peepers singing down at the river, the night had grown remarkably quiet.

He drew his pistol and then resumed his movement. Approaching the bus, he could see that the windows had been painted black. Quietly approaching the rear corner, he stooped down, turned on his flashlight again and looked for a pair of feet behind the bus. Seeing none, he turned off the light and rose again, aimed his pistol at the open door and proceeded ahead. Fifteen feet away, he stopped.

'Sal Erickson?' he said. He set his flashlight on the ground. 'Sal, why don't you come out now? I'm armed, and I'd rather not come in after you.'

He tried to listen, but the peepers were singing much too loud. He noticed a drop of blood on the bottom step, still liquid. As he wrapped his fingers around the stainless steel rail, he imagined getting shot in the face, and he thought bitterly (as he often did lately) how little cops were paid.

'Sal, I know you're hurt. Let me know if you're in there, please. I want to help you.'

He climbed onto the first step, leaning back so that his head and body remained outside the door. He raised his weapon beside his ear.

'Mr Erickson?'

His suspicion grew that he was talking to himself, and that made him feel at once relieved yet frustrated. Nevertheless, he had to know for sure. He took a breath, counted to three, then poked his head and gun through the door, scanned the inside of the bus in a glance, then pulled out again. Registering what he had seen: table and seats on the left, halfway down; Styrofoam cooler on the right; cola cans strewn all over the aisle. The only place to hide was behind the table.

He swung in again, propped his pistol arm against the railing, aimed just over the seat. 'If you're behind there, Sal, put your hands up. I'm not going to shoot.'

Gratefully, then, Shepherd noticed the mirror at the back corner of the bus, a round wide angle that confirmed he was alone in the bus. He turned quickly, in case Sal was behind him – and that's when he noticed the overturned cardboard box on the ground, the spilled clothing. He stepped down, picked up his flashlight and illuminated the box. Blood was smeared on the cardboard flap, and there was blood on the ground. With Sal wearing a fresh shirt, there'd be no more blood to track, for a while.

'Shit,' said the detective.

Consumed by cold and weakness, Sal sat high on the bluff above the bog. He had come through the underbrush directly behind the Royals' property and then, to avoid both paths, through a savagely dense growth of pines. Without a light to help him see, and with the thatched ceiling too thick to allow moonlight in, he had scraped his wall through the stiff branches, his wounded arm hanging inside his flannel shirt, taking punishment again and again. Now, in the open moonlight above the river, still wearing his wet jeans and boots, the shirt did little to warm him. The intensity of his shivering, of his pain, made it hard to focus his thoughts.

She would come down, he knew that. She would have to come down – if she wasn't there already, waiting for him. But trying to hear footsteps was futile over the incessant screeching of peepers below. Likewise, the ground fog down on the river made it impossible to see the bank – or even to know how high up he was perched. He pushed himself forward until he felt gravity tugging at his backside. He stared down into the softness, knowing that he had no real choice, this was how he was getting down, wondering if he would survive the fall, wondering why he had come here in the first place, why he didn't just roll back in the grass, close his eyes and let unconsciousness take him. He lost that option when his boot heel lost its purchase on the side of the bluff. Starting to slide, he reached out listlessly, caught a clump of grass, knowing that he lacked the strength to hold on. And then he plummeted, fell ten feet before his legs hit the vertical bank, where he slid another twenty feet down hardpack, trying to slow himself with the sides of his boots and his single hand, but managing instead to turn himself onto his injured side before he was dropped into the air again. He hit bottom twice, once on his heels and again on the flat of his back, with a deafening thud.

Lying there inside the cover of fog, Sal knew he should get to his feet and find cover, but he lay there anyway, dazed, the impact reverberating through his bones. After a minute had passed, he rolled onto his right side and stared off where he thought the path should have been, but the thick, gray gauze in front of his face was all he could see. The only sound in the night was the chorus of peepers. He was surprised they hadn't been silenced by his fall. Shivering weakly, he pushed himself to his knees and rose out of the fog. Suddenly exposed, his heart skipped. The flat surface of fog was three feet high and moonlit nearly white; trees seemed to grow out of it. Sal looked off down the path, watching for movement. But even with the moonlight, the trail diminished into obscurity thirty or forty feet away.

He struggled to his feet and turned to the fishing pool, looked out over the table of fog. Unable to see even the ground beneath him, he stepped gingerly until his boot found a solid surface – his fishing rock. He crouched inside the fog and, finding the edge of the rock with his hand, sat down with his legs over the edge. Pushing off, his boots met soft resistance, than sank in the mud. Immediately the peepers stopped – a sudden, conspicuous silence. He remained as still as he could, even tried to stop shivering, but he could not, with the freezing water oozing into his boots. Out beyond the sandbar, the river lay quiet, no longer running to the sea, but lolling, fattening, breathing against its banks – the incoming tide.

Because the pool was lower than the bank, Sal now found himself standing up to his neck in fog, and that made him feel safer. He ducked his head and was once again hidden – but now he could not see, either. He stooped to feel the water with his hand and found it about six inches deep.

To reach the river debris, he turned to his right. But when he tried to pull his left foot out of the mud, the bog was reluctant to let him go. Unable to use his left arm, even for balance, he found it easier to lower himself to his knees to break the suction at his heels. Holding the fishing rock with his right hand, he pulled his left leg forward and set it down, then went down to his right knee.

In this way he worked around the rock until finally his knee struck a floating object. He reached out and felt plastic, a hollow handle. He knew he was lifting an empty milk jug out of the pool. He reached out and set it on the grassy bank to his right, then felt around him again, found a plastic sandwich bag – put that on the bank too. In the same way he removed and identified each bit of trash: a deflated kickball; a rectangular plastic bottle that might have once contained motor oil; a hollow doll with a missing leg; a plastic ice cube tray; a rubber glove, its fingers stuck together. He folded the glove and stuffed it in his pocket, then felt for more: a small plastic bottle with a cone top – maybe a mustard dispenser; a fishing bobber attached to a few feet of line; a short string of Christmas tree lights; a flat slab of Styrofoam that might have been insulation or the broken lid to a cooler; Sal skimmed his hand over the water and couldn't find anything more – until he reached under the bank. That's where he found the empty tube, and then something close to warmth went through him. Stuffing the tube in his other pocket, he crawled onto the bank and then quietly lowered the rest of the debris back into the pool.

It was the tube of hair cream that Davey had joked about when they were fishing, the hair goop. It was his one chance – if he could convince anybody that this wasn't some last-ditch fantasy of his. He was about to stand again when he heard the noise out ahead of him – a slight crack. He stopped moving.

Cocked his ear to the left and heard it again. He looked ou
over the fog toward the river, where the trees stopped. Ther
he knew the firm bank gave way to a grassy sandbar that curve
around to form the outer boundary of the pool, holding out th
river on its other side. He heard a squirrel start to chatter ahea
on the path, a nervous warning.

He stepped over the rock and very slowly, very quietly, mad
his way along the edge of the bank, past the last scrub alder
until he felt the ground soften under his feet. As the bar curve
around to the left, heading downriver, the sand became eve
softer and wetter, spreading into a grassy swail, the inlet for th
reversing tidal waters. When Sal felt water filling his boot
again, he turned and climbed back onto the bar where the gras
grew thicker and the sand was firmer. There he sank to hi
knees beneath the fogbank, to wait.

It seemed a fair place strategically, across the pool so h
could see both approaches – that is, if someone came with
flashlight. He knew that Noel would come in from the lef
(where he had heard the noises); the police, if they came at all
would follow the path down from the right.

Sal had no idea what time it was – two? three? four o'clock?
nor if his position was indeed as advantageous as he'd firs
thought. Now it occurred to him that he had trapped himsel
on the sandbar along with the only piece of evidence that migh
incriminate Noel. The river behind him was twenty feet across
and the woods beyond thick and unfriendly – assuming he ha
enough strength to mount an escape, which he doubted. Hi
body was dominated by uncontrollable shivering and pain. Ye
he felt nothing as much as his fatigue.

He pulled the tube of hair cream out of his pocket, intendin
to bury it in the sand beneath him. But needing to preserve th
silence, and wanting to warm himself, he closed the tub
tightly in his hand and pulled his knees into his chest, makin
as compact a shape as possible in the marsh grass. With th

toes of his boots, he dug small holes in the sand, thinking even that might help warm him. He laid his cheek in the grass and stared into the cold, blind fog that surrounded his face, shivering, keeping his ears attuned for the slightest rustle.

But the night had fallen so brutally still. The night, the pool, the river. The only sound he heard was the little plop of a tree frog going into the pool in front of him. It wasn't long before a frog on the opposite bank called out with a single, daring peep. Moments later, there came an answering peep from off to his right. An unsolicited response from the left. Then two and three and four more, and all at once the entire bog was once again awash in the mating concerto. The music surrounded Sal, became synonymous with his shivering, a pleasant, buoyant life raft on which he willfully floated away from his weariness and pain. The loss of feeling, the loss of heat, the loss of blood – the accumulation of losses finally took his consciousness.

A whisper gave it back. He was aware of nothing at first, and then a sudden, furious cold – but it was the whisper that had roused him. The whisper of water. He realized that he was hearing the falls reversing, the tidal waters fighting their way over the rocks down-river – and then he remembered where he was. And why. He opened his eyes and could see nothing but an impenetrable grayness, black wires of marsh grass in front of his face. He had fallen asleep, he didn't know for how long. Now he was awake; cold, stiff and shivering to his core. The falls whispered on, the unnatural act continuing, tidal water flowing uphill, washing the darkened woods with ocean life. The sound was so soothing he started to doze again. But something else—

He realized that something else had awakened him: The peepers had stopped.

She was there.

* * *

He caught his breath. Silently he lifted his cheek off the sand, his eyes out of the grass, afraid of even a rustle of cloth, the snap of cartilage. And he saw her. On the far side of the pool, a bare dot of light appeared to float in the air, and then it lowered to the pool, making a smudge reflection. She was bending, looking through the debris—

The hair cream. He realized that the empty tube was still in his hand.

He knew she wouldn't have come down without her gun. He knew also that he had given her no choice but to use it – unless he could hide the tube.

He looked up through the fog, saw that the sky was half a shade lighter than the bog, just enough to give objects a shadowy definition. But where he lay, forty feet away, he realized that he must have looked no more distinctive than any other part of the bank, if she could see the sandbar at all.

As slowly as he could manage, he raised his body enough to free his right arm. Then he lowered his hand until he felt the flat bottom of the tube meet the sand. He pushed it about a half inch deep and very slowly plowed a short furrow.

Suddenly in front of his face, he heard a snick of sound – a tiny shadow leaping out of the grass – a tree frog – and then its small splash in the pool.

The light whipped around in the fog, no bigger than a dim, searching eye. It hovered above the water, not moving.

The moment remained motionless, poised. Sal stared, wondering if his own eyes reflected the light back to her, bracing for the muzzle flash, the clap of gunpowder. When he couldn't wait any longer, he rose to his knees.

'I got what you're looking for,' he said, his voice slicing the fog.

For a moment, her light remained still. Then it rose into the ir, and he heard her leg suck out of the mud. He knew that she was aiming her revolver at him.

'I buried it,' he said.

She pulled her other foot up, made a soft, water sound as she took another step. 'I really don't know what you're talking about. Buried what?'

Gradually he could make out the outline of her head and shoulders in the fog, then her torso and hips. He moved his hand, furtively plowing sand over the tube as he talked. 'It's all in your book,' he said. 'Hair cream and swimming pool cleaner. It's how Jerry Royal's house burned down.'

'Jerry's house?'

She took another step, and her outline suddenly became clearer, her light beam brighter. 'I'm not sure I understand how that relates to me.'

'Jerry knew what you did, Noel. He put it in a letter, to protect himself. And then he tried to blackmail you. That's why you burned down his house, to destroy the letter.'

'You really are delusional,' she said. 'That's what people say about you, you know, that you've had a breakdown.' Her foot made a sucking sound.

'It didn't make sense at first, I mean why he didn't turn you in. But then I realized – he couldn't. Because it was Jerry who killed Eliot Wicker.'

Noel sighed. 'Sal, you know you murdered Wicker, just like you deceived Bobby. Like you deceived me into coming down here so you could attack me.'

Now he could make out her features enough to see that she was barelegged under a dark, hooded sweatshirt. And that she did indeed have her pistol with her. Aimed squarely at him.

'Psychologically, it's not hard to understand. You had sex with me. You betrayed your best friend and your wife, and now you need someone to blame. Poor, innocent Salvatore, victimized by the evil seductress.'

389

She took another step, and then she stopped. The light flared in his eyes.

'So, I guess whatever it is you buried,' she said—

and that's when Sal realized his fatal mistake—

—'well, that's exactly what I was planning to do.'

She hesitated, as if giving him a chance to respond. But he just stared into her light without recourse, exhausted, targeted. A wave of weak emotion passed over him, knowing he was about to die. He lowered his eyes. He pictured Iris .. Davey...

With no trace of regret, she said simply, 'Nobody's innocent, Sal. And you're nobody's victim.'

A thick shaft of light flashed across the bog.

'*Noel, don't you move!*'

To Sal's left, at the source of the light, all he could see was the shape of a man standing amongst the vaporous trees.

'Drop that gun in the water, Noel.'

It was Shepherd, perched at the foot of the sandbar, no thirty feet away. His light, diffused through the fog, gave Noel's face a reddish, eerie glow. She shielded her eyes with the hand that held her own penlight, but her revolver remained point-blank at Sal.

'I'm sorry, *Detective*, I need to protect myself. In case you haven't heard, he broke into my apartment and tried to kill me earlier. He murdered Bobby. I came down here because I knew this was where he'd be.'

'You came down to get something out of the water,' Shepherd replied. 'I've been right here watching you.'

Standing up to her knees in the pool, Noel sneered. 'You're just so clever. But if you'll take your flashlight out of my eye and shine it on him, you'll see that he also has a gun in his hand.'

Shepherd didn't budge. He kept his flashlight – and his eye – on her. 'Noel,' he said, softening his voice, 'I know you can'

ee me here, but I have a nine-millimeter semiautomatic aimed
t you. I have fourteen rounds, and you're making me very
ıervous. Drop your weapon now.'

She smirked. 'Do they teach you to talk like that at detective
chool, or did you pick it up at the movies?'

'Drop it.'

'He murdered my husband,' she said, 'and he murdered
Eliot Wicker. He's got nothing to lose by killing both of us.'

'Mr Erickson, did you kill those men?'

'Oh, right, ask him, asshole.'

'Noel—'

'I've done a lot of things I can't undo,' Sal said. 'I'm a drunk.
destroyed my family. But I've never killed anybody.'

'Sal, I found your wallet,' Shepherd said.

For a moment, the only response was the sound of the pool
quietly rising up its banks. 'Okay,' Sal answered.

'I have it with me.'

'I don't mean to sound ungrateful, Detective, but I don't
ıeed my wallet right now.'

'Sal, you need to explain your driver's license,' Shepherd
old him.

Noel broke in, keeping her gun on Sal. 'You are questioning
ıim,' she said, 'but you are still shining your light on me. I find
hat extremely annoying.'

'It's a Rhode Island license with your picture on it, Sal.'

Noel continued. 'Are you going to let him murder me in cold
blood while you're standing right there?'

'You keep quiet.'

'Look at him! He has a gun!'

'Noel, I'm not taking my eyes off you. Sal, I want you to
xplain the name on your license.'

'What name?'

There was a pause. 'Dale Newman.'

'*Bastard!*' Noel said.

'*Noel!*' Two corners of the triangle leaned in, Noel aiming her light and gun at Sal, Shepherd aiming at Noel.

'He murdered my husband!' she snapped. 'I have the right to protect myself!'

'You do anything other than dropping that gun,' he replied, 'and I'll shoot you dead.'

'I'd love to be there when you explain that,' she replied.

Shepherd kept his pistol trained on her chest. 'Sal, we have more than enough evidence for an indictment. I need to know why I shouldn't arrest you.'

Sal dug his fingers in the sand.

'*He's got a gun!*'

'*Sal – Don't you move!*'

Sal pulled out the tube and tossed it. It hit Shepherd's leg made him jump back, ready to swing toward Sal. 'Jesus Christ I said don't move!'

'Hair cream,' Sal told him. 'She burned down Jerry Royal's house with it. He was blackmailing her.'

'With hair cream—?'

'You mix it with swimming pool cleaner to start a fire. The directions are in a book she had in her apartment. I saw the empty tube here yesterday when I was fishing with my daughter.'

'We have videotape of the area,' Shepherd said. 'If it was in the water, we'll see it.'

Noel glared down the barrel at Sal. 'And you'll send it down to the lab for analysis, and you'll find my fingerprints on it. So what? Of course my fingerprints are on it. I sell that brand of hair cream in my store.'

'I don't think so,' Sal said. 'You're too smart to leave finger prints.' He leaned forward, his right hand going behind him.

Hearing the movement, Shepherd tensed again. 'Just tell me!'

'*Watch him!*'

'*Noel!*'

Sal snapped the glove from his pocket. Shepherd caught his breath, remained riveted on Noel.

'It's a rubber glove,' Sal said. 'I don't have a gun.'

'Okay, that's enough,' Shepherd told him. 'I'd rather you didn't say any more.'

Noel sighed impatiently. Her right leg moved in the water. 'Detective, if I agree to—'

'Noel, don't you even think about turning toward me or I'll shoot you.'

'The fingers are stuck together,' Sal said, 'like they've been melted.'

'*Enough!*' Shepherd told him. 'Don't you say another word.'

Sal heard the detective's foot enter the pool, saw the light beam shift on Noel's right side. 'Okay, I'm coming out where I can see you both. Noel, for all I know, you could be thinking that the only way out of this is to kill me first, and then shoot him.'

'I'm sorry, but you have it exactly wrong, as usual,' she scoffed. 'He's the one who has to get out of this, and right now he's aiming his gun right at the side of your face.'

Shepherd put his other foot in the water. 'Calm down, Noel. Now I need you to drop your weapon in the water.'

'I don't believe this,' she said. 'A tube of hair cream and a rubber fucking glove. Listen to me – I have a seven-thirty flight!'

Shepherd kept his gun on her, while his voice grew steady and soothing. 'It's important that we all stay calm. There's nothing we have to solve here and now. That's what lawyers are for. Now lower your weapon, Noel. Nice and easy.'

But she kept her revolver trained on Sal.

As Shepherd came closer to her, his beam intensified on the side of her face, her shining eye. 'That's right, everyone stay cool, and we'll all get out of here without anyone getting hurt.'

Sal knew differently. There were three possible ways this would end, none of them calm. Only one way had him walking out alive. He swallowed.

'Detective Shepherd,' he said.

'Not now—'

'Is it possible to take fingerprints from inside a rubber glove?'

Shepherd stopped. Extended his gun toward Noel.

'Don't move, Noel—'

Her green eye, sideswiped by the light, narrowed in the fog.

'Noel, please,' he said quietly. 'Drop it in the water.'

For several beats, the only sound in the pool was breathing.

'Noel, we're about one second from becoming very bloody here.'

Her mouth contorted in a crooked, haughty smile. 'Are you serious?' she said, turning toward him.

The gunshots cracked off the bluff – three, in quick succession, from Shepherd's pistol.

Sal fell back.

Noel dropped into the pool as if she'd been pulled down by the legs. She curled away from Sal, looking like she wanted to return fire at Shepherd, but her feet were stuck and she couldn't seem to raise her arm. Slumping forward, she managed to draw a knee up under her. In the water, her small haze of light drifted away.

Sal pulled himself to his feet, legs shaking.

Shepherd took a step toward her, his gun trained on the top of Noel's head, his flashlight beam searching the murky water for her right hand, her weapon.

'Let go of the gun, Noel. Let me help you.'

As the pool rose to her face, Noel turned her head groggily, her eyes rolling over to Sal, dark and glazed.

He stepped toward her in the mud.

'You stay back,' Shepherd told him, but Sal wasn't hearing. He took another step.

Noel continued staring at him as the pool licked her chin. Her head hitched forward once. Then, sucking in a shallow breath, she slid under.

Sal pushed through the muck, sloshing forward. Shepherd moved forward, trying to stop him. 'Get back—'

Sal dropped to his knees, got his right arm under Noel's arm and started to lift. She felt heavier than possible, at first, then suddenly weightless—

'*Look out!*'

Her face flew out of the water, gasping the air, eyes flaring. Her elbow followed, the revolver splashing up.

Sal froze in front of her, pinned.

The pistol shot blew behind Sal's ear with tremendous volume, the echo absorbed by the dense fog, the surrounding trees, and as Sal watched, horrified, Noel slipped heavily from his arms, seeming to dive away from him, moving the water back.

For most of a minute, the entire bog lay perfectly still. Neither man moved.

Than Sal rose to his feet.

Shepherd let out a low sigh. 'You can't help her now,' he said.

Engulfed by shivering, Sal took a step deeper into the pool. Shepherd slogged toward him, caught hold of his shirt with his flashlight hand. 'Listen—' His right arm went around Sal's back, to keep him from falling. 'She did it herself.' He raised his flashlight to the middle of the pool as the body stopped drifting. 'She did it herself,' Shepherd said again.

'I know. I know.'

Sal stared into the dusky fog. From where he stood, the lifeless form that protruded from the pool, still as one of the rocks or tussocks around it, could have been mistaken for anything – another rock, a discarded milk jug, a child's broken kickball. But it was Noel Swift in the water, Bobby's Noel, the last part of her cooling body to go down, her buttock and thigh.

16

The morning newspaper ran a photo of Jerry Royal's body draped out of the front window of the Ericksons' house, with the headline 'Suspect at Large in Gravity Carnage,' although the accompanying article failed to draw a relationship between the deaths of Jerry Royal and Sergeant Murdoch and the pursuit of Sal Erickson. By the time the papers came off the trucks, Sal was in the emergency ward of Downeast Memorial Hospital with a mild case of hypothermia, serious blood loss and a fractured shoulder.

By seven o'clock, Lieutenant Boggs found himself standing in front of television cameras lamenting Sergeant Murdoch's untimely death and painting him as a hero, telling the viewing audience that even after Murdoch was mortally wounded, he had taken down his assailant while the man engaged police in an armed standoff. Boggs went on to say that a second suspect in the case was now in custody, although he did not make it clear what Sal was suspected of.

Reporters, eager to profile Sal Erickson and his family and photograph the house where Murdoch and Jerry Royal had been gunned down, were kept away from the scene in the early morning, until evidence technicians had finished processing the house. Then, when a crew of carpenters and cleaners took over, there was nothing newsworthy to see, nor anyone knowledgeable to interview.

Michael Kimball

Despite the calamitous events – or maybe because of them –
a stony reticence overspread the town. Even the coffee crowd,
who had gathered outside the closed Superette to discuss the
news, steadfastly refused to talk to reporters. At seven-fifteen,
when they all went off about their day's business, the
newspeople gave up and returned to Bangor to await the police
report.

It wasn't that townspeople were unmoved about what had
befallen the victims; they were just relieved that the ordeal
was finally over. They longed for the Gravity they knew,
slow and warm in the summertime, with haying and berrying
and lawn-mowing and half-witted tourists and lobster bakes;
with their Fourth of July parade, their oxen pulls, their
Blueberry Queen.

For Iris, the hours that followed were, in various ways, the
saddest yet most liberating time of her life, and so she was
careful with her emotions. At seven-thirty in the morning, after
staying up all night talking to Helen, she telephoned the clinic
to say she was taking a month off (despite protests from the two
doctors, who owed her twenty-four weeks in accumulated
time). At eight, she called the university and canceled her
summer semester. It was the first time in her memory that she
had no schedule to keep. Then, leaving Davey with Helen
Swan, Iris walked out to her car and began the long journey of
reclaiming her life.

She started by visiting an Ellsworth funeral director. In the
slow hours before dawn, over two pots of tea, Helen had told
Iris that one day she would learn to forgive her brother. By the
time Iris had finished making arrangements for Jerry's burial,
she believed that one day she would.

After leaving the funeral home, she drove to the hospital to
visit her father. She brought him a can of vegetable juice and a
straw from the cafeteria. She held his hand while she told him

about Jerry. She didn't tell everything. When the nurse brought lunch, she fed her father with a spoon; she brushed his hair with a soft baby brush; then she stayed for a while and watched him sleep.

Before she left the hospital, she stopped at the desk to ask for Sal. She hadn't planned to, not exactly. But thinking that she might, she had brought a tulip that Davey had picked from Helen's bulb garden, along with a get-well card that Davey had made. The receptionist told Iris that Sal was recovering from surgery and that, since he was still in police custody, he could not have visitors.

She went up to the recovery room anyway and looked in the window while Sal slept. He looked old – that was Iris's first thought – whether because of the cast on his arm, his pallid complexion, his growth of beard or the weight he had lost. A uniformed policeman sitting in the room with him glanced up from his magazine. Iris held the flower and card to the window. The cop set his magazine on the radiator and came to the door to take them.

It was another twenty-four hours before Sal opened his eyes. When he did, the tulip was the first thing he saw. The card beside the red plastic vase said 'I love you Daddy.' He went to reach for the card but found his arm unmovable, bound in a stiff cast.

'Still pretty tender, I guess,' a voice said.

Sal raised his head, saw Alston Bouchard sitting at the foot of his bed. The constable lifted two pill bottles from his shirt pocket. 'I've got a ten-day supply of painkillers for you,' he said. 'Plus tetracycline, to ward off infection.'

Sal cleared his throat, coming to full, painful consciousness. His shoulder throbbed intensely, his back and ribs hurt when he breathed. Even his jaw still ached where Bouchard had punched him.

'I thought you were in jail,' Sal said, his voice raspy from the long sleep.

'They let me go,' Bouchard told him. 'Detective Shepherd stopped by a while ago. He said they found that book you were looking for. It was in her dumpster with a lot of other things she was throwing out.'

Sal laid his head back on the pillow. Memories began seeping in, carrying far more pain than he felt physically.

'Also' – Bouchard leaned forward in his chair – 'he wanted me to show you this.' He took a Polaroid photo out of his pocket, got to his feet and came to Sal's bedside. 'They went through her suitcases and such. 'Course, they found her round-trip plane ticket to Tampa.'

He put the picture in Sal's hand, a close-up of a green airline ticket.

'This one they found in the lining.'

Sal's eyes sharpened. 'Swissair?'

'Miami to Zurich,' Bouchard said. 'The money'd been transferred to Switzerland.'

Sal's eyes stung. He closed them, the photo hanging from his fingers.

'See the name on the ticket?'

Sal opened his eyes again, saw the way Bouchard was looking at him. He didn't have to look at the ticket.

'They found black hair dye too. She would've been on that plane today.'

Sal remained silent. Bouchard took the photo from him.

'I brought you a change of clothes. They want to check you over once more, then you're free to go.'

Sal laid his head back on the pillow.

Bouchard's car radio didn't work, so it was a quiet ride back to town. Sal wore a pair of corduroy trousers and a dark cotton shirt that Bouchard had brought for him; the left sleeve was cut off at the shoulder to make room for his cast and sling. Sal had shaved before he left, and he'd eaten some mashed potatoes and apple sauce, his first solid food in days.

They drove on over the frost-heaved road, the late afternoon sun flickering through the windows. Sal put his visor down, opened his window. The warm air, laced with lilacs, fluttered against his face.

'Windy,' Bouchard said, the only thing he had said since they'd left the hospital.

Sal did not respond. They drove on further, eventually crossing into Gravity.

'Your motorcycle's up to my place,' Bouchard told him. 'But with that arm...'

'I'll get my car,' Sal agreed.

'I'll drop you off at...' Bouchard flipped his hand. *Your house* were the words he did not say.

They drove the next three miles without speaking. When they reached the Superette, the building was deserted, ringed with yellow police tape. Sal stared straight ahead out the windshield as they drove by. Crossing over the bridge to the stop sign, Bouchard stepped on his brakes, then started to turn.

'I'll get out here,' Sal told him.

Bouchard pulled over, shifted into neutral. Sal pushed against the door, popped it open. He got out, then reached into the back seat with his good arm and picked up the plastic bag containing his clothes. Somebody at the hospital had laundered them. Halfway out, he stopped. 'Listen—'

'Yup.'

'I've been thinking, next time you go to one of those meetings...'

Bouchard nodded, his hands rubbing the steering wheel. 'I was going to say, you ever go fishing and want some company...' He jerked his wrist.

Sal nodded, shut the door. Looked in the open window.

Bouchard raised his fingers off the steering wheel. 'Anyway, about those meetings, we'll be going every night for the next three months, you and me . . .' He made a fist, bounced it twice off the wheel.

Sal gave him a long look. Then he smiled a little. 'I'm thinking about it,' he said. 'Maybe one of these days I'll come up with a higher power.'

Bouchard gave another nod. Then he drove off.

Sal looked down the road toward his house, and he started walking. It was a bright afternoon, windy and warm. He could hear a lawn mower going, he could hear songbirds in the trees. Off in the eastern sky a noisy flock of Canada geese rode the wind northward in a V, following the coast. Any other day like this, after supper, he'd be mowing his own lawn, or out in his garden, or playing catch with Davey, or heading down to the fishing pool with his rod and net. Now that he was this close to home, his heart sank inside him, knowing that those days were gone. The wind gusted behind him, pushing him down the road. But he held back, favoring his left ankle. He was in no hurry.

He figured he'd drive into Ellsworth and buy a newspaper, start looking for a job, maybe do some house painting. Or he'd go up to the university and see about giving private lessons. Approaching his house, he saw Mrs Abraham standing in her sunporch, looking out at him. Sal knew she'd be on the telephone in the next minute.

When he could see his own house, the first thing he noticed was the new front window and patch of new shingles around it. His shoulder ached.

Then he saw them both, Iris and Davey, out behind the house in the garden. He was glad their backs were to him. It looked like Iris was pushing the rototiller, fighting to steady the machine while it rocked her along. He could hear the motor sputtering. Davey was crouched in the garden behind her – weeding? He could see the row of pea plants – already up past Davey's ankles. The row of spinach was thick and green. A twinge of pride mixed with his sadness. They were doing without him.

Sal reached the property without their seeing him, cut across the front lawn so they were out of sight behind the house. He went to his car, looked in the window and saw the back seat packed with cardboard boxes of his things. What he wanted to do was to go out to the garden and see them both, tell them that he'd been cleared, but he figured they must already know. He'd wait till he looked better, dressed in clothes that fit him; without the cast. He'd come back when he was settled and he felt stronger, when he could face Davey without feeling ashamed. When he could face them both – although right now he couldn't see that day ever coming. He opened the car door and slid in on the seat. He reached in the ashtray and took out his spare key, and that's when he heard the rototiller die. He put the key in the ignition and sat for a moment to listen, while Iris pulled the starter cord again and again, and the rototiller did nothing but cough. He heard Davey's voice, like a sweet song; Iris's voice, patient and soothing.

Sal took a long breath, got out of the car. He walked up the driveway and then stopped tentatively between the garage and the house, where he could see them: Davey kneeling in the peas, Iris bent over the machine. 'This must be the choke,' Iris was saying, making an adjustment. Sal walked under the clothesline while she gave another pull. This time the motor sputtered, and Iris adjusted the choke until the motor evened out. She increased the throttle, and the rototiller sang. She started the tines revolving and then went churning up the dark soil.

Yes, they would do without him. He started to turn, wanting to get out of there before he was spotted.

Michael Kimball

But then Davey turned too, as if she had sensed his presence. At first she gazed with disbelief, then she sprang to her feet and came running through the garden, and she was in his arms. Iris stopped tilling, looked back at them both, Davey with her long limbs wrapped around her father, hugging Sal as if she'd never let him go. Sal held her just as tightly with his one good arm, his face reddening.

Iris disengaged the tines, slowed the throttle, took off her glasses to wipe her dirty face with the back of her arm. She stopped the motor with her foot and then walked across the soft dirt, taking long, purposeful strides toward him.

Sal watched her uncertainly, not knowing what he could possibly say. He cleared his throat and started anyway. 'They let me' – his words caught in his throat. Still holding Davey, he closed his eyes and took a breath. He shook his head, unable to speak.

Iris took another step toward him. 'Be careful of Daddy's shoulder, love.'

The wind came up again, whipped Iris's hair around. Sal could see where her face had been colored by the sun. And then he couldn't look at her anymore.

'Davey, I gotta put you down,' he whispered.

But Davey held him tighter, her strong legs squeezing his waist.

'Honey, I have to go.'

'Don't—'

Iris's voice seemed to blow off on a gust of wind. Sal looked at her again. Was she speaking to Davey? She was looking at Sal. A dizziness came over him, and he teetered a bit under Davey's weight.

'Hon, you gotta get down now,' he said to Davey, but he was still captivated by Iris, by the look she was giving him – like she was looking right through him.

She took another step closer, until she was within touch, and

404

hen she said clearly, 'Sal, I don't want you to go.' Just like that. So clear there could be no mistake, and Sal lost his balance, lost his legs and staggered backwards, landing softly in a row of soft dirt and radishes. Davey laughed. Still holding on, she braced her feet on the ground to keep him from falling onto his back, and she laughed at him.

And then Iris was there with them both, on her knees, working one arm under Sal's, the other around Davey. The three of them holding one another against the wind, Sal's face caressed by their hair, Iris's mouth at his ear. 'You were right,' she said to him. 'I did come looking for you, Sal. And I found just what I was looking for.'

He leaned into both of them, cradled by their skulls. 'No,' he breathed. 'No.' And Iris angled her face until they found each other's eyes through her hair. 'I came looking for you,' he said. 'And I never even knew it.'

They held each other. They swayed, the three of them in the late afternoon sun, wrapped together like some wild, burgeoning bush. In the soft dirt, in the wind, it was a wonder how they stayed upright.

ACKNOWLEDGMENTS

Thanks to all of you who generously offered or agreed to read this novel in all of its varied forms and then gave me your valuable suggestions and encouragement:

Ron Bourassa
Rich Connor
Chris Fahy
Nancy Gish
Joel Gotler
Rick Hautala
Kyle Jones
Glenna Kimball
Jesse Kimball
Stephen King
Tabitha King
Sue Locsin
Bo Marks
Art Mayers
Allison Mullen
Alan Philbrook
Jessa Reifsnyder
Peter Reifsnyder
Justin Smith
Laurie Stone

Michael Kimball

* * *

For help with research and other things, thank you:

Ladd Alcott
Walter Chapin
David Crook
Meredith DeLoca
Roy Gallant
Dan Guerin
Brent Harrell
Bill Harwood
Al Hendsbee
Joe Jackson
Phil Jones
Ronald Kaufman
Sarah Kimball
Peter and Paula Layton
Bob MacMahon
Dorothy Morang
Howie Nielsen
Andy Pratt
Henry Ryan

Very special thanks to:

Jennifer Hershey, my Avon editor
Billy Massey, my Headline editor
Howard Morhaim, my agent

Bless you, Lou Aronica